ROBERT JOSEF KONIG

OF GOOD AND EVIL:

PRELUDE TO THE HOLOCAUST

A HISTORICAL FICTION DEDICATED TO THOSE WHO PERISHED IN THE HOLOCAUST. MAY THEIR MEMORY BE BLESSED FOR ALL TIME.

To Darlene and Paul
Our long time friends

Bob

REISEPASS ON THE FRONT COVER IS THE GERMAN PASSPORT MY FATHER USED TO LEAVE AUSTRIA AFTER THE ANSCHLUSS

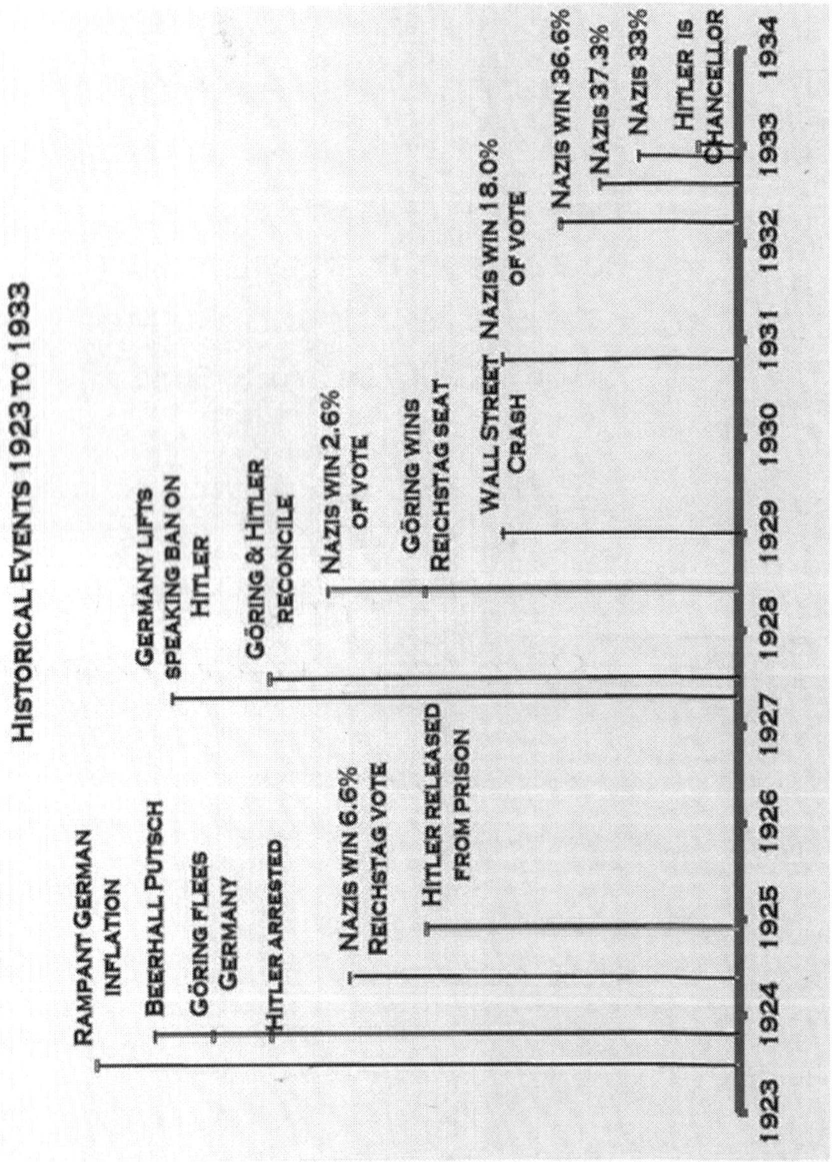
HISTORICAL EVENTS 1923 TO 1933
RAMPANT GERMAN INFLATION
BEERHALL PUTSCH
GÖRING FLEES GERMANY
HITLER ARRESTED
NAZIS WIN 6.6% REICHSTAG VOTE
HITLER RELEASED FROM PRISON
GERMANY LIFTS SPEAKING BAN ON HITLER
GÖRING & HITLER RECONCILE
NAZIS WIN 2.6% OF VOTE
GÖRING WINS REICHSTAG SEAT
WALL STREET CRASH
NAZIS WIN 18.0% OF VOTE
NAZIS WIN 36.6%
NAZIS 37.3%
NAZIS 33%
HITLER IS CHANCELLOR
1923
1924
1925
1926
1927
1928
1929
1930
1931
1932
1933
1934

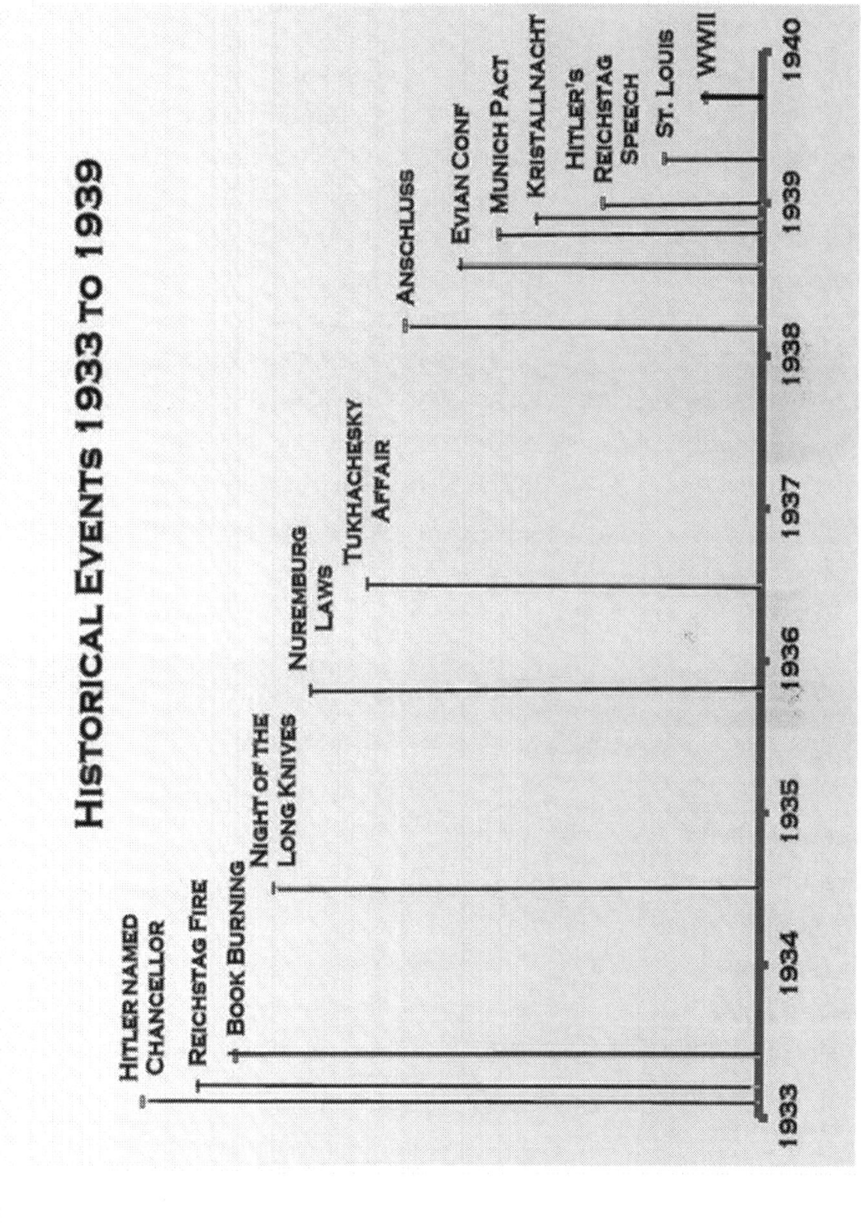
HISTORICAL EVENTS 1933 TO 1939
HITLER NAMED CHANCELLOR
REICHSTAG FIRE
BOOK BURNING
NIGHT OF THE LONG KNIVES
NUREMBURG LAWS
TUKHACHESKY AFFAIR
ANSCHLUSS
EVIAN CONF
MUNICH PACT
KRISTALLNACHT
HITLER'S REICHSTAG SPEECH
ST. LOUIS
WWII
1933
1934
1935
1936
1937
1938
1939
1940

CAST OF CHARACTERS

NAZIS - HISTORICAL

Canaris, Admiral Wilhelm	1887-1945	Chief of Abwehr Spy Network
Eichmann, Karl Adolf	1906-1962	SS Lieutenant Colonel
Göring, Hermann	1893 -1946	Hitler's 2nd in Command
Hanfstängl, Helene	1893 – 1973	Prevented Hitler's suicide
Hanfstängl, Putzi	1987 – 1975	Hitler confidant
Heydrich, Reinhard	1904 – 1942	SS General
Himmler, Heinrich	1900 – 1945	SS Commander (Reichsführer)
Hitler, Adolf	1889 – 1945	Führer, The Third Reich
Kantzow, Baroness Carin	1888 – 1931	Hermann Göring's wife
Kliest-Schmezin, Evan	1890 – 1945	Attorney, Germany
Oster, Hans	1887 – 1945	General, Germany
Röhm, Ernst	1887 – 1934	Chief SA (Storm Troopers)

NAZIS - FICTIONAL

Billingsworth, Elisabeth
Blick, Erik
Braun, Wilhelm
Freund, Rupert
Hauptman, Bruno
Heintz, Rolf
Kepner, Fritz
Kleindienst, Bruno
Kreutzer Family:
Bruno, Otto, and Irena

Littner, Max
Mayer, Claus
Nagel, Wilhelm
Schmidt, Werner
Schlossberg, Ernst
Schwartz, Franz
Stroller, Ingrid
Wasserman, Peter

CAST OF CHARACTERS

THE OTHERS – HISTORICAL

Berenson, Lawrence		Attorney, JDC*
Brú, Frederico Laredo	1875 - 1946	President, Cuba
Churchill, Winston	1874 -1965	Minister, House of Commons
May, Jonas		Leader, Kitchener Camp
Schröder, Gustav	1885 – 1959	Captain, The *St. Louis*
Schuschnigg, Kurt	1897 – 1977	Chancellor, Austria
Sinclair, Admiral Sir Hugh	1873 – 1939	Director ,MI6
Tukhachesky, Mikhail	1893 – 1937	General , Soviet Union
Troper, Morris	1887 – 1945	Executive, JDC*

*Jewish American Joint Distribution Committee

THE OTHERS - FICTIONAL

Amerati, Vincenzo
Billingsworth Family:
Cecil, Elisabeth, & Margaret
Bleiman, Nathan
Dewalt, Ludwig
Goldstein Family:
Chaim, Mordechai, Rachel, & Schlomo
Hirsch, Phillip
Isaacson Family:
Joshua, Hadassah, & Judah
Kaiser Family:
Avram, Deborah, Eszter, Johannes & Yaakov
Klein Family:
Gustav, Otto & Margarette
Klientraub, Hans
Kleinschmidt, Manfred
Labandter, Willy
Lukasik, Malka
Mannheim, Siegfried
Mayer Family:
Heinrich, Hermann & Liesel
McAllister, Ian
Rheinbaum, Hertha
Smyth, Sean
Solomonson Family:
Mendel, Rachel, & Sarah
Turnbey, Reginald
Weisskopf Family:
Moshe, Sarah & Solomon
Wollinski, Irma

The world is a dangerous place to live;

not because of the people who are evil,

but because of the people who don't do

anything about it.

~ Albert Einstein ~

FOREWORD

The first German Jews arrived at the Auschwitz Death Camp on December 10, 1942. I was born five days later, in London England. Two days after that, British Foreign Secretary Anthony Eden informed the House of Commons that the Nazis were annihilating European Jews. By the time I was three, Hitler's Holocaust had slaughtered over six million Jews.

Although Hitler's rise to power didn't affect me directly, the story of my families' exodus from hell changed my life. It compelled me to write this Historical Fiction.

I began by learning about Adolf Hitler's rise to power. What I found disturbed me. Why would Germany, a respected constitutional democracy, surrender itself to a rogue, anti-Semitic, police state? I then expanded the scope of this book to answer that question, and its ramifications to Germany and the world.

Of Good and Evil is a work of fiction. Nonetheless, historical events drive the plot, while the wants, needs, hopes, aspirations and fears of historical and fictional characters bring those events to life.

Robert Josef Konig

INDEX

CHAPTER ONE -- CLAUS MAYER

9th June, 1923 - Munich – Claus begins his new life

An earsplitting noise and flash of light caught Claus Mayer's attention as he passed an alleyway. He walked toward it and watched as a soldier's right hand dropped limply to his side. *Is he holding a pistol?* He inched closer and saw blood streaming from his right temple. Claus reached for the gun, forced it from the dead Captain's grip, and opened the chamber. *He left me four bullets. This must be an omen.* Claus checked to see whether anyone was watching, closed the chamber, and slipped the gun into his coat pocket. His pulse raced as he dashed home.

Entering his apartment, he grimaced seeing the crumpled eviction notice lying where he'd tossed it last week. He took the revolver from his pocket, set it on the table, and sat staring at it. *If I Act now I won't become another starving, forgotten, German roaming Munich's streets.*

A tear came to his eye thinking about his family. Claus didn't want them to know how far he'd fallen since losing his last job. *If only I could become successful at something, anything, I'd go home with my head held high.*

Disgraced, hungry, and exhausted, he fell asleep and dreamt of a time, seven years earlier, when he was still happy. Twelve-year-old Claus hugged his older brother Heinrich. "Even if we weren't brothers, I'd consider you my best friend."

Without warning, Rolf Heintz leapt between them and bludgeoned Heinrich. When Heinrich refused to defend himself, Claus jumped in and felled the neighborhood bully with one punch.

Heinrich's face reddened as he yelled, "Violence is a last resort."

Claus shook himself awake, then smiled. *Heinrich would never get that angry with me*. His smile wilted when he picked up the gun. W*hat made him do it?* His stomach fluttered. *I have no choice either. The police will force me out me today.*

Claus thrust the barrel in his mouth and pulled the trigger.

The click unnerved him.

He let the pistol fall to the table.

His hands trembled when he again took hold of it and opened the chamber. *It rotated past the misfired bullet.* He closed the chamber, relaxed for a few moments, then heard the landlord use the bathroom. *I must act before he brings in the police*. He aimed the gun at his temple, closed his eyes, pulled, and felt the click. *Another bad bullet*?

Claus' rage erupted when his weapon failed a third time. *Can't I even be successful at killing myself?* He hurled the firearm at the eviction notice. It exploded, and the landlord blew through the door moments later. After glancing at the weapon, which was beyond Claus' reach, he yelled, "That's it Mayer. I'm not waiting for the police. *Get out.*" He grabbed him, pushed him out of the apartment, and through the open front door.

Claus stumbled out to the pavement. *I need food and somewhere to sleep.* He walked to a poverty-stricken neighborhood where the homeless seemed to be everywhere. Those not asleep on the sidewalk shuffled around in a state of confusion. Putrid garbage lined the gutters, making him feel nauseous.

He made his way to an affluent district where well-dressed men and women darted across the street as soon as they spotted him. Claus' spirits bottomed seeing his sunken blue eyes, sallow skin, and unwashed blond hair reflected from a shop window. Forcing himself on, he caught sight of a restaurant. *Will the owner take pity on me? No, he'll probably order my arrest.* He stopped at the door and gave a long low sigh. *Jail may be my only escape from starvation.*

He hunched his shoulders, entered the eatery, staggered to the darkest corner, and collapsed into a chair. The proprietor eyeballed him, ran his finger down a list next to the telephone, and placed a call.

He must have called the police. I won't be here long. Claus blocked out further thoughts of suicide by visualizing Heinrich urging him to pursue good instead of evil. His brother's goodness and decency shone as a beacon of hope, easing Claus' anxiety.

Someone approached him. Claus looked up expecting to see a policeman. Instead, a stocky scar faced man wearing a shabby Great War uniform stood over him. Angry at the vagrant for interrupting his brief break with reality Claus stood up, clenched his fists, and stepped forward to tower over him. "Why are you pestering me?"

The stranger grasped his hands and spoke in a guttural yet kindly tone of voice. "I'm the answer to all your prayers, young man. My name is Ernst Röhm, and I hold your ticket to fame, fortune and a life of honor in the new Germany."

Claus shook himself free. "Your scarred face and worn out uniform prove you can't even care for yourself. Go away."

Determination filled Röhm's eyes when he replied. "I may bear the scars of a noble war against Germany's enemies, but it was the Jews that vanquished our country, making it impossible for Aryans like you and me to survive. We must oust them to build a mighty Fatherland where *we* shall rule supreme."

Confused, Claus asked, "How can *we* rule?"

"By helping Adolf Hitler forge a new Germany governed by Aryans."

Claus felt a glimmer of hope. "What will you do for me today?"

Röhm pulled a thick wad of Billion Mark Banknotes from his wallet. "I'll pay for your meal and offer you a position in the SA."

Obsessed by Röhm's bankroll he asked, "SA, what's that?"

"The military wing of the National Socialist Party. We helped Adolf Hitler rise from obscurity after the Great War. Two thousand of us now follow him. What's your name; where do you live?"

"I'm Claus Mayer from Berlin." His lips quivered as he asked, "You offered me a job, sir?"

"Yes. You won't earn much, at first, but you'll never lack for food, shelter or a sense of belonging to a righteous cause." Röhm paused for a few moments then said, "I'll buy you a meal, then introduce you to your new comrades at the barracks."

Röhm watched quietly as Claus wolfed down his food, then asked, "Would you like a beer?" After he nodded yes, Röhm hailed the waiter and ordered two. When they arrived Claus said, "I drink to you, Herr Röhm. Thank you for coming to my aid."

After he finished eating, and the pair toasted Claus' good fortune over a second beer, Röhm said, "Let's walk to my barracks. It's not far."

"Do you mind if I ask you a question?" asked Claus as they set out.

"Go ahead."

"When I came in the restaurant, the owner placed a phone call. Soon after that, you approached me. Did he tell you about me?"

"Yes. After I paid him, he pointed you out and I walked over to meet you."

"Do you often recruit men that way?"

"I do, and I'm glad to say you appear smarter than most of them. We're at the barracks. Let's go in and I'll introduce you to your new compatriots."

Two months working for Röhm bolstered Claus' spirits. He had food, shelter, and Adolf Hitler's dream of a new Germany free of the Jews and Communists who caused all his problems. Despite that, he became conflicted whenever Röhm commanded him to assault anyone defaming Adolf Hitler or the National Socialist Party. Such overt aggression tore at the nonviolent values Claus' brother ingrained in him. After summoning his courage, he approached Röhm to declare his misgivings. "May I speak with you, sir?"

"Later, Mayer, gather on the parade ground with the others. I have an important message for you all."

Röhm's nostrils flared when he stepped up to the speaker's platform. "The Führer's warriors must regard compassion as the most hated of all weaknesses. It is our duty to obey Adolf Hitler's decrees without comment or reservation. I will purge our ranks of anyone whose misplaced sense of morality keeps him from promptly acting on my orders."

Claus' chest tightened. He had two choices: reject the values Heinrich instilled in him, or rejoin the legions of starving, forgotten men still roaming Germany's streets. *Heinrich had my best interest at heart, but his advice caused my downfall. Now I must pursue success by obeying Röhm's orders.*

Claus spent the next few weeks devising a ritual that focused his mind until it was razor sharp, replacing compassion with cold-hearted indifference. He began his daily rite by splashing ice-cold water over his body. Claus then mouthed the solemn oath of his personal faith twelve times while gazing at a portrait of Adolf Hitler.

Whatever benefits Führer and Party is ethical.
Hitler's authority is absolute.
Complying with his decrees will never torment me.
His vow to drive all Jews from our Fatherland is my most sacred mission.
Adolf Hitler's will is my moral compass.

Claus consecrated himself to his Fuhrer every morning. After spending the next two months purging his ethical constraints, he was reborn as Mayer and embarked on his new life. Guilt no longer plagued him while attacking those who defied his Führer and Party… so long as he began every workday by reciting his morning sacrament.

9th November, 1923 - The Munich Beer Hall Putsch

The hall telephone rang. Mayer stepped out of his apartment and lifted the receiver.

"The Führer needs you. My limousine will pick you up in ten minutes." Röhm hung up before he could reply.

Mayer's heart raced at the thought of standing beside his idol, Adolf Hitler. He strode back into his living quarters, slipped into a formal SA uniform, checked his reflection in the mirror, and made for the street. A black Mercedes, swastika flags flying on both fenders, drove up as he reached the curb. It was the meeting of two machines… human and automobile. Both were in perfect working order. Both obediently performed their duty. Neither had a conscience.

The chauffeur stepped out, raised his arm in a National Socialist salute, barked "Heil Hitler," and opened the passenger door. Mayer smiled as he entered the limousine, grateful Röhm transformed him from an aimless nonentity to a respected Storm Trooper Lieutenant. As an officer, he now lived in his own apartment instead of the SA barracks.

Half an hour later, the driver stopped and turned to him. "We've arrived, sir. The meeting is in the Führer's second-floor apartment."

Mayer walked in and chatted with SA friends until his gaze locked on Hermann Göring, the aviator whose daring exploits enthralled him during the Great War. Göring cut a dashing figure in a jet-black shirt and Pour le Métite medal, Germany's highest military honor, draped around his neck.

Moments later, Mayer snapped to attention when Adolf Hitler entered the room with General Lundendorff, a senior commander in the Great War. Hitler wore an unassuming blue suit while Lundendorff personified the role of battle-tested warrior in his ceremonial army uniform.

The room hushed when Hitler told everyone to sit. "Mussolini marched on Rome last year to launch a Fascist regime and become Italy's dictator. We shall follow his lead, launching Germany's own putsch."

Mayer rose and applauded with the others.

Hitler continued after they retook their seats. "Agitation by our SA brethren resulted in uprisings throughout Germany. The Weimar government gave Gustav von Kahr dictatorial powers to restore order. Kahr will address the SA at the Bürgerbräukeller Beer Hall this evening. We shall enlist his support to depose the governments of Bavaria and Berlin and replace them with a National Socialist administration."

Röhm stood, faced the Führer, gave a straight-arm salute, and barked, *Sieg*. The others rose, lifted their arms, and responded, *Heil*. The room came alive as Mayer joined his compatriots chanting *Sieg - Heil* until Hitler raised his hand and looked to the leader of his SA.

"Göring, gather your troops outside the Bürgerbräukeller at eight this evening." Addressing the others, he added, "Tonight, we shall stage an uprising that will shake the world."

The apartment shuddered as everyone stamped their feet in concert with repeated *Sieg - Heil* choruses.

After the room quieted down Mayer saw Hitler speak with Röhm, then break into a smile as he strode toward him. "Röhm tells me you are always among the first to deal with anyone who dishonors me or the Party. Keep up the good work Mayer. You will go far."

Mayer blinked, mesmerized by a gaze that seemed to drill into his deepest thoughts. He stammered incoherently.

Hitler took him in a firm handshake. "I know you are one of the many who joined our struggle to avenge the governments' crimes. Together, we will depose them and establish a Third Reich that shall strike fear and envy throughout the world."

Shaking off Hitler's hypnotic spell, Mayer replied, "Thank you, my Führer. I will obey your commands without question or regret, offering my life to make your dream of a Jew-free Germany a reality."

"You bring nobility to our cause," said Hitler.

Mayer's head spun anew, as his deity strode away.

"I know," said Röhm as he approached Mayer. "Hitler has that overpowering effect on us all. Now, prepare for tonight. Be at the beer hall before the Führer arrives to make sure no problems arise. Fritz Kepner, my newest SA recruit, will help you. Meet him outside the hall at seven forty five. He'll wear a red scarf over his black leather coat."

That evening, he recognized Kepner at once. "I'm Lieutenant Mayer. Have you been inside the Bürgerbräukeller yet?"

"No sir, it sounds like they're having a party. I thought we were planning to overthrow the government?"

"Munich's beer hall patrons always enjoy a few rousing songs before listening to political speeches. We'd better go in before the Führer arrives."

Mayer found the warmth created by a crowd of 2,000 to be a welcome respite from the biting cold outdoors. He gazed at the wall-to-wall array of SA troopers and civilians crowded around large circular tables. Swastika flags surrounded the huge hall. Mayer sensed that the hall's air, heavily laden with perfume and tobacco smoke, predestined the launch of his Führer's new Aryan paradise.

Mayer leaped onto a chair to get a better view of the crowd. His gaze froze on a willowy young woman with long flowing brown hair, pearl white skin, and regally slender neck sitting at a table to his left. He felt a surge of lust as she stared into her beer stein, looking like the loneliest person in the world.

⌘⌘⌘⌘⌘⌘⌘⌘

Elisabeth Billingsworth arrived in Munich a day earlier. This was her final stop on a tour of continental Europe arranged by her prosperous parents. They'd hoped she would return eager to abandon her unquenchable appetite for excitement and self-gratification. Yet it was the exhilaration of danger, promised by hotel acquaintances, which prompted her to arrive early. Now she yearned to be free of the annoying patrons singing their tiresome German songs. *There's nothing exciting about this place. Had I left for London yesterday I'd be having fun at one of Marilyn's wild parties. Will this day never end?*

⌘⌘⌘⌘⌘⌘⌘⌘

Kahr walked to the podium, diverting Mayer's attention. It was time to prepare for Hitler's arrival. He sought Kepner in the crowd, jumped off his chair, and headed toward him.

Moments later, Adolf Hitler threw open the doors of the Bürgerbräukeller. Göring, Lundendorff, and other top leaders followed. Hitler shoved his way to the center of the packed hall, leapt on a chair, fired two shots into the ceiling, and yelled, "The Munich Putsch has begun. Our SA troopers occupied the army and police barracks. Both rallied to the swastika, deposing the governments of Bavaria and Berlin. I will replace them with a National Socialist administration."

Two thousand stood to cheer their messiah's declaration.

Looking to his left, Mayer saw the brown-haired beauty's blue eyes blaze as she joined her new compatriots chanting *Sieg–Heil*. He was about to make his way to her side when Röhm grabbed his arm and gestured toward the exit. Hundreds of SA troopers stood outside in combat gear, aiming their machine guns away from the beer hall. Pointing at them, Mayer asked, "What are they doing, Ernst?"

"They're making sure government soldiers can't get inside to arrest the Führer. We're in control here, so I need you to check whether our Putsch is advancing elsewhere around Munich." He handed Mayer his keys, and told him where to find his car.

After finding Kepner, and retrieving Röhm's car, Mayer drove the pair through Munich's streets to gauge the coup's progress. Seeing an SA lieutenant friend leading a storm trooper squad, Mayer stopped to ask, "How is the Putsch proceeding?"

"It's going well. We haven't seen many government troops and easily overwhelmed those we encountered."

After confirming the SA overcame resistance throughout Munich, Mayer took a shortcut to the Bürgerbräukeller that took them through the Jewish District. "Look," said Mayer, pointing at four SA comrades forcing old Jews to kneel and clean the gutter with their long coats. "They're doing god's work. We'll soon help them make progress toward the emergence of a new Germany."

"How will we do that, sir?"

Mayer thrust out his chest. "This is how," pulling typed lists from his coat pocket. "I broke into a Synagogue this afternoon and forced the Rabbi to give me these Jewish addresses. We can't become a great nation until we force them off our land. After I report our findings to Röhm, we'll gather a squad of troopers to rid our nation of that vermin."

Mayer drove back to the beer hall where he returned Röhm's car keys and told him the SA controlled every Munich neighborhood he'd visited. Mayer then jumped on a nearby chair. "My SA brothers, who will help me rid the Fatherland of its Jew filth?"

A sea of hands signaled Mayer would have no trouble recruiting volunteers. Kepner helped him select twenty, and they left together.

9th November, 1923 – Munich - 9:30 PM - Mayer invades the Goldstein home

After returning to the Jewish district with the troopers, Mayer looked down at his list of addresses and pointed to a large house across the street. “My brothers, we will now rid our Fatherland of its Jews.”

“What if they won’t go?” yelled one volunteer.

Mayer smiled when he replied, “You can do whatever you want to them.”

The troopers cheered.

Mayer strode to the door and pounded on it with his fist. A white-haired man with a long beard and prominent curled sideburns opened it and asked, “Why are you here?”

“All in good time Jew, first tell me your name.”

“I am Mordechai Goldstein. Why are you bothering me?”

Mayer pushed him into the house. Kepner and several troopers followed. Mayer faced Mordechai and glared at him. “You desecrate the holy ground that is Germany. When will you leave our beloved Fatherland?”

“What?”

“It’s simple. When can we rid ourselves of your Jewish presence?” Mayer clenched his jaw.

“I don’t understand. We have lived here for many generations. My youngest brother served in the army with distinction during the Great War, winning the Iron Cross. The French killed my oldest…"

"... I didn't ask for your family history. I want to know when you will leave Germany."

Mordechai took a step toward Mayer. "We will *not* leave *our* homeland."

Recalling the picture of an old man hugging a young woman, he'd seen while entering the room, Mayer asked. "Where is your daughter?"

"What business is that of yours?"

Mayer grabbed Mordechai's beard, tugged him closer, and growled, "Is she here?"

"Get out of my house."

Mayer drew back his knee and drove it into the old man's groin.

Mordechai doubled up, but didn't cry out.

A young brown-haired woman ran in, kneeled at Mordechai's side, then helped him stand. She was tall and slender with luminous skin. Her eyes shone with sapphirine fire as she glowered at Mayer. "*I* am Mordechai Goldstein's daughter. What do you want?"

Mayer touched the base of his neck, trying to remember where he'd seen this Jew. Satisfied he'd never laid eyes on her, he turned to Mordechai. "Tell me when you will leave

Germany, or I'll feed your daughter to the enraged SA troopers outside."

"Leave my Rachel alone," cried Mordechai, his lips quivering.

Mayer saw the fear in Mordechai's eyes as he stepped back and said, "What if I leave in a week?" in an unsteady voice.

"With your daughter?"

"Yes, with Rachel."

Mayer pointed at Rachel, who was still glaring at him. "I'm taking her to the street. My SA brothers won't harm her now, but if you are here a week from today, *she* will pay with her life."

"How do I know you won't hurt her?" asked Mordechai, his eyes blinking rapidly.

"I have nothing to gain by harming her; I will have everything I want when you are both gone."

"Take me," pleaded Mordechai. "I'll go if you leave my Rachel here."

"No, this is *my* responsibility," said Rachel as she strode toward Mayer. Their noses almost touched when she stopped. "Let's get this over with Mr...."

The fearlessness of Rachel's approach, and her sudden closeness, caught him off guard. Ill at ease, he replied, "Lieutenant Mayer is my name."

"Take me," repeated her father.

"No, Papa, stay here. I'll soon be back," Turning to Mayer she added, "Isn't that right, *Lieutenant?*"

"You're a brave woman," said Mayer, captivated by her beauty and indomitable spirit.

"Can we get on with this?"

"Of course," replied Mayer, giving a slight bow. "Follow me out."

Outside, Mayer addressed his SA volunteers. "This is a wise family. They will leave our Fatherland." The crowd cheered. Mayer raised his hand and motioned Rachel to his side. "If you see this Jew after a week has passed you may do whatever you please with her." Mayer paused, waiting for the troopers to stop cheering. "We have what we want here."

The troopers moved away.

Rachel turned and walked toward the house.

Mayer looked at her, saying, "You're a courageous woman."

Rachel continued through the door without acknowledging him.

9th November, 1923 – Munich - 10:00 PM - Mayer attacks the Weisskopf home

Mayer couldn't get Rachel out of his mind as he strode away from the Goldstein home. *I didn't know Jews could be so bold.* His body stiffened. *That sow brushed aside my authority, and I did nothing to reprimand her. Röhm would be furious if he knew.*

Mayer's temper grew as he stopped, looked down at his list of Jewish addresses, and pointed at a house across the street. "Jews live on the second floor. Fritz, give me your rubber club."

He took the weapon, sped to the door, and pounded on it with all his strength.

⌘⌘⌘⌘⌘⌘⌘⌘

Solomon Weisskopf gasped hearing the deafening blows. The family just finished a late Sabbath eve dinner and was reciting *Birkhat ha-Mazon*, the ancient grace chanted by observant Jews after a meal.

"Open this door you fucking Jew bastards," screamed someone from the street.

"You have one more chance," yelled a second voice.

"Let us in or we'll break it down," roared another.

Solomon Weisskopf stood and planted his hands on the table. He spoke calmly, looking his brother in the eye. "Moshe, take Sarah into the bedroom and hide in our large wardrobe. I will attend to the strangers downstairs."

Solomon stashed the evening's dishes in a cupboard while Moshe and Solomon's wife hurried away. *If the strangers come upstairs, they must believe I'm alone.*

Earlier, when he first heard the noise from below, Solomon shuddered seeing the color leave his brother's face. *Moshe ran from confrontation as a child. Growing older made him no more courageous. That never concerned me before...*

Tears filled Solomon's eyes as he placed his hand over his heart and prayed: "Eternal God, should I perish give Moshe the strength to protect my Sarah from those who would do her harm."

After hearing the wardrobe close, Solomon dried his eyes and moved toward the head of the stairs. Looking down, he heard several loud thumps then saw the front door blow apart.

⌘⌘⌘⌘⌘⌘⌘⌘

Mayer calmed his rage before stepping through the shattered entry. Looking up he said, "May I join you, old man?"

"What do you want?"

"Angry soldiers are waiting in the street. You could invite me up, or take your chances with my unruly friends… It's your choice."

Solomon's face mutated into a pained smile. "Please come upstairs, officer."

Nodding his acceptance of the invitation, he mounted the stairs two at a time, saying, "My name is Lieutenant Mayer."

"Welcome, Lieutenant, I'm Solomon Weisskopf. What can I do for you?"

Mayer paused midway to look down at Kepner. "You see, Fritz, Weisskopf is very reasonable." He then continued upstairs, stopping inches from Solomon. "Isn't that right?"

Solomon grimaced. "What do you want, Lieutenant?"

Mayer allowed his anger to grow as he pushed Solomon back into his apartment then faced him. "Leave Germany within one week, *or face the consequences*."

Solomon's eyes widened. "Excuse me?"

"You and your race are no longer welcome here."

"Lieutenant, my family lived here for over three generations. My brother fought on the Western Front, giving his life for our Fatherland."

Mayer clenched his fists and leaned toward Solomon. "We don't care about your family, or what they did. We want *you out*."

Solomon set his jaw. "We are Germans and intend to stay in *our* country. Leave my home. You are no longer welcome."

Rachel's bold indifference to his authority flashed through Mayer's mind, intensifying his rage. His muscles quivered as he grabbed Solomon's coat and dragged him toward the head of the stairs. Releasing his coat, Mayer walked around him, placed his boot in the middle of Solomon's back, and said, "This is how we treat Jews who insist on remaining where they're not wanted," then gave him a brutal shove.

Solomon grasped for the banister, couldn't grip it, and careened down the stairs.

Mayer followed him down, snarling as he stepped over Solomon's body. Turning, he locked his boot into his arm, raised it, gripped the collar of his coat, and dragged him through the shattered doorway. Solomon groaned when Mayer tugged him over the three steps of his concrete stoop, then cried out as he heaved him into the street.

The Storm Troopers surrounded Solomon, behaving like a pack of hungry wolves ready to pounce on their wounded prey.

"My brothers," yelled Mayer. "This is the Jew, Weisskopf. He refuses to leave our beloved Fatherland. He thinks *he* is *our* master. What say you? What shall we do with this swine?"

One said, "Kill him."

"Yes, kick this vermin, showing him no mercy," yelled Mayer. The mob drew their legs back as one, then drove their steel-toed boots into Solomon until nothing but a hideous mass of bloodied flesh, muscle, and bone remained.

Satisfied he'd vanquished his prey, Mayer ran into the house. The troopers followed him up the stairs and into Solomon's living room. Mayer grinned when the troopers found pillowcases in a linen cabinet and filled them with Solomon's valuables. Rachel's likeness flashed though his mind. *Never again will a Jew get the better of me*. He then rejoined the Storm Troopers in the street.

⌘⌘⌘⌘⌘⌘⌘⌘

Minutes earlier, Sarah felt Moshe shiver next to her in the wardrobe. She whispered prayers to calm him. When her husband cried out for mercy, she grabbed Moshe's arm. Sarah clenched her jaw when someone outside yelled, "Kill him." Unable to contain the fear her beloved would die alone, she released Moshe and said, "I must go to him."

"No, stay with me, that's what Solomon wanted."

"My place is at his side." She placed a gentle kiss on Moshe's cheek, then left the wardrobe, closed it and opened the bedroom door.

Hearing the sounds of many feet clambering up the stairs, Sarah flattened herself against the wall. She waited for several minutes, then craned her neck to see what was happening. Men, a few of whom she recognized as trusted neighbors, were pillaging through her belongings. Tears of humiliation rolled down her cheeks, she felt dizzy, and stepped forward to steady herself.

A uniformed trooper approached her, breaking into a maniacal laugh. "Come on, Grandma. Why don't you join the celebration downstairs? It will be great fun."

She stepped back; he lunged forward, grabbed her, then forced her out of the bedroom and down the stairs. She kept from stumbling by sliding her hand along the banister. The mob screamed joyfully as they followed. When the soldier pushed her out of the house, Sarah saw a line of laughing men standing in her way. A scream froze in her throat when they moved aside to expose her husband's blood soaked remains in the street. Anguished, she fell to the pavement. The troopers cheered. Then they lifted Sarah, throwing her onto Solomon's warm corpse. Sarah's caterwaul of grief rose from the depths of hell. Her cry subdued the marauders. Then one said, "The sow misses her pig husband. Isn't that a shame?" and they resumed their celebration.

Sarah turned her tear and bloodstained face upward, begging the Almighty to receive her husband's soul.

⌘⌘⌘⌘⌘⌘⌘⌘

Exhibiting no emotion, Mayer strode to where Sarah lay. He gazed deeply into her woeful eyes and pointed at

Solomon. "This was *his* fault. *He* refused to leave *our* country. We will treat your Jew friends the same way if they stay where they're no longer wanted."

Satisfied he'd won forgiveness for failing to discipline Rachel's brazen lack of respect, Mayer turned toward the euphoric troopers and held up his hand to silence them. "This Jew paid the price for being unwilling to leave Germany. Let's find more Jew vermin and continue performing our sacred duty."

9th November, 1923 – Munich – 10:30 PM –Moshe Weisskopf is reborn

Moshe cowered alone in the wardrobe after Sarah left. His heartbeat clanged like a huge drum pounding inches from his ears. Terror settled into his embattled mind.

A force greater than Moshe's fear calmed him; his breathing became more even; his pulse slowed. That strange power transported him to his Synagogue where the Rabbi gave his sermon on Yom Kippur… the most solemn day of the Jewish year.

⌘⌘⌘⌘⌘⌘⌘⌘

"The Talmud teaches that Pharaoh consulted his three advisers, Bilaam, Yisro, and Iyov saying: T*he Jews grow strong. We must exterminate them so they cannot defeat us by joining our enemies during a war. How shall we destroy them?*

"Bilaam, an evil man, spoke first. *Kill every firstborn Jewish male in Egypt, my Pharaoh.* Yisro rejected the Pharaoh's plan, saying *The Jews committed no crime, my Pharaoh. It is wrong to make them suffer.* Iyov believed as Yisro. Yet he remained silent, endorsing Bilaam's evil intent."

The Rabbi continued, "We are taught that the Eternal dealt with Pharaoh's advisors according to their deeds. Bilaam died at the hand of those he sought to destroy. Yisro settled in Midyan, where Moses married Yisro's daughter Tziporah many years later. His descendants rose to prominence as judicial leaders of the Jewish people. Iyov, afflicted with a lifetime of pain and suffering, raised his voice in protest, but the Eternal would not lessen his anguish. Thereby did he learn it was *his duty* to speak out against evil, even if he knew his protests would go unheeded.

"It is our obligation, as Jews, to dissent whenever evil is visited upon our family, our friends, our neighbors... and yes even if visited unjustly against our enemies."

⌘⌘⌘⌘⌘⌘⌘⌘

With those words ringing in his ears, Moshe found himself back in the wardrobe, his will strengthened by heaven-sent faith. Moshe's strong posture reflected his newfound courage as he rose and made his way down the stairs.

Moshe's eyes fell on Sarah, lying motionless on his brother's battered and bloodied corpse. His body was steady as he went to stand over her. He swayed back and forth chanting the ancient Kaddish, prayed by untold generations of Jews after they lost loved ones.

As the final words of his prayer reverberated through the street, Sarah looked up at him. Her bloodshot eyes were full of tears. He fell on his knees next to her. "Today *Elochainu* opened my mind to the curse of evil."

"Why are you risking your life? My beloved Solomon is dead. You must hide, the killers may return."

"A great injustice was done here. I must answer it."

Sarah shrank back. "How can you seek vengeance for your brother's death? You are but one man." She fell weeping on her husband's lifeless body.

Moshe lifted Sarah and held her tightly. She continued shedding tears as he whispered, "The Eternal shall seek vengeance. I must learn what He expects of me, and how I may do his bidding."

10th November, 1923 – Munich – 8:00 AM – Mayer saves Göring's life

Mayer woke to Kepner screaming, "We are needed," as he banged on the door. Mayer flashed back to Rachel Goldstein taunting him with her unyielding intensity. *Why can't I get her out of my mind?*

He opened the door. "What do you want?"

"Röhm needs our help. Our Putsch is unraveling, sir. The government retook a few of their buildings, and the SA is trying to regain the upper hand."

Shocked to his senses, Mayer said, "Come in, I'll put on a clean uniform, and we'll be on our way." Moments later, the pair was running through the streets of Munich searching for their Führer and his SA troops. Mayer heard Storm Troopers nearby. They were chanting, "Out with the Jews." Pointing in their direction, he said, "That's where we will find our SA brothers." His heart leapt as he rounded the corner. Adolf Hitler, Hermann Göring, Heinrich Himmler, and Ernst Röhm marched toward him leading the SA army. Röhm yelled, "Come join us Claus." The pair fell in line with their leaders.

"What happened, Ernst?" yelled Mayer above the tumult of two thousand troopers.

"Everything went well, then the Putsch fell apart this morning. We must take the Defense Ministry to regain our momentum."

"And so we will. Let anyone try stopping us," said Mayer.

Soldiers blocked their way as they approached Odeonsplatz Square, in central Munich. Mayer drew his pistol, aimed at the soldiers, and continued marching forward.

A shot rang out.

The street came alive with gunfire.

"Kepner, stay close in case I need you."

"Yes sir."

Looking to his left Mayer saw Göring fall to the ground. Holstering his weapon, he yelled, "Follow me, Kepner," as he ran to Göring's aid.

The hail of bullets slowed.

Out of the corner of his eye, Mayer saw Hitler stumble, then fall.

He was about to leave Göring's side when Hitler regained his footing and got into a car that sped away.

Mayer feared the worst when he turned his attention to Göring. His hero hadn't moved. Mayer pointed at a bank's open door. "The shooting's ended. Let's get him in there, Kepner."

The pair lifted Göring, carried him into the bank, and laid him on a large cushioned couch in the entry hall. A man raced toward them saying, “Göring needs help,” in a shrill voice. He then ran into an office, dialed the phone, and yelled, “It’s Oscar in the bank, Doctor. You’re needed. Please come.” Oscar ran back to Mayer, saying, “I’m the bank manager. Doctor Katz is on his way… there he is.”

Katz rushed to Göring’s side, took scissors from his medical bag, and cut the bloodstained clothes away from his lower body. After examining his patient, he said, “He’s close to death. I must extract the wood lodged in his groin. Get me clean sheets, hot water, and soap.”

Kepner looked at Oscar. “Can you find what he needs?”

“Yes, I have it upstairs.” He turned and dashed up the stairs.

“What can I do to help, doctor?” asked Mayer.

“After excising the wood I’ll need Dakin’s solution to clean out the wound. Send someone to get it from a pharmacy.”

“I’ll do that,” said Kepner as he ran from the bank.

“What can I do?” repeated Mayer.

“A prayer wouldn’t hurt. Your friend needs divine intervention to survive.”

"I can't pray anymore," said Mayer under his breath. He'd regularly attended religious services with his parents and brother, but hadn't been to church, or even thought about Christianity, since leaving home. Looking at his incapacitated hero he whispered, "I wish I knew how to pray."

The doctor kept his eyes on Göring, as he said, "I'm about to operate." He took a stiff brush from his medical bag and scrubbed his hands using newly arrived soap and water. After drying them, he retrieved surgical instruments and placed them on a clean sheet. He then used a scalpel to remove solid wood and splinters from the wound. As he was finishing he asked, "Where's your friend with the Dakin's?"

"I have it," said Kepner as he ran up to hand the doctor a large glass bottle containing a colorless liquid. Kepner then turned to Mayer. "Do you still need me, or should I see whether I can help the SA?"

"Go work with the SA, then come to my home in the morning."

After two hours, the doctor wiped his brow, stepped back, and smiled for the first time. "I believe the worst is over, this man will live."

Mayer felt drained from the evening's attacks on Munich's Jews, and hours spent saving Göring's life. His strength gave way, and he collapsed into a chair. The doctor looked at him. "You worked valiantly to keep your friend alive. He would have died without your intervention."

Mayer's eyes opened wide as he jumped out of his chair. "Don't you know who he is?"

Katz studied Göring's face. "Is he the Great War airman who took over the Flying Circus after Baron von Richthofen died?"

"Yes, and he is my greatest hero of the Great War."

"What was he doing in that melee outside this morning?"

"He reports to Adolf Hitler as commander of the SA."

The doctor's face turned an ashen color. "He leads the Brown Shirts?"

"That's right, and we are eternally in your debt for saving our leader's life."

A whisper from Göring diverted Mayer's attention. He rushed over and moved his ear close. "Could you please repeat that sir?"

"Who are you, soldier? Where are we?"

"I'm SA Lieutenant Mayer. We're in a bank on Residenzstrasse near the Hofgarten."

Göring grabbed Mayer's shirt. "Is Hitler all right?"

"I saw him fall, then get up and leave the field of battle in an automobile. What can I do for you, sir?"

"Contact my wife, the Baroness Carin von Kantzow. Her address is on a card in my wallet. Let her know I'm fine. She'll be frantic with worry. Don't let her come here."

Mayer returned with the Baroness several hours later. She ran up to Göring, tears running down her cheeks. She held his hand. "How could you order Claus to keep me away? My place is at your side when you're in danger."

After speaking with his wife and the doctor, Göring turned to Mayer. "Doctor Katz tells me I owe my life to your swift action, Lieutenant."

"My honor sir, I only wish the soldiers injured me instead of you."

"Don't worry about me. I can survive a little pain on my way to recovery." Goring paused, then said, "Carin told me the government overwhelmed our Putsch, and Hitler is in hiding. It doesn't look good for our cause. We agreed our most prudent alternative is to retreat and resume the fight another day. Are you willing to help us?"

"Of course, sir."

"Carin will make the funds available for our exit from Germany. You must join us. That's the least we can do."

"That's unnecessary, sir. The government doesn't know me. I can best support the Party by remaining here. When you return, I'll be ready to serve you, and the noble National Socialist cause."

"I won't forget this," said Göring, patting his face as if he were his own child. "I *shall* come back, and when I do, you will be among the first I turn to for help. We will rise like the Phoenix from the ashes, claiming a victory that elevates Hitler to ruler of all Europe." Göring winced as he grabbed Mayer's hand and pulled himself up. "Your steadfast loyalty to our Führer, to me, and to the Party, will earn you a place of honor in our new order."

A month passed since the failed Putsch. Göring was in exile. Hitler awaited trial on charges of high treason. The future of the National Socialist Party was uncertain, and Mayer was again friendless, forlorn, and penniless.

When the thought of facing life alone became unbearable, a package arrived from Innsbruck. Mayer opened it, pulled out a sheet of crimson parchment having a light, pleasant fragrance, and read a note written in exquisite calligraphic script.

Dearest Claus,
How can I ever repay your kindness?
You risked your life to save my beloved husband.
Were it not for you, I would now be in deep mourning.
I know the small gift enclosed with this note is pitifully inadequate.
Please accept it as a small token of my heartfelt appreciation
Yours Eternally with Love,
Carin

Scribbled below was written:

I shall never forget your loyalty, Claus,
Commander Hermann Göring,
December 1923.

Mayer gasped after removing velour wrapping from the package. Beneath it was a cigarette box fashioned from a rosewood limb. Heart shaped red rubies circled a swastika carved into the lid. Fine silver calligraphy surrounded the rubies:

To Claus Mayer, a great German patriot.
Carin and Hermann Göring.

Inside the cigarette box, he found another envelope. He opened it and read the note.

I fear for your safety, Claus. It may be years before Hermann and I can return, and the Party won't have the funds to continue paying SA Troopers. I asked a relative to open a bank account in your name. She will keep replenishing your funds until we get back. You'll find the bank's information on a card in this envelope.

Carin

Tears came to his eyes. *I'm rescued a second time. First Röhm snatched me from poverty, and now Carin will pay for my shelter and food. I shall be forever grateful to her and the Party.*

He ran his right index finger over the rubies on the cigarette box, placed it on the top shelf of his bookcase, and headed to Carin's bank.

CHAPTER TWO -- RACHEL GOLDSTEIN

9th November, 1923 – Munich – 9:00 PM – Rachel reacts to Claus Mayer's intrusion

When Mayer and his troopers walked away from Rachel's home she turned, went inside, and closed the front door. Moments later, she felt nauseous and reached for a chair to steady herself. She then stood erect, held her hand over her heart, and whispered, "I curse you Mayer for the monster you are. Never again will you or your kind have such power over me."

Mordechai rushed to Rachel's side and took her in his arms. "Thank God you are safe, my child?"

"Never again can we allow a band of brutes to enter our home and act as they did tonight," said Rachel.

He led her to their couch and sat down with her. "You are overreacting to this evening's events, my child. The government will soon put an end to Mayer and his thugs. Then our lives will return to normal. We've lived in Germany for many generations, and with God's help we'll live here for many more."

Rachel's heartbeat raced when she said, "Don't you understand, Papa? It's only a matter of time before a political party holding anti-Semitic views takes power. No Jew will rest easy after that happens." Rachel's voice rose to a crescendo when she added, "I *won't* stay here. I'll find a better life elsewhere before someone like Mayer can rise to rule our lives."

Mordechai's demeanor went from irritation to anger and finally rage as Rachel bellowed her intention to leave Germany. "How dare you scream at me in my home? I taught you better than to act so disrespectfully."

Rachel turned, stormed to her bedroom, and slammed the door shut.

The next morning, Rachel reproached herself for yelling at her father. She found him in the kitchen. "Papa, please forgive me for yelling. I never intended to hurt you. I'm emigrating to escape Mayer and his thugs. Please give me your blessing."

Mordechai walked over to Rachel and hugged her. Gently brushing a loop of hair from her brow he said, "My darling child, you are the light of my life, but it would be wrong of me to keep you from acting on your deeply held beliefs. I *will* bless your going."

She hugged her father and felt his tears kiss her cheek. "I love you, Papa."

"Do you want me to help you become established in a foreign land?"

"Yes I would, Papa."

"You have a cousin, Uncle Chaim's son, Solomon, who lives in England. He could help you adjust to your new life."

"You never told me about this cousin, Papa."

Mordechai gazed at the floor, as if collecting his thoughts, then looked at Rachel. "When Solomon was little older than you are now, he also feared anti-Semites would come to rule our land and told Uncle Chaim he would emigrate. Chaim took this as a direct attack upon his leadership of the family, warning he'd disavow him if he left Germany. Solomon tried reasoning with his father, but Chaim refused to discuss the issue further. Solomon left the house that evening, and my brother hasn't spoken of him since that day."

"I'm glad you didn't give me an ultimatum, Papa. It would have broken my heart."

"Mine too, my darling child, mine too."

"How did he prepare himself to leave Germany?"

"Cut off from his family, he spent two years living with a friend in Berlin. It took that long for him to get the documents necessary to enter England legally. Once there, he found a job working for the British government. Several years later he changed his name to Sean Smythe."

"How did you know this, Papa?"

"I remained in contact with Sean, but told no one. Your Uncle Chaim would never have forgiven me if he knew. I shall write, asking Sean to help you."

"Thank you Papa," said Rachel hugging her father again. "I'll find a safe place for us in England and bring you there when the anti-Semites seize our land."

"Perhaps, my child, but it's also possible you'll return to Germany after recognizing that Friday evening's intrusion was nothing more than a bump in Germany's long road to tomorrow."

⌘⌘⌘⌘⌘⌘⌘⌘

Mordechai wrote to his nephew the next day. Smythe replied quickly, eager to help Mordechai in any way. He included a recent picture so she would recognize him when she arrived. A week later, Mordechai approached her holding the newspaper. "Today's paper is filled with reports of many in Munich, including 4,000 University students, who protested Hitler's power grab. The unrest continued for three days, concluding after the protesters heard the army arrested Hitler and charged him with high treason. It's just as I told you, my child. The German people will never allow a fanatic like Hitler to seize power. You don't need to leave home."

"I'm sorry Papa; I still believe our safety will one day depend on my moving beyond Mayer's reach."

The next day, Rachel traveled to the British Embassy in Berlin and applied for an immigration visa. She then went back to Munich, took a job as a waitress to pay for her move to England, and learned how to write and speak in English from a friend. The days passed slowly as she waited for the British Embassy to approve her visa. When she mentioned it to Mordechai, he suggested she join the young singles club at his Synagogue to fill her time. She smiled at the idea. "Are you hoping I'll meet the right someone who will convince me to stay here?"

He answered with a mischievous smile. "Would that be so bad?"

She thought about it for several minutes before saying, "I don't like my life being on hold while waiting for word from Britain, so I will ask the Rabbi about the club."

The next day the Rabbi told her, "The next meeting is this Sunday afternoon, at the Temple. I hope you'll join."

She replied, "I will be there," with a smile.

When she walked into the Temple on Sunday, many of her school friends walked up to greet her. Among them was Benjie Kornblum, the first boy she'd ever kissed. She tried to hide her disappointment when he told her he was engaged and invited her to the wedding. After a few weeks, she stopped going to the young singles group. Instead, she regularly attended the Temple's morning and evening services, with her father, to deepen her commitment to Judaism.

⌘⌘⌘⌘⌘⌘⌘⌘

Over the next two years, Adolf Hitler's popularity fell as the German economy steadily improved. Even so, Rachel was thrilled to receive a letter from the British Embassy telling her she could pick up her immigration visa. The next day, she took a bus to Berlin and shed tears of joy exiting the embassy with the visa stamped in her passport. She booked passage on a ship to Dover, then boarded a bus back to Munich.

Rachel paused as she approached her front door. *Am I making the right decision? In a few days, I'll leave the only home I've ever known. It holds a lifetime of happy memories.* After thinking about it for several more minutes, she dismissed any further thought of remaining at home.

When Rachel opened the door, her heart ached seeing the anguish in her father's eyes. He walked with her to the couch where they sat and wept.

Mordechai was the first to speak. "I hope it won't be long before we're reunited." He kissed her and then asked, "When do you leave for England?"

"My ship leaves Hamburg in one week."

"Would you like me to go with you to the port?"

"I would love it."

When they arrived, Rachel and Mordechai waited quietly for the order to board. Then Mordechai said a final prayer and kissed Rachel. They held each other until a ship's employee told her the ship was about to leave. Rachel gave her father a final kiss, then embarked, and waved to him from the promenade deck as the ship began moving. She went to the back of the ship and cried until her father disappeared from sight. Then she made her way to the front of the vessel at a snail's pace, wiping the tears from her eyes. Scanning the horizon, she looked for her new home, certain her life in England would be free of evil men like Claus Mayer.

10th November, 1925 – Dover – Rachel Arrives in England

Rachel scanned the faces of those on the dock as the ship tied up in Dover. Her pulse raced when she spotted her cousin Sean. After disembarking, Rachel went through the immigration process and then ran up to hug Sean. Speaking in German, she said, "I recognized you from the picture you sent my papa. I'm so glad to meet you."

"Welcome to England and your new life. Let's get your baggage, then I'll take you home. It's almost impossible to find a flat in London, so I arranged my extra room for you. Stay as long as you want."

"Thank you, Sean."

He helped Rachel find her suitcase, then showed her to his car. "It should take us about two hours to reach my apartment. Make yourself comfortable."

Rachel smiled. "This is a real treat. I rarely rode in a car. We usually take public transportation in Germany."

"It's been about two years since your papa told me you were immigrating. Did the visa take that long?"

"Yes, I applied a few days after Papa wrote to you."

"What did you do while you waited?"

"I took English lessons from a friend and worked as a waitress to pay for my move."

Sean stopped at a traffic light, turned to Rachel, and asked, "Would you feel comfortable speaking to me in English?"

"Yes, I'd like that," said Rachel in English with a German accent.

After the light turned green, Sean asked, "Your papa never told me why you left Germany."

She told him about Mayer's Beer Hall Putsch visit, and her fear that anti-Semites would one day rise to rule Germany. "Papa told me you work for the British government. What do you do there?"

"My work is in Britain's national interest."

Rachel didn't understand what that meant, but felt awkward asking for an explanation.

A week later, Sean found her a job translating German newspapers into English for Alistair Sedgwick, a co-worker of his. While driving to the office, on her first day, Sean said, "Before you begin, I must warn you of two things. First, Alistair is blind, so you must read your translations to him. Second, he is a stickler for the King's English. He will expect you to pronounce each word as if you were born and educated in London and he'll correct you every time you make a mistake."

"How long did it take to lose your German accent?"

"About four months, but it wasn't easy. A friend helped me."

"Do you think he'd be willing to help me?"

"I'm sure he would. I'll invite him to the apartment next weekend."

Wanting Sean to be proud of her progress, Rachel threw herself into her work. She worked with Sean's friend most evenings and only spoke English with her cousin. After four months, she navigated an entire week's worth of daily translations without interruption. Soon after that, Anthony Glasgow replaced Sedgwick as her supervisor. Rachel found it strange they'd made the switch, but decided her bosses must have a good reason.

On their first day, Glasgow told Rachel she would meet many of the Englishmen who visited his office. "Our section has a strict policy against hiring foreigners. Sean persuaded us to make an exception in your case, so it will go badly for him if any of my guests discover you aren't British."

Not wanting to cause her cousin any problems, Rachel replied, "They won't know."

⌘⌘⌘⌘⌘⌘⌘⌘

Five months after Rachel arrived in England, Sean invited her to visit his office. He led her through areas of the building she'd never seen. When they stopped at a checkpoint, an armed guard said, "Good morning Colonel."

Rachel glanced sideways at Sean, surprised he held a military rank.

The guard pulled a manila folder from a file cabinet at his desk and said, "I have the pass you requested for Miss Goldstein's visit to the high security area."

Sean took a badge out of the folder and handed it to her. "Please attach this to your blouse, then we can continue."

Rachel felt uneasy pinning on the badge. The pair then walked past the officer, wound their way through a maze of corridors, and paused at a secretary's desk. "Is he ready for us, Ducky?"

"Yes, sir."

Sean escorted Rachel through a door behind Ducky's desk. Inside, detailed maps of several European countries blanketed the windowless office. The map of Germany was large enough for Rachel to see the small towns she'd visited with her father as a child. Looking across the room, she saw a man with a full black beard gazing at her. He stood, extending his hand. She offered hers, and he shook it vigorously. "Welcome, Miss Goldstein. I've been looking forward to meeting you."

Rachel tilted her head to one side and felt her eye twitch.

He sat down. "No need for distress, Miss Goldstein. Please take a seat so we can talk more comfortably." He waited for her to sit, then continued. "Sean told us you believe the National Socialist Party, or its equivalent, would one day rise to rule Germany."

"That's true, sir."

"Would you be willing to keep Hitler from establishing a National Socialist regime in Germany?"

Rachel sat bolt upright, a fluttery feeling growing in her chest. "I would gladly do so, sir."

He leaned toward her. "You'd be embarking on a perilous assignment that could lead to torture and death. There's no turning back if I continue. Are you sure you want me to proceed?"

"Yes. I am certain, sir."

He sat back in his chair. "My unit oversees Germany for Britain's Directorate of Military Intelligence Section 6, commonly known as MI6. We believe Germany, and Herr Hitler in particular, may one day pose a threat to our island nation."

"Thank God, someone will do something about that monster," blurted Rachel, biting her lip to keep from crying out for joy.

"That is our greatest wish, Miss Goldstein. Unfortunately, many in MI6 consider Communism, not National Socialism, Britain's main source of danger. They believe we should *support* Adolf Hitler."

"Are you joking, Mr…?"

"I apologize. My name is Reginald Turnbey, and no, I am not joking. The bulk of MI6s staff would like to see Hitler take power, certain he would build up Germany's military and become England's first defense against a Soviet invasion."

Rachel was pleased Turnbey considered Hitler a threat, but dismayed that others in MI6 wanted to advance Hitler's ambitions. *Perhaps Turnbey's unit could keep Hitler from gaining power.* "How many people oversee Germany for you, sir?"

"There are four of us; Sean, myself, and two others who will soon be here."

"May *I* join your section?" asked Rachel.

"You already have."

Rachel looked at Sean. "Were you responsible for that?"

"Yes," he replied with a sheepish grin.

"What have I been doing?"

"Everyone in our section reads, writes, and speaks German fluently," replied Turnbey, "so we didn't need you to translate newspapers for us. We did want to know whether you could learn to speak like a London native."

The door opened and Turnbey pointed at the newcomers. "You already know Alistair Sedgwick and Anthony Glasgow. Alistair is not blind. We used his faux blindness as an excuse to improve your English speaking skills. The elocutionist who trained you is also an MI6 employee. We then tapped Anthony's wide assortment of British contacts to make sure Alistair perfected your English fluency. To your credit, all his unwitting language detectives believed you were a native Londoner."

Sean leaned forward. "We want to send you back to Germany as a spy, but you cannot return as Rachel Goldstein. You will get a name identifying you as the daughter of an established British family, and a religion consistent with your new station in life."

Rachel sagged into her chair. The thought of remaking herself into an Adolf Hitler devotee hadn't occurred to Rachel. That meant she'd have to abandon her Judaism to become one of them. *I must think and act like Claus Mayer if I'm to defeat him and his kind, but how...*

"I know what's going through your mind," said Sean. "Judeo-Christian ethics underpin every fiber of your being, and we're asking to turn your back on all you hold dear. However, doing so is vital to your feeding us information that can prevent Hitler's rise to power. There is also a chance he will one day rise to rule Germany, so you must establish yourself as a devoted member of the National Socialist Party. You could then send us reports on his regime while funneling crucial funding to those who defy him." Sean paused for a moment, then added, "When you embark on this assignment you will help heal a broken world... *tikkun olam* in Hebrew... which is consistent with the highest of Jewish ideals."

Which is worse? Acting like a National Socialist, or turning down an opportunity to destroy Hitler. The answer is obvious. "But Papa will be inconsolable when he hears I abandoned my Judaism," blurted Rachel.

"He'll never know about your Christian identity," replied Turnbey. "After you accept this mission, we'll stage your death in an accident and a Jewish agency will inform your father."

Rachel clutched at her stomach. "Must my father know I am dead? He will be heartbroken. Is there no other alternative?"

"No, my dear," said Turnbey. "Your family must be certain you are dead. Should one unintended slip of the tongue come to the SA's attention, they will torture you for information and then kill you."

Rachel frowned, then her features became firm. "I *must* accept this responsibility. Rachel Goldstein will cease to exist, for a time, so I can battle Hitler's perverted beliefs. My father will weep, but with the Almighty's help I'll rejoin him in a Germany purged of monsters like Claus Mayer."

Despite her valiant declaration, Rachel feared that purging her religious beliefs would turn her into a hard-hearted monster. So she vowed to keep a trace of Rachel's ethical self to act as a moral gatekeeper over her soul, to make sure that the National Socialists couldn't corrupt her.

15th August, 1926 - Berlin – 7:30 pm – Mayer attends his brother's graduation party

In December 1924, the German government released Adolf Hitler from Lansberg prison and he resumed his duties as leader of the National Socialist Party. Mayer rejoined the SA as a trooper in early 1925 and notified Carin Göring she no longer needed to support him financially.

Mayer hadn't contacted his family since being fired from his last job in the early 1920s. Proud of his successful SA career, he yearned to rekindle his close relationship with Heinrich. A newspaper story hailing his brother's graduation at the head of his medical school class, and inviting friends and family to a party for Heinrich on 15 August 1926, gave him that opportunity. Mayer's heart raced at the thought of reestablishing a close relationship with his family at the party.

The familiar whiff of his mother's beef goulash made Mayer's mouth water when he entered the banquet hall. Heinrich ran over to hug him. "We haven't heard from you in years, Brother. I'm delighted you came." He turned to his parents. "Look, Claus joined our celebration." The three of them embraced Mayer, bringing him to tears.

⌘⌘⌘⌘⌘⌘⌘⌘

Moments earlier, one guest grimaced when Claus Mayer arrived at Heinrich's party. Turning to the person next to him, he pointed at Mayer and huffed. "I'm appalled that Heinrich's brother had the gall to show up here. He's an SA thug who attacks Jews at Social Democratic Party meetings. He enters the hall with his goons and orders them to assault anyone wearing a skullcap or having a long nose. Heinrich will be furious when he finds out."

The listener told other guests. News of Mayer's affiliation spread.

⌘⌘⌘⌘⌘⌘⌘⌘

After kissing his mother, Mayer turned to Heinrich. "I'm not surprised you graduated at the head of your class. You were always much smarter than me."

"That's not true," replied Heinrich. "I was always proud of you, and it looks like you have done very well for yourself. What are you doing now?"

"I supervise an employee section."

"Where do you work?"

Reluctant to explain his responsibilities, afraid his brother wouldn't understand the importance of his duties to the future of Germany, he said, "Please excuse me, Heinrich. I must call my boss about a serious issue."

"When you're done come sit next to me at our family table."

"Yes, I'll join you as soon as I can."

Mayer walked over to a phone, pretended to place a call, and acted as if he was busy. After Mayer's father asked the guests to take their seats, friends and family began toasting Heinrich. Mayer then hung up the phone and took the empty seat next to Heinrich. His father was making a toast when someone approached Heinrich and whispered in his ear. Mayer's stomach tightened when he turned to him and asked, "I just heard something ridiculous. You couldn't be a storm trooper… could you?" in a shaky voice.

I remember that look from our childhood. Heinrich always saw the best in me, refusing to believe an accusation of guilt unless I confirmed it to be true. He expects me to deny I am a trooper. As a child I lied to make him happy, but why should I lie about joining the SA? It's the best thing I've done in my life. It is my life.

Mayer replied, "I am proud to be a Storm Trooper Lieutenant."

Heinrich's cheeks slackened and his voice quivered as he asked, "Are you teasing me? I can't believe you are a Brownshirt."

"I told you the truth, Brother."

Heinrich's voice and facial features firmed. "Disavow those beasts, Claus. You don't belong in that devil's brigade. Come home. We will care for you until you find yourself. I beg you to give up this alliance with evil."

Mayer stood up and stuck out his chest. "Germany's Democratic Republic destroyed everything good in our country. Patriots like me must right the wrongs perpetrated by the Social

Democrats, Jews, and Communists. I beg you to join our cause. It is our duty to liberate Germany and create a new Reich that will become the envy of the world."

Mayer's words, coming from deep conviction in Hitler's agenda, rose to a crescendo that reverberated throughout the banquet hall. Seeing he was now the center of attention, Mayer sat and continued in a hushed and respectful tone.

"I was at my lowest ebb, Brother, when fate brought me to Adolf Hitler's side. He felt my pain when I told him how I tried to better my lot and failed. He said I was not responsible for my situation. Far from it, I was an innocent soul victimized by the tyranny of an unfeeling state. Hitler knows what it takes to return our nation to its former greatness. All he asks is that we trust him. I cannot refuse Adolf Hitler's plea, and neither should you."

⌘⌘⌘⌘⌘⌘⌘⌘

Mayer's parents stood and clutched each other. Their tear-filled eyes mirrored disgust at the evil now at the core of their family. His father sobbed. His mother gazed despondently at her son, seeking *any* evidence he was not a monster. After a few moments, she buried her face in her husband's chest and wept the tears of a parent mourning the death of a child.

⌘⌘⌘⌘⌘⌘⌘⌘

The turn of Heinrich's mouth confirmed his outrage at the brother he cherished as a soul mate since childhood. "I am horror-struck that you now court the devil. You have made your choice and so must I. Divorce yourself from that amoral band of thugs or we shall be strangers until death."

Mayer's voice was firm when he stood to reply. "Mine is the only sure path to Germany's revival. I will make any sacrifice, in Adolf Hitler's name, to make sure our Fatherland is reborn as a respected world power."

Heinrich rose, took his brother's face in his hands, placed a soft kiss on his cheek, and whispered, "So be it," in his ear. He then walked to the other end of the banquet hall where his friends enveloped him in a sheltering cocoon of sympathy, support, and solidarity.

Heinrich's ultimatum surprised and saddened Mayer. Even so, Hitler's charismatic hold on him, and National Socialism's promise of privileged status in a resurgent Germany, far outweighed his love of family. He glared at the crowd surrounding Heinrich. "One day you'll see that National Socialism is the only true path for our Fatherland. When that happens, I shall welcome you all with open arms."

Mayer's words again shook the hall, but his brother did not look in his direction… confirming they now lived in separate worlds. He turned and walked toward the exit. Looking back, he half expected somebody to stop him. Instead, the circle tightened around Heinrich.

Someone ran into Mayer when he opened the door. He glowered at him for a moment, then clasped him in a warm hug. "Bruno Hauptman, what are you doing here?"

"Your brother invited me to show his appreciation for the support I gave you when four of your workers assaulted you."

"I'm glad he asked you and would like to buy you a drink."

"Shouldn't we go into the hall?"

"No, I wore out my welcome in there." Mayer remained silent until the pair exited the banquet building. He then continued. "What happened after my employees insisted I attacked them without cause, and my boss fired me?"

"They badgered me until I resigned. Since then, I've been going from job to job, unable to hold any of them for long." Bruno paused before adding, "Your manager wanted to keep you on, but his director heard of your reputation as a bully and forced him to fire you. I met with the director to let him know your workers attacked *you* without reason. He refused to change his mind, saying you might have been innocent in that case, but he knew of many other times when you were not."

Mayer slowed his pace. "I also had trouble holding jobs after they fired me. By 1923, I was starving and homeless. Ernst Röhm came to my aid, offering me a new life with the SA. Now I am a respected Storm Trooper Lieutenant." He paused to face Bruno. "You lost your job because of me. The least I can do is repay my debt of gratitude by enlisting you as a member of my storm trooper section. The pay isn't great, but you'll always have a roof over your head and food in your stomach."

"Thanks Claus, but that's not the life for me."

Mayer pulled a wad of Reichsmarks from his wallet and handed them to Bruno. "There's little else I can do for you now. Please call me if you ever need anything."

CHAPTER THREE -- ELISABETH BILLINGSWORTH

13th November, 1923 – London - Billingsworth returns from Germany after the Putsch

Elisabeth Billingsworth's heart raced when Adolf Hitler stormed into the Bürgerbräukeller, leapt on a chair, fired two shots into the ceiling, and yelled, "The Munich Putsch has begun." Then, when he added, "Our SA troopers deposed the governments of Bavaria and Berlin," she stood and screamed praise for her new messiah with 2,000 compatriots.

When someone called for volunteers to help him rid the Fatherland of its Jew filth, she attempted to enlist. However, a jostling crowd of SA troopers, battling to join his unit, blocked her way. She stamped her feet in anger when he left the beer hall with his recruits.

⌘⌘⌘⌘⌘⌘⌘⌘

SA Lieutenant Bruno Kreutzer smiled seeing Billingsworth's tantrum. *I must meet that woman. She's gorgeous and spirited.* He approached her saying, "I'm sorry you couldn't join Lieutenant Mayer's squad, but you're welcome to become my first recruit."

She tilted her head to one side. "Will you enlist others?"

"Yes, would you like to help me choose them?"

"I would."

Billingsworth helped Kreutzer select twenty storm troopers and left with them. After they reached the Jewish District, she pointed at an SA Lieutenant ordering his men to kill an old Jew. “Isn’t that the squad I wanted to join?”

“Yes, that’s Claus Mayer.”

Billingsworth watched as Mayer’s gang surrounded an old man. Her sexual excitement grew as they kicked him to death. Then she trembled hearing a woman’s unearthly howl after the troopers hurled her onto his dismembered body.

“What’s the matter,” asked Kreutzer.

“Nothing at all,” she replied, her heartbeat again racing.

“Did that excite you?”

“More than anything I’ve ever experienced.”

“When we get to know each other better, I’ll introduce you to delights you may enjoy even more.”

“Yes?”

“This evening, I’ll tell my men to treat the Jew vermin we find in ways that will take you to new heights of arousal.”

Billingsworth delighted in her newfound pleasures, watching the troopers humiliate and torture defenseless Jews until dawn. Before they parted company, she told Kreutzer, “Tonight convinced me to make National Socialism *my* political cause. I will dedicate the rest of my life to championing Adolf Hitler’s goals and methods.”

"I can help you," said Kreutzer, gazing at her in a way that again aroused her. He wrote his phone number and address on a slip of paper. "Take this and contact me when you're ready."

Billingsworth took the note. "I'm returning home tomorrow, and will support Hitler as soon as I can." She then went back to her hotel room, dropped onto her bed fully clothed, and fell asleep as soon as her head hit the pillow.

When Billingsworth's parents picked her up at the Dover seaport, she told them, "I will support Adolf Hitler's goal of restoring Germany to its rightful status as a world leader."

Cecil and Margaret were ecstatic. This was the first time in their daughter's life she showed signs of outgrowing her unquenchable appetite for excitement and self-gratification. That evening, Margaret asked her husband, "It seems like sending Elisabeth on a European tour made her grow up, but what do you know about Hitler?"

"Only what I read in the newspapers." The next morning, Cecil wrinkled his brow as he approached Margaret. "I called a few of my German friends and asked them about Hitler. They told me he's an evil man, and his National Socialists are anti-Semitic Fascists." He paused for a few moments, then added, "Reginald Turnbey works for MI6. He may know how we should handle this situation. I'll call him tomorrow."

When Cecil phoned to tell Turnbey about Elisabeth's fascination with Hitler, Turnbey invited him to his office. Later that day, Turnbey stood up when Cecil's secretary showed him in. He shook Cecil's hand then pointed to a chair and sat down next to him. "I wouldn't like Elisabeth to become involved with Hitler or his party. A few days ago, they tried to overthrow Germany's government. The army stopped them, and the police arrested Hitler. He will stand trial for high treason."

"What do you think we should do?"

"Warn Elisabeth, in no uncertain terms, that both of you oppose her joining Hitler's thugs."

That evening, Cecil called his daughter into the library, closed the door, and asked her to sit down with him. "You have no business supporting an evil madman like Hitler."

"You don't understand, Daddy. Hitler wants to restore Germany to its rightful status as a world leader."

Cecil's body tensed. "He attempted to overthrow the German government, but the army stopped him. The police arrested him and he'll be tried for high treason."

"That's why I *must* support him. The German government is corrupt, and I will help Hitler take power."

If I tell her not to help Hitler, she will do the opposite. Perhaps it's best if I let this situation play out. "I will not stand in your way. However, if you disgrace our family, I will force you to leave our home."

Billingsworth invited her friend Marilyn and several other companions to her house and convinced them to help her raise money for Hitler. A week later, Billingsworth met a rich Londoner eager to finance Hitler's dream of building an anti-Semitic Fascist State in Germany. He invited Billingsworth, her friends, and his similarly minded wealthy compatriots to his mansion. After a meal and several rounds of cocktails, Billingsworth spent over an hour describing the Beer Hall Putsch and its brutal aftermath in graphic detail. The guests praised her devotion and donated generously to Adolf Hitler and the National Socialist Party. Many promised to continue contributing, so long as she remained faithful to the anti-Semitic Fascist ideal.

The next day, Billingsworth wrote to Bruno Kreutzer asking where she should send the donations she'd raised. He replied that the National Socialist Party assigned him to work with British donors and asked her to mail him the funds.

⌘⌘⌘⌘⌘⌘⌘⌘⌘

Several weeks later, Turnbey called Sedgwick into his office. "A few weeks ago Cecil Billingsworth told me his daughter wanted to help Hitler and asked what he should do about it. I told him to warn Elisabeth that he and his wife Margaret strongly oppose it. He did so, but she raised money for Hitler, anyway. Yesterday, I checked with a German friend. He told me she's raising more money than anyone expected. Hitler and his Social Democratic Party must be delighted with her. I'd like you to find out whether she'd be willing to join MI6. She could keep us informed about Hitler's activities.

Two weeks later, Sedgewick walked into Turnbey's office. "Elisabeth Billingsworth would never consider becoming an MI6 agent."

"Why not?"

"I phoned her using a German accent and said I wanted to donate a significant amount to Adolf Hitler and the National Socialist Party. She asked me to meet her at a small restaurant in Whitechapel the next morning. During that meeting, I told her that Adolf Hitler's speeches convinced me to support his Party. She smiled, then said she'd dedicated her life to championing Hitler's goals and methods. The rest of our conversation convinced me she'd *never* consider working with MI6."

"That's too bad. We need someone like her working with us. Please ask Glasgow to join us."

Sedgewick returned with Glasgow a few minutes later. After they sat down, Turnbey said, "It's time we find someone respected by Hitler's National Socialists to become an agent. That's the only way we can know what they're planning. See if you can find someone like that, and I'll ask Desmond, a police department friend, to be on the lookout."

⌘⌘⌘⌘⌘⌘⌘⌘

Kreutzer often visited Billingsworth in London to help with her fundraising. After they'd been working with each other for two years, Kreutzer told her the lack of excitement in their lives frustrated him.

A smile crossed Billingsworth's face when she said, "Why don't we shake up my Dad's exclusive men's club. They're a bunch of stuffy old men, and we need to teach them a lesson." He agreed, and they went there that evening.

The next day, the Club's president called Cecil. "Your daughter and her German friend instigated a drunken brawl at our club yesterday. It resulted in serious injury to several longtime members. The pair also caused extensive damage to our facilities. My board insists you pay all medical and repair costs. If it happens again, we shall ask you to resign your club membership."

Livid after hanging up the phone, Cecil stormed into his daughter's room. "I warned you of the consequences if you didn't cut off all ties to Hitler and his Fascist Party. We will no longer put up with your wild and irresponsible behavior. Leave this house at once and don't come back until you dissociate yourself from Kreutzer and his thugs." He knew she would return as soon she'd spent her own meager funds.

After checking into a London hotel, that afternoon, Billingsworth called Kreutzer, who'd returned to Germany after the incident at Cecil's club. "My parents threw me out of the house because of my work in behalf of the Party. I moved into a hotel, but can't afford to live here for more than a few days. What should I do?"

⌘⌘⌘⌘⌘⌘⌘⌘

Kreutzer, who was falling in love with Billingsworth, realized he could exploit Elisabeth's predicament to his advantage… but he needed time to come up with a plan. "Tell me where you are staying."

"I'm at the Ritz London, in Piccadilly."

"stay there. I'll send a cable giving them permission to charge all your expenses to my Berlin bank."

"Can you afford that?"

"Yes, a wealthy maiden aunt died last year leaving me a sizeable fortune. I'll book passage on the first ship back to England and will join you as soon as I can."

Kreutzer considered his options after getting off the phone. *I want to make her mine. If Elisabeth returns home, her parents will make sure we never see each other again. I must decide how to keep her away from them.*

When Kreutzer's ship docked, he took a taxi to the Ritz London and sat down with the concierge. "I am Bruno Kreutzer. My friend Elisabeth Billingsworth is a guest here."

"Yes sir. We received your cable a few days ago. I will prepare a statement detailing Miss Billingsworth's expenses."

"That's fine, but I'm interested in buying a home in an affluent London neighborhood. Can you help me?"

"Certainly, sir. Kensington Palace Gardens is one of the most prestigious neighborhoods in Europe. I can recommend an agent to show you all the available properties."

"Can your hotel vouch for that agent, and when would he be available to show me the properties?

"Many of our guests used him, and none lodged a complaint with us. I'll call his office to find out when he can meet with you."

Ten minutes later, the concierge told Kreutzer the agent had cancelled all his appointments and was on his way.

The agent spent the next three hours showing Kreutzer homes for sale in Kensington Palace Gardens. After lunch, Kreutzer called his Berlin bank and ordered them forward a certified check to him, at the Ritz London, for a 10% deposit on the most expensive mansion they'd seen. He then returned to the concierge's office and called Elisabeth's room. "This is Bruno. I have a surprise for you."

"What is it?"

"Come downstairs and you'll see."

He hung up the phone and asked the concierge to arrange for a limousine and chauffer.

"I can have it for you in five minutes, sir,"

Elisabeth exited the elevator as the limo arrived. "What's your surprise?"

"Come with me and I'll show you." Bruno led her to the limo, and they got in. After they drove for a few minutes he said, "Close your eyes."

"Why?"

"Trust me; it'll be a pleasant surprise."

They drove a little further, then slowed.

"Can I look now?"

"Not yet."

The limo turned, a gate squeaked open, and they stopped a few moments later.

"You can open your eyes now."

She did so, stepped out of the auto, and stared at a huge mansion. It had three floors, was seven windows wide, and had a huge carved ivory central doorway. A ten-foot high steel fence surrounded the building. "Why did you bring me to a museum? They bore me."

Bruno laughed, then took Elisabeth in his arms. "Welcome to your new home. You'll never again have to live with your parents."

"Is it yours?"

"If you like it it's yours. I will buy it for you after we sign a written agreement."

"Why would you do that?"

"I love you and want to make you happy."

She stepped back. "What do I have to sign?"

"That the mansion will be available whenever I'm in London."

Elisabeth tilted her head to one side. "This place must be expensive to run. I can't afford that."

"I'll give you enough money to meet all your wants and needs. If we marry, I'll name you as my sole beneficiary. That will also be part of our agreement."

"You won't be sorry," said Elisabeth as she embraced Kreutzer and kissed him.

Overwhelmed by Kreutzer's generosity and glad she wouldn't have to return home, Billingsworth hired a tutor to improve her German language skills.

A few weeks later, Kreutzer decided it was time to ask Elisabeth to marry him. He bought her 3-carat ring and travelled back to London. As soon as he arrived at her mansion Kreutzer whispered, "Where is she?" to Daphne, her maid.

"She's in her room, sir. Do you want me to call her?"

"No, I want to surprise her." He tiptoed up the stairs, opened her door, and saw her getting dressed in the large closet. She hadn't yet seen him, so he took out the ring and held it out as he approached her.

She swung around, grinned when she saw his face, then her eyes sparkled when she looked down at the ring. "If that's an engagement ring, my answer is yes. If not, why are you waiting?"

"I showed the ring to my parents, and they insisted we get married at our home in Berlin. They can't wait to meet you."

The following week they sailed to Germany where Kreutzer's parents threw them a lavish wedding.

After they married, Billingsworth spent the next two years in England raising funds for Hitler. Kreutzer, who was rising in the National Socialist Party, remained in Berlin, but visited Elisabeth in London as often as he could. Billingsworth's fundraising prowess, and marriage into the well regarded Kreutzer family, brought her to the attention of German Party leaders.

⌘⌘⌘⌘⌘⌘⌘⌘

Elisabeth Billingsworth died in mid-1926. The investigating Police Detective, who had known the Billingsworths for many years, called on them to break the news.

"What happened, Desmond?" asked Cecil Billingsworth with a distant stare.

"Daphne, her maid, told our constable that Kreutzer killed her."

"How?" asked Margaret, dabbing the tears from her eyes.

"Daphne said it happened when Kreutzer performed Erotic Asphyxiation, a lovemaking technique he taught Elisabeth soon after she moved into the mansion."

Margaret covered her mouth with her hand and sobbed. Cecil's eyes became glassy when he asked, "What is that?"

"Kreutzer cut off Elisabeth's air supply during their lovemaking to intensify her sexual climax. He added to his own sadistic pleasure by watching her thrash about, desperately fighting for life. Yesterday, Kreutzer deprived Elisabeth of air long enough to kill her."

Seeing them both in tears, Desmond asked, "Would you like me to stop?"

"No, please go on," said Cecil, as he walked over to comfort his wife.

"Yesterday, Daphne heard strange noises when she walked past Elisabeth's room. When Daphne opened the door, she saw Kreutzer bring his lovemaking to its lethal climax. She ran screaming from the house and hailed a police constable walking past the front gate. He hurried in with her, arrested Kreutzer, and took him to Scotland Yard."

"Did Kreutzer force her to take part?" asked Cecil.

"No. Elisabeth told Daphne the sexual exhilaration she felt when Kreutzer took her to death's door, and back, was beyond anything she'd ever experienced. It became an obsession. Elisabeth demanded he perform Erotic Asphyxiation at least once each time he returned to her mansion." Desmond paused for a few moments, then continued. "Why would Elisabeth share such intimate details with her maid?"

"To embarrass and humiliate her," answered Cecil. "She knew such shocking comments would disgust Daphne. It was a flaw in our daughter's personality."

When he returned to Scotland Yard, Desmond telephoned Turnbey. "A few years ago, you asked me to tell you if I found anyone like Elisabeth Billingsworth who you could recruit as an MI6 agent. I thought you'd like to know that Elisabeth's husband murdered her yesterday."

As soon as he hung up, Turnbey called Sedgwick and Glasgow into his office. "Elisabeth Billingsworth is dead. I knew her as a young adult. If I remember correctly, she resembled Rachel." Turnbey stroked his beard as he added, "If Rachel can impersonate Elisabeth, we could send her back to Germany as a spy."

Sedgwick stood. "I took a clandestine picture of Billingsworth when we first considered her as an agent. I'll get it." Sedgwick smiled when he returned a few minutes later. "She could be Rachel's identical twin. Here, take a look."

Examining her picture, Turnbey said, "Stupendous, if we add a few inches to Rachel's hair, and she puts on a few pounds, Rachel could pass for Billingsworth." Stroking his beard, Turnbey added, "I'll dine with Cecil Billingsworth tomorrow. He will most likely welcome an opportunity to help us undermine Hitler."

The next evening, Turnbey met Cecil in a private room at their favorite restaurant. After toasting their first drink, he leaned toward Cecil and whispered, "Would you be willing to help MI6 contain Adolf Hitler's ambitions in Germany?"

"I'm definitely interested. Please tell me more."

"I can't go into much detail now, but someone who could pass for Elisabeth is on my staff. We'd like to send her back to Germany as a spy, but can only do so if you help her adopt Elisabeth's speech and mannerisms."

A smile crossed Cecil's face. "You bet I will. Have her visit us tomorrow morning. Margaret and I will do all we can, and I'll introduce her to Daphne. She took care of Elisabeth from birth to the day she died."

"Can we rely on Daphne to keep Elisabeth's death a secret?"

Cecil nodded his head. "Without a doubt; she'd do anything to get back at those Fascist goons for killing Elisabeth. I'll talk with her tomorrow."

The next morning, Turnbey contacted Scotland Yard to arrange for Kreutzer's transfer to a top-secret MI6 facility outside London. He then met with MI6 director Admiral Sir Hugh 'Quex' Sinclair to brief him on Billingsworth's murder and his plan to have Rachel step into her shoes as a spy in Germany.

"If you want this to succeed," said Sir Hugh, "you must do something about Kreutzer before Rachel returns to Germany. What do you suggest?"

"My staff believes it's best if we stage a fatal accident, eliminating him as a threat to Rachel."

"I agree, but Hitler mustn't know it was our doing."

Two weeks later, Kreutzer washed up on a remote stretch of beach south of Margate. The police identified the decomposed body after finding an engraved waterproof timepiece in his swimsuit. His parents gave it to him on his twenty-first birthday. Margate authorities ruled his death an accident, concluding that a deadly undertow caused his drowning after he swam too far from shore. The British government notified Adolf Hitler, with its deepest condolences, and flew his body to Berlin. The SA buried him with full military honors.

15th March, 1927– London - Rachel learns to become Elisabeth

The day after Sir Hugh approved her assignment as a sleeper agent, Rachel walked into Reginald's office. "I heard you have good news for me."

"Yes, we can soon send you back to Germany as a spy."

Rachel felt her excitement growing as she sat down. "Please go on, Reg."

"Elisabeth Billingsworth, daughter of an esteemed London family, died a few days ago. She could be your identical twin, and Hitler's followers regard her as one of their own."

"That's marvelous. What's our next step?"

"Tomorrow morning, you'll meet her parents and their maid. They'll help you to adopt her look, mannerisms, and personality traits."

Rachel felt her stomach tighten as her taxi approached the Billingsworth estate. *How will they feel about me stepping into their deceased daughter's shoes*? The car drove through a gate made of hammered iron with relief décor and a double-headed eagle. Beyond the gate was an exquisite garden. Cecil later told her he'd patterned the house and grounds after the Winter Palace built by Peter the Great for his daughter, Empress Elisabeth, in St. Petersburg, Russia. He named Elisabeth after the Empress.

An English butler met Rachel at the door. As he took her through the sizeable entry foyer and into what he said was the drawing room, she thought, *I've seen nothing this large and spectacular*. Cecil walked over to her as soon as she entered the room. "I'm Cecil Billingsworth. My wife Margaret and I are pleased you will assume our daughter's identity."

The unease drained from Rachel's body as Cecil guided her to a settee opposite Margaret and sat down with her. "You resemble our daughter in looks, but it's impossible to overlook your kindly manner. It's not good to speak ill of the departed, but our daughter didn't have a compassionate soul. She sought malicious friends and evil causes. By stepping into her shoes, you will make it possible for Elisabeth to live on as a good person, fighting wickedness instead of embracing it. Don't you agree, Margaret?"

"Oh yes, I do," answered Margaret as she turned to face Rachel. "You look like our Elisabeth, but if you're to assume her identity, you must treat us as she did. She showed us no respect, calling us by our Christian names at home and in public. You should also act hard-heartedly toward her friends if you want *them* to accept you."

Later that day, Cecil introduced Rachel to Daphne. After he left, Daphne said, "Mr. and Mrs. Billingsworth told me you look just like my darling Elisabeth, and you really do. I will do everything I can to help you impersonate her, but we have a great deal of work to do. She didn't have your demeanor."

"How do you mean?"

"It's your eyes, they radiate compassion. She only acted kindly toward those who did things for her. Everyone else was unimportant, and she let them know it."

Rachel crinkled her nose. "I don't think I could act like that. It goes against everything I believe."

"I can see that, dear, but I'm certain you will succeed if it's for a good cause… and I'll be there to correct you whenever you step out of character."

Rachel smiled, walked over to Daphne, and hugged her. "I'll love working with you, Daphne."

"Me too dear, me too," said Daphne, giving Rachel kisses on both cheeks moistened with her bittersweet tears. "I'll come to your mansion tomorrow morning to begin your makeover. Mr. and Mrs. Billingsworth will meet us there to help in your transition."

Rachel, who'd lived with her cousin since arriving in England, moved into Elisabeth's mansion the next morning. Daphne was there to help her unpack. She then took her on a tour of her new home.

"I can't believe the size of this place," said Rachel. "Were you and Elisabeth the only people living here?"

"Bruno, her husband, visited often, but that was it."

"I suppose we should get to work on my transformation. The sooner we start the sooner I can help my people in Germany."

Daphne began Rachel's transformation by saying, "Elisabeth always entered a room with a cold, belligerent demeanor, as if she dared anyone to get in her way. We'll begin with that, then move on after you feel comfortable impersonating that aspect of her personality."

Rachel steeled herself to the task, but found it difficult to take on Elisabeth's combative manner. When Rachel told Daphne, she said, "Perhaps it would be easier if I talked to you about the character traits that contributed to Elisabeth's aggressive behavior."

"Please do."

"She always expressed her own feelings, needs, rights, and opinions, but never respected other people."

"Can you expand on those four traits so I can better understand them?"

"Yes. First, she forced her feelings on others by acting self-centered, irate, and tactless toward them. Second, Elisabeth acted as if her needs were paramount by dismissing or ignoring those of others. Third, she stood up for her own rights by insisting that only her opinions were worthy of contributing to a discussion. In other words, Elisabeth always aimed to win at the expense of others."

Rachel worked with Daphne for almost six months before Daphne and the Billingsworths agreed that Rachel was taking on Elisabeth's personality. After Cecil telephoned Turnbey to let him know she was ready to go ahead, Turnbey called Rachel and asked her to meet with him at MI6 headquarters the next morning.

When they met, Turnbey said, "Before sending you back to Germany we must be certain you are able to think and act like Elisabeth. To do so, I asked Alistair Sedgwick and Anthony Glasgow to test your readiness."

The pair asked associates, who had personalities ranging from easygoing to belligerent, to assess Rachel's ability to act aggressively toward them. Two weeks later, Glasgow told Turnbey, "Rachel convinced all our colleagues that she was ready to embark on her assignment in Germany."

The next day, Turnbey stood when Rachel walked in and sat down next to her. "Sedgewick and Glasgow are convinced you are prepared to move ahead. Now it's time for you to sever ties with Elisabeth's friends. Daphne told us they are untrustworthy, which could become a problem if they contact Hitler's people after you return to Germany. Daphne told you about her friend's names, temperaments, and physical appearances, but she couldn't tell you about inside jokes, gossip, or other details they'd expect you to know."

"Then I must deal with them swiftly, forestalling any lengthy conversations about bygone days."

"Quite right," said Turnbey with a smile.

A week later, Elisabeth drummed her fingers on the table while she waited for her namesakes' friends at one of their favorite hangouts, a small restaurant in London's Soho district. She smiled when they all walked in together.

The redhead, who Elisabeth recognized as the principal troublemaker from Daphne's description, was the first to speak. "Where in the hell have you been? The least you could have done was phone us." The others nodded in agreement.

"Shit, Marilyn, what do you think I am… your nursemaid?" said Elisabeth, rolling her eyes.

"No, but..."

"... but what? Are you too stupid to understand the impact Bruno's death had on me?"

"Yes, but..."

"... stop with the buts, you imbecile. I grieved for months after he died, almost destroying my mansion at one point. Then, when I thought about Bruno, it became obvious how completely he dedicated his life to Adolf Hitler. If I'm to recover from his death, I must follow in his footsteps and dedicate myself to the Führer. Such selflessness demands I grow up and act responsibly, something you're not intelligent enough to understand."

"You can't talk to Marilyn that way," said one of the others angrily.

"What do you expect me to do, sink to her level," spat Elisabeth, glaring at her.

"All right, miss high and mighty, maybe it's time we find someone else to call our friend," yelled Marilyn with an angry huff.

"That's fine with me. But you'd better not show your faces in Germany, or I'll have Ernst Röhm and his SA teach you a lesson you won't soon forget."

"You can keep that pack of animals all to yourself," screamed Marilyn, slamming her fist on the table. "We're no longer interested in them, right?"

"Yes," said the others in unison. They stood up and stormed out of the restaurant.

Elisabeth took a deep breath, savoring the moment.

"Rachel, we're proud of your progress," said Turnbey, beaming at his protégé the next morning at MI6 headquarters. "Now comes the hard part. Kreutzer's replacement, Wilhelm Nagel, tried to contact you after we returned Kreutzer's body to Germany. Nagel broke off his attempts two months ago, most likely assuming your fascination with Hitler died with Kreutzer. He probably told his Party bosses you didn't respond, so it's essential you quickly restore Elisabeth's good name with the National Socialists. If you fail, we can't send you back to Germany."

After thinking for a few moments, Rachel said, "It's time I offer Bruno's parents my belated condolences. Daphne told me Elisabeth met Bruno's parents only once, and that was when they welcomed her as their daughter-in-law. If Elisabeth were in my situation, she'd assume the Kreutzer's would be eager to help her mend fences with Hitler's followers. And so should I."

"Excellent my dear. You have shown great insight, despite having little experience in the secret agent world. It is now high time we begin addressing you as Elisabeth Please send a telegram to the Kreutzer's, letting them know you'd like to see them, and asking when they could receive you."

12th January 1927 – Berlin – 3:00 PM - Elisabeth meets Kreutzer's parents

A few days later, when Elisabeth disembarked her ship in Hamburg, she saw a uniformed chauffeur holding a sign for Fräulein Elisabeth Billingsworth. After she identified herself he directed her to a 1923 Heine-Velox limousine. She got in and settled into the comfortable back seat. Elisabeth felt a twinge at the pit of her stomach when the driver said, "We are almost there," in German. After he stopped the car, the chauffeur opened the door, and a butler ushered her into the house. *This is even more spectacular than the Billingsworth's home*, thought Elisabeth as he escorted her through the entry hall and into the Kreutzer's library. A pair she recognized as Irena and Otto Kreutzer, from pictures Turnbey showed her, awaited her arrival.

Irena's mouth tightened, as if she'd tasted something bad, when she hissed, "Why weren't you at Bruno's side when he died?"

Elisabeth replied in German with a British accent. "Bruno said he was on a special mission for our Führer, and I knew better than to ask him about his clandestine activities. He'd always get so angry. Now I blame myself for not insisting. Had I done so, he might still be alive."

Elisabeth's gaze froze on Adolf Hitler's portrait on the wall behind Irena. *Those eyes… those damned piercing…* she shifted her focus to Otto, who gave her an understanding nod, as if offering her an olive branch. "We know how difficult Bruno could be about his work. You had to let him have his way."

"Why did you take so long before contacting us?" interrupted Irena.

Elisabeth swallowed hard. "After Bruno died, I drowned my sorrows in an endless diet of alcohol and pills. After that, I became angry with myself and tore our mansion apart. Then I spent time in America to escape my grief. Only recently did I feel strong enough to visit you. Believe me; you wouldn't have enjoyed my company while I mourned Bruno's death."

"It seems you've changed since you were last here," said Irena, her eyes narrowing. "I find your manner to be more… compassionate."

"Yes, my anguish transformed me," replied Elisabeth, covering for her reversion to Rachel's personality. "I now look at life anew, knowing if I give solace to others, they will do the same for me. That's why I'm here, eager to help *you* recover from Bruno's tragic death."

Irena's stare remained frozen.

She hates me. Perhaps it'll be impossible for me to…

Irena's facial expression softened into a tearful smile. "I also went through hell after Bruno died. It must have been worse for you. I wish you would have cabled or written us. Perhaps we could have helped you cope during those early dark days."

"You're so sweet," replied Elisabeth, her nervousness dissipating. "Standing here, I'm sorry I didn't reach out to you. Can you ever forgive me?"

"You've done nothing we need excuse," replied Irena in a kindly tone. "I must stop asking heartless questions and help you. Is there anything Otto or I can do for you, anything at all?"

Elisabeth's heart skipped a beat. *This is what I've been hoping for, but I must tread softly.* "You're too kind, Irena, but it's wrong of me to impose on your generosity."

"That's silly, my dear. We both want to help you. You are our daughter-in-law and it would honor our dear Bruno's memory if you consider us your family and make our home your home. Don't you agree, Otto?"

He smiled, nodding his head in agreement.

"My life was best when Bruno and I worked as one to support our Führer. His death created a void I can only fill by resuming my efforts in behalf of the Party. You must have friends who could help me."

"That would be our greatest joy. Isn't that right, Otto?" asked Irena as she stood up.

"Yes, if you stay with us for a few more days, I'll invite our close friends over for dinner," replied Bruno.

Irena walked to Elisabeth and took her hand, "That's marvelous. What do you say?"

"Oh yes, Irena. I'd love to stay."

Irena kissed Elisabeth's cheek. "Then it's settled, Bruno's room will be yours whenever you are in Berlin. My oh my, you've been standing here all this time. Please sit with us while we talk about your future." Irena walked to Otto's couch and sat Elisabeth between the two of them. Still holding her hand, she added, "It will take time, but you will eventually follow in our beloved Bruno's footsteps. Otto and I will see to that."

Elisabeth squeezed Irena's hand as she said, "I'm so happy to be with you both again." *This couldn't have gone better.*

"So are we," said Irena. "But, you look exhausted after your trip. Please go to Bruno's room. He's on the second floor, the last door on the left. Get a good night's sleep, and we'll talk again tomorrow morning."

Elisabeth stopped cold after turning on the light in Bruno's room. The walls radiated with evil, brought to life by myriad red, black and white swastika flags filling the walls. It took all Elisabeth's resolve to keep Rachel from crying out. Elisabeth turned out the light to block the hideous sight from her eyes… *but Hitler's vindictive stare is still drilling into my innermost thoughts*. After undressing, she fell uneasily onto Bruno's bed.

Her eyes filled with tears, her body shook. Rachel's emotional needs went into dormancy after she was reborn as Elisabeth. On this restless evening, Rachel thought back to a gentler time when togetherness and Jewish tradition filled her formative years. Although thoughts of her uncomplicated life before Mayer's attack comforted her, Rachel feared her days could never again be so overflowing with family, love, and meaning.

Without warning, Elisabeth's vow to fight Hitler as an MI6 agent tugged at Rachel's conscience. *The Kreutzers accepted me. I must now harden my heart, doing whatever is necessary to become a devoted National Socialist. If I don't, I may as well return to England, resign from MI6, and turn my back on the Jews of Germany.*

15th March, 1927 – Dover – 10:30 AM – Elisabeth gives her first report to Turnbey

Elisabeth breathed a sigh of relief when her feet touched British soil in Dover. She'd spent two months in Germany becoming acquainted with the Kreutzers and their friends. While she was away, Daphne maintained her Kensington Palace Gardens mansion. She also arranged for Elisabeth's limousine to meet her at the dock.

Elisabeth nodded as she approached her Rolls Royce Phantom. Reginald Turnbey, dressed as a chauffeur, was holding the door for her in a deferential manner. Elisabeth pursed her lips, maintaining an arrogant pose until Reginald seated her. As soon as Turnbey closed his door, Elisabeth laughed so hard tears poured down her cheeks. "Reginald, I see the British Government promoted you to an appropriate position."

"Hilarious, Miss Billingsworth," said Turnbey, his eyes on the road. "It looks like you've made a complete transition to your namesakes' vile and ugly personality."

"I'm sorry, Reginald, I couldn't help myself. You looked so… so…"

"… *demeaned* is the word you were searching for, my dear."

After Elisabeth recovered her composure she asked, "Why did *you* meet me at the dock?"

"I met you there instead of MI6 headquarters because our sources tell us Hitler's SA is watching you. Two agents sailed onboard your ship." He narrowed his eyes, gazing through the rearview mirror. "If I am not mistaken, they've been tailing us since we left the port."

Elisabeth grimaced. "Why are they doing that? I can't do them any harm from here."

"Our sources believe you've made a positive impression, and they'd like to confirm you're not a spy."

"Do they have any evidence to suggest I am?"

"Not as far as we know. They'll stop following you when they're certain of your loyalty. Do you have other questions?"

"I don't, but you must have several for me."

"Yes, after the Beer Hall Putsch, while Hitler was still in prison, the National Socialists won 6.6% of the Reichstag vote. A few months after his release, they garnered only 3%. Did that poor performance disappoint the Kreutzers?"

"Many Germans wrote Hitler off as a viable candidate. The Kreutzers were not among them."

"Why's that?"

"The government prohibited Hitler from speaking publicly after his release from prison. Bavaria lifted its speaking ban on him before I left Germany. The Kreutzers are sure the government will soon allow him to speak freely throughout the country. When that happens, they believe Hitler's personal magnetism will propel him to certain victory on the national stage."

"Did Hitler learn anything from the Putsch experience?"

"Yes, that he can't take Germany by might, alone."

"Will he no longer rely on force to get his way?"

"He'll still use the SA to intimidate his foes, but will also market himself as Germany's best choice for a national leader." Elisabeth paused for a few moments, then said, "Hitler's performance at last year's Party rally impressed the Kreutzer's."

Turnbey looked at Elisabeth in his rear-view mirror. "What happened there? It seemed innocuous."

"He elevated his *Blood Flag* to the status of a major religious icon... something like his Holy Grail."

"Blood Flag? Holy Grail? How can *that* help him?"

"That flag, stained with the blood of martyrs killed during the Beer Hall Putsch, became a symbol of the supreme loyalty his followers owe Hitler as their leader."

"How did he make that happen?"

"He used the flag in a solemn ceremony known as the *blutfahne*. The Kreutzer's described Hitler's sacred rite with tears in their eyes."

"You're joking, right?"

"No. Hitler's ritual is best described as a mass, with the flag as its crucifix. He clutches a corner of the blood flag in his right hand then, as the standard-bearer stops briefly, he grips the corner of each flag with his left hand. His followers believe the *blutfahne's* mystical power flows through Hitler's body, consecrating every flag he touches."

Elisabeth saw Turnbey's smirk in the rearview mirror. "Reg, the Kreutzer's showed me movies of the *blutfahne*. Believe me it's moving… especially to those who accept Hitler as their personal messiah."

"Enough of that, have you learned anything we could use?"

"No. While the Kreutzer's accept me as a genuine sympathizer, the Party regards me as their English daughter-in-law."

"How do the Kreutzer's treat you?"

"I have free run of the house, can travel where I want, and they invite me to most of their dinner parties."

Turnbey raised an eyebrow. "Do they host Party leaders?"

"Yes, quite often. They hosted Hitler once, but kept me out of sight that evening."

"Did you meet any Party leaders?"

"Yes, Hermann Göring. Many in Germany still see him as the Great War fighter ace."

Turnbey looked at her in the rearview mirror. "He still lives abroad. I suspect he returned to Germany to re-establish himself as a major figure in the Party. Did he attend any meetings while there?"

"After dessert, the Kreutzer's make their library available for private discussions. Göring met there with Party leaders."

"Are the Kreutzer's also invited?"

"Never. Armed SA guards keep all but top Party leaders from entering."

"Did the Kreutzer's ever discuss their feelings for Hitler?"

"They worship him as a divine being."

"How do they deal with the brutality of his SA?"

Elisabeth hesitated before answering. "They're aware of SA cruelty, but view it as a necessary evil. To them, it's akin to a doctor cutting off a gangrenous leg to save a patient's life. They see the slaughter of Hitler's opponents as a small price to pay for Germany's rebirth."

"That stands to reason. Being conspicuously loyal to Hitler, they have little to fear from the SA."

"Exactly."

Turnbey paused for a moment. "Did you dislike anything about the Kreutzers?"

"They hate Jews like the plague. If they knew Jewish blood flows through my veins, they'd turn me over to the SA without a second thought."

"Do you know *why* they hate Jews so much?"

"They believe Jews stabbed the army in the back by forcing Germany to surrender when Great War victory was within their grasp. Then they caused the hard times that followed. They're convinced Germany can't become a great world power until they drive the Jews from their country."

"Do they hate only Jews?"

Once again, Elisabeth took a few moments to frame her answer. "The Kreutzers despise all inferior races, including Jews, Poles, Russians, and Gypsies. They believe their presence damages Germany."

"Why's that?"

"Germans treat eugenics as a science. While I was there, eugenics experts presented their latest findings at two well-attended meetings in their home. The presenters warned that intermarriage between Aryans and inferior races make Germany incapable of returning to its rightful place as a world leader."

"Eugenics is not a new concept," said Turnbey, keeping his eyes on the road, "An English scientist coined the term late in the last century. It encourages society elites to improve coming generations by having more children. Some eugenicists propose legalizing sterilization to eliminate 'defectives' from the gene pool."

"The Kreutzer's told me the United States Supreme Court heard a case to legalize enforced sterilization. That *was* Party propaganda, right?"

"I'm afraid not. Justice Oliver Wendell Holmes Jr. recently upheld the Buck vs. Bell case. His majority opinion endorsed a Virginia statute allowing compulsory sterilization of the mentally retarded for the protection and health of the state."

"That's monstrous. The Kreutzer's believe the rest of the world mirrors Hitler's feelings about the inferior races and prove it by trotting out evidence like the Buck vs. Bell Supreme Court case."

Elisabeth paused for a moment, looked at Turnbey in the mirror and asked, "Would you be interested in a conversation I had with Helene Hanfstängl, after the Nazi leaders retired to the library one evening?"

"She's the American born wife of Ernst, Hitler's Foreign Press Secretary, right?" said Turnbey with obvious interest.

"Yes, Ernst, known as Putzi in Nazi circles, graduated from Harvard in 1909, and befriended New York State Senator Franklin Delano Roosevelt at the New York Harvard Club. Helene told me Hitler stumbled and fell during the Munich Putsch. Walter Schultze, the storm troopers medical doctor, escorted him to the Hanfstängl country house in Uffing. Two days later, Police Lieutenant Belleville came looking for him. Convinced his political career was at an end Hitler held a gun to his head and was ready to pull the trigger when Helene walked in. She disarmed him, then ordered him to act the part of Germany's greatest leader. Helene insisted he would have killed himself if she hadn't intervened."

"It's a shame she walked in on him," said Turnbey with a glum expression.

"You won't get an argument from me. Helene's persuasion worked. After Hitler regained his composure, she led Belleville to his room. Belleville took him to prison as he found him, wearing white pajamas and an arm sling for his dislocated shoulder. A few days later, Hitler again became despondent and went on a hunger strike. Asked to intervene, Helene again convinced him not to commit suicide."

"Did you know that wasn't the first time Hitler fell into a deep depression?" asked Turnbey.

"No I didn't."

"While serving as a soldier at the front, during the Great War, Hitler believed Germany was on the verge of victory. He spent several weeks in a hospital after a poison gas attack blinded him. While there, he heard that Germany surrendered. Certain his country was winning the war, Hitler saw Germany's capitulation as an act of betrayal. According to several reports, he became melancholy, and contemplated suicide. Hitler recovered from his depression stronger than ever. He used his newfound energy to take control of the Nazi Party."

"That's ominous," mused Elisabeth. "Hitler hits his lowest ebb on several occasions, contemplates suicide, and then snaps back stronger. How can we deal with such single minded determination?"

8th January 1928 - Berlin - Göring returns to Germany

Over one and a half years passed since Mayer attended his brother's graduation party in 1926. During that time, he lost two benefactors, shattering any hope of becoming a Party leader. His first patron, Ernst Röhm, resigned in mid-1925, after Hitler wouldn't support his proposal to realign the Storm Trooper corps. Then, Hermann Göring couldn't return to Germany because the government would arrest him for his part in the Beer Hall Putsch.

The hall telephone rang, waking Mayer. Seeing it was eight fifteen, he turned on his side to get more sleep. Someone answered the phone, tapped on his door, and said, "It's for you."

I wish they'd leave me alone on a Sunday morning. He scrambled out of bed and stumbled outside to the telephone. "Yes, can I help you?"

"Is this Claus Mayer?"

"Yes, who are you?"

"This is Göring. I'm in Berlin and want to see you."

Mayer's heart jumped as he replied, "Certainly sir, I would be honored."

"I'm staying at the Kaiserhof, next to the Reichschancellory. Meet me in the main dining room at seven this evening for dinner."

"Yes, sir."

Mayer rifled through his clothes trying to find anything more appropriate, for his meeting with Göring, than SA uniforms, and an unkempt suit. Feeling uneasy approaching the Kaiserhof dining room Maître d' in his disheveled suit, he asked, "Could you please show me to Commander Göring's table?"

The Maître d' rolled his eyes, sneered, and then waved for a waiter to approach. "He'll take you to the street. You'll find him there."

Göring sprang up and strode toward the Maître d'. "I will seat my good friend." He curled his lip adding, "Tell the wine steward to bring a bottle of your 1918 Chateau Gruad Larose Red Bordeaux St. Julien for my guest." Göring led Mayer to his table, then turned his nose up as they took their seats. "That arrogant imbecile treated you like scum. When Hitler becomes Germany's Führer we'll no longer tolerate such petty insolence."

"It's an honor to see you, sir, but isn't it still unsafe for you in Berlin?"

"No, the government granted me amnesty, so I'm no longer in danger of arrest. Claus, I asked you to dinner so I could thank you for saving my life during the Putsch. You are a true patriot, and I shall never forget it. I also want to know whether you'd like to work for me."

"I would, sir. What do you have in mind?"

"The Führer set his sights on becoming Germany's Chancellor. The Putsch taught him he must use legal means to win the hearts and minds of German voters. As a first step, he asked me to run for a seat in the Reichstag. I must prepare for the spring elections and need you to keep me informed on topics ranging from the mood of our country to exploitable weaknesses I can use against my opponents."

"Exploitable weaknesses, sir?"

"Yes, I want you to uncover *anything* in my opponent's backgrounds we can use to defeat them. I'll also need Storm Troopers to deal with my more difficult rivals. You know who's best suited for that, right?"

"I do, sir," replied Mayer with a smile.

"Many of my backers belong to the upper class. As my representative, you must wear fashionable clothes." Mayer leaned forward to interrupt. Göring pulled a card from this jacket pocket and handed it to him. "I gave my tailor instructions to outfit you at my expense. This is his address, visit him soon."

"How can I ever repay your kindness, sir?"

"By keeping me out of trouble."

The next morning, Mayer telephoned Kepner. "Commander Göring asked me to work for him, and I will need your help."

"I've been waiting for this since the day we saved his life. What can I do?"

"Göring will run for a seat in the Reichstag in the May 1928 elections and needs two things from us. You will take care of the first by selecting an elite Storm Trooper corps. You will then train and lead them to make sure Göring's rivals can't run effective election campaigns. While you do that, I will give Göring direct support."

Mayer and Kepner spent the next two weeks selecting forty troopers. Kepner then directed his storm trooper corps as they roughed up Göring's opponents and incited violent confrontations in the streets of Bavaria. Kepner routinely advised journalists about upcoming free-for-alls and waited for them to arrive before initiating the violence.

Göring's fame as a Great War pilot helped him win his first Reichstag seat in May 1928. Nazi popularity surged after 1929 when the global depression led to high levels of German unemployment. The Reichstag elected Göring as its President in 1932.

In the July 1932 elections the National Socialist Workers Party, now known as the Nazis, won 37.3% of the Reichstag's seats. Four months later, in the November elections, they won only 33% of the seats. It seemed as if the Nazis were doomed to failure. Hitler again contemplated suicide.

On the morning of 30 January 1933, German President Paul von Hindenburg surprised the world by swearing Adolf Hitler in as Germany's new Chancellor. That afternoon, Kepner burst into Mayer's office, closed his door, and whispered, "I'm glad Hindenburg made Hitler Chancellor, but why did he do it? The Nazis didn't win 50% of the vote."

"Hindenburg's advisors told him Hitler would stem the Nazi violence, now tearing Germany apart, after taking power. When Hindenburg asked whether a Dictatorship would be worse than Nazi aggression, his counselors convinced him they would make sure Hitler could never establish a German dictatorship."

Both men laughed.

⌘⌘⌘⌘⌘⌘⌘⌘

Göring's secretary asked Mayer to meet with him on 27 February 1933. When Mayer walked into his office, Göring stood up saying, "Our day of destiny is at hand. The Führer appointed me Minister of the Interior for Prussia, and ordered me to prepare our Fatherland for Nazi dictatorship. My first priority is to silence the large minority opposing Adolf Hitler and the Nazi Party."

"How may I help, sir," asked Mayer.

"We must first neutralize the Communists and Social Democrats."

The telephone rang. Göring lifted the receiver and Mayer heard the caller scream, "The Reichstag is on fire." Göring flew out of his chair, threw on his big camel-hair coat, and ran for the door bellowing, "Follow me Mayer."

Mayer smelled smoke when they reached the street. The pair ran toward the fire. Göring grunted as they approached the Reichstag. Fire and police officers were standing idly by while Germany's parliament building blazed. Göring's body shook as he screamed, "Why aren't you containing the fire?"

The Fire Chief replied, "There's nothing we can do," then flames broke through the cracked glass dome.

Göring charged into the building yelling, "We must save the tapestries." Mayer followed him in and grabbed Göring when a powerful air current threatened to draw him into the debating chamber. The chamber became a roaring furnace, consuming everything including the tapestries.

The pair retreated to the lobby. Hitler and Goebbels stampeded toward them. "What happened, Göring?" demanded Hitler.

Rudolf Diels, Göring's head of the Prussian Police, ran into the lobby. Göring turned to him. "What do you know about the fire, Diels?"

"A few minutes ago, I interrogated the man responsible for the fire. He's a Russian madman who..."

"... This was a carefully planned Communist plot," interrupted Hitler, working himself into a rage. "It is time for swift action. The German people won't tolerate clemency. We must hang every Communist deputy we find, and there will no longer be leniency for the Social Democrats."

Göring turned toward Mayer and whispered, "The Führer never lets a serious crisis go to waste."

17th May 1933– London MI6 Headquarters – 9:30 AM – Elisabeth talks to Turnbey about Hitler.

Elisabeth was returning to London for the fourth time since meeting the Kreutzers. She'd been an MI6 agent in Germany for over ten years and the Nazis now acknowledged her as an esteemed Party member.

She trembled the entire ocean voyage home and was still shaking when she entered Turnbey's office. He jumped out of his chair. "You look terrible. Take a seat. Tell me what's wrong?"

Elisabeth voice wavered as she said, "Hitler is now Germany's Dictator." She sat down and added, "Does England still see him as someone else's problem?"

"I won't lie to you. It will take many more years before Britain pays off its Great War debt. Until then, we have limited funds to keep him in check."

Elisabeth thought for a few moments. "Do you know of anyone holding political power who opposes Hitler?"

"Winston Churchill consistently takes positions supporting Jewish causes. As early as 1904, he made an impassioned plea against adoption of the Conservative Party's Aliens Bill, which opposed Jewish immigration from Tsarist Russia. He held a Conservative seat in Oldham then and knew he'd face defeat by continuing to argue against that legislation. He resigned and won a seat in Manchester North-West in the next election. A third of the voters were Jewish, allowing him to continue opposing the Aliens Bill."

"You're reasoning that Churchill's support of Jewish causes could also show him to be a Nazi foe, right?"

"Exactly."

"Is it possible for me to talk with him?"

"I've never met Churchill, but a friend, Ian McAllister, works for him. I'll call him to arrange a meeting."

The next day, McAllister's secretary showed Elisabeth into his office. "Miss Billingsworth, Reginald insisted I meet with you at my earliest opportunity. Please take a seat and let me know how I can help you."

After sitting down, Elisabeth said, "Reginald told me you work with Minister Churchill, and that he is a man who has done much to show his support for the Jewish people."

"That's true."

"Is he openly opposed to Hitler's rule of Germany?"

"He definitely is. Last month, during a debate in the House of Commons, the Minister warned that a militarized Germany could easily conquer Poland, extending Hitler's hateful anti-Semitic rule to another country."

"I'm glad to hear that *someone* in Parliament criticizes him. Is Hitler aware of Mr. Churchill's anti-Nazi views?"

"Yes, and it infuriates him. He's been trying to court Western opinion since taking office, and Winston's speeches, especially his indictments of Germany's anti-Semitism, hit a raw nerve. Last month a *Birmingham Post* correspondent in Berlin reported that their newspapers had sharp warnings for England. One headline referred to Churchill's 'impudence.' I'm surprised you didn't see those reports."

"I live in Berlin with my in-laws. They make sure my feelings aren't hurt by hiding insults leveled against England in the German press."

A rotund man charged into the room chomping on a cigar and barked, "Ian, give me half a glass of my favorite whiskey and top it off with water." Churchill then turned to face Elisabeth. "Who is this young lady?"

"Miss Elisabeth Billingsworth, Mr. Churchill. She'd like to see Hitler thrown out of office. The sooner the better."

Elisabeth shot to her feet at the mention of his name. Churchill appeared somber when he asked, “Why do you find our Mr. Hitler so objectionable, Miss Billingsworth?”

“I was a Jew born in Germany, and his SA victimized me during the Beer Hall Putsch,” replied Elisabeth as she sat down. “That experience prompted me to emigrate. Had I not done so, I’d be another of Hitler’s victims. Today, as an MI6 spy, I can fight to undermine his anti-Semitic regime.”

Churchill’s expression softened as he walked over to shake Elisabeth’s hand. “Good for you, Miss Goldstein. It’s a shame we don’t have more like you working for the government. Then we could do away with that paperhanger.” Churchill smiled when Elisabeth made a barely audible sound at the mention of her real name. “I looked into your background after Ian said you wanted to meet me.” He then downed his drink and handed his glass to McAllister for a refill.

“What did you learn, sir?”

“That you’re a plucky lady, and it’s good you’re helping MI6 deal with that boil on civilizations’ arse… if you’ll excuse my crude language.” Churchill moved a chair next to Elisabeth, sat down, and asked, “Why did you want to meet with me?” as Ian handed him a fresh drink.

"This is my first trip home since Hitler became Chancellor, and Reginald dismayed me by saying Great Britain couldn't devote funds to containing his ambitions."

"He's correct, and you're right to be disheartened. It's distressing that Hitler plans to build up Germany's military strength, while we talk about downsizing ours. As a result, we may, one day, be looking down the barrel of an invincible German fighting force."

"Are you saying Great Britain will do nothing to stop him? If that's the case, we may as well capitulate today."

Churchill stood, cigar smoke filling the air as his face took on the look of an attacking bulldog. "Nothing can be further from the truth. I will fight to make sure the military balance never swings in Germany's favor. One day, I'll prevail and spare our beloved England its first foreign invasion since the Normans in 1066." Churchill sat down, his features softening. "I understand your frustration, Miss Billingsworth. Is there anything *I* can do to help you succeed in Germany?"

"Do you ever receive reports of prominent Nazis who oppose Hitler's regime?"

Churchill sat back, twirling his cigar between his index finger and thumb. "Have you ever met Erika or Wilhelm Canaris?"

"They often come to the Kreutzer's parties, and Erika invited me to their home several times." Elisabeth frowned as she added, "Did you know Wilhelm and General Heydrich served together in the Navy, and are close friends."

"Wilhelm also befriended influential Jews, so don't dismiss him out of hand."

"You're right, sir."

"I understand Otto Kreutzer has a wide range of friends who control powerful Nazi and foreign agencies."

"Yes, Irena invites many of them to her parties. I've cultivated friendships with their wives, and they often ask me to their homes. Now many of their husbands also consider me a friend."

Churchill took another puff on his cigar, downed the rest of his drink, and leaned toward Elisabeth. "You are a self-driven woman, able to do much for MI6. I'd like to meet with you whenever you are here. Let Ian know your schedule, and he will make the arrangements." Churchill handed his empty glass to McAllister and charged out of the room.

Elisabeth smiled. "Mr. Churchill is overwhelming. He displays a sense of resolve that gives one confidence in his ability to get things done under the most adverse conditions."

"He has an indomitable spirit, and may, one day, become the savior of Western civilization," added Ian.

"Why does Mr. Churchill call Hitler *that paperhanger*?"

"Hitler is proud he was a painter before entering politics. The Minister contends he painted houses, not pictures, hence his nickname." Both of them laughed.

McAllister's secretary walked into the office. "Excuse me, sir. Mr. Turnbey left this urgent message for Miss Billingsworth while you were meeting with Minister Churchill."

Elisabeth took the folded note, opened it, and read it silently. *Please come to my office before returning to Germany. I have important news.*

"Please pardon me, Ian. Reginald asked me to meet with him."

"Of course, Elisabeth. Ask Reginald to let me know when you visit England and have a safe trip back to Germany."

Elisabeth thought about her meeting with Churchill as she left McAllister's office. *Churchill changed my mind about Wilhelm. He may well be a valuable Nazi contact.* She walked into Turnbey's office. "You wanted to see me, Reg?"

"Siegfried Mannheim, an Austrian citizen, approached our Viennese consulate offering to help us fight the Nazis."

"What do we know about him?"

"He has no known Nazi ties, and his birth certificate is on file with the Office of Jewish Registrations in Vienna, so he most likely *is* a Jew."

"How can I meet him?"

"I'll ask our consulate to send me that information and forward it to you in a sealed package from the Billingsworth's. That's still a secure way to send notes to you, right?"

"Yes, the Nazis would never intercept mail going to them."

"How was your meeting with Mr. Churchill?"

"It went well. He'd like to spend time with me whenever I visit home and asked that you let Ian know my schedule."

"I'll be glad to do that."

"Do you think it would be all right if I spend a few weeks in England before returning to Berlin?"

"Yes, you deserve a rest."

The news that Elisabeth would spend time with Cecil and Margaret Billingsworth before returning to Germany delighted them. They insisted she join them at their Southold summer cottage.

12th June, 1933– Berlin – 9:30 PM – Elisabeth returns to Berlin

During her visit to England Elisabeth felt safe, protected by reasonable, predictable, and non-intrusive laws legislated by England's freely elected parliament in the light of day.

When she disembarked in Hamburg, legalized criminality hung as a dark cloud over Berlin's streets. Bands of SA Brownshirts seemed to be everywhere on her route home. On three occasions, they bludgeoned victims who didn't fit Nazism's rigid Aryan stereotype. She hid her face each time, afraid someone would see the disgust in her eyes, note the limousine's license plate, and report her intolerance to Otto Kreutzer.

Elisabeth sighed when the limousine parked at the Kreutzer's mansion. She forced a smile walking through the front door and asked Greta, their maid, to have someone bring her bags from the car.

"My darling, it's you," exclaimed Irena running out of the Kreutzer's ballroom. "You're just in time. Our Dr. Goebbels is about to show his new movie about the book burning that took place outside the Berlin Opera House last month."

"I was sorry to miss that spectacular occasion, Irena. Please give me a moment to freshen up from my trip, and I'll be right back."

The last thing Elisabeth wanted was to see Goebbels' film celebrating the destruction of books written by Upton Sinclair, H. G. Wells, Jack London, Helen Keller, Ernest Hemingway, Sigmund Freud, Bertold Brecht and over 50 others. She'd seen enough of the Third Reich's ill will on her drive home. Nonetheless, she had to lavish praise on the Doctor's movie to counterbalance the well-known liberal leanings of her English parents.

The ballroom, packed with the cream of Nazi society, rose and applauded when Elisabeth arrived. Dr. Goebbels strode over, bowed slightly, and kissed her outstretched hand. "Let me be the first to welcome you home, Fräulein Elisabeth." Guests responded with warm smiles and a second round of applause. After they took their seats, Goebbels walked to a large movie screen and addressed his audience.

"We must always remember the book burnings of the tenth of May as a glorious tribute to our Führer's greatness. What many of you may not know is that on the sixth of April, less than three months after Adolf Hitler became Chancellor, the German student's Association proclaimed a nationwide *Action against the Un-German Spirit*. It was they, the future leaders of our great Reich, who made the magnificent book burning possible. It was they who demanded Germany rid itself of the destructive influences that continue to plague our land. And yes, it was they who penned their twelve theses detailing the evil forces which we must purge from our society." The guests rose to their feet and applauded.

Goebbels bowed slightly, handed a large envelope to the Kreutzer's butler, whispered something to him, and then turned to face his audience. "You will each receive a commemorative copy of the twelve theses. Please display them in your homes or places of business to honor our German students. With that, I shall take my seat, and let you enjoy my new film."

The screen flickered with the movie credits and went dark. Fiery torches brandished by students dressed in identical military uniforms pierced the stark blackness of night. They walked eight abreast in an endless line, forming a blazing oval around an enormous bonfire. The soundtrack barked Goebbels' praise for the youngsters as they broke ranks to throw their torches on the bonfire, grab armloads of banned books from a huge mound, and heave them into the flames. Elisabeth was deaf to his rants, silently praying for someone… anyone… to stop Germany's descent into barbarism.

After it ended, the audience gave the movie, and Goebbels, a standing ovation. Elisabeth stood, faced the guests, and raised her hand to silence them. "My friends and fellow devotees to the National Socialist ideal, this evening we witnessed history in the making. Dr. Goebbels' brilliant epic shall live as long as our Thousand-Year Reich. Let us praise Dr. Goebbels and our Führer, whose inspiration is at the root of everything good in our Fatherland."

"Well said Elisabeth," boomed Reinhard Heydrich from the back of the room "Let us salute all in our country inspired by our Führer. Sieg,"

"Heil," said the guests in union, their arms raised in a straight-arm salute.

Moments later, Elisabeth excused herself. "Irena, I am so sorry. My long journey exhausted me."

After kissing Irena on the cheek, Elisabeth made her way out of the ballroom. Affectionate guests praised her as she passed them.

Elisabeth's persona crumbled when she locked the door to her room, which Irena redecorated in a soft feminine motif after her first visit. Rachel's eyes filled with tears, her spirit spent. *God forgive me for praising the Nazis. Give me strength to keep fighting until they are all defeated. Show me the way, Eternal One, to end the madness infecting the people of Germany.*

Elisabeth fell into an exhausted sleep, imagining a brighter day when she would no longer have to voice admiration for Adolf Hitler and his lawless Nazi sentinels.

Two weeks later, Irena glared at Elisabeth as she approached her holding a sealed package. "An SA friend seized this before dispatching it to the Gestapo. I convinced him to hand it to me. It's addressed to you and came from England. What do you know about it?"

Elisabeth fought to hide the fear turning her stomach. *It must contain Reginald's note telling me where to meet Siegfried Mannheim*. "Please let me look at it."

Irena handed it to her without a word.

She opened the package and smiled. "It's from my mother. We went shopping while I was home. I took a liking to this hat, but didn't tell her. She must have noticed and bought it for me."

"Let me look at it."

Elisabeth pulled a hat from the box. The box still contained a note. She hid it under newspaper stuffing before handing the hat to Irena. Elisabeth bit her lip when Irena poked around the rim, hoping she wouldn't lift it. Irena inspected the hat for a few more moments, then gave it back to Elisabeth. "I'm sorry, darling. The Gestapo took a sudden interest in anything mailed from England. They tell me the British are trying to enlist our countrymen as spies."

"How terrible," said Elisabeth with a frown. "They should be ashamed of themselves."

After Irena left the room, Elisabeth retrieved the hidden note. *You should try the pastries at Vienna's Éclair Restaurant. They are simply delicious.* She looked inside the hat's brim and read *27 June at 7 PM.*

Elisabeth burned both notes, arranged a two day shopping trip to Vienna, and walked into the Éclair restaurant at the appointed time. Siegfried was the only man there, so she approached him and asked, "Are you Herr Mannheim?"

He stood up, shook hands, and asked, "Do you mind if we meet at my Synagogue, It's a short walk from here, and would be safer for the both of us."

She replied, "Yes that would be fine," and accompanied him there. He unlocked the door, led her to the Rabbi's study, and pointed to a wall filled with pictures.

"These photographs show me growing up as a member here." He showed her the pictures of his Bar Mitzvah, Confirmation, and installation on as a member of Temple's board. "As you can see, I'm a Jew. I would like to help you fight Hitler and the Nazis."

Elisabeth interviewed him for another hour, then said, "I must clear you with my higher-ups at MI6 before offering you the position. Can we meet here again tomorrow at ten in the morning to answer any questions they may have?"

"Yes, of course."

Elisabeth phoned Turnbey at an unlisted number in London and said, "He is definitely Jewish, and appears to have the qualifications we need to hire him. I recommend that you do so."

Turnbey replied, "You have my approval," and hung up.

The next day, Elisabeth met Siegfried outside the Temple. He unlocked the door, they walked in and sat in a pew at the back of the sanctuary. Elisabeth shook his hand and said, "I can hire you now. Do you have any questions?"

"How long have you worked for MI6?"

"I joined almost eight years ago."

"Hitler was still recovering from the failed Munich Putsch. What prompted you to join MI6 then?"

"I was a Jew in Munich, and Hitler's followers attacked our home during the Putsch. Convinced that an anti-Semitic group would eventually rule Germany, I joined MI6 to keep that from happening."

"Then I am honored to work alongside you until we rid Germany of the Nazis."

19th January, 1935 – Berlin – 9:30 PM – Elisabeth joins Abwehr

Over eighteen months passed since Elisabeth met with Churchill. She'd seen Wilhelm and Erika Canaris several times since then, and was now looking forward to their arrival at Irena's party to celebrate Wilhelm's promotion to Commander-in-Chief of Abwehr, Germany's MI6.

Elisabeth greeted Erika and Wilhelm at the door. "I'm so pleased for you, Wilhelm. Your appointment to Abwehr is a great honor." Turning to Erica, she added, "And it must thrill you to be coming home from Swinemünde."

"I am," replied Erika, "though I loved waking to the beauty of the Baltic every morning."

Later that evening, Elisabeth approached Erika. "It's a mild evening for mid-January. Would you like to join me in the garden?"

Erika smiled and replied, "Yes."

They walked out to Irena's rose garden and sat down on a wooden bench overlooking a babbling brook. A few minutes later, Elisabeth turned to Erika. "It's been many years since I actively supported our Führer, and I would like to once again taste the thrill of doing so. Working with Wilhelm, at Abwehr, would give me that opportunity. Do you think he'd consider hiring me?"

Erika answered with a blank stare.

Elisabeth took her hand. "Erika, limiting myself to attending parties and buying clothes is wasting my life. I could spend my time better by helping Wilhelm improve our Reich."

Erika's expression softened. "I'll talk with him about it, but can't make any promises."

"That's all I ask," replied Elisabeth with a smile.

Canaris called Elisabeth the following morning. "Is it true you're interested in working with me at Abwehr?"

"I am."

"Would you object if I take advantage of the good will you cultivated with many Nazi and foreign leaders?"

"I don't understand, Wilhelm," lied Elisabeth.

"Abwehr is one of seven agencies established by Hitler to gather intelligence. I aim to transform my agency into the best informed of them all. Irena Kreutzer invites leaders of many Nazi and foreign agencies to her home, and you established a kind-hearted rapport with many of them. That relationship could help win them over as confederates, helping me strengthen Abwehr."

"I'm speechless."

"Does that mean you will accept the position?"

"When do I start?"

"Be at my office tomorrow at ten so we can dispense with formalities."

The next morning, Canaris stood when his secretary ushered Elisabeth into his office. He walked around his desk, shook her hand, pointed to a chair, and sat down next to her. His tone was somber when he said, "Abwehr's work is top secret, and I must trust you to keep everything you see and hear in the strictest confidence. Should you breach my trust, in any way, I shall have to dismiss you and refer your behavior to the Gestapo. Is that understood?"

Elisabeth swallowed hard before answering, "Yes, of course, Wilhelm."

"Since Abwehr is a branch of the Army, you must take the Führer Oath before enlisting. Please stand up, give the Hitler Salute, and say the words on this page aloud."

Elisabeth stood, looked down at the oath, held her arm erect, and forced herself to mouth the loathsome words with great reverence:

> *I swear by Almighty God this sacred oath to Adolf Hitler, Leader of the German Reich and Supreme Commander of the armed forces. I pledge unconditional obedience to Adolf Hitler and am prepared to give my life to honor this oath.*

"Excellent, now you are officially one of us," said Canaris, again shaking her hand.

Canaris' secretary walked in and said, "The Führer asked that you meet with him later today to discuss your new duties."

"Elisabeth, we can discuss your Abwehr role tomorrow morning. In the meantime, introduce yourself to Hans Oster, my second in command."

"Yes sir," *I'm glad that oath's done.*

CHAPTER FOUR -- JOHANNES KAISER

16th September 1936 – Vienna – 10:30 AM – Irma Wollinski Visits Johannes.

Johannes Kaiser was a well-regarded partner in Der KleiderKaiser, the women's clothing company established by his father, Avram. Johannes was twenty-seven years old, somewhat portly, five feet six inches tall, with thinning black hair. He always wore the best and most fashionable clothes and exuded a sense of charm and self-confidence that put most people at ease.

"Hello Johannes," said someone as he headed up the stairs to the KleiderKaiser office.

He turned and ran down with a wide smile. "Irma Wollinski. It's wonderful to see you again. Did you move back to Vienna?"

"No, I'm immigrating to England, and wanted to visit my Austrian friends before leaving. Do you have time to talk?"

"Yes, we can meet in the office. Would you like a bratwurst sandwich for lunch?" She nodded yes. After entering the office, Johannes sat down at his desk, telephoned an employee, and asked him to buy their food. After hanging up, he asked, "Why did you leave Germany?"

"Haven't you heard about the anti-Semitic laws enacted by Adolf Hitler after he became Chancellor?" asked Irma, disbelief ringing in her tone.

"Yes, but weren't those claims exaggerated? I can't believe the German people would allow the Nazis to pass such evil decrees against us."

A tear fell from her eye. "The Germans did nothing to stop him. Isaac Isaacson, our attorney, paid for that with his life. I met with him several weeks ago to discuss legal matters. After we finished, he told me ruffians looted his home. When he reported their names at the police station, the officer on duty told him the thugs were Nazis, and warned him against taking the issue any further. Undeterred, Isaac swore out a complaint. After hearing nothing from him for several weeks, I went to his apartment. His wife was in mourning. The police arrested him the day after he swore out the complaint. She received a letter from the Gestapo a week later declaring that a guard shot him while trying to escape. A friend, briefly held with him at Dachau, told me..." Irma stopped to dry her eyes. "He said a guard tied him to a post, gave him fifty lashes with a whip, then slit his throat. Guards forced all the other prisoners to watch."

"That's insane. Aren't there laws against murder in Germany?"

"Not any more. A few weeks after Hitler became Chancellor, he accused the Communists of burning down the Reichstag to overthrow his government. The legislators panicked, passing the Reichstag Fire Decree suspending citizen rights to privacy, assembly, and the press. Soon after that, the Enabling Act established Adolf Hitler's dictatorship. *He* now decides who commits a murder."

Someone knocked on the office door, opened it, and handed Johannes two sandwiches. He offered one to Irma. She took it, laid it down, and asked, "Do you remember Aaron Goldberg?"

"Yes, he's a jeweler who moved to Berlin when you did. I heard his store is doing well."

"Not any more. Storm Troopers painted a swastika on his window, along with the inscription: *Jews own this store - Don't buy here*. They returned every morning to keep customers from entering. A few days later, the troopers didn't appear and an angry mob broke down the door. The police watched from across the street as barbarians looted Aaron's store. Aaron filed a police report giving the names of those he knew. The policed arrested none of them."

Johannes felt his throat tighten. *Thank God, we don't live in Germany.*

Irma picked up her sandwich, took one bite, and put it on the table. She got a brochure from her bag and handed it to Johannes.

"What is this?" asked Johannes.

"*The German Catechism.* It's required reading for all German students. It teaches them that all good students must fight the Jews because they want to destroy Germany's culture. Similar lies appear in the newspapers, over the radio, and at the movies. Someone told me it was Goebbels' great invention, resting on the principle that if a lie is audacious, and repeated often enough, the masses will believe it is true."

Irma dabbed tears from her eyes before continuing. "Nazi propaganda turned all but the most principled non-Jews into anti-Semites. Many of my Gentile friends refused to recognize me when we passed on the street. At first, I cried every time it happened. Later, it became an everyday part of my life."

Irma took another bite of her sandwich then put it down and continued. "Hitler's Nuremburg Laws, passed at this year's Nazi Party rally, bar German Jews from Reich citizenship, leaving them at the mercy of an unscrupulous anti-Semitic state."

Irma finished her sandwich and said, "I must now go to the airport. Please take my words to heart, Johannes. Leave Vienna before Hitler invades Austria, country of his birth."

Johannes' heart throbbed after Irma left. *I'm frightened for Germany's Jews. Thank God, Hitler won't enter Austria. The rabbi told us about the German-Austrian Agreement of 1936, recognizing Austria's sovereignty and agreeing that neither country would interfere in the other's internal affairs.*

Relieved, Johannes put the German situation out of his mind. His attention returned to business, and his commitment to Der KleiderKaiser's success.

16th October 1936 – Vienna – Bruno Hauptman joins Der KleiderKaiser

In October 1936, still downhearted by his repeated failures to find and keep a job, Bruno Hauptman saw a sign in Der KleiderKaiser's window advertising a training position. He went home, put on his finest suit, returned to the store, and told Avram, "My name is Bruno Hauptman. I am interested in interviewing for your training position, sir."

"Please come upstairs to my office so we can talk in private."

During the interview, Hauptman impressed Avram as a hardworking and honest person. He offered him the position.

Johannes became Bruno's instructor, teaching him the many facets of the tailoring trade. Bruno took great pleasure in learning how to cut and sew fabrics, finding his patience, attention to detail, and manual dexterity were perfect traits for the job. He soon grew to be a competent tailor, giving Bruno a feeling of self-satisfaction. Self-satisfaction grew to confidence, and finally to skill at his new profession. Avram and Johannes were very pleased with Bruno's progress, giving him a large increase in pay. Bruno credited Johannes' support for his success.

Several months later, Johannes caught Bruno reading Der Stürmer, a newspaper supporting the Nazi Party's anti-Semitic policies in an often perverted and vicious manner.

"Herr Kaiser, please don't report me to your father. A friend gave me this newspaper last night. While I know the Nazi Party serves Germany's greater good, I don't believe the ugly things this paper says about your people. You and your father have shown me nothing but respect and kindness since I became your employee."

"Bruno, I'm not a political animal, and don't care who runs the government, so long as they leave me alone to earn a living and enjoy my life. We will keep this between us, but never again bring that newspaper to work. If my father catches you reading it, he will dismiss you."

"Thank you, Herr Kaiser. I won't forget today's kindness or the many days you devoted to helping me master the tailoring trade. If the Nazis take power in Austria, and make you suffer, I will do what I can to help you."

10th June 1937 – The Tukhachesky Affair – A turning point for Canaris

It was eighteen months since Elisabeth joined Abwehr. During that time, she helped Canaris grow Abwehr from less than 150 employees to almost a thousand.

Elisabeth was working alone one evening when she heard Canaris curse as he stormed into his office and slammed the door shut. She wondered what upset the unflappable Canaris. A few moments later, someone pounded on his office door and Canaris yelled, "Who is it?"

"It's Oster, we need to talk."

Elisabeth placed an empty water glass against her shared wall with Canaris, put her ear against it, and heard Hans Oster ask, "Did you hear that Abwehr became embroiled in the Tukhachesky Affair?"

"Yes, Heydrich borrowed my best agents almost a year ago. Today I found out he asked my agent to comb through our Abwehr files for the names of every Soviet military man who visited Germany since Stalin took power. Then, Heydrich had my agent create false documents identifying Tukhachesky, and other Soviet visitors, as conspirators in a plot to overthrow Stalin. Heydrich then had those documents delivered to Stalin."

"He admitted that to you?" said Oster.

"Not only that, Heydrich bragged that Stalin had Tukhachesky, Chief of Staff of the Red Army, executed after reading the forged documents. When I asked Heydrich why he became involved in such an underhanded scheme, he told me Hitler ordered him to do it, and he was proud to obey."

"He could *never* have done it without your help. Thousands of innocent Soviets might still die as Tukhachesky's co-conspirators." Oster was silent for a moment, then added, "Does that convince you we must stop Hitler and our Nazi leadership?"

Elisabeth heard nothing for several minutes and was about to remove the glass from the wall when Canaris answered. "You've been right about Hitler and Heydrich. They're steering our country into a moral abyss. If we don't do something, they will irreparably harm Germany."

Thank God, Wilhelm now realizes that Hitler and Heydrich are evil. She put down the glass and returned to her desk. *How can I help Canaris do something about those Nazi monsters without letting him know I'm a spy?*

CHAPTER FIVE -- THE ANSCHLUSS

12th March 1938 – Vienna – 6:30 AM – Johannes learns about the Anschluss.

Der Kleiderkaiser's business was flourishing in mid-February of 1938. Johannes visited the fashion capitals of Europe to buy new clothing styles to meet growing customer demand. He spent two weeks placing orders at firms in Paris, Rome, and Milan, followed by a week of skiing with friends in the Swiss Alps. His plane touched down in Vienna after midnight on the twelfth of March. Worn-out from his long trip, Johannes slept all the way home in the taxi, paid the driver, clambered up to his apartment, dropped onto his bed fully clothed, and fell into a deep sleep.

At seven that morning, loud banging on his door woke Johannes. Still half asleep, he stumbled down to open it.

"I must talk with you," insisted Otto Klein.

Reacting to his best friend's alarm, Johannes asked, "What happened?"

"Come outside and you'll see."

Johannes followed Otto into the street and shivered... not from the cold of a mid-March Viennese morning... but from gut wrenching, bone chilling terror.

The neighborhood was awash with swastikas. Someone had staked a few in open soil along the pavement. More hung in apartment windows up and down his block. One massive swastika hung like wash on a clothesline strung between two balconies across the street from each other.

Then he noticed the writing scrawled on his building.

Jew pigs leave while you still can.

Recalling Irma Wollinski's visit, Johannes felt trapped by the Nazi anti-Semitism that forced her to flee Germany. Beads of sweat formed on his brow, his pulse quickened, he became lightheaded, and his legs buckled.

"Now isn't the time. Pull yourself together," said Otto grabbing his friend and walking him back into his apartment.

After taking a few minutes to recover, Johannes said, "I must see what the Nazis did to our district. Will you walk with me?"

"Can you keep your emotions under control while we're out there?"

"Yes, of course."

After walking together for several minutes, Johannes turned to Otto. "Over two years ago Irma Wollinski visited me after leaving Germany. She'd lived there since 1930." He recounted Irma's accounts of Nazi atrocities and watched as Otto's eyes filled with fear. "For the first time, I see Hitler and the Nazi Party as *my* problem, and it terrifies me. I'm sorry I didn't tell you sooner. Perhaps our families would have fled Austria before the Nazis invaded."

"Don't blame yourself. In your shoes I might have done the same."

Johannes pointed to the Nazi flags surrounding them. "The Austrian government banned Nazism before I left on my buying trip. What changed?"

"Hitler intends to annex our country as a German province."

"Are you serious?" asked Johannes with a shudder. "What did Chancellor Schuschnigg say about that?"

"Last week, he visited Hitler at his mountaintop retreat in the Bavarian Alps. When he arrived, Hitler warned him he'd invade if Schuschnigg blocked Germany's annexation of Austria."

"How do you know that?"

"A friend of mine in the Diplomatic Corps told me. I didn't believe him then, but all these Nazi flags confirm he told the truth. After Schuschnigg returned from Germany, we heard reports of an imminent German invasion. When I asked my friend about them, he said Hitler made his threats public to scare Schuschnigg into surrendering. Others may have buckled, but Schuschnigg scheduled a plebiscite for tomorrow. Austrians will decide whether Germany should annex our country."

"Good for him," said Johannes. "Why should we surrender?" His jaw dropped when he pointed to a notice scrawled in thick red paint on the side of a building.

Plebiscite cancelled for 13 March
Heil Hitler

"What's that?" asked Johannes.

"It can't be good."

The pair returned to Johannes' apartment. A soft Viennese waltz was playing when Johannes turned on the radio. The lilting melody soothed him as they sat down at the kitchen table.

"Perhaps we're making too much of this," said Johannes. "I can't believe Hitler would seize Austria. The French and the British would certainly come to our defense."

"I hope you're right."

An announcer interrupted the music. "Attention, Attention. Chancellor Schuschnigg will make an important announcement."

"What now?" asked Otto, as Johannes turned up the radio's volume. The Chancellor was brief. Germany would invade if Austria didn't surrender to Nazi rule. Schuschnigg continued, "President Miklas asked me to let you know we are bowing to violence. He refused to shed blood if Hitler attacks and ordered our troops to surrender. "

Tears flooded Johannes' eyes. "How can England and France do nothing while Hitler attacks Austria? What will stop him from invading Czechoslovakia or Poland or any other neighboring state?"

Later that evening, the pair heard Dr. Seyss-Inquart, the Austrian Chancellor Hitler selected to replace Schuschnigg, read a statement on the radio stating he would maintain order. He then directed the army to offer no resistance when the Wehrmacht crossed the border.

"Well, that's that," said Johannes, his lips trembling. "It's just a matter of time before Austria ceases to exist."

Following the Seyss-Inquart broadcast, Johannes heard singing in the street. Looking outside, he saw young people singing and waving swastika flags as they walked by his building. "Do you know that song?"

Otto wrinkled his nose. "It's a German anthem written by Horst Wessel, a Nazi troublemaker who died violently in 1930."

The two friends turned from the window and grasped each other, trying to shut out the evil taking control of their birthplace.

When Otto prepared to go home, Johannes said, “Stay here, you can use my spare bed.”

“Thanks, I’d rather not be alone tonight.”

14th March, 1938 – Vienna – 6:30 AM – Mayer meets Eichmann

The morning after he arrived in Vienna, Mayer smiled hearing the pealing church bells. *Göring predicted the Viennese would welcome Hitler's annexation. How right he was.*

Mayer thought back to the day he accepted the Vienna assignment. It was during an Anschluss planning meeting when General Reinhard Heydrich mentioned he was looking for someone to deal with Jewish troublemakers in Vienna. Mayer suggested himself for the post.

Following the meeting, Göring called him into his office. "I knew you would volunteer and have already begun the paperwork for your promotion to SS Obersturmbannführer, under General Heydrich. I will miss you as a member of my staff, but believe this move will be good for your career."

When Mayer first spoke with Heydrich, in his new capacity, the General suggested he meet with Adolf Eichmann. "Eichmann, who also joined my Austrian staff, is our foremost expert in Jewish affairs. He will help you prepare for your new duties. You should also hire Erik Blick as your interrogator. He is our ablest practitioner in the art of torture. Those familiar with his work named him *The Grand Inquisitor*. You will need his services to extract information from tight-lipped Jewish troublemakers."

The telephone rang as Mayer was shaving. It was Adolf Eichmann. “I lived in Vienna until 1933, when the Austrian government outlawed the Nazi Party. Since you are new here, I’ll come to your apartment and act as your guide.”

Eichmann knocked on Mayer’s door at 10 that morning. After they shook hands he asked, “Would you like to see our offices in the newly acquired Metropole Hotel. We’ll be stationed there with the Gestapo.” He then held up the latest issue of the *Völkischer Beobachter,* Nazism’s daily newspaper. “This says that Austrians lined the roads at the German border, throwing flowers at the feet of our troops. Several papers are now calling our Anschluss the *War of the Flowers*. The *Beobachter* also reported Hitler would speak at the Heldenplatz in Vienna. We should go there after visiting our workplace.”

Later that afternoon, Mayer looked on in amazement as supporters surrounded Heroes Square screaming for Hitler to show himself. Turning to Eichmann, he said, “A few days ago, Schuschnigg warned his countrymen that Germany was about to invade Austria. Now, these people are hailing Hitler as their liberator.”

A few minutes later, the pair watched Hitler walk out on the balcony to the adoring screams of the crowd, and say, “As Führer and Chancellor of the German Nation, I report the entry of Austria, my homeland, into the German Reich.”

"The Führer strengthened Germany since taking office in 1933," yelled Mayer over the hysterical cheers, "and has now annexed Austria without shedding a drop of blood."

"That's true, but it poses an enormous new problem for him."

"How so?"

"The Reich added more Jews today than fled Germany in the years since he took power."

14th March, 1938 – Vienna – 6:30 AM – Hitler enters Vienna

Pealing church bells woke Johannes out of a deep sleep. Then a thunderous roar made his windows tremble in their casings. Running to look outside, he shivered seeing a line of military tanks with swastika markings roll past his building. Young people carrying Nazi flags paraded alongside the combat vehicles. Occasionally, a helmeted soldier looked out of the tank's turret and waved. The crowd cheered and waved back.

"What's all that commotion, Johannes?" asked Otto, rubbing the sleep from his eyes.

"It's the Germans. They're moving their panzer divisions into Vienna."

Otto rushed to the window. The two friends looked on nervously as the military spectacle passed below them. Otto whispered, "Perhaps Hitler should have allowed us to have our plebiscite. He may have won."

Otto dressed quickly then left to look in on his parents. Johannes did the same.

Johannes's parents rushed to greet him as soon as he entered their apartment. His mother held him for over a minute, her tears kissing his cheek. "You worried us, why didn't you call?"

"I'm fine, Mama. Otto and I spent the night together. Are *you* all right?"

"Don't worry about me. The Nazis can't scare me by rolling a few tanks through our streets."

Father and son laughed, then gave Eszter a loving embrace. "Johannes and I must talk," said Avram. "Could you please make us a pot of tea, and perhaps a few of the delicious cookies you baked yesterday?"

Father and son walked solemnly into the parlor.

"Johannes, never repeat what I tell you in this room."

"Of course, Papa."

"I was a young boy when I first experienced anti-Semitism. It was my first memory. Our family was living in the eastern territories..." Avram stopped to wipe tears from his eyes. "Yossele was my best friend. We did everything together until that cold grey afternoon. I'd spent the day with him and was leaving for home when the townspeople came. They screamed obscenities at me as they surrounded the house. Then they set it on fire."

"Did they come after you?"

"No, they shouted that I should tell my Jewish friends they'd get the same treatment if they didn't leave." Avram's body shook when he said, "Yossele ran out of the house, and the mob cheered as their bullets cut him to pieces. His mother, father, brothers, and sisters all burned to death that day."

Overcome by emotion, Avram felt for a chair and sat down. He said nothing for several minutes before continuing. "Yossele's family wasn't alone. Large-scale anti-Jewish rioting, known as pogroms, rocked the eastern territories. Twenty five hundred Jews died in the 1905 Odessa pogrom. Fearing for the family's safety, your grandparents moved us to Vienna. The pogroms continued, sending a steady stream of Jews to Vienna. Jewish refugees now make up almost 10% of our population.

"Why Austria, Papa?"

"We had a constitution promising equal rights to everyone, including Jews. My father, and many other Jewish immigrants, built successful businesses here. After the Nazis did away with Germany's constitution, they handed many Jewish owned businesses to Aryans. They may do the same here."

"Will you leave Austria, Papa?"

"I've thought about it, but most countries closed their borders to all but a few of our people. I can't believe our countrymen will tolerate the violent anti-Semitic attacks that became commonplace in the Eastern provinces, so it should be safer for us to stay here."

"During the Great War, you served with distinction in the Austrian army. Do you think the Nazis will give you special consideration?"

"Wilhelm Braun and Rupert Freund, Gentile friends who served with me in the Great War, called after Schuschnigg told our army to surrender. They promised to watch out for your mother and me. Wilhelm told me emissaries from Berlin asked him to help with the Anschluss last year. He saw the handwriting on the wall and joined the winning side before it was too late." Avram's eyes turned to the floor when he added, "Sadly, we must now entrust our lives to those who abandoned our nation in its hour of greatest need."

18th March, 1938 – Vienna – 10:30 AM – Gustav Klein is Attacked

When Otto got home, he found his parents' door open with the lock broken. His heart pounded as he rushed in and looked for them. He found his mother in the bedroom. She lay in a fetal position on the bed. He hurried to her side and brushed the hair from her face. "What's the matter, Ima?"

Margerette's eyes were red and swollen. She attempted a smile, then wept.

"You're scaring me Ima," pleaded Otto as he sat down next to her. "What's the matter?"

She continued sobbing for a few moments, then spoke in a whisper. "Rolf Heintz and Franz Schwartz broke in this morning and asked where your father was. I would not tell them. When they threatened to beat me, Abba came out of the bedroom. They grabbed him yelling they would get even with him now that the Nazis ruled Austria. Heintz tore the yarmulke from his head, threw it on the floor, stomped on it, and then the pair dragged him out of the apartment." Marguerite broke into tears again.

"Why would they do such a thing?"

"The boys stole newspapers and magazines from Abba's newsstand last year. Officer Kleinschmidt caught them and made them return his property. Abba pressed no charges, but Officer Kleinschmidt told their parents. They spanked them both for what they had done. The boys blamed their beating on Abba, and took it out on him today."

Otto comforted his mother for a short while, then said, "I must find Abba, will you be all right?"

"Yes, but be careful *you* don't get hurt."

Otto hurried out, asking everyone he met if they'd seen his father. He spotted Kleinschmidt after turning down the street where his father sold newspapers. "Manfred, my friend, I am glad to see you."

"I haven't seen you since last year. How are your honored parents?"

"Rolf Heintz and Franz Schwartz dragged my father out of the apartment, and I can't find him. Will you please help me?"

"Of course."

As they walked, Otto asked, "Is there anything you'd like to share with me? You look worried."

Kleinschmidt turned to him. "You haven't changed. When we were in school, you always showed concern for your upset classmates." He paused for a moment. "Before the Anschluss, Heintz and Schwartz came to the police station and told us they would become policemen after the Nazis annexed Austria. The Nazis will then dismiss any officer caught helping a Jew. Many of my fellow officers cheered. I was heartbroken."

"I knew the Nazis hated Jews," said Otto, "but didn't think they'd attack us so soon. Should you be helping me? I don't want you disciplined on my account."

"Screw those fucking Nazis. I won't stay in a country that dismisses policemen for helping those in danger. My older brother moved to Holland after graduating from school and is now a high-ranking official with Amsterdam's police department. When I told him about the Nazis, he invited me to join him. I'm moving there next week."

It took over an hour before the pair found Otto's father unconscious in an isolated alley. Dried blood and bruises covered his face and his clothes were torn. Otto sat next to him and placed his head on his lap. "Abba, I'm here. You're safe now. Officer Kleinschmidt and I will take you to the hospital."

Otto tended to his father while Kleinschmidt ran to the police station to get a stretcher. Otto's father was conscious and in great pain when he returned. The pair moved him onto the stretcher and hurried him to the hospital. When they got there, Heinrich Mayer was the only doctor on duty. After examining his new patient, he asked, "Are you related to this gentleman?"

"Yes, he's my father," answered Otto. "Will he be all right? Can you ease his pain?"

"How did he receive these injuries?"

"We're Jewish. Two Nazi thugs invaded our home, dragged him out into the street, and beat him."

Heinrich looked away, covered his mouth, and remained silent for several moments. He then told Otto, "Your father is very fortunate. He sustained severe bruises, but no bones appear broken. With your permission, I will admit him to the hospital to make sure he doesn't go into shock. He needs to rest now, so please don't stay here too long."

Otto thanked the doctor then turned to Officer Kleinschmidt. "Our Jewish tradition believes if a man saves one life it is as if he saved the entire world. You helped my father, despite the risks to your own safety. May God grant you peace and keep you safe when you move to Amsterdam."

⌘⌘⌘⌘⌘⌘⌘⌘

Heinrich's anger flared up after the pair left. *I came here to escape Nazi laws forbidding me to take care of Jews. How long will it take them to extend those laws to Austria? Never again, shall I run from my responsibility. From this day on, I will devote myself to combating the Nazi curse Claus helped unleash on humanity.*

When his anger subsided, Heinrich realized he couldn't confront the Nazis until he contacted the Austrian resistance.

13th April, 1938 – Vienna – 1:30 PM Heinrich Mayer contacts the Viennese resistance

A month after Heinrich treated Otto's father, he returned from lunch to find two patients in the waiting room and no doctors on duty in the treatment area. A tall man brandishing a revolver stepped in front of Heinrich, startling him. "Stay calm and I won't hurt you," said the stranger.

"What do you want?"

"Someone shot a friend of mine. He needs medical attention."

"What have you done with my staff?"

"They'll be safe if you stay quiet and help my friend." The gun shook in his unsteady hand.

Heinrich calmly strode to a chair and sat down facing the stranger. "You can shoot me if you wish, but I won't treat your companion until you give me that pistol."

The man grimaced, then handed the firearm to Heinrich.

He stood, took his weapon, locked it in a cabinet, and turned to face him. "Where is he?"

The intruder opened the door to one of the treatment rooms, and pointed.

Heinrich approached the wounded man and cut the clothes away from his midsection. Blood ran onto the table, then dripped to the floor. "How did this happen?" asked Heinrich, his gaze fixed on the patient's injuries.

"I'd rather not say."

"Was it the Nazis?"

"Will you report him?"

"What will happen if I do?"

"You're German, right? I can tell by your accent."

"Yes, I am."

"Are you one of *them*?" His voice cracked with fear.

"How do I know you're not?" responded Heinrich, lifting his eyes.

The stranger opened his shirt, revealing a large Star of David hanging on a bulky silver chain. "I'm Jewish. If this doesn't convince you, I'll pull down my pants to show you where the *mohel* circumcised me when I was eight days old."

"That's unnecessary." Heinrich sighed, relieved a trap wasn't being baited for him. He carefully lifted the patient to examine his back. After laying him down he said, "The bullet missed your friend's vital organs and exited through his back. He'll be weak from loss of blood, but should recover after I treat the wound."

"How can I repay you, Doctor?"

He continued working on his patient as he said, "Release my staff. They must be anxious."

"No one was here when I arrived, so I took no hostages."

"How stupid of me, the staff took a long lunch to celebrate the head nurse's birthday."

"Is there anything else I can do?"

Having cleaned and sutured the patient's wounds, Heinrich looked up and stepped away from him. "Do you know anyone in the Austrian resistance? I can no longer stand by while the Nazis victimize those who disagree with their insane policies."

The stranger pointed at his friend and replied, "He's the only one I know."

"What are your names?"

"I'm Judah Isaacson and he's Siegfried Mannheim."

Siegfried was unconscious when Judah helped Heinrich carry him to Heinrich's apartment. The next evening, Siegfried woke with a start. "Where am I? Who are you?"

Heinrich rushed to his side. "The Nazis shot you. Judah brought you to my hospital, and I took care of you. I'm Doctor Heinrich Mayer."

Siegfried tried to lift his body then winced and fell back.

"It's best if you don't move. The bullet exited your body, but you lost a lot of blood. It will take time for your injuries to heal."

"Are you Jewish?"

"No, but I'd like to help Jews who are in trouble with the Nazis."

Siegfried narrowed his eyes. "Why would you do that?"

"I left Germany to escape Nazi laws forbidding me to take care of Jews. Last month, I treated an old man who'd been beaten by two Nazis because he was Jewish. Realizing it'll soon be illegal for me to treat Jews in Austria, I decided it was time for me to combat the Nazi curse. What can I do to help you?"

Siegfried thought for a few moments. "Our greatest challenge is hiding Jewish fugitives until we can get them out of Austria."

"I'll see what I can do."

The next morning, Heinrich visited Nathan Bleimann, the hospital's administrator. After closing the door and turning on the radio, he said, "Last month, we talked about taking care of Jews in trouble with the Nazis. Yesterday, I met someone who needs our help."

Bleimann raised an eyebrow. "Tell me more."

Heinrich told him he'd treated Siegfried, a member of Austria's underground who needed a safe hideout for escaping Nazi fugitives.

Bleimann leaned toward him. "What do you know about Siegfried?"

"Only what Judah Isaacson, the friend who brought him to the clinic, told me. I'm inclined to believe Judah is Jewish and I suspect that Siegfried is also a Jew."

Bleimann sat silently for several minutes, then said, "We *must* trust someone in the underground if we're to help Jewish fugitives. Are you willing to take a chance on Judah and Siegfried?"

Heinrich nodded his head in agreement. "Do you know where we could build a hideout?"

“There’s another level below the basement. I found it while replacing the tile down there.”

“How could we keep the Gestapo from discovering it?”

“Infectious Disease Clinics must strictly limit entry to make sure that diseases aren’t spread.”

“I’ll suggest it to Siegfried tonight.”

Siegfried thought the plan had merit and told Elisabeth about it. She sent a coded message to Turnbey asking him to investigate Heinrich and Bleimann. Turnbey told her that both of them cared for Jews in Germany until Nazi laws forbad him from doing so, then they immigrated to Vienna. Elisabeth scheduled an interview with Heinrich the following week and told Irena she was visiting Vienna to shop for clothes.

“Siegfried told me you saved his life,” said Elisabeth after meeting Heinrich at his hospital.

“Yes, and I’d like to help others threatened by the Nazis.”

“I understand you could build an Infectious Disease Clinic in the hospital’s basement.”

“Yes, such facilities restrict visitors, giving us the cover we need to hide our fugitives.”

"Will someone in the hospital's administration help you?"

"Yes, but we'd rather not give you those details until we can trust you. I'm sure you did the same before contacting me."

Elisabeth smiled, then asked, "Won't you need Berlin's approval?"

"Yes, we know someone who authorizes construction of such facilities. Should we begin the permitting process and let you know what's needed to build the clinic?"

"Yes, build a list of items you need, then hand it to Siegfried. He'll send it to me and I'll let him know when we've bought everything." Elisabeth paused for a moment. "I'll also get you an ambulance. You'll need it to secretly transport fugitives to and from the hideout after it's built."

Elisabeth then bought some clothes, called Irena to tell her when her plane would arrive, and flew back to Berlin.

25th April, 1938 – Vienna - 10:00 AM- Der KleiderKaiser is boycotted

It had been forty days since the Anschluss. Der KleiderKaiser's revenue dipped at first and then recovered. Avram was optimistic the firm would survive under Nazi occupation.

Johannes was opening the store when a storm trooper painted "Jewish owned business–don't buy here," in huge black letters on the outside of his display window. *Why didn't I act on Irma's warning while there was still time*? He shuddered as five Storm Troopers turned one of his best customers away at the door. After they kept another twenty from entering, Johannes exited the back door and rushed to warn his father.

"Who's minding the store?" asked Avram.

"Nazis boycotted us this morning. They sent all our customers away." When Avram showed no reaction, Johannes asked, "Doesn't that upset you, Papa?"

"No, it's happened before. A police friend of mine resolved those situations. I'll talk to him tomorrow."

The next morning, Avram went to the police station and told his friend about the boycott.

He replied, "After the Anschluss, the Nazis assigned a new supervisor to my department. He threatened to arrest any officer unwilling to enforce the boycott against Jewish stores. I can't help you," said the officer as he led Avram to the door.

Avram cried as he broke the news to Johannes.

Every morning after that, Johannes watched from inside the store as storm troopers turned KleiderKaiser customers away. Two weeks after the boycott began, the troopers didn't appear. Johannes opened the store and called his father with the good news. Thirty minutes later, a mob raced in and stole everything not bolted to the floor. Three police officers stood idly as they watched the plunder from across the street.

When Avram arrived, he tried to stop the looters. Fearing for his father's life, Johannes forced him out the back door.

"The Nazis will never allow us to reopen," said Avram, as they walked away from the store. "Even if they do, it would be foolhardy to restock. The thieves will return and steal our new merchandise. What are we to do?"

Johannes stopped and faced his father. "Many months ago, I caught Bruno reading Der Stürmer."

"He read that anti-Semitic rag?"

"Let me finish, Papa. Bruno didn't want you to know…"

"… rightfully so. I would have fired him on the spot..."

"… and asked me not to tell you. Relieved that I kept it to myself, he promised to help us if we ran into trouble with the Nazis. Should I ask Bruno what he can do?"

"Be very careful, my son. Nazis have no scruples. They'd rather kill a Jew than give him the time of day. Be very careful."

"Of course Papa."

That afternoon, Bruno greeted him solemnly at the door. "Please come in Herr Kaiser. I saw the looting this morning. Your nerves must be shattered."

Johannes swallowed hard before saying, "Two years ago, you offered to help us if we ran into trouble with the Nazis. I realize the situation has changed since then..."

"... You need go no further." interrupted Bruno.

Johannes felt his throat tighten.

"You accepted me as a trainee and patiently taught me the clothing business. Then, you didn't dismiss me after catching me read Der Stürmer. Grateful for your acts of human kindness, I called my good friend, a respected Nazi, to ask what he could do to keep you from bankruptcy. He suggested it would be best if Der KleiderKaiser were no longer a Jewish owned enterprise."

Johannes shivered.

"Don't worry Herr Kaiser. We're not setting a trap for you. Claus recommended that I buy your firm and declare it an Aryan owned business. That way the store can reopen, there would be no more boycotts, and the police will arrest anyone caught looting."

"Do you have the money to buy our store?"

"I couldn't hand it to you in a lump sum, but if you and your father agree, I'll give you an immediate down payment, then pay the rest from my profits."

"You know all the clothing and fixtures must be replaced before reopening."

"I also discussed that with Claus. Do you carry insurance?"

"Yes, but I haven't yet submitted a claim."

"That's good. Had you done so, the Reich would have assessed one fine after another, leaving nothing for you. If I become the Aryan owner, they will honor my claim in full."

"What will happen to my father and me?"

"I'll keep you both on as employees, giving you the same wage you paid me. You'll keep all proceeds of the sale and remain in Vienna for the foreseeable future."

"The foreseeable future?" repeated Johannes.

"I have no way of knowing what new rules the Party may impose on Jews. They could force you and your family to leave Austria. If that happens, I'll do everything in my power to help you."

"I'll tell my father what we discussed. If he agrees, I will call you to arrange a meeting at the store to work out the details."

"Excellent, but let's meet at your father's apartment. That way nobody can overhear details of our transaction."

Johannes outlined Bruno's proposal for his father. Although Avram was skeptical, at first, he agreed a negotiated settlement was better than receiving nothing for the store. The pair analyzed the firm's books to decide on a reasonable transfer price, then all three met at Avram's apartment the next morning to agree on terms of the transaction. The following day, Bruno handed Johannes an envelope with the down payment. That evening, all signs designating Der KleiderKaiser a Jewish establishment disappeared. Two weeks later, Der KleiderKaiser's sales returned to pre-boycott levels.

CHAPTER SIX -- MAYER'S 15TH ANNIVERSARY PARTY

22nd June, 1938 – Vienna – 8:30 AM – Claus Mayer arrives at his Office

It had been three months since the Anschluss. During that time, Mayer established a Viennese SS section and hired Blick to interrogate Jewish troublemakers identified by the Gestapo. Mayer then had the Gestapo dispatch those found guilty to the Dachau concentration camp.

Mayer got out of bed, gazed at the stranger in the mirror, then splashed icy water on his face to begin the daily ritual he devised in 1923 to replace compassion with cold-hearted indifference.

He then took one of his many identical SS uniforms from a large wooden clothes closet and examined it in minute detail to make sure every button was in place and that no imperfection marred the unspoiled blackness of the fabric. If he saw any defect, he put the uniform aside for necessary corrections. He then selected a second uniform and repeated the process.

Before shaving, Mayer scrutinized his body to make sure no hair was out of place and no blemish marred the perfect whiteness of his skin. The casual observer may have mistaken this practice as self-aggrandizement or vanity. Nothing could be further from the truth. His appearance, his will, and his absolute obedience belonged to the Nazi state.

After bathing and dressing, Mayer telephoned for his limousine and sat down to a breakfast of porridge with a dab of jam. Thirteen minutes later, he walked out of his apartment, locked the door, and strode down the six steps to the sidewalk. The limousine drove up to meet him at the precise moment his shoe touched the curb. The chauffeur jumped out, ran around the car, opened the rear passenger door, and closed it behind Mayer. Twenty-three minutes later, the limousine came to a stop at Vienna's Gestapo Headquarters and the driver let Mayer out.

The two-man SS honor guard snapped to attention, clicked its boots in unison, gave a synchronized straight-arm salute, and barked "Heil Hitler." Mayer smiled inwardly as he returned their salute. Although they were duty bound to hide their emotions, the guards' facial expressions couldn't conceal their pride at his arrival. They and their compatriots idolized his ruthless conformity to the basic laws of the SS: *Show human kindness to your own kind while acting with cold-blooded brutality toward all others*. Adolf Hitler, and all who served him, considered Mayer an exemplary Nazi.

Mayer entered the building, mounted the stairs two at a time, strode into his second floor office, and shut the door. Seconds later, someone knocked.

"Enter."

"Heil Hitler Obersturmbannführer," barked his aide-de-camp as he clicked his heels and saluted.

"Stand at ease, Kleindienst. Any burning issues this morning?"

"The Gestapo arrested an old man last night, Herr Oberst. He's suspected of being the ringleader in a Jewish conspiracy to undermine the Reich."

"What do we know so far?"

"That's the problem, sir. The prisoner refused to speak."

"Was he interrogated?"

"Yes, Blick spent over three hours with him."

Mayer leaned forward. "He refused to speak despite Blick questioning him for over three hours?"

"Exactly, sir, it baffled me too. Blick *never* goes beyond two hours without getting a full confession."

Mayer sat back in his chair. "Send Blick to my office, and arrange for me to interrogate the prisoner at…" Mayer checked his schedule, "… at ten thirty."

"Yes sir. Can I do anything else for you sir?"

"Carry on with your duties."

Moments later, there was a light knock on the door.

"Enter."

Blick walked in, approached Mayer's desk, clicked his heels, and saluted.

Noting the fear in his eyes, Mayer nodded toward an armchair. Blick sat down.

"You had trouble interrogating a prisoner?"

"Yes sir." Blick squirmed.

"Can you offer an explanation?"

"I used my most effective techniques, but he was unresponsive to them all."

"Did you learn *anything* about him?"

"No sir. I knew less after I finished than when I began."

"Explain." The tone of Mayer's voice reflected his growing impatience.

"Before starting an interrogation, I assess each prisoner to discover his or her exploitable fears. Finding none, I proceeded expecting to increase his pain sufficiently to make him yield. After three hours, I'd exhausted all my non-lethal treatments. My only options were to try again and risk killing him, or delay the cross-examination. I chose the latter."

Mayer sat forward. "I hired you on General Heydrich's recommendation. Your performance was exemplary until this morning. Need I say more?"

Blick looked to the floor. "No, Herr Oberst."

"I shall meet with the prisoner at ten thirty. You have one hour to rectify this situation." Mayer paused for several moments, then added, "Do you understand?"

"Yes sir."

"You may leave," said Mayer, taking a folder from his in-box and laying it on his desk. He opened it after Blick closed the door behind him.

Fifteen minutes later, Adolf Eichmann strode in followed by two aides carrying a huge cake. “Don’t get up, Claus,” said Eichmann with a smile. “No matter how much you protest, you can’t weasel out of this celebration. Reichsminister Göring, Reichsführer Himmler, and SS General Heydrich arranged for it.” Eichmann instructed his aides to place the cake in front of Mayer.

Mayer winced. *I have no time for this nonsense. Eichmann is such a sentimental fool.* He looked down at the cake. Its top was silver with a Nazi flag made of colored bonbons in the center. Circling the flag were the words *Honoring Oberst Mayer's fifteen years of devoted service to the Reich* in black icing. Goose-stepping SS militiamen, their arms raised in the Nazi salute, decorated each of the cake’s four sides.

Members of Mayer and Eichmann’s staffs walked into Mayer’s large office. Well-wishers who reported to neither man also crowded in. Mayer wanted to eject them, but that was pointless. The Nazi chain of command insisted that subordinates respect certain protocols…, which included celebrating the number of years they’d served the Party. *Forgetting the importance of this day was an obvious oversight, but not a major blunder. It won’t happen again.*

Eichmann walked around Mayer’s desk and tore the pen from his hand. “My friend, forget your duties for a few moments while we celebrate your great accomplishments as a Nazi.” He slapped Mayer on the back, as if to punctuate the point.

"You're right. The work will wait. My well-wishers won't," replied Mayer, frustration ringing in his voice.

22nd June, 1938 – Vienna – 10:30 AM – Mayer meets the strange prisoner

The anniversary party ended at ten. Mayer was reviewing critical funding documents when there was a knock on the door.

"Enter."

"It is 10:30, Herr Oberst," said Kleindienst. "The prisoner is in your private interrogation room."

"Did Blick contact me?"

"No sir. He hasn't yet returned."

"Order him to see me as soon as I get back."

"Yes, sir."

Mayer proceeded to the third floor where SS engineers had transformed a twenty by twenty foot office into a soundproof interview chamber. The walls were a drab green color. Thick gray bars secured the only window. A small cot having leather restraints at each corner rested uneasily against one wall. The captive sat shackled to a metal armchair at a large table in the middle of the room. When Mayer walked in, Kepner, his trusted second in command, got up from a chair behind the prisoner.

"Fritz, please unchain our guest."

He unlocked the shackles in a fluid motion, revealing he'd often prepared a detainee for his superior.

"Was he any trouble?"

"No sir. He didn't say a word and sat where I put him." Kepner then left the room.

Mayer eased himself into a cushioned armchair facing the hostage. He studied him for a few moments. The prisoner looked to be in his sixties or seventies, with thick white hair. Dried bloodstains covered his ripped shirt and numerous cuts and bruises were visible through slits in the fabric. The man's left arm hung limply at his side, and his right hand bore a red heart-shaped mark. Drawing on his interrogation experience, Mayer concluded he had suffered a vicious beating. Yet, he appeared to be a man at peace, his bearing holding no clue to the unspeakable tortures he'd endured.

A mysterious energy radiated from the prisoner's brown eyes, captivating Mayer. Emotions purged during his morning ritual reemerged, percolating into every muscle, bone, and sinew of his body. He couldn't decide whether he was feeling fear, or hope, or even desire of a mystical nature. An aura of tranquility descended over him.

"Are you having a problem with the subversive sir?" asked Kepner, unexpectedly appearing at the door.

Startled for a moment, Mayer remembered following Eichmann's advice to install a one-way mirror in the wall. A trusted aide could then watch the interrogation and intercede when necessary.

"No, Fritz. Everything is all right. Carry on with your duties." He nodded to his boss and retreated through the door.

"My name is Lieutenant Mayer. I'm sorry my interrogator treated you so badly…"

He often used those words to begin an interview, but his time he felt genuine remorse. A lump formed in his throat. "… but I can make sure your treatment improves." The lump grew, immobilizing his vocal cords. After taking a few minutes to settle down he continued. "Please tell me your name." The captive remained motionless, not uttering a sound. His expression remained unchanged.

⌘⌘⌘⌘⌘⌘⌘⌘

Mayer experienced a sudden pang of extreme heartache as his mind drew him back twelve years to the day his brother spurned him. Tears came to his eyes reliving Heinrich's final kiss, ending their close relationship.

⌘⌘⌘⌘⌘⌘⌘⌘

Kepner reappeared at the door: "Is there anything I can do for you, Herr Oberst?" His voice registered concern.

The captive's strange power had immobilized Mayer's protective shield. His conscience breathed freely for the first time in fifteen years.

"Return him to his cell," said Mayer in a rasping tone. "Have his injuries seen to and get him a clean set of clothes."

When he looked up, Kepner hadn't moved. Mayer clenched his jaw. "Did you misunderstand my order?"

"No sir, but…"

"… but what?"

"Will you resume the interrogation, Herr Oberst?"

"Come outside with me."

When they were several yards from the door, Mayer turned and glowered at Kepner. "I want the prisoner fed, treated for his injuries, and given clean clothes. I'll see him again at two. Bring our more cooperative Jews to the viewing room, one at a time, until someone identifies him. Then tell me who he is."

"Now I understand, sir. You want him cleaned up before he's seen by other Jews."

"Not that it's any of your business." Mayer couldn't shake off the detainee's lingering hold over his senses. "Will you obey my order before it's time to go home?"

"Of course, sir."

When the pair returned to the interrogation room, Kepner grabbed the prisoner's arm. Mayer reacted angrily. "I want no more bones broken… do you understand me?"

"Yes, sir," replied Kepner, looking blankly at his boss.

22nd June, 1938 – Vienna – 11:30 AM – Heydrich congratulates Mayer

Mayer returned to his office and slumped into his chair. *What made me so powerless in the presence of a shackled Jew? Why am I at peace after failing so miserably to perform my duty? How can I fulfill my obligations to Führer and Reich while harboring such feelings…?*

"… Herr Oberst," interrupted Kleindienst, peeking around the opened office door. "Please forgive me. I know you instructed me not to intrude, but Colonel Eichmann insisted I ask you to join him for lunch to celebrate your anniversary."

Mayer, still trying to make sense of the morning's events, scowled at his aide. His first impulse was to reprimand him for ignoring his express orders. He then blurted, "I… I… oh damn it, come in Adolf."

When Kleindienst stepped aside, Eichmann walked in and glared at Mayer. "Haven't *you* been out of sorts today?"

"I don't know what you mean."

"Your interrogation of the old Jew, it's turned you into a different man. I've never seen you like this."

Mayer sighed loudly and replied, "Oh that."

"Yes, that. What happened to your razor sharp, single-minded focus?"

"You and the rest of the office diverted my attention during my anniversary party, making it impossible for me to concentrate while interviewing the prisoner."

"It sounds like you need a few days away. When was your last vacation?"

"I don't remember."

General Heydrich marched into the room.

Mayer shot out of his chair and approached his boss with a smile. "What brings you to our little outpost of the Reich, Reinhard?"

"Why you, Herr Oberst, I came to congratulate you on your fifteenth anniversary with the Party."

"You're playing with me. Why are you *really* here?"

"I'm here on a classified mission for the Führer. This morning, as I was leaving his office he stopped me and said, *Tell Mayer how much his efforts are appreciated by the Party, and by me personally.*"

"Truly Reinhard, did our Führer ask you to convey such high praise?"

"I swear by the Swastika, Claus. He's very appreciative of all your efforts, from the first time he met you, to your exemplary performance identifying, questioning, and dispatching Jewish troublemakers to Dachau."

"Do you remember when *we* first met?" asked Mayer.

Heydrich was silent for a moment. "For the life of me, I can't."

"This may embarrassing for both of us," said Mayer suppressing a grin.

"Go ahead, Claus. We're all friends here, right Adolf?" said Heydrich, winking at Eichmann.

"It was at a party given by the Führer a few days after he became Chancellor. I walked in and there you were, playing the violin. Hitler looked enchanted, and you appeared to be in a different world. I thought you were an itinerant musician, hired for the evening."

Heydrich laughed until his face flushed and tears drained from his eyes. "I remember now. We were younger, and it was such a carefree time. I so enjoyed playing the violin, but have little time for such trifles today. We now have a world to rescue from the Jews, and no allies committed to help us in that monumental task. Look, Claus," said Heydrich, his voice unexpectedly reflecting a worried tone. "It troubled me when I heard about your interrogation of the old Jew. What happened?"

"It's nothing to worry about, sir. The emotions I felt during my fifteenth anniversary party clouded my judgment, making it hard for me to deal with a difficult prisoner."

"You had trouble dealing with a Jew?" asked Heydrich, as if reprimanding a child.

"It wasn't a physical issue, sir. He showed no response to Blick's interrogation, and you know how effective *he* is at loosening a troublemaker's tongue."

"Has he slipped?" asked Heydrich, concern echoing in his voice.

"On the contrary; Erik *reduced* the time to get a worthwhile confession."

"So what happened when *you* questioned him?"

"I couldn't provoke a response. It was almost as if his mind detached itself from his body and was floating above us."

Heydrich's eyes bulged as he screamed, "Have you taken leave of your senses, Mayer? Are the Viennese pastries turning your brain to mush? You're dealing with a fucking Jew, not a circus freak. I want to hear no more of floating minds."

"I haven't lost my mind, General. When have I ever given less than my soul to you, our Führer, and the Reich? Have I not followed both the letter and the spirit of all your orders? In your heart, you know that is true."

"I agree, Claus. You *have* been a model Nazi, combining your superior Nordic breeding with an unbending will. I wish we had more like you in the SS."

"Thank you, Reinhard. My only goal is to serve the Reich to the utmost of my ability. To do less is a crime against Führer and Fatherland."

"If you need help with the prisoner, just ask. Now I must go to my appointment," said Heydrich in a friendly tone, as he left Mayer's office.

"That was a close call, Claus," said Eichmann. "It looked like the General was ready to fire you, but you handled it well."

Mayer was still reviewing funding documents when Kleindienst stuck his head around the door. "It's two o'clock sir, the prisoner is ready for your interrogation. Can you meet with him?"

"Yes, I'm on my way."

Mayer stood up, checked if his uniform was in order, and left the office. Approaching the interrogation room, he stopped, walked into the viewing room, and gazed at the prisoner. He wore a spotless shirt. His tranquil demeanor hadn't changed. Mayer was trying to fathom how this Jew could have overpowered him when Kepner walked in. "Are you ready to restart the interrogation, sir?"

"Yes, I'm going in there now." He stood up, walked out into the hall, and saw Heydrich striding toward him.

"Mayer, you have a new assignment. I need you to familiarize yourself with it as soon as possible."

"Of course, General, I'll have the captive returned to his cell, then we can talk in my office."

"I will handle that for you, sir," said Kepner, heading into the interrogation room.

"Do you think Kepner is ready to shoulder your duties?" asked Heydrich as Mayer closed his office door.

"Yes I do," replied Mayer, trying to hide his relief at the possibility of surrendering his unyielding captive. "Nobody is better acquainted with my responsibilities."

"Then prepare the paperwork for my signature."

"I'll do that today, sir. What can you tell me about the assignment?"

"The Führer phoned to tell me the American cripple, Roosevelt, scheduled an international conference to discuss the Jewish question."

Mayer cracked a smile, "Is Roosevelt also trying to get rid of his Jews?"

"No, Hitler thinks Roosevelt wants other countries to take them off *our* hands." Heydrich chuckled then added, "Probably, so he's not forced to do so himself."

"How can I help, General?"

"Hitler wants you to work with Göring."

"The Reichsminister, sir?"

"Yes, Heinrich asked that you be reassigned to him, and the Führer agreed."

"That's wonderful." Mayer beamed at the thought of reuniting with his former boss. "When should I leave for Berlin?"

"He's expecting you tomorrow. The conference begins on the sixth of July."

CHAPTER SEVEN -- THE EVIAN CONFERENCE

23rd June, 1938 - Berlin – 9:00 AM – Mayer meets with Göring

The next morning, Göring stood up as Mayer entered his office. "Claus, my dear friend, it's been much too long." The two clasped in a warm hug.

"Yes, Herr Reichsminister, it truly has."

"I wish we had more time to talk, but we have a great deal to discuss and the Führer asked me to sit in on an important meeting in a few minutes. Please take a seat." Göring sat next to him. "I need you to learn all you can about Roosevelt's Evian Conference, then find someone reliable, but not German, to attend for us."

"Is that necessary, sir? I'd be glad to represent you."

"Germany wasn't invited since we're ridding ourselves of the Jews. Our *Völkischer Beobachter* reporters will be there as observers, but I need a more impartial account than they'd be willing to offer. Here is a copy of the agenda," said Göring, handing it to him. "It takes place at the Royal Hotel, in Evian-les-Bains, which sits on the shores of Lake Geneva in France. Over thirty countries will attend. The second page lists their names. We expected Roosevelt to select Secretary of State Cordell Hull as his representative, but he announced that Myron Taylor will head the American delegation."

"Myron Taylor, who's that?"

"He's a close friend of Roosevelt's and a former U.S. Steel CEO. Since Roosevelt called the conference, Taylor will also act as its chairman." Göring paused for a moment. "You appear puzzled."

"Do you think his choice as conference chairman will limit its chances for success?"

"Had he chosen his Secretary of State it would have signaled a high level of commitment. Taylor's choice sends a less positive message. We can only hope attendees will believe otherwise." Göring appeared deep in thought for a moment, then added, "The world's democracies haven't lifted a finger to help our Jews immigrate. If they continue doing so at Evian, it will doom the conference to failure. If so, our Führer may have to develop his own solution to the Jewish problem. I must go now, Claus. Please keep me informed."

Mayer studied the agenda after Göring left the room. He then turned the page and ran his finger down the list of invited countries. *How could over thirty nations attend, then refuse to accept our Jews? Britain, France, and the United States will take a few. That should convince the others to increase their immigration quotas.*

Mayer then returned to his hotel room. With no plans for the afternoon, he decided to visit the Kreutzers. He enjoyed their company and hadn't seen them for over a year. He lifted the phone and asked the operator to connect them.

"You are in Berlin, Claus?" exclaimed Irena. "Otto and I will be upset if you don't attend our dinner party this evening. We're welcoming Elisabeth Billingsworth, our daughter-in-law, home from London. I've wanted you to meet her for the longest time. You must come, I insist."

"I wouldn't miss it for the world."

27th June, 1938 - Vienna - Otto learns about the Evian Conference

Otto Klein was heartbroken that the democratic nations of the world denied entry to thousands of Jews trying to flee Nazi persecution. Then he read that the United States scheduled an international conference to rescue Germany's Jews. He was rushing to share the good news with Johannes when he ran into an old friend. "Hello, Peter. It's wonderful to see you."

⌘⌘⌘⌘⌘⌘⌘⌘

Peter Wassermann scowled at Otto, rage percolating from the pit of his stomach. Clenching his fists, he punched him in the face, sending him sprawling to the pavement.

Wiping blood from his nose, Otto said, "Why did you do that, Peter? We've been friends since childhood."

Wassermann spat on him. "You filthy Jews defile our nation's honor and pollute our race's blood. It is my destiny, as a Nazi, to purge you and your parasitic leaders from our Fatherland. If I see you again, I'll have the Gestapo drag you off to a Concentration Camp."

Towering over Otto, Wassermann saw himself as Hitler's mythical, all conquering superman. Lean and tall, his blond hair, blue eyes, and classic Aryan features affirmed his supremacy over Otto and the Jewish race. He strode away thankful Adolf Hitler had lifted him from despair and given him purpose. *It wasn't my fault I couldn't find work befitting my station after school. The Jews were to blame. They stole my birthright. Hitler is reversing the sins of the past, returning what they stole from me. He's creating a new Germany where Aryans will reign supreme; where I shall reign supreme.*

⌘⌘⌘⌘⌘⌘⌘⌘

Otto took a detour to the hospital, so Dr. Mayer could tend to his injuries. A bright brass plate bearing the inscription, *Dogs and Jews not permitted beyond this point* greeted him. Tears filled Otto's eyes as he stared at it. He turned and slowly made his way toward Johannes' apartment.

As soon as he opened the door Johannes blurted, "What the hell happened to you?"

"I met Peter Wassermann on my way here. He hit me then launched into a tirade, saying I was filth and he would have the Gestapo send me to a concentration camp if he saw me again."

Johannes led Otto into the bathroom to tend his injuries. "That looks painful, but it doesn't appear that the bastard broke anything."

"It wasn't for the lack of trying, but I have exciting news. The American President called for a conference of nations in France."

"Yes, I heard about that. After it convenes, we'll be able to emigrate, escaping Hitler and people like Wassermann."

The friends spent hours talking about the wonderful places they would visit, and the fantastic things they would do after emigrating. Then, their conversation took on a tone of sadness. They didn't want to leave their beloved homeland, but what choice did they have?

28th June, 1938 – Berlin – 3:30 PM – Elisabeth returns to Germany

Mayer knocked on the Kreutzer's door and Greta, their maid, opened it. "Herr Oberst, the Kreutzers are looking forward to seeing you."

Mayer smiled and gave her a small hug. She showed him into the drawing room. Otto and Irena walked in a few moments later. "My dearest Claus, I am so angry with you," chided Irena, giving him a light slap on the arm. "It's been much too long since you called on us."

"It's good to see you, Irena. I'm sorry I couldn't visit you sooner. Trying to cope with Austria's Jewish problem overwhelmed both Colonel Eichmann and me."

"Better you than me," replied Irena with a scowl. "I wouldn't deal kindly with them. They overstayed their welcome in our Reich, but we shouldn't aggravate ourselves on a joyful day like today. Otto and I have wanted you to meet Elisabeth Billingsworth, our dear daughter-in-law, and you will finally do so this evening." Irena glanced at her watch pendant, "But now I *must* go. We still have much to do before our guests arrive."

Soon after Otto and Irena left the drawing room, Greta ushered Adolf Eichmann in carrying a glass of red wine. Mayer jumped out of his chair. "What are you doing in Berlin?"

"General Heydrich asked me to brief him on progress of my project this morning. Then he insisted I join him after the Kreutzers invited him to this party." He paused for a moment. "You are friends with Otto and Irena, but I don't think you know Elisabeth. She married Bruno, their dear departed son."

"I knew Bruno from my storm trooper days, but haven't met Elisabeth. Tell me about her."

"You're in for a treat. She is beautiful and has an engaging personality. Who knows, perhaps your bachelor days are numbered."

"We'll see."

28th June, 1938 – Berlin - the Kreutzer Mansion – 8:00 PM – Mayer meets Elisabeth Billingsworth

The butler ushered Mayer and Eichmann into the grand ballroom at eight. They chatted with Reichsminister Goebbels, his wife Magda, and Generals Heydrich, Rommel, and Keitel before Irena approached them. “Elisabeth will soon arrive. I’ll show you to your seats at the head table.”

Irena seated Mayer with Eichmann on his left, then sat down at the end of the table. She pointed at an empty chair between her and Mayer. “Elisabeth will be there, next to you.” Otto sat at other end of the long rectangular table. Members of the Nazi elite sat between Otto and Eichmann. The other guests were at round tables arranged in a semicircle around the head table.

Waiters moved about the assembled company filling everyone’s glass with their apéritif of choice. Mayer ordered a Jägermeister, took a sip, and placed it on the table. A musical ensemble, comprising a piano, two violins, a viola, a cello, and a clarinet, played light classical music from a stage at the other end of the hall.

The door opened and Elisabeth walked in, her long brunette hair flowing behind her. She wore a lilac chiffon dress, a lavender sash accentuating her trim waist.

The guests all rose, faced Elisabeth, and applauded.

She walked to the round tables, stopping to chat with a few friends. When she turned toward the head table her smile wilted, she felt dizzy, and reached for a chair to steady herself. "These new shoes from London are terrible. I almost fell on the floor."

"Are you all right Elisabeth?" cried Irena as she hurried to help her.

"Of course, Irena. It's nothing more than a bad pair of shoes. I'm fine."

Irena took Elisabeth's hand and led her to the empty chair held by Mayer. "My darling, this is Herr Oberst Claus Mayer, but you *must* call him Claus." Turning to Mayer, Irena continued, "And I'd like to introduce my daughter-in-law, Elisabeth Billingsworth." Irena then sat down.

Elisabeth extended her hand. Mayer bowed and kissed her white lace glove. Her heart beat so loudly she feared Mayer would hear it over the voices of the guests. Mayer moved her chair away from the table and slid it under her as she sat. He bent over her left ear and whispered, "May I get you anything?"

She replied, "No, I'm much better now," in a stiff tone of voice.

Mayer remained standing until all the guests took their seats. He then lifted his Jägermeister and faced Elisabeth. "I offer a toast to our beautiful guest-of-honor and hope this will be the first of many times we sit together."

Rachel was deaf to Mayer's toast, her mind racing. *Why didn't that louse die? Does he remember me? If so, I can no longer be an MI6 spy. If he doesn't...*

The guests rose, repeating, "To Elisabeth," in unison.

They were about to retake their seats when Heydrich stood up and held his glass high. "To our Führer, may he long guide our nation to greatness."

Everyone repeated, "To our Führer," sipped his or her drinks and sat down.

Irena took Elisabeth's hand in hers and said, "My dearest Elisabeth I *know* you and Claus will become the best of friends, perhaps even more."

Smiling, Elisabeth squeezed Irena's hand, saying nothing. *Friends with a worm like that, impossible.*

Irena turned to Mayer. "Is Elisabeth not the vision of loveliness?"

"Thank you for inviting me, my dearest Irena." He turned to face Elisabeth and smiled.

She tilted her head downward. “Thanks for your gracious toast,” *you serpent.* Looking at him she added, “Please excuse me, Herr Oberst. I have a terrible headache and must take an aspirin.” Her voice was icy.

“Of course, but you *must* call me Claus. Irena will be unhappy if you don’t.” He stood, pulled out her chair, and she strode quickly away.

Eichmann touched Mayer’s arm after Elisabeth left. “She’s gorgeous, right?”

“Yes, but is she always so off-putting toward people she just met?”

“No, perhaps she felt ill at ease after almost falling in front of everyone.”

“Yes, that’s possible. I’ll reserve judgment for now.”

Rachel’s hate consumed her as she closed the bathroom door. *That insolent pig... how dare he... I’ll make him suffer for the way he behaved toward us... yes that’s what I’ll do... that snake will pay a heavy price.* Elisabeth’s stomach churned seeing Rachel’s enraged expression in the mirror. I must c*alm down. Everyone will know something is wrong. I’ve made too many sacrifices to ruin everything because of my hatred for Mayer.*

Elisabeth went to her room and sat down to purge the rage from her mind. She waited until her pulse and respiration felt normal, then smiled into the mirror until her cheerfulness appeared genuine. Feeling more relaxed, she returned to the ballroom and said, "I am sorry for acting so rude, Claus, but I couldn't have gone on without an aspirin and some rest. Can you forgive me?"

"No apology is necessary. I hope you are feeling better now."

"Yes, I am, and thank you for being so understanding."

By the time waiters served the main meal, featuring a tender shoulder of venison on an austere art déco plate, the pair talked as if they were alone in the crowded room.

After the waiters served desert, General Heydrich, and other Nazi dignitaries left for the library. Eichmann winked at Mayer as he followed them out. Mayer and Elisabeth continued their conversation for several more minutes. Then, a smile lit Mayer's face. Elisabeth's muscles tensed when he said, "I *knew* this wasn't the first time I saw you."

She forced a smile. "When was that, Claus?"

"During the Putsch."

Dear God, this can't be happening. He knows I'm Rachel. Act as if nothing is wrong. Looking around the banquet hall she said, "You didn't join the other leaders in the library."

"Would you like me to leave?" asked Claus, pretending to rise from his chair.

"Don't you dare. It's refreshing to see a member of our Führer's elite who isn't all business."

"To tell you the truth, I *am* usually all business, but, I've never had such charming and attractive company to keep me from my duties."

Elisabeth smiled at Mayer's compliment, then took another sip of her after-dinner brandy. "Claus, I need to powder my nose. Would you like to meet me outside when I return? It's a lovely evening for a short stroll."

"I would," said Mayer, as he got up to move her chair. "I'll be in Irena's rose garden."

Opening the bathroom door Elisabeth thought, *Claus must have met the real Elisabeth during the Putsch. I'll bury my feelings for him now and build on that relationship.* She primped herself in the mirror and set out to conquer an Obersturmbannführer.

⌘⌘⌘⌘⌘⌘⌘⌘

After going outside, Mayer sat down on a wooden bench overlooking a babbling brook in Irena's rose garden. *She intrigued me when I first saw her from a distance, but I was only eighteen. I'll spend time with her to see whether we're meant for each other. How will I do that... of course... as an Englishwoman, she's eligible to attend the Evian Conference.*

⌘⌘⌘⌘⌘⌘⌘⌘⌘

"My oh my Claus, you certainly are deep in thought," said Elisabeth as she sat next to him. "What could be so important?"

"I was thinking about my meeting with Reichsminister Göring this morning."

"That puts me in my place, doesn't it Herr Oberst?" said Elisabeth with a little pout.

"No, you misunderstand, Elisabeth."

"I apologize… again… Claus. I was just cracking a small joke at your expense."

He gave her a stern look, then broke into a nervous chuckle.

She laughed coquettishly.

They locked eyes, and he embraced her. Seconds later, he pulled back. "My deepest apologies, I should not have done that. It was inappropriate."

She touched his arm and whispered, "I'm not complaining, Claus." *Excellent... this is going better than I expected.* Intent on winning Mayer's love, Elisabeth suppressed Rachel's impulse to spit in his face.

Mayer kissed her, first gently then passionately. Rachel felt like choking. *How can I go through with this? I'll pretend he's Benjie Kornblum. I still loved him when we met again at Temple before I left Germany.*

Irena walked out of the house and stood looking at them. She then said, "Lovebirds already," in a singsong voice. Continuing in a more serious tone, she added, "And exactly what I expected after you met." Irena looked at them for a few more moments, as if etching the scene into her memory, then went back into the house.

"I loved that woman for as long as I've known her," said Mayer, "and now I know why. She has an extraordinary gift for matchmaking."

Elisabeth smiled. "I find her taste in men to be impeccable."

Later that evening, when they were sitting alone in the library, Mayer brought up the Evian assignment.

"I'd love to attend with you. My in-laws told me Evian is beautiful." *How perfect, I can be there when the world's great powers open their doors to my people.*

"Unfortunately, I'm not invited. It's only for delegates from countries willing to accept Germany's Jews. Germany doesn't fit that category, but Britain does." After thinking for a moment, Mayer continued, "We can meet afterwards, in Switzerland, to discuss your findings."

"I'd prefer attending with you, but spending time with you in Switzerland later would be wonderful."

After the party, Elisabeth stretched out in her bed. *I'll make him fall in love with me and use his connections to benefit my MI6 responsibilities.* Elisabeth then fell into a sweet, pleasing sleep.

29th June, 1938 – Berlin – 1:00 AM – Eichmann discusses his Reich Bureau for Jewish Emigration

Heydrich's limousine dropped Mayer and Eichmann off at their hotel. Mayer was heading toward the elevator when Eichmann said, "I'm too wound up to fall asleep, let's have a nightcap."

"I'd like that, Adolf."

After ordering their drinks, Eichmann turned to Mayer and smiled. "Well?"

"Well, what?"

"Earlier, you found Elisabeth to be cold. Did you change your mind about her?"

"Yes, I remembered seeing her sit at the table next to mine when the Führer launched the Putsch in 1923. Although she didn't see me, she caught my attention." He looked down at the Benedictine he'd ordered. "She may be the one I've been looking for all my life."

"That's wonderful news, Claus. It's high time you settled down and started a family. I'm thrilled for you."

"Before dinner, you mentioned talking with Heydrich about a project. Are you free to discuss it?"

"Yes, earlier this year he asked me to set up a process for purging Austria of its Jews.

"The General mentioned that, but offered no details. Was it a difficult mission?"

"It was, at first. When I arrived in Vienna, the agencies serving Vienna's Jewish community weren't active and I couldn't proceed until they reopened."

"Did the Jews shut them down to thwart us?"

"No, in their zeal to solve the Jewish problem the Gestapo closed them and arrested their leaders."

"What did you do?"

"I looked over the records of everyone they'd taken into custody and asked the Gestapo to release those I needed. They're now free and willing to help me."

"How will your new office help the Reich? We're already taking their money."

"It simplifies our process. Jews wishing to emigrate must now visit offices scattered throughout Vienna, making it difficult for us to know whether they paid all their bills before emigrating. I'll move all the various Reich and local representatives to one building. Then we will make the Jews pay us all they owe before permitting them to leave."

"Where will you house those officials? Our building is bursting at the seams."

"At the Albert Rothschild Palace. It was one of the first places commandeered by the SS and now stands almost vacant. Heydrich gave me permission to use it this morning."

"Will you also help émigrés get the paperwork required by receiving nations?"

"No, since our emigration authorization expires two weeks after it's issued, they must have all their receiving country paperwork in hand *before* entering the Palace."

"Do you have room for my people there?"

"I'm glad you asked. I've set aside an area for your department."

5th July, 1938 – Evian France - Elisabeth attends the Evian Conference

The next morning, Elisabeth sat down to have breakfast with Irena. "Claus asked me to attend the Evian Conference for him next week."

"Will he be there?"

"No, he can't go. Attendees must be from countries willing to accept Germany's Jews."

"When *will* you see him?"

"I'll report my findings to him afterwards, in Switzerland."

"Good, so you will spend time alone with him." Irena paused for a moment. "I remember Otto telling me something about that conference, but can't remember what it was." She went out into the hall and called for him to join her. He was still upstairs getting dressed. When he came in, she asked, "Didn't you mention the Evian Conference a few days ago?"

"Yes, I told you Wilhelm Nagel will be there with reporters from the *Völkischer Beobachter*. His plane will stop in Paris before going on to Evian. He knew I planned to visit Paris and asked whether I'd like to go with him."

"Will you go, dear?"

"No, I have important Party meetings here."

"Claus asked Elisabeth to attend the Evian Conference for him. Can she take your seat?" asked Irena.

"I don't see why not. In fact, I prefer it. There will be lots of Jews there, and he'll make sure they don't pester her."

"There," said Irena, turning to face Elisabeth. "It's all arranged. You will attend the conference with Wilhelm."

Six days later, Elisabeth and Nagel were waiting in line to check into the Royal Hotel when a page walked by calling out her name. After she identified herself, he led her to the front desk and introduced her to a uniformed member of the hotel's staff. Speaking in flawless Kings English he said, "We made special arrangements for your stay, Miss Billingsworth. Please come with me."

She narrowed her eyes. "Who are you?"

"My name is Philippe."

Nagel mouthed the words, *what's happening*? when Elisabeth passed him walking alongside Philippe toward the elevator. She shrugged her shoulders mouthing, *I don't know*.

She felt uneasy getting into the elevator with him. When it stopped, Philippe stepped out saying, "This is our most exclusive floor, Madam. Your room is here." He then walked down the hall.

Elisabeth asked the elevator operator to wait, then said, "I must talk with your manager before going any further."

"There is no cause for alarm, Madam," said Philippe as he unlocked the fifth room on the right and gestured for her to join him. She didn't move.

Sean Smythe poked his head out behind Philippe and waved for her to approach.

Elisabeth walked forward while Smythe slipped out of sight. She entered her room, then Phillipe followed her in and looked around. "Everything appears to be in order. Is there anything else I can do for you, Madam?"

"No, I apologize for causing such a fuss."

"No apology needed. If you need anything, please call the Bell Captain. He's instructed to contact me at once."

When she fished in her bag for a tip, Philippe said, "That's unnecessary. The hotel took care of all costs associated with your stay." He then backed out of the room and closed the door.

Moments later, Elisabeth heard a faint knock. Turning, she noticed another locked door and opened it. Sean smiled at her asking, "What do you think of your accommodations?"

"Accommodations, Sean? What are *you* doing here?"

"We got word you'd attend the conference. Since I was already here Reginald decided we should meet, and I suggested connecting suites."

"How do I explain this upgrade to the Kreutzers?"

"A Royal Hotel executive is on MI6s payroll. Turnbey had him award them a complimentary stay in a master suite. The hotel called Kreutzer about the award after you left for the airport. As expected, he asked the hotel to transfer his credit to your account."

"I have high hopes for this conference's success, Sean."

Smythe tilted his head to one side, saying nothing.

"What's wrong?"

"There are countries where Jews cannot live, and countries where Jews cannot enter. I'm afraid this does little to change that."

"How can you prejudge the conference before the first session is called to order?"

"Punsters in England had a field day with the fact that Evian spelled backward is naïve."

"That proves nothing, Sean. I don't appreciate your wisecrack."

"I also have deep German Jewish roots, Elisabeth, and am disappointed the conference will do little to help Germany's Jews. But the handwriting is on the wall."

"What makes you so pessimistic?"

"The Jewish Agency for Palestine wanted to offer Germany's Jews a home there, but the British ruled Palestine out as a Jewish haven."

Her heart sank.

Smythe took a copy of the conference invitation out of his pocket, and read, "No country must receive a greater number of immigrants than its existing legislation allows."

"Sean. I've heard enough. Every time it looks like the world's democracies will do right by our people, they disappoint me. Will this never end?"

"I'm sorry, Elisabeth. There's a lot more to tell, but you'll learn that as the conference unfolds."

The next morning, Elisabeth was on her way to meet Nagel for breakfast when someone rushed up to her speaking in German. “Rachel Goldstein, I haven’t seen you in years.”

Recognizing her as a Jewish school friend from Munich, Elisabeth stuck up her nose and said, “I don’t know you. Leave me alone,” in Kings English. She then turned, stormed away, and made for the closest bathroom to calm her nerves. After regaining her composure, she joined Nagel for breakfast in the restaurant. “Did you hear anything about the conference, Wilhelm?”

“Yes, after talking with quite a few delegates I learned that most countries in attendance don’t have large Jewish populations, and they want to keep it that way. It doesn’t look like this conference will solve our Jewish problem.”

Elisabeth’s chest tightened.

“Why so gloomy? If the conference fails, it’ll bear out our Führer’s claims that the democratic countries hate the Jewish race as much as we do.”

“It’s not that. If other nations won’t accept our Jews, how can we hope to get rid of them?”

“Don’t worry. If the conference doesn’t succeed, Adolf Hitler will come up with his own plan to solve his Jewish problem.”

Elisabeth looked down at her watch. "We'd better get going. The opening session is about to begin."

Ambassador Taylor was reading his introductory remarks when the pair arrived. They took the last two adjacent seats as he said government-sponsored persecution was forcing six hundred thousand people to seek sanctuary, and that number was increasing daily. Elisabeth's spirits soared. *Perhaps he will take a strong stand in support of Germany's Jews and encourage other countries to follow suit.* Taylor then dashed her hopes by declaring that the United States wouldn't increase its existing immigration quotas and didn't expect other nations to do so.

Elisabeth felt like crying. Fearing Nagel would see her despair, she forced a smile. *Thank God for small miracles. He's turned his attention to the podium.*

Taylor's opening remarks set a standard for inaction. Elisabeth listened mournfully as each delegate bemoaned the plight of Hitler's unwanted Jews, then offered excuses for not accepting them. After a while, she became disenchanted and stared through the huge panel windows behind the speaker. A squirrel, scurrying about in a tree, looked into the hall then quickly returned to the chore of finding acorns. She smiled. *I know how you feel. I'm also having trouble concentrating on these proceedings*. Disgusted at her own lack of interest, she began making detailed notes on each speaker's excuses for not accepting Germany's Jews.

That evening, Smythe knocked on their adjoining door and looked into her room. "Come in, Sean," said Elisabeth, then added, "I have a problem. One of my Jewish school friends from Munich recognized me this morning. Please get rid of her. If my Nazi companion finds out about her, he'll tell the Kreutzers."

"Give me her name and describe her in as much detail as you can. I'll locate her and her companions and convince them to go home."

Elisabeth wrote her friend's information on Royal Hotel stationary and handed it to Smythe. "You were right. This conference won't help our people. It makes me want to cry."

"I knew you'd feel that way, but if you're to continue as MI6s ears and eyes in Germany you must condemn the world's refusal to take in Hitler's Jews, while agreeing that Nazi anti-Semitism isn't a bad thing."

"Not only that. I'm seeing Claus Mayer afterwards to convey my thoughts about the conference."

Smythe lifted an eyebrow. "Is that the same person who victimized you during the Beer Hall Putsch?"

"Yes, Irena Kreutzer introduced us at the homecoming party she threw for me last week."

"Did he recognize you?"

“He recognized me as the real Elisabeth. He must have met her in1923. I think they were close because he kissed me when we were alone.”

“How did that intimacy make you feel?”

“It made me want to throw up, but I forced myself to return his affections with as much sincerity as I could. A relationship with Mayer could open new doors for me in Nazi Germany.”

“When will you share your conclusions with him?”

“We’ll meet in Switzerland after the conference, then he’ll pass them on to Göring, his boss.”

“Becoming intimate with a Göring confidant will improve your Nazi credentials, but please be careful. It could become your death sentence if he finds out who you are.”

“Don’t I know it.”

Smythe pointed at the balcony. “Perhaps you’d like to go outside with me to look at Lake Geneva. It’s a magnificent sight.”

Her eyes filled with tears as she walked out. “How can the Democratic countries allow Hitler to persecute our people? Why don’t they condemn him, or at least open their doors to us?”

"That's why our MI6 work is so vital. If the world doesn't care about us, we must help the Jews get out of Nazi Germany as quickly as possible."

15th July, 1938 – Evian, France – 2:30 PM Elisabeth prepares to leave for Lausanne

Elisabeth was packing her clothes on the last day of the conference when someone knocked on her door. She answered, and Philippe said, “I have an envelope for you, madam.” He handed it to her and backed away.

She thanked him, closed the door, and read the enclosed note.

Dear Elisabeth,

When General Heydrich heard I was meeting with you in Lausanne, he made his private plane available. Please be at Evian’s airport at four this afternoon.

I hope you had a pleasant time and look forward to seeing you soon.

Respectfully,

Obersturmbannführer C. Mayer

He signed the typewritten note Claus.

That proves it. The Nazi top brass wants us together. Why else would Heydrich offer Claus his plane? Smythe knocked on their adjoining door and stepped into her room.

“Look at this note,” said Elisabeth, handing it to him.

He looked at it, then at her. "It looks like you've made a positive impression on both Mayer *and* Heydrich. That's a good thing." He paused for a moment, then asked, "What will you do if Mayer wants to take your relationship to the next level in Switzerland?"

"I don't know how I'll do it, but I must act as if I'm falling in love with him. If he suspects I'm pretending, the consequences could be dire for me and my role as an agent."

"I can't offer any advice other than to take no unnecessary chances. If you suspect he's on to you get out of Germany and cable MI6 your location. We'll take it from there." Smythe was silent for a few moments, then asked, "Have you decided what you'll tell him about the conference?"

"I know what I want to say… this conference will leave a dark stain on the reputations of every attending country, but I know I can't tell him that."

"Yes you can, but you must focus on how the outcome benefits the Third Reich. I'd better get back to my room so you can finish packing." Sean hugged her, and she kissed him on the cheek.

After closing her bags, she called for a bellhop to take them downstairs. He did so and placed them next to the bell captain. The bell captain then asked, "Would you like me to call a limousine for you, madam?"

"Yes, I'm going to Evian's airport."

After calling for a limousine the bell captain asked, "Did you attend all the conference proceedings, madam?"

"Yes, they were important."

"You were in the minority."

"What do you mean?"

"Many delegates didn't attend all the meetings. A few chose pleasure cruises on the lake; others gambled at the casino; still others took mineral baths at the Esablissement Thermal; some traveled to Chamonix for summer skiing; while a small number went riding. Evian has many pleasures beckoning nearby, making it difficult for delegates to sit inside and listen to speeches all day."

His comments broke Rachel's heart. Elisabeth's eyes were moist when she entered the limousine. *That's disgusting. With Jewish lives in the balance, delegates took a vacation.* After feeding her regret for a few more moments, she pulled out her conference notes and reviewed them.

About ten minutes later, the driver parked next to a two-engine airplane, its tail adorned with a huge swastika. He ran around the car and opened Elisabeth's door. She stepped out into the cool summer breeze, approached the airplane stairs, and gasped looking up.

"My heavens," said Mayer, filling the airplane's doorway, "you're even more beautiful than I remember."

"I'm glad to see you too, Herr Obersturmbannführer," said Elisabeth affectionately, as she drew close to him.

He stroked her face gently, then took her into his arms. She melted into Claus' embrace, pretending he was Benjie Kornblum.

A uniformed Luftwaffe officer approached the couple. "I'm Horst, the pilot. We must leave. I have to be in Berlin for the General tonight."

"Of course," said Mayer, a flush crossing his cheeks.

Horst accompanied the couple to their seats. "Is there anything else I can get you before we leave?"

"Yes, please bring us the General's champagne and two glasses."

The General sent champagne. He's toasting our relationship. How wonderful. Now I must convince Mayer I'm falling in love with him.

Moments later, the couple sat facing each other, their glasses filled. "Our first toast must be to Irena Kreutzer, without whom this moment wouldn't have been possible," said Mayer.

She replied, “I shall always be indebted to my wonderful mother-in-law,” with forced delight. They clinked glasses as the airplane rocketed from the runway.

“Tell me about the conference. Did it succeed?”

“No, none of the delegates increased their immigration quotas.”

“I’m surprised.”

“Why’s that?” asked Elisabeth, trying not to show her astonishment.

“Looking over the conference agenda I felt certain the United States, Britain, and France would let a few Jews immigrate. That would have convinced other countries to follow suit.” He paused for a few moments before adding, “Were there any other surprising outcomes?”

“Yes, the delegates passed no resolutions condemning our Nuremberg Laws. They didn’t consider our treatment of Germany’s Jews to be their problem and wanted to keep it that way.”

The airplane touched down a few minutes later, and Horst approached the pair. “It’s been a pleasure having you both on board. Your luggage is being loaded into the limousine, and it will take you to your hotel.”

Mayer reserved a suite at the Hôtel de la Paix Lausanne. He'd never visited there, but when he called Irena about it she said, "Elisabeth loved vacationing there, and it has marvelous views of the Alps and Lake Geneva."

The General Manager met their Mercedes limousine when it pulled up to the hotel. He opened Elisabeth's door and helped her out. "It is my great pleasure to welcome you back, Miss Billingsworth. You and the Obersturmbannführer will stay in our Royal Penthouse. It has two bedrooms sharing a living and dining room area. We tried to anticipate all your needs. If you need anything else, please call our bell captain."

Elisabeth became conflicted after closing her bedroom door. *It's easy to talk about falling in love with Claus, very hard for me to surrender myself to him... but that's what I must do.* She decided to unpack later, join him, and take it from there.

When she walked into the living room, Mayer was sitting in an overstuffed armchair facing the beauty of azure blue Lake Geneva. Elisabeth trembled when he stood and turned toward her. A surge of fear-laced adrenaline electrified her as he approached. She tried in vain to maintain her composure, but felt her left eye twitch.

He stopped, extending his right hand to her.

Their fingers touched. His smile deepened. She thought about Benjie.

His voice was soft as a flowing stream as he said, "Please join me on the sofa. The view is incredible."

As she sat down, he eased himself beside her leaving ample space between their bodies.

They looked at the scenery silently. He then turned to face her. "Elisabeth, it's been years since I was alone with a woman. Please let me know if anything I do makes you feel uncomfortable." He was silent for a moment, then asked, "Do you mind if I smoke?"

"Not at all, Claus."

He lit a cigarette, drew the smoke deeply into his lungs, then slowly exhaled it through his nose. Somehow, her fearful anticipation of this moment, and intense desire to make him fall in love with her, awakened long dormant sensual yearnings within Elisabeth. She felt her heart flutter.

Mayer placed his cigarette in an ashtray at his side, leaned toward Elisabeth, and brushed strands of hair from her brow. She touched his hand. He brought her hand to his mouth, gently kissing her fingers. She moved closer to him. *I love you Benjie.* Her breathing became shallow. Her heartbeat quickened. Their lips touched. He put his arms around her. They kissed. *Benjie, my love.*

She put her arms around him and they kissed hungrily. Mayer released her, turning his gaze toward her bedroom and back to her eyes. She smiled. They walked there hand in hand. He closed the door.

The weekend passed like a warm summer's eve. Elisabeth enjoyed having sex with Mayer while fighting to keep Rachel's hatred for him at bay. They spent every moment together.

While returning to Berlin in Heydrich's plane, Elisabeth said, "The conference accomplished nothing. Is there any point in discussing it further?"

"I still want your honest assessment of the arguments made by delegates, and would also like to see any notes you took. They'll be useful when I talk with the Reichsminister tomorrow morning."

18th July, 1938 – Berlin – 9:30 AM Mayer reports to Göring on the Evian Conference

“Elisabeth Billingsworth attended the Evian Conference for me and reported her findings this weekend,” began Mayer the next morning.

Göring smiled. “Is that all you have to say?”

“Well, Herr Reichsminister, we met at the Kreutzers’ home, and have since developed a closer relationship.”

“I congratulate you, Claus. Elisabeth is an excellent choice as a companion, and perhaps more.”

“Yes she is, sir.”

“Claus, I have an advance copy of the *Völkischer Beobachter* with a direct quote from our Führer about the conference: *It is a shameful spectacle to see how the whole democratic world oozes sympathy for the poor tormented Jewish people, but remains hard-hearted and obdurate when it comes to helping them.* Can you outline what the delegates said?”

“Certainly, Herr Reichsminister, but before doing so, here is an excerpt from a recent article written by American journalist William Shirer: *I doubt if much will be done. The British, French, and Americans seem too anxious to not offend Hitler. It’s an absurd situation. They want to appease the man who was responsible for their problem.*"

"It's always nice to know world leaders fear and respect our Führer, isn't it Claus?"

"I agree, sir. Here are specifics from the conference."

Mayer referred to Elisabeth's notes as he detailed the conference outcomes, then concluded by saying, "During the meeting, delegate after delegate rose to express sympathy for the Jews, then most countries, including the United States and Britain, gave excuses for not accepting more refugees."

"Are you telling me no country opened its doors to our Jews?"

"The Dominican Republic offered visas to some of them."

"Was that a good faith gesture, or did they cite other factors?"

"They would accept 100,000 in exchange for a multimillion dollar payment from the American Jewish Joint Distribution Committee."

Göring almost fell off his chair laughing. "Those pigs will make themselves rich off our Jews." He fished through a pile of newspapers on his credenza, then said, "The fourteenth of July issue of our newspaper had this headline summing up the Evian Conference." He held it up for Mayer to see.

JEWS FOR SALE AT A BARGAIN PRICE—WHO WANTS THEM? NO ONE.

Heydrich strode into Göring's office. "The Führer wants to discuss the Evian Conference with us."

"Claus, will you share Elisabeth's findings with the Führer?"

"Of course, sir."

Mayer's report surprised nobody. After he concluded, and took his seat, Heydrich said, "The world's refusal to accept any of our Jews confirms what we have been saying. They hate them as much as we do. Perhaps the most remarkable result was they wouldn't pass any resolutions condemning the Nuremburg Laws. Dr. Goebbels will use that failure to great effect when responding to the democracies' endless whining about our treatment of the Jews."

"I agree," said Göring.

"Let's strike while the iron is hot," said Hitler. "Heydrich, arrest at least fifteen hundred able bodied German and Austrian Jews with any police record, then detain them at Dachau until their families raise the funds for them to emigrate. If the world doesn't act after that, keep tightening the noose around our Jews' necks until they do. Are there other items to discuss? If not, I'll meet with Goebbels."

"We're done here, sir," answered Göring. "We'll meet in my office to tie up any loose ends."

"Are you returning to Vienna today, Claus?" asked Heydrich as he closed Göring's office door.

"Yes, I am sir."

"Eichmann is flying home in my plane. If the Reichsminister agrees, I would appreciate it if you go with him and ask whether he can use your help with the new assignments our Führer gave him this morning."

"I agree," said Göring, turning to Mayer, "if you have the free time to do so."

"I welcome the opportunity, sir. Might I add, General, I'm grateful you made your plane available for our flights to Lausanne and back to Berlin."

"I understand you had a most charming companion," replied Heydrich.

"Yes, Fräulein Billingsworth joined me in Evian."

"You can be proud that Elisabeth cares for you. She exemplifies the best we, in the SS, seek in the perfect Nazi woman and wife."

"Thank you General. I cannot agree with you more."

Eichmann appeared deep in thought when Mayer sat down across from him in Heydrich's airplane.

"Adolf, the General suggested I go home with you so we can talk about the assignments Hitler gave you today."

Eichmann smiled weakly.

"I've never seen you so preoccupied. Has something happened to your family?"

"No, Göring called me before I boarded the plane. He met with the Führer after we left the Reichschancellory. Hitler acknowledged that our efforts are being hampered by the unwillingness of other nations to accept our Jews, but insisted we do more to speed up their departure from the Reich."

"Did they agree on a course of action?" asked Mayer.

"Yes, Hitler accepted Göring's recommendation that we use *all necessary force* to speed up the Jewish exodus," answered Eichmann. "But before doing so we must steel ourselves to the extreme brutality it will take to meet Hitler's goals. We can't allow a misguided conscience to blunt our efforts."

"Gentlemen," interrupted the co-pilot. "Please buckle your seat belts. We are about to leave. Thank you."

As the airplane lifted from the runway, Mayer thought about Eichmann's comments. *Prior to my encounter with the strange prisoner, I felt no guilt when ordered to inflict extreme pain on those opposing Hitler's rule. However, since that day I find myself reluctant to use violence, even if commanded to do so. Eichmann must have dealt with such misgivings.*

"Adolf, how do you prepare yourself to obey an order that calls for the inhumane treatment of unarmed people?"

"Experience taught me to *never* question the merits or morality of any command given by my superiors. Nothing can be more fundamental to a loyal Nazi than acting on directives that are personally distasteful."

"But, you're a married man. How do you reconcile repugnant actions on the job with being a good husband and father at home?"

Eichmann smiled. "Do I sense that your relationship with Elisabeth is deepening?"

"We spent a wonderful weekend together in Lausanne, and yes, our relationship did deepen."

"Congratulations, Claus. She's quite a catch. Getting back to your question… all of us, even the best Nazis, have times when we have a guilty conscience. That's when I remind myself that any order, whether moral or not, is my obligation to Hitler, not something I do of my free will." He looked at his watch. "We must cut this discussion short. Today's meetings exhausted me and I need some sleep before we land in Vienna. If you like, we can continue this conversation tomorrow."

Sitting back in Heydrich's airplane, Claus's embryonic ethical self was comforted when Eichmann didn't spell out the force needed to rid Austria of its Jews. Mayer's amoral self, still controlling his mind, was also comforted. *I won't allow my conscience to interfere the next time we discuss this.*

CHAPTER EIGHT – JOHANNES MUST LEAVE AUSTRIA

20th July, 1938 – Vienna – 2 PM – The police arrest Johannes

Three police officers walked into the store while Johannes was serving a customer. When the redhead asked a sales clerk something, the clerk pointed at Johannes. All three officers approached him. The redhead asked, "Are you the Jew, Johannes Kaiser?"

Johannes shuddered. "Yes officer. What can I do for you?"

"Come with us, you are under arrest."

Johannes' stomach tightened. *Did they find out why Bruno bought Der KleiderKaiser? Perhaps not. I must push back.* "Three of our best Nazi customers will complain if I don't finish their tailoring work this afternoon."

The policemen faked a smile then glared at him. Johannes shrugged off their mistrust. "Please let me call the owner. He'll confirm I'm telling the truth." His mouth went dry as the officers considered his request. *How can I convince them to give me extra time? I must talk with Bruno...*

"Stay here, Jew," said the bald officer. "Where's the proprietor? I'll get him. You'll be sorry if you lied."

Johannes swallowed hard before answering. "Herr Hauptman is busy. Take those stairs. He's in the second office on the left."

When Bruno returned with the bald officer, Johannes blurted, "Herr Hauptman, I told these officers about the three suits I must complete this..."

"... shut up Jew," bellowed the bald officer. "Speak only when spoken to." He turned to Bruno. "Do you need this Jew to finish some work today?"

"Yes, I must deliver three suits this afternoon. My customers need them for a special occasion tonight. If they aren't ready they may never shop here again. Is there a problem, Officer?"

"Yes, we're arresting him under authority of the Gestapo."

"What's he being arrested for?" asked Bruno.

"All we know is the Gestapo classified him as an undesirable and sent us to get him. There are another hundred on our list, and they must all be in custody tonight. We don't have time to return."

"No problem officers, I guarantee he'll be at the police station in the morning."

"We will trust you this once, Hauptman," said the redhead, "but if he doesn't show up, we'll arrest the both of you."

"I understand, Officer. He will be there." Turning to Johannes, he snarled, "Right?"

"Of course, Herr Hauptman."

The police officers glared at Johannes, nodded to Bruno, turned, and left the store.

Bruno and Johannes walked silently up to the office. Bruno closed the door and sat down next to Johannes. "Last month, the Gestapo imprisoned hundreds of Jews in Germany having police records. Were you ever arrested?"

He thought for a minute. "No, but I got a citation for driving through a red light. Do you think they're arresting me for that, or did they find out why you bought the business?"

"They'd have arrested us both if it was the sale."

The telephone rang. When Bruno answered, he smiled at first, then frowned. "What's the intent of this new apprehension order?" after a few moments he added, "Yes Claus, I'll see you for breakfast tomorrow morning. Have a safe flight home." He hung up and turned to Johannes. "The Gestapo is arresting at least fifteen hundred German and Austrian Jews having police records." He paused for a moment. "They probably asked the police to arrest a few of them."

"Can your friend intercede in my behalf?"

"I'm afraid not. It may prompt a formal investigation into our relationship, which neither of us wants. Go to the police station and I'll talk to my friend about getting you released."

Johannes went to his parents' apartment. Eszter shivered when she heard what happened. He took her in his arms to calm her. "Mama, I've overcome difficult times before and will get through this too."

"I'll pray for you," said Eszter tearfully. "May God find it in His heart to spare you." Avram and Johannes held Eszter until she stopped trembling. Avram then led Johannes into the parlor.

"My son, is there anything I can do for you?"

"Don't worry Papa. Bruno is helping me. I'll come and see you after the police release me."

⌘⌘⌘⌘⌘⌘⌘⌘

The next morning, Bruno met Mayer for breakfast at a small restaurant close to the Rothschild Palace. "It was a stroke of luck you called while Kaiser was in my office," said Bruno. "He relaxed after hearing the order for his imprisonment had nothing to do with my purchase of Der KleiderKaiser."

When Mayer turned his eyes downward, Bruno asked, "Is there a problem, Claus?"

"Possibly, the Gestapo ordered the Jews held overnight. They'll send them to the school on Karajangasse today."

"What happens there?"

"It's a gathering point. They'll bus them to Dachau today and hold them there until their families make arrangements for them to leave Austria."

Bruno jumped up. "I must stop Johannes before he leaves home." He rushed to a telephone at the other end of the restaurant, dialed, and waited for over two minutes before replacing the receiver. After looking at his watch, he slowly returned to the table.

Bruno's voice quivered as he said, "It's after nine. He's on his way to the police station. Can you do anything to help him, Claus?"

"Perhaps, I'll let you know after talking to a few people."

20th July, 1938 – Vienna – 9 AM – Johannes is imprisoned

Johannes walked into the police station at nine the next morning. He gave his name to the officer on duty who picked up a note on his desk, then looked up at him. "You're the Jew who promised to show up here this morning?"

"Yes, sir."

"Good thing you did. The Gestapo ordered us to arrest you, your entire family, and your employer if you weren't here by noon."

The officer winked at someone behind Johannes, then looked back at him with a grin. "Come with me, Jew. We have a fine place for you to spend the next few hours."

He led Johannes downstairs to a cell compound filled with men in their late teens to mid-forties. Johannes recognized many of them from the Synagogue and later heard everyone there was Jewish.

Moments later, three police officers came thundering down the stairs and headed toward a fire hose at the other end of the jail. The bald officer unfurled it while the redhead turned toward the captives. "You've been filthy long enough, Jews. It's our duty, as Aryans, to wash the filth off your bodies."

The redhead turned on the water. Two others clung to the hose and aimed it into the first cell. Johannes heard men shrieking. A few minutes later, the officers aimed the hose into Johannes' cell. Johannes cried out when the powerful spray propelled him into fellow prisoners and against the brick cell wall. Both officers grinned as they directed the spray at each man. After soaking them all, they moved on to the next cell.

Soon afterwards, the redhead turned off the water and started toward the stairs. He glared at the prisoners in Johannes' cell. "We should have liberated Austria years ago. That way you swine wouldn't have been so filthy, and we could have saved water." He and his compatriots laughed as they scrambled up the staircase.

When he arrived at the police station, Johannes wore a good quality blue suit, bright white shirt, and red tie. The hosing incident ripped his clothes and bruised his hands, face, and self-esteem. Feeling powerless, he sat down, took his head in his hands, and sobbed. A stranger approached him, knelt down, and took hold of his hands. "Don't give them the satisfaction. The Nazis want to make us all feel like defenseless animals."

Johannes felt his confidence return as he gazed into the newcomer's eyes. "Who are you?"

"My name is Ludwig Dewalt."

"Are you Jewish?"

"My birth parents were. They died in a tragic auto accident when I was eight."

"Losing them at such a young age must have been terrible."

"It was. When I was thirteen, a friend invited me to his Christian boy's club. That experience changed my life. After that, I attended church services every week. Years later, I studied at a

Lutheran seminary and became an ordained minister. I now teach at that seminary. Yesterday, the police barged into my classroom and arrested me."

"How could they do that if you're no longer Jewish?"

"My students also asked that question. One of the Nazis pulled out a legal looking document and told us it was the First Decree of the 1935 Reich Citizenship Law. He then read that *A Jew is one who practices Judaism or has at least three Jewish grandparents*. Since the Reich annexed Austria, it now applies to us."

"A friend of mine warned me about the Nuremberg Laws before the Anschluss," said Johannes. "I wish I would have taken her advice seriously and left Austria."

Later, when the three police officers returned, Johannes expected a second assault. Instead, they opened the first cell and herded the prisoners past Johannes, and up the stairs.

One prisoner passed Johannes' cell asking, "Where are you taking us, sir?" The bald policeman struck him in the groin with his nightstick, saying, "Shut up, Jew." Five minutes later, the guards returned to empty a second cell. Soon after that, the bald Nazi emptied Johannes' cell and directed the prisoners up the stairs, out the door, and into a waiting bus. Johannes sat next to Ludwig on the rear seat.

"Do you know where they're taking us?" whispered Ludwig.

"No," answered Johannes, holding his hand over his mouth so the policeman watching from the front couldn't see him talking. When the bus turned onto Karajangasse, Johannes leaned toward Ludwig. "There's a secondary school down this street. I wonder if that's where they are taking us."

"You back there," said the officer. "What are you doing?"

Johannes checked to see whether anyone reacted to the order. Everyone was gazing down at the floor. He looked back at the police officer, who signaled him to stand. "Were you talking to someone, Jew?"

Johannes stood up and felt his throat tighten. He tried to speak, but couldn't. The guard barked, "Get over here, pig."

Johannes was making his way to the front of the bus when it stopped cold, jolting him forward. He'd almost regained his balance when it lurched ahead for a moment, sending Johannes backward toward the floor. He fell to the floor with a loud thump. The officer laughed. "That's the most fun I've had all day. You can be first off the bus."

Johannes stood up, straightened his clothes as best he could, and continued toward the officer. He expected him to taunt him further, but he didn't. When he entered the school a policeman directed him upstairs and another pointed him toward a classroom. His bus mates followed him in, then the officer closed and locked the door.

"I wonder what happens next?" asked Johannes when Ludwig joined him.

"I don't know, but at least we can see the street." Approaching the barred window Johannes said, "Look, the policeman who let me off the bus is blocking pedestrians coming from the left and sending them to the other side of the street. Another officer's doing it on the right. A line of busses is pulling up."

Moments later, Johannes heard footsteps passing the door. He looked out the window and grimaced. "They're loading them onto the first bus. I wonder where they're taking them." Johannes' fingers felt like ice.

The first bus drove off, then Johannes heard the adjoining classroom empty. A few moments later, he saw men boarding the second bus. "We're next," said Johannes, his voice quivering.

As if on cue, a police officer opened the door. "Is Kaiser here?"

Johannes and one other prisoner raised their hands. The officer looked down at the note he was holding. "Johannes Kaiser?"

Johannes was now the only one with his hand raised. His muscles tightened.

The officer pointed at Johannes. "Everyone except him, follow me."

He felt like vomiting.

Looking surprised, Ludwig embraced Johannes. "Remember what I said; don't give them the satisfaction. May God be with you, my friend."

Johannes choked back a tear as he wished his new friend well.

After everyone else left the room, a policeman walked in and asked, "Do you have papers to leave Austria?"

"Yes sir," lied Johannes.

"Why the hell didn't you tell us sooner?"

"I didn't know I should. A friend of mine also has papers. Shouldn't he also be here?"

"It's too late now. They'll process him out at Dachau."

"Dachau?" Johannes' throat went dry.

"Everyone without a visa goes there. Follow me, Jew."

The officer directed him downstairs, then ordered him to stand in a line behind several other prisoners. A few minutes later, a stern looking man wearing a black uniform strode to a table, sat down, and organized his forms, rubber stamps, and stamp pads in a precise fashion. He then motioned the first in line to approach.

I told the guard upstairs I had papers to leave the country. I don't, but Bruno said Austrians could cross into Italy with only a passport. If that guard lets me out, I'll go home, get mine, and leave Austria.

Ten minutes later, the officer motioned him forward and asked his name.

"Johannes Kaiser, sir."

"To where are you emigrating?"

"Italy, sir."

"Where are your papers?"

He doesn't know I don't need papers to enter Italy. I'd better handle this carefully. Johannes leaned closer. "I ordered them several weeks ago, but they haven't yet arrived. If you'd let me call home, I'll see if they came in today's post."

The captain summoned an elderly man wearing a German Great War uniform. "Take this Jew to the phone. He can call home to ask if his visa arrived. Don't let him say anything else. If he does, disconnect the call, and let me know."

The soldier led Johannes down a hallway. When the captain was out of hearing range he said, "I'm sorry about this. I don't like what the Nazis are doing to you poor Jews. Say whatever you need to your family. I won't tell him."

Johannes thanked him and dialed his parents' number. The soldier moved to the other end of the hall and lit a cigarette. *I don't know whether he's trying to trick me into saying more than I should, so...* Avram answered the phone. "Hello Papa. Yes, I'm doing fine. I can't speak freely. Did my Italian visa arrive today?"

Avram understood, telling him, "I have your visa. Please take care of yourself."

"Thank you Papa. I'll be fine."

When Johannes hung up, the old soldier walked back toward him. "Did it arrive?"

"Yes, my father has it."

The old soldier led Johannes back to the captain. "This Jew's exit papers arrived, sir, and he said nothing out of the ordinary to his family."

The captain retrieved two blank forms from one of his neat piles, asked Johannes' name, address, and age, and listed them on both forms. He then took a rubber stamp, inked it, and pounded it twice on each document. Looking up he said, "Sign these statements, promising to leave the Reich within two weeks, and you're free to leave. You must register at your local police station every day until you leave the Reich. If you're still here in two weeks, we'll send you to Dachau."

The captain handed Johannes one of the signed copies. Johannes took it and bowed. "Thank you, sir."

Johannes shuddered when he reached the street. *I could be going to Dachau.* He took a deep breath and offered a silent prayer of thanks. Seeing his reflection in a shop window, Johannes smiled. *I have torn clothes and bruises all over my hands and face, but I am free.*

The Nazis didn't steal his money, so Johannes took a taxi home, had a relaxing hot bath, put on a clean white shirt, fashionable red tie, and black suit. Looking at himself in the mirror, he made final adjustments and set out for Der KleiderKaiser.

Bruno jumped up when Johannes walked into his office. "You look terrible, what happened?" He offered him a chair and sat down next to him.

Johannes told Bruno about his treatment at the Police Station. "One policeman singled me out and sent everyone else to Dachau. Then they set me free. I don't know why I was so fortunate."

"Claus Mayer stepped in to help you. He told the senior officer at the school you had permission to leave the country and ordered your immediate release."

"You must have asked your friend to do it."

"I did, and I'm glad you're safe."

"What should I do next?"

"Arrange for a German passport."

"Can't I use the one I have from Austria?"

"No, Germany invalidated all Austrian credentials after the Anschluss. The Gestapo now issues German permits to Jews. You must go to their headquarters in the former Hotel Metropole on Morzinplatz."

Johannes felt his limbs shake as he asked, "The Gestapo, is there no other way?"

"No, there isn't. Be sure to take two passport-sized photographs with you. If you don't, they'll force you to leave, have your picture taken, and stand in line again."

Johannes was still quivering when Bruno got up to wish him well. "Try calming yourself before going for your passport. You'll need your wits about you while there."

"I will, Bruno, and please thank Herr Mayer for contacting the officers at the school. I'd be in Dachau now if it weren't for him."

After leaving Der KleiderKaiser, Johannes started out toward his parents' apartment. Not wanting to worry them, he forced himself to relax. Eszter hugged him at the door, then grimaced looking at his bruised face. "What happened to you, Johannes?"

"We were all treated badly. I was luckier than most…"

"… Thank God you got away from the Nazis." interrupted Avram, then added, "What did they tell you to do next?"

"I must apply for a German passport," not letting his mother know he had to do so at Gestapo headquarters.

"Hundreds of Jews apply for them every day. You'll have a better chance of getting through the queue sometime tomorrow if you stand in line this evening."

Johannes was preparing to leave when Eszter asked, "Would you like something to eat?"

The ordeals of the day had killed his appetite. Now that he was safe, Johannes realized he was famished.

"Thank you Mama, I could eat a horse."

"Sorry Johannes, I have no horses," said Eszter with a smile, "but I have your favorite, schnitzel and potato salad." Johannes and Avram laughed. They hugged Eszter, and she said, "My precious Johannes. What's to become of you? Will we ever see you again?"

"That is now in the God's hands, Mama, but I'm sure we'll be reunited in better times."

Before Johannes left, Avram prayed for God to guide and protect him.

21st July, 1938 – Vienna – 10 PM - Johannes applies for his German Passport

Johannes arrived at Gestapo headquarters at ten that evening. Seventy-five men were already in line. Trying to occupy his mind, he studied the architecture of the four-story building, decorated with Atlases and Corinthian columns. The person behind him said, “They built the Hotel Metropole for the Vienna World Exhibition in 1873.” The man next to him added, “They take prisoners inside to interrogate, torture, and kill them.” Johannes shivered.

The queue grew throughout the night. At nine the next morning it moved toward the door marked *Jewish Passport Applications*. Several applicants left cursing that they didn’t get their photos taken.

Once an hour a Gestapo official came outside, pointed to the first in line, and barked, “Go to the back.” Looking at the Nazi, Johannes guessed there was a time he enjoyed this part of the job, but it now bored him.

The closer Johannes got to the door the more anxious he became. His heart beat loudly when the guard motioned him to enter. A man wearing a black uniform, sitting inside, asked for his pictures. Johannes trembled handing them to him. The man compared them against Johannes’ face, gave them back, and pointed to six men standing in a line leading to an officer seated at a small table. “Go wait there.”

Remembering Bruno's advice, Johannes forced himself to relax. The Nazi asked for his pictures, then stapled one onto a large record, and the other onto the second page of a brown passport. He then asked for Johannes' name, profession, birthplace, birth date, and marital status. The Nazi wrote the responses on the record and in the passport. He then handed them both to Johannes asking him to review and sign them if they were correct. After he returned them, the officer struck the permanent record with a rubber stamp three times, and the passport picture page two times. "Now, write your address on this form. We'll mail your passport in two to three weeks."

Johannes fingers tingled. *I only have two weeks before they send me to Dachau.*

After handing back his completed form Johannes asked, "Is that it?" meekly.

"Yes Jew. Leave before I change my mind."

Johannes looked at the official, glanced at the passport application, still sitting on his desk, and said, "Thank you sir."

Johannes went to his local police station the next morning and asked where he should report. The officer on duty directed him to the other end of the building. Johannes' heart skipped a beat seeing he would report to a former KleiderKaiser customer.

"Johannes Kaiser. It's been a long time, hasn't it?"

"Yes Officer, it has."

"Did the police take you to Karajangasse yesterday?"

"Yes sir."

"Did the Gestapo give you a form permitting you to stay in the Reich for two weeks?"

"Yes sir," said Johannes, handing it to him.

He recorded Johannes' name and the date in a book and handed the form back. "Sign this and report back here every day you're still in the country."

"Yes sir, I will."

Johannes anxiously awaited the mail carrier every morning then went to sign in at the police station in the afternoon. After a week, his customer asked, "You know what happens next week, right?"

"Yes sir, I do."

On the two-week anniversary of his Karajangasse visit, the officer pounded his fist on the table. "Why didn't you heed my warnings? Do you *really* want to go to Dachau?"

Johannes' lips quivered as he said, "No sir, but my passport hasn't yet arrived. As soon as it does, I'll be on an airplane to Italy."

The official glared at him, "If it doesn't arrive tomorrow, you must write to Vienna's Gestapo headquarters, asking permission to stay here until you get it."

"Yes sir," said Johannes, his voice again cracking with fear.

He spent much of the next day waiting outside for the mailman, then trembled carrying the envelopes into his apartment. He leafed through them. It was not there. He looked again, just in case. *It hasn't arrived.*

Johannes reluctantly pulled out his typewriter, typed the letter, mailed it, and took a carbon copy to the police station. His hands were shaking when he handed it to his customer. "I mailed this, as you instructed. What happens now? Should I return tomorrow?"

He read Johannes' letter and returned it to him. "No, I'm no longer in control. It's up to the Gestapo now. Nothing will happen if they grant your appeal. If they don't, they'll send you to Dachau. Leave Austria the day your passport arrives."

"Yes I will and thank you for your help."

21st July, 1938 – Vienna – Peter Wassermann applies to join Adolf Eichmann's organization

In early 1938, Peter Wassermann coordinated the bureaucratic documentation for Austria's transition to a Nazi dictatorship. He completed his assignment two months after the Anschluss and returned to work at Himmler's Propaganda Ministry in Berlin. While reviewing confidential memos, he found one reporting that Hitler authorized Eichmann to use all necessary force to rid Austria of its Jews. Wassermann called Eichmann's office to ask for an interview.

The next morning, Eichmann's secretary pointed Wassermann to an open door behind her desk. "The Colonel is ready to see you, sir."

"Please take a seat, Herr Wassermann," said Eichmann as he entered his office. "I talked to your superiors in Berlin. They praised your accomplishments in Austria and told me you're interested in helping me rid Austria of its Jews. Is that correct?"

"Yes, sir."

"Tell me about yourself, and why you'd like to work on the Jewish question?"

Wassermann told Eichmann about his early training at a Paris art institute, and his bitterness at finding no work after graduation. "That all changed when I attended my first Hitler rally. Our Führer put it in plain words. I didn't fail, the Jews triumphed. Their power and influence weakened our Fatherland, making it possible for them to steal everything we valued. On that day, the Führer transformed me from a rudderless drifter to his loyal servant in the Nazi Party. If you hire me, I vow to act decisively as I purify our race. Under my watch, no Jew will deny Germany its rightful place as the Aryan master of Europe."

Peter's zeal could serve him well when he faces the moral issues Claus and I debated in Heydrich's airplane. Eichmann voiced his only concern. "Peter, I admire your fervor, but I fear it could be blunted by a conscience that rails against the monstrous force needed to cleanse our land of its Jews."

"Colonel, with all respect, I disagree. I will use all means necessary to achieve our Führer's wishes. My conscience shall remain peaceful as a sleeping child, even as I ruthlessly punish one thousand obstinate Jews unwilling to leave our Reich."

"I commend your exemplary attitude, and would like you to join my organization for a thirty day probationary period. If either of us decides this position is not right, you can return to the Propaganda Ministry with no questions asked. Is that acceptable to you?"

"Yes, Colonel."

Eichmann had second thoughts as soon as Wassermann left his office. He knocked on Mayer's door, walked in, and said, "I've been thinking over the conversation we had on the flight back from Berlin, and decided my department *shouldn't* use undue force to increase Jewish emigration."

"How did you arrive at that decision?"

"It would be reckless to use strong-arm tactics before allowing the process I designed to succeed. Our problem doesn't lie at the Palace, but in ensuring the Jews leave Austria within two weeks of visiting there. I believe the Gestapo should handle that task, and will ask Heydrich whether he agrees."

"Then you envision no changes in your procedures?"

Eichmann answered with an impish smile. "Not quite, I plan to be on duty every day dressed in my SS uniform. My demeanor will let them know, in no uncertain terms, that they'd better leave our country as quickly as possible."

"I sense you had another reason for changing your mind."

"You know me better than I know myself, Claus. I met with Peter Wassermann yesterday. Do you know him?"

"No, I don't remember that name. Is he from Berlin?"

"He grew up in Vienna and is seeking a post where he can rid the Reich of its Jews. He's enamored of the rough stuff, such as brutally disciplining those unwilling to cooperate. I was sufficiently impressed to offer him a probationary position. After he left, I realized his brand of violence could disrupt the orderly flow at the Rothschild Palace. When I brought him to Heydrich's attention, he thought Wassermann was worth watching as a future Party leader. He ordered Ernst Schlossburg, who identifies Jewish subversives for Vienna's Gestapo, to hire him, so my decision turned out to be good for everyone concerned."

12th August, 1938 – Vienna – 11 AM - Otto Klein fights Heintz and Schwartz

Five months after the Anschluss, Otto was returning home when he spotted Rolf Heintz and Franz Schwartz beating Joshua Isaacson, an elderly friend of his father's. Infuriated that the pair had previously assaulted his father, Otto clenched his fists and charged toward them. "Why don't you scum pick on someone your own age?"

He rammed his fist into the base of Schwartz's skull, sending him headfirst to the street. Seeing he was unconscious, Otto turned to help Joshua. Heintz released him, then approached Otto pulling something black and shiny from his pocket. Otto rushed toward him reaching for the shiny object. The two struggled, there was a blast, and Heintz's body slumped to the ground.

Otto was now holding a black revolver and blood was oozing from a hole in Heintz's jacket. He dropped the gun and fell to his knees next to him. Heintz looked up at Otto, his lips quivering. "Otto, don't let me die. I'm afraid. Please help me. Please…" His eyes closed, and he stopped breathing.

Otto, who was still kneeling, reached out to the lifeless body. He trembled, and his eyes filled with tears as he begged God's forgiveness for having taken a life. Looking up, he saw Schwartz coming toward him wielding a long knife. He grabbed Schwartz's right leg and twisted it with both hands, bringing him crashing to the pavement. The knife fell next to Otto.

Otto's anger broke free of his conscience. He seized the knife and snaked toward Schwartz, who sprang up, turned, and limped away.

Looking back at Heintz's lifeless body, the enormity of what he had done came rushing back. His anger melted into guilt. Tears welled in his eyes.

Schwartz turned at the corner. "Now you've done it Klein, you fucking Jew pig. I'll have the Gestapo arrest you and your family."

Although Otto looked directly at him, Schwartz's words couldn't penetrate the haze of his intense grief.

Schwartz disappeared around the corner.

Joshua Isaacson approached Otto. "You had no choice. If you hadn't killed him, he would have taken *your* life." Patting Otto's face he added, "You and your parents must flee to safety before that thug tells the Gestapo. He'll make sure they arrest you all."

Joshua's warning broke through Otto's anguish. "What should I do?"

"Bring them to my home. I'll have resistance fighters there to take you out of the country."

"Are you sure you're all right," asked Otto.

"Yes, now get your parents."

⌘⌘⌘⌘⌘⌘⌘⌘

Schwartz limped to Gestapo headquarters. He entered the building out of breath and dripping with perspiration. The officer on duty told him to sit down. "What happened to you?"

"Otto Klein and Joshua Isaacson attacked me and killed Rolf Heintz."

"Wait here," said the officer. "I'll ask the Gestapo Chief how we should handle this."

The officer returned ten minutes later and asked, "What is your name?"

"I'm Frantz Schwarz. What did the Chief say?"

After jotting Schwartz's name down in his notepad, the officer said, "Three Gestapo agents will go with us to find Klein and Isaacson. Follow me to our garage."

Schwartz, the officer, and three agents got into their black car. Schwartz directed the driver to Otto Klein's home. Finding nobody there, the sergeant asked Schwartz, "Do you know where Isaacson lives?"

"Yes, it's less than a five-minute walk from here."

The sergeant took the notepad from his pocket and handed it to Schwartz. "Write his address down." He then pointed at one of his officers. "Stay here with me." Turning to the other two, he said, "Go to Isaacson's home with Schwartz. I'll phone the station and have them dispatch another car to that location. He will blow the horn three times when he gets there."

After Schwartz handed the Sergeant the notepad, with Isaacson's address, he led the two Gestapo agents to Isaacson's building. The three of them barged into his apartment and arrested Joshua and two other men.

⌘⌘⌘⌘⌘⌘⌘⌘

MI6 agent Siegfried Mannheim was on his way to visit Joshua Isaacson when he saw Schwartz and two Gestapo agents turn the corner. They hadn't yet looked in his direction, so he ducked into an alcove and watched them enter Joshua's building. A few minutes later, a dark blue car drove up, and the horn blew three times. Siegfried shuddered when two fellow resistance fighters hobbled out of the building. Their clothes were torn and bloodied. The two Gestapo agents pushed them into the blue car's back seat, Schwartz got in front, and the driver raced off leaving the two agents behind.

Guessing Schwartz told them to arrest Joshua's son, Siegfried left his alcove and set out to find him. He found Judah moments before he and his mother turned the corner onto their street. "Come with me. The Gestapo entered your house then arrested your father and two resistance fighters. Two agents are now waiting there to capture you."

"What should I do?"

"I'll have a resistance comrade escort you and your mother to Palestine. You can either stay there or return to Vienna."

"I'm coming back to join the resistance."

"Are you sure?"

"Yes."

"When you're ready to return, send me a telegram saying *my son will be born on* and add the date you expect to arrive in Vienna. We'll rendezvous outside the Éclair Viennese pastry shop at eight the evening after you arrive. If you're not there, I'll return each evening at 8 until we meet."

12th August, 1938 – Vienna – 4:00 PM - Johannes' passport arrives

Johannes' German passport arrived two days after he mailed the letter to Gestapo Headquarters. He walked into his parent's apartment waving it. "The good news is I have all I need to leave Austria." His jaw dropped. "The bad news is I *must* now leave Vienna."

Johannes sat down at the kitchen table to look over his childhood home. His gaze froze on Eszter. He wept seeing the sadness in her eyes.

Eszter moved her chair next to his and sat down. "Until now, I prayed for the hate to wither in our beloved Austria so you wouldn't have to leave. That was an impossible dream. Now I pray we will soon reunite in a world free of Nazism."

⌘⌘⌘⌘⌘⌘⌘⌘

Avram watched Eszter and Johannes from the kitchen doorway. He yearned for Solomon's wisdom. *What can I say or do? I may never see Johannes again.* He went to the dining room cabinet and retrieved the *yarmulke* and *tallit* he carried to the Synagogue every Sabbath. He placed the skullcap on his head then mouthed a blessing while draping the prayer shawl over his shoulders.

Avram then paged through his Bible to Psalm 121, approached Johannes, spread the embroidered *tallit* over both their heads, and recited the prayer in a reverent voice. He said the last two lines while looking into Johannes' eyes:

The Eternal will guard you from all evil; He will guard your soul.

The Eternal will guard your going out and your coming in from now until eternity.

Avram folded the skullcap and prayer shawl, placing them alongside the Bible in the bag his grandmother made for him and handed it to Johannes. "Take these as you travel. Wherever you go our prayers will unite, imploring the Almighty to bring us together in health and happiness."

After leaving his parents' apartment, Johannes went to visit his grandparents. When he walked in, Debora said, "Your mama called to say you were on your way."

"How did she know? I didn't decide until a few minutes ago."

"A mother always knows."

Seeing the Sabbath eve candles still burning brightly, Johannes' eyes again filled with tears. "Omi, watching you light the Shabbat candles will always be one of my most cherished memories." *I wish I could have seen you do it this one last time.*

⌘⌘⌘⌘⌘⌘⌘⌘

Knowing this would be the last time they'd be together, Yaakov and Debora decided they wouldn't cry when Johannes visited. Debora's steadfastness held for a few minutes, then she wept. "I'm sorry Johannes. It's not right for me to burden you with my tears."

Johannes took his grandmother into his arms, "Omi, you've been strong all my life. How many times did I come crying to you when I was a child? You were like a rock, counseling me, and consoling me. Your strength will always bolster me."

"I am very proud of you, my dear Johannes." Debora dried her eyes. "The Nazis make it impossible for you to remain here, but I know you will thrive wherever destiny takes you."

⌘⌘⌘⌘⌘⌘⌘⌘

After leaving his grandparents apartment Johannes went to visit Otto. He hadn't spoken with him for over a month and wanted to see him before leaving Vienna. Approaching his building, he flinched seeing no lights on in his apartment. *His parents always keep a lamp lit all night.* After one of Otto's neighbors entered the building, a tall man got out of a black car and followed him inside. Walking toward his building, Johannes saw the tall man return to his car saying, "That's not Klein." *Otto must be in trouble. I'd better check his apartment using the hidden entry we discovered as children.*

He circled the building, staying in the shadows until he reached an adjacent alley. There, to one side of the dimly lit pathway, was a small storage shed. After checking if anyone was watching, Johannes dug a key from the ground to the left of the building. *Thank God, it's still here*. He unlocked the shed door, moved several boards out of the way, slid a panel to the left, and stepped into the basement of Otto's building.

Checking for lookouts, he went upstairs to his friend's apartment. *Good, the door's unlocked*. Johannes' heart raced as he tiptoed in, then breathed a sigh of relief finding no strangers there. *The moonlight is bright enough for me to explore without turning on a light.*

He saw unfinished sandwiches and half-empty water glasses on the table. *Otto and his parents must have taken off in a hurry.* Finding no other clues to their disappearance, Johannes left for home. The black car still sat in front of Otto's building. Johannes sensed its occupant's eyes locked on him as he passed them.

When he got home, Johannes found a note stuffed under his door. *Don't come to my apartment. Gestapo looking for me. Meet me behind your store at eleven. You are my last hope. Otto.*

Johannes checked his watch. It was ten thirty. His heart pounded as he double backed several times to make sure nobody was following him. At eleven fifteen, he saw Otto peek out from behind a brick wall Johannes' father built to keep snow from accumulating at the store's back door in winter.

"Were you followed?"

"No, I checked along the way. I have a key; let's go into the store."

When they got inside, Johannes said, "I saw the Gestapo outside your apartment building, went home, read your note, and rushed over here. What happened?"

Otto told Johannes he'd killed Rolf Heintz while saving Joshua Isaacson's life. "Schwartz threatened to have the Gestapo arrest me and my parents. I raced home and told them Herr Isaacson's resistance friends would get us out of the country. After helping them pack one suitcase each, I turned all the lights out so our friends would know we were in danger. Then, we used our secret passage to leave the building. Turning onto Herr Isaacson's street, we saw the Gestapo loading him and two other men into a dark blue car. It looked like the Gestapo physically abused all three of them. My parents were frantic with fear, so we left."

"What did you do then?"

"My father suggested we go to see Christian Bodenbaum. He treated him well, even after the Anschluss. I had no better idea, so we went there. Herr Bodenbaum was glad we came to him for help, but warned us his son would be back from the Hitler Youth Camp tomorrow evening. If we were still there, he'd report us to the Gestapo."

"Incredible," gasped Johannes. "What's happened to our country? Good Austrians never acted like that before the Anschluss."

"I agree, but it is what it is." Otto's lips shivered when he added, "If I can't move my parents somewhere safe, the Gestapo will arrest them. Do you have any ideas?"

"No, but my father may. Go back to your family. Don't leave until I get there."

Johannes hurried to his parents' home. "Why are you back? Is there a problem?" asked Avram.

"Otto and his parents are in danger." Johannes told his father about their circumstances and asked whether he knew anybody who could help them.

"Yes, one of my friends gave me the name of someone in the underground." Avram looked through papers hidden in a credenza drawer and smiled. "You must talk to Doctor Heinrich Mayer at the

Central Vienna Hospital. He's not Jewish, but makes it his business to help Jews in trouble with the Nazis. Show the receptionist this card, say your name is Braun, and tell her you need to talk with Mayer. He'll take it from there."

Johannes took the card. It had a ten-digit number typed on it. Johannes thanked his father, embraced his mother, and rushed to the hospital.

Heinrich Mayer was in the final stages of treating a patient with a near fatal gunshot injury. He'd removed the bullet and was suturing the wound when a nurse approached him. "Doctor, a man handed me this card with one of the Austrian resistance's authorized codes and said his name is Braun. We have no reason to believe the Nazis discovered the code. Would you like him to wait?" asked the nurse.

He looked up and replied, "No, take him to my office. I'll meet him there in a few minutes. Before you go, please arrange a hospital bed for this patient. He's had a narrow escape, and the nurses will need to watch him." After finishing with his patient, Heinrich went to his office.

"Are you the person who wanted to talk with me?"

"Yes doctor. I need to help a friend's family escape from the Nazis. Can you help me?"

"Are they Jewish?"

Johannes' muscles tightened. "Yes they are. Is that a problem?"

"Not at all. Is it safe for your friends to be seen on the street, or should we arrange for an ambulance to transport them?"

"It's best if you use an ambulance. I'll direct you to where they're hiding."

"Please give me a few minutes to check whether all is well with my last patient of the day, then I'll go with you."

Half an hour later, Johannes and Heinrich arrived at the Bodenbaum's building and walked upstairs to their apartment.

Otto and his parents jumped up when someone knocked on the door. Bodenbaum opened it and said, "It's for you, Otto."

Johannes walked in saying, "I brought someone to help you, Otto."

Otto stared at Heinrich. "What are you doing here, Doctor Mayer?"

Heinrich smiled. "I'm here to keep you and your parents safe from the Nazis, Herr Klein."

"You two know each other?" asked Johannes.

"Yes, this is the doctor who cared for my father after Schwartz and Heintz attacked him."

"It was Heintz who beat your father?" asked Heinrich.

"Yes, Doctor," replied Otto.

"I just removed a bullet from his chest."

"Will he live?" asked Otto.

"Yes, lucky for him the bullet just missed his heart."

"Lucky for me too, you lifted a great weight from my mind."

"Do we need Herr Kaiser to stay here?" asked Heinrich. "If not, let him get on with his life."

"Yes, Johannes you must go."

"I have a German passport and must leave Austria tomorrow." Johannes summarized everything that happened to him since his arrest and added, "I pray we will soon be together in a world free of Nazis." The two friends hugged, then Johannes went to clear the few remaining items from his apartment. He took them to his parents and spent the night with them.

13th August, 1938 – Vienna - 11:30 AM - Johannes leaves Vienna

The next morning, Johannes took a deep breath as he left the taxi and walked into the airport. When he handed his ticket to the Deutsche Luft Hansa agent she said, “May I please see your passport, sir?” He got it from his jacket pocket and handed it to her. She opened it to the first page, then returned both documents. “Please take these in there,” pointing to a door marked *Private–Security Police*. “The Gestapo must approve your ticket before I can allow you on the plane.”

“Does everyone need that approval?”

She looked down, as if embarrassed, and said, “No sir, only the Jews.”

Johannes’ stomach muscles tightened as he walked toward the security office. When he entered, an officer waved him to come forward and asked for his passport. He opened it, and said, “Another Jew is leaving our beautiful country,” in a sarcastic tone of voice.

“Yes, sir.”

“Where are you going?”

“To Milan, sir.”

After checking the passport against several pages filled with names, he said, “You’re not on the list. You can board the plane as soon as I authorize your ticket." Johannes handed it to him, he stamped and signed it, then returned it with his passport.

He was heading toward the door when the officer added, "You're one of the smart ones. Tell all your *yid* friends to get out of my country while they still can."

As *much as I love Vienna, I won't miss the unbridled hatred of my countrymen.*

Johannes had a bounce in his step when he reentered the ticketing area. He walked over to the agent and handed her the signed authorization. "Which plane are we flying today?"

"You'll be taking our Junkers G-38."

"Some seats are in the wings, right?"

"Yes, you get a pilot's eye view. Unfortunately, they're often the first to go."

"Are any still available?"

She looked at the plane's seat map, put a large X through one of the seat locations, wrote a number on the ticket, and handed it back to Johannes. "You have the last wing seat, Herr Kaiser." She pointed to the right. "The waiting area is through that hallway. A gate agent will tell you when it's time to board. I hope you'll have an enjoyable flight."

Johannes entered the boarding lounge as a plane was taxiing in for arrival. He moved toward the window to get a closer look at what was then the largest land based airplane in the world. Time passed quickly while Johannes watched airline workers prepare it for departure. As soon as the gate agent invited passengers to board, Johannes bounded outside and up the G-38s stairs. He found his seat on the left. Sitting down, he saw the front of the airplanes' fuselage to his right and one of the four engine blades to his left. Directly ahead, was an unobstructed view of the plane's flight path. Johannes was looking up to see the pilots' second floor cockpit when someone moved next to him and bellowed, "Get out of my seat, *Jew*."

A tall SS officer glared down at Johannes. He sprang out of his seat and moved cautiously around the SS officer. *I hope he doesn't attack me or throw me off the plane*. After the Nazi let him pass, the airplane door slammed shut, and the stewardess announced, "Will everyone please take their seats. We're about to leave."

Looking toward the back of the plane, Johannes saw a seat next to an attractive young woman. He approached her asking whether he could sit there. She replied, "Please do," with a smile.

After Johannes sat down, she leaned toward him and whispered. "I saw what happened. That could have been me. I'm also a Jew leaving Austria."

A tear came to his eye as he said, “What a wonderful coincidence.”

“I don’t believe in coincidences.”

“Have you visited Milan?”

“No, how about you?”

“Yes, I studied there and often return on business. What do you do for a living?”

“I’m a seamstress.”

“And I’m a tailor who believes our meeting is a wonderful coincidence. Perhaps that Nazi is really a yenta matchmaker dressed up like an SS officer.” They both laughed.

“My name is Malka Lukasik. I’m pleased to meet you.”

“I’m Johannes Kaiser.”

The pair spent the rest of the flight talking. Startled, when the pilot announced they were about to land, Johannes said, “I can’t believe how fast the time passed. It’s been a pleasure talking to you. I hope we can meet in Milan.”

“That would be wonderful. I know nobody there.”

"I have an idea. Let's have lunch at Ristorante Savini. It's my favorite restaurant, and I have their business card." He fished it out of his wallet and handed it to her.

"When would you like to do that?"

"How about a week from today at one? We'll both be settled in by then."

After leaving the airport, Johannes rented an apartment, then visited Milan's Jewish Committee Office. He spoke to the reception desk attendant in Yiddish. "My name is Johannes Kaiser. I'm Jewish and just arrived from Vienna. Is there anyone here who could help me get a visa to a Nazi-free country?"

She replied in German. "You're not the first to ask that question. Many Jewish newcomers fear Hitler will export his Nazism to Italy and want to set up an avenue of escape. We assigned Joshua Klein to handle such matters. I'll introduce you to him."

Klein told Johannes that a consul at Milan's Mexican Embassy was selling visas.

"Are any visas available to countries other than Mexico, Mr. Klein? I have no interest in moving there."

"I'm afraid not. Most countries closed their doors to Jewish immigration, but if you move to Mexico, and then want to enter the United States, you'll only have to cross one border."

Johannes thought for a moment. "You're right. I have a friend who might also be interested. Can you arrange for that too?"

"Yes, that would be no problem."

A week later, Johannes arrived at Ristorante Savini five minutes early, took a table overlooking the street, and looked for Malka. He saw her almost immediately. She was a few inches shorter than he was and had a slender athletic looking body. Her dark hair blew gently in the breeze and her eyes sparkled as she approached him. He stood up, offered her a chair, and sat next to her.

"It's good to see you, Malka. What have you been doing since we arrived?"

"I rented a nice apartment, then looked for work. It's been frustrating because I have no contacts in Milan."

"You told me you're a seamstress, right?"

"Yes. Many say I'm good at my work, but it's difficult for a foreigner with no local references to be hired on her own recommendation." Malka frowned.

Johannes leaned toward her. "An old friend of mine, who owns a clothing factory here, allows me to use his machines after seven every evening. I make women's coats and dresses for a growing list of customers and would love it if you'd work with me."

"Are you sure that's all right?"

"It's better than all right. I have more orders than I can fill on my own. With your help, I could double my output. My customers would be delighted, and I'd be thrilled to have you working with me. Please say yes."

Malka smiled as she nodded her head in agreement. "I'd love to work with you, Johannes. Thank you."

"Before I forget, I applied for a Mexican visa and was wondering whether you would also like to get one."

"Is it necessary?"

After Johannes explained they could use the visas to escape Italy, if Mussolini began enforcing Hitler's anti-Jewish laws, she replied, "That sounds sensible."

After lunch, the pair went to the Mexican Embassy to have their passports stamped with the visas prearranged by Joshua Klein. They then spent the afternoon exploring Milan. Afterwards, Malka accompanied Johannes to his friend's clothing factory for the first time. They worked from seven to midnight on weekday evenings and were free to do whatever they wanted during the day and on weekends.

Johannes wrote a letter to his parents telling them he had safely arrived in Milan. He also told them about meeting Malka Lukasik on the plane.

CHAPTER NINE -- THE MUNICH PACT

19th August 1938 – London – 10 AM Ewald von Kleist meets with Churchill

In mid-1937, the Tukhachesky Affair convinced Canaris the Nazi leadership had fallen into a moral abyss. He concluded that irreparable harm would come to Germany if nobody stopped their leaders. When Hitler encouraged Konrad Henlein, leader of the Sudetenland Nazis, to demand a union with Germany Canaris knew it was time to act.

In August 1938, Canaris sent his emissary, Ewald von Kleist, to tell Sir Robert Vansittart, British Undersecretary of State for Foreign Affairs, that Germany's senior army officers would depose Hitler if he invaded the Sudetenland region of Czechoslovakia. When Vansittart told Chamberlain, he discounted Kleist's report and did nothing.

The following day, Churchill rose from his chair when Kleist walked into his office. "I welcome you as a true friend of peace. What news do you have, sir?"

"Hitler finalized his plans to invade the Sudetenland. If he attacks, our generals will depose him. But if Britain hands the Sudetenland to Hitler, we will be powerless to act."

"Why are you telling me this?" asked Churchill, narrowing his eyes.

Kleist leaned toward him. "If Hitler isn't stopped, he will embroil us in a conflict neither of us wants."

After speaking with him for over an hour, Churchill said, "Herr Kleist, would it help your cause if I sent you a message claiming Hitler's invasion of the Sudetenland will lead to renewal of world war?"

Kleist thought for several minutes. "The worst that can happen is he disregards your message. Please send it."

Kleist received Churchill's letter the next day. He immediately handed it to Canaris, who gave it to Hitler. After reading it, Hitler looked up with a sneer. "Churchill doesn't have the political power to stop me, and Chamberlain has lost his will to fight. I risk nothing by proceeding."

23rd September, 1938 – Berlin – Mayer discusses the Sudetenland with Göring

It had been two months since Mayer arranged for Kaiser's release from the Karajangasse School. Curious whether Kaiser was safe, Mayer requested a Gestapo report listing all Jews who recently immigrated to Italy. *Good*, thought Mayer after opening the report. *He's safe. I could lose my job, and perhaps my life, if Göring finds out, but helping Kaiser escape was the right thing to do.*

The phone rang. It was Göring's secretary. The Reichsminister wanted to meet with him the next morning. Mayer caught the last plane to Berlin, overnighted at the Kaiserhof, and met with Göring at 10 AM.

"The Führer wants to scare the Czechs into handing him the Sudetenland," began Göring. "He's ordered the Second Motorized Division from Stettin to roll through Berlin tomorrow on its way to the Czech border. He hopes Berliners will show the same enthusiasm they did in 1914 when thousands tossed flowers to our troops leaving to fight the Great War. Hitler often talks about how young girls ran up to kiss them."

"Wasn't that the biggest demonstration ever held at the corner of Linden and Wilhelmstrasse, sir?"

"Yes, it was. I'd like you to go there tomorrow then let me know if it's repeated."

The next day, Mayer approached the intersection at Linden and Wilhelmstrasse expecting to see large crowds. To his dismay, few people were there. When the motorized divisions appeared, Mayer grimaced seeing most of the civilians duck into a subway station. Those who remained stood silently at the curb. *This is no repeat of Hitler's 1914 experience.*

When a policeman announced Hitler was reviewing troops from his balcony at the Reich Chancery, Mayer rushed there. He found less than two hundred people standing quietly on Voss Strasse. Hitler appeared grim watching the passive onlookers. He gave the troops a half-hearted salute then stormed back inside and slammed the door. *The Germans don't want another war… that's for sure.*

The next morning, when Mayer walked into Göring's office, Göring said, "No need to tell me what happened yesterday. The Führer was furious, describing the Berliner's mood as monstrous and unpatriotic. He contemplated ordering the SS to cart them off to Dachau, but thought better of it at the last second."

Göring's secretary poked her head around the door. "The Führer wants to meet with you, sir."

Göring thanked her and turned to Mayer. "Would you mind waiting? I don't think I'll be long." He checked to make sure his clothes and hair were in order, then rushed out of the office.

Göring's eyes sparkled when he returned an hour later. "Our Führer's done it again. We'll soon control the Sudetenland, and it won't cost one bullet."

"How is that possible, sir?"

"British Prime Minister Neville Chamberlain, French Prime Minister Edouard Daladier, and Italian Dictator Benito Mussolini will meet with him in Munich tomorrow. They will force the Czechs to hand us the Sudetenland. Chamberlain and Daladier must believe the Führer's oft-repeated claim that he'll have no more territorial demands in Europe. This is another master stroke that will baffle Hitler's critics."

Göring strutted to his credenza and retrieved a large bottle. "Claus, this extraordinary brandy is reserved for special occasions. Join me in a toast to our great Führer and his bloodless Sudetenland conquest."

Göring poured two glasses and handed one to Mayer, who said, "May Hitler long lead the Reich from glorious victory to glorious victory."

The two men spent a few minutes savoring their drink, then Göring placed his empty glass on the desk. "We should get back to work, Claus. Would you mind attending the Munich conference for me tomorrow?"

"Not at all, Herr Reichsminister."

"I'd also like you to board the Führer's train tomorrow. He will meet Mussolini, and may need your help if any problems arise along the way." Göring then took a document from his file cabinet and handed it to Mayer. "Chamberlain and Daladier refused to sign this agreement when they last met with the Führer. During tomorrow's meeting, Mussolini will hand it out as a new proposal. Mark my words, Claus, *they will* all sign it this time."

Walking back to his hotel, Mayer noticed that most people appeared cheerful as they passed him. Several mentioned the Munich Conference with a smile. *Goebbels must be reporting it to everyone. How marvelous.*

After entering the Kaiserhof lobby, Mayer approached the concierge. "Did you hear the news, Herbert?"

"Yes I did, Oberst Mayer. The radio announced the Munich Conference about an hour ago, and they broke into regular programming every few minutes to give updates. Imagine, we will annex the Sudetenland without losing one German life. I'm so happy we won't go to war." The concierge smiled as he added, "Is there anything else I can do for you on this day sent from Heaven?"

"No thanks, Herbert. Long live our Führer, and his good works."

The next morning, Mayer watched from the train as Hitler greeted Mussolini at Kufstein, on the former Austro-German border. The two Axis leaders then disappeared into Hitler's private car. About an hour later, Mayer heard Hitler's bellicose voice above the din of the speeding train's wheels. He appeared to be referring to a map while trumpeting his intention to occupy all of Czechoslovakia soon. Then Hitler roared, "… and the time will soon come when we must fight side by side against France and England." Mayer didn't hear Mussolini's response, but was certain he agreed.

Following their arrival in Munich, Mayer went to his hotel room and changed from his uniform into civilian clothes. It was too early to leave for the conference, so he went to the Kaiserhof bar for a drink.

The bar was packed. Half the people wore badges identifying them as members of the press. Many others had the dour look of government bureaucrats. Mayer sat down at a table with an empty beer stein and soiled napkin. He was thinking about what he'd heard on Hitler's train when a tall man with a handlebar moustache, and wearing a tweed jacket, approached him. "I say old chap, you took my table."

Knowing little English, Mayer gave the newcomer a blank stare.

The Englishman then spoke in German. "I'm sorry, but I was sitting at this table."

"My apologies, I thought this was the only open place."

The Englishman looked around, then back at Mayer. "It *is* quite full, but there's plenty of room for us. Let's share a drink."

"That's very considerate of you. I'm surprised how many people are here, with the conference about to begin."

"You're right. We'd better order our drinks before it's too late." The stranger hailed a waiter and asked for a Guinness stout. "Would you also like to drink?"

"I've never had an English beer. It's high time I try a Guinness." The Englishman caught the waiter's eye and held up two fingers.

"Incidentally, I'm Ian McAllister from London."

"And I'm Claus Mayer from Vienna. What brings you to the conference?"

"I'm here in an unofficial capacity representing Winston Churchill, a member of Britain's Parliament."

Mayer winced. "Isn't he the Englishman who sees our Führer as a threat to the peace and stability of Europe?"

"Guilty as charged."

"It looks like we're here in similar capacities. I work for Reichsminister Göring."

"Göring, isn't he the chap who replaced the Red Baron in the Flying Circus during the Great War, and is building Germany's new Air Force?"

"Yes."

"We have similar interests on both sides of this…. eh…. how should I put it… this situation and we may be able to help each other, Claus."

"I see no problem with that, so long as you don't expect me to divulge any state secrets."

McAllister gave a rousing laugh, raised the large elegantly adorned beer stein, just delivered by the waiter, and barked, "Let's drink to that."

"Do you know where Chamberlain and Daladier met to prepare for the conference?" asked Mayer as he put down his stein.

It was now McAllister's turn to wince. "They never met."

"You're joking. They must have shook hands to wish each other well."

"No, they came to Munich in separate planes and are staying at different hotels."

Mayer looked at his watch. There was barely time to get to the conference before it began. "Ian, I'm afraid I have to go. I'm sorry we couldn't talk more. Would you like to exchange telephone numbers?"

"Certainly Claus, if you're ever in England, please contact me. If I get back to Germany, I'll call you."

Mayer waited outside the Great Hall of the Führerhaus for Hitler, Chamberlain, Daladier, and Mussolini. After they arrived, two men who said they were representatives of the Czech government approached Mayer asking whether they could attend the conference as observers. Mayer told them to wait and went inside to ask Hitler. He replied, "Tell them to wait *outside* the building," in an irritated tone of voice.

After Hitler called the meeting to order, Mayer closed the door and took a seat against the wall. He'd heard that Hitler liked to schedule negotiations when the sun shone through a large window behind him. Mayer smiled seeing Daladier and Chamberlain squint every time they addressed him. The talks made little headway until Mussolini distributed his own proposal. Mayer looked at his copy, confirming it mirrored the draft Göring handed him. The leaders of

England, France, Italy, and Germany then signed the Munich Pact, handing the Sudetenland to Germany on terms Daladier and Chamberlain earlier rejected.

Mayer thrust out his chest seeing his Führer strut from the meeting. He also saw Chamberlain looking pleased with himself as he headed toward his suite at the Regina Palace Hotel. Göring later told him Chamberlain pulled off a clever face-saving stunt by signing a joint communiqué with Hitler that said, in part, "We regard the agreement signed last night… as symbolic of the desire of our two peoples never to go to war with each other again."

Hitler asked Mayer to summon the Czechs so a member of Chamberlain's staff could talk with them. When they arrived, Chamberlain's representative showed them a map of the Sudetenland detailing areas non-Germans had to vacate within ten days, leaving behind all their personal possessions. When the Czechs disapproved, Chamberlain's representative glared at them, saying, "If you do not agree, you must settle your affairs with Hitler yourselves."

Mayer felt sorry for them. Göring had told him that Chamberlain promised to keep the Czechs' interests in mind during the Munich Pact negotiations.

⌘⌘⌘⌘⌘⌘⌘⌘

The morning after the Munich Conference, Elisabeth was working in her office when someone entered Canaris' office and slammed the door shut. She heard Hans Oster yell, "Hitler didn't foil our plan to oust him. It wasn't even the SS or the Gestapo. It was Chamberlain. That fool handed Hitler the impenetrable defenses Maginot built in the Sudetenland. With those defenses, the Czech army could have easily repelled a German invasion. Not only that, the Czech warehouses will provide vital weapons and munitions for over 100 German divisions. Hitler can now grab the rest of Czechoslovakia whenever he wants, and might even consider invading Poland."

There was dead silence for several minutes. Then, Canaris yelled, "It's time for us to take matters into our hands. We must reach out to the British." Oster's response was inaudible, then Canaris bellowed, "It's obvious we can't trust Chamberlain. He'll probably *tell* Hitler, hoping to get something… anything… in return."

She couldn't hear Oster's reply, then Canaris loudly exclaimed, "Perhaps, but it's too dangerous for our people to travel back and forth to England, and I don't think Churchill will visit Germany anytime soon."

Elisabeth jumped up and strode into Canaris' office without knocking. The pair greeted her with a blank stare. "I wasn't eavesdropping, Wilhelm, but couldn't help overhearing. I can make it possible for you to communicate directly with Churchill."

"Sit down, and tell us how," said Canaris.

She pulled a chair and sat next to Oster. "I've known Churchill since I was a little girl. He used to bring me bonbons and rock me on his knee. Many years ago, I told Winston that the Führer won my loyalty. He showed no interest until Hitler began ridding Germany of its Jews. Then he begged me to turn against him. What if I tell him the Munich Pact changed my mind about Hitler, and offer to open a direct channel of communication between the two of you?"

Canaris leaned toward her and asked, "What do you need?"

"Get me a secure two way radio." *The Gestapo has been extra vigilant recently, making it difficult for me to communicate with MI6. If this works, I could also use it in emergencies.*

"What do you think Hans?" asked Canaris.

"It's worth a try, but we'd better make sure the Gestapo can't spy on us."

"I can handle that," said Canaris.

Elisabeth didn't move a muscle as she gave an inward scream of delight.

CHAPTER TEN - THE NIGHT OF BROKEN GLASS (KRISTALLNACHT)

9th November, 1938 – Vienna – 7:30 PM - Judah Isaacson returns from Palestine

Judah Isaacson approached the Éclair Restaurant thinking how quickly the three months passed since he'd taken his mother to safety in Palestine. Siegfried Mannheim bumped into him, apologized, and pressed something into his palm. Judah continued on his way, then turned down the first street, stopped under the sole streetlight, and looked around to see whether anyone followed him. Feeling secure, he opened a note from Siegfried. M*eet me at our favorite place at ten tonight.* They'd never felt the need for privacy as children, so they often met at the grand waiting room in Vienna's main rail station. Judah arrived there at 9:45.

"Welcome home, my friend," said Siegfried, approaching him from the rear. "Let's sit on those benches against the wall. We can see anyone approaching us from there." After they sat, he turned to him with a grim expression. "You returned from Palestine to join the resistance. If you do, and the Nazis arrest you, they'll make your life a living hell."

"They already have." Judah's eyes became red and puffy. "The partisans who brought me across the border said the Gestapo tortured my father for days, and he died in agonizing pain. I won't rest until I avenge his death."

"He was a great man, never revealing the names of fellow resistance members under brutal torture."

"What shall I do after joining?"

"The Nazis want every Jew out of their Reich. Those who keep their noses clean, and get the necessary documentation, won't need our help. The troublemakers will."

"People like Otto Klein?"

"Exactly, he almost killed the Nazi who attacked your father."

"What happened to Otto?"

"He's been a hunted man since the day he shot Rolf Heintz and is under our protection."

"When can I see him?"

"After you enlist in the resistance and visit our secure hideout."

"I'm ready to join. What should I do? I can't go to my parent's home. Somebody else is probably living there."

"Go to my apartment. You'll live with me for as long as necessary. I'll leave first. Wait four or five minutes, then follow me."

Siegfried went to the main exit, stopped to talk with someone, then turned and walked back slowly. His face was pale when he sat down next to Judah. "The Nazis set the Jewish district on fire. We're needed there. I know you want to get even with them, but take no risks without my permission. Do you understand?"

"Yes, I'll follow your lead."

9th November, 1938 – Vienna – 10:30 PM – Kristallnacht begins

The pair left the station and headed toward a sky glowing orange and yellow. A storm trooper startled Judah when he sprinted past yelling, "Your time is up, Jews. We'll teach you a lesson you'll never forget." Tears came to his eyes when a scantily dressed pregnant mother came running toward him carrying a squealing toddler. She slowed for a moment, clenched her jaw, shook her head as if in denial, then sped past him. He tried to follow her with his eyes, but she vanished into a sea of inhumanity. A few minutes later, Judah's blood boiled seeing six Nazis cheer as they kicked an old Jewish man bloody. Unable to control his emotions, he broke stride and stepped toward the Nazis. Siegfried grabbed his arm and pulled him back. "Judah, no, stay shoulder to shoulder with me so we don't get separated."

Judah grunted. *I'll teach those Nazi bastards a lesson they'll never forget.*

Turning a corner, Judah saw four youths commanding a defiant old Jew to urinate on an open Torah scroll in the street. Seconds later, three more thugs ran past him pushing a young woman toward the elderly man. One yelled, "We have your granddaughter, Jew. Piss on that good-for-nothing scroll, or we'll rape her right here in front of you."

She screamed, "You're not man enough to rape me," then turned to look at her grandfather. "Don't listen to them, they won't harm me."

Judah's outrage vented itself in a lion-like growl. "I'll take the three attacking her. You handle the others."

"More Nazis might join them."

Judah's fury climaxed, his entire being bent on avenging the savagery surrounding him. "*I don't care.*"

"Take this," said Siegfried thrusting brass knuckles into his hand. "Do you know how to use it?"

"No."

"Put your fingers through the open loops and nestle the curved part in your palm. Use a rolling punch, hitting him at an angle to maximize damage. A hard enough blow to the nose, skull, sternum, or spine should incapacitate him."

Judah slipped Siegfried's weapon on his right hand, crept behind the Nazi holding the girl's right arm, and heard a dull sound as his brass knuckle connected with the bones at the base of the Nazi's skull. His victim crumpled to the street. The other two froze in place. Taking advantage of their momentary confusion, Judah summoned all his strength to drive his iron fist into the head of the man holding her body. He felt a flutter of exhilaration when the Nazi fell to the ground. The girl gave a small scream, broke free of the assailant holding her left arm, wheeled around, and kneed him in the groin. He squealed like a pig, then dropped to the ground grasping his crotch. Judah walked to where he lay, glared at him for a moment, then kicked him senseless. "That's a down payment for what you bastards did to my father."

Looking at Siegfried, Judah saw one of his four Nazis was unconscious. Two of the remaining three grabbed the old man from behind. The third, who was preparing to kick the captive, turned toward Judah. Taking advantage of the distraction, Siegfried stepped behind one of the two holding the old man and drove his armored fist into the base of his skull. When the other Nazi turned to see what happened, Siegfried struck him in the face with his brass knuckle. The Nazi remained in place for a moment, fell backwards screeching in pain, then hit the ground with a loud thud. The only attacker still on his feet turned and sprinted away.

"Did those animals hurt you, Sarah?" asked the elderly man as he ran to his granddaughter.

She rolled up the Torah, lifted it, and kissed it gently. "No, Grandpa, those two men stopped them." She then pointed at one of her unconscious attackers with an ugly twist to her mouth. "And I kneed *him* in the groin."

Her grandfather looked where Sarah was pointing, smiled, and said, "Good for you, my sweetheart."

Siegfried asked her, "Did those thugs recognize you?"

"Yes, one of them was in my Gymnasium class."

"Those beasts will soon wake up and rush to your home. Is anyone there?

"Yes, my grandmother."

"We must get there before they do. Where do you live?"

"Close by, I'll lead the way."

Judah and Siegfried held the old man up as they followed her.

⌘⌘⌘⌘⌘⌘⌘⌘

Peter Wassermann, wearing civilian clothes, watched from behind a building as two youths overwhelmed seven Nazis. After they left, he marched toward the six who still lay on the ground. When one stirred, he kicked him in the side. "You incompetent imbecile; how could you let two subversives, a girl, and an old man do this? I'm ashamed of you." Wassermann handed him a small black notebook. "Write your comrades' names and addresses in here."

"Why should I do that?"

"Because I'm a Gestapo agent."

He stood up, gave a straight-arm salute, said, "Of course sir," and took the notebook. After writing in it, he gave it back.

"Who are you?"

"I'm Werner Schmidt.

"Did you recognize the old man, the girl, and the two subversives who attacked you?"

"The old man is Mendel Solomonson, and the girl is his granddaughter Sarah. They live close to here. I didn't see the others. One of them must have knocked me out."

"The coward who ran away is a disgrace to the Aryan race. What's his name?"

"I was unconscious, can you describe him?"

"He had red hair."

"That's August Meitzmann."

"Do you know where he lives?"

"Yes, I do."

"Contact him to find out what he knows about the two who attacked you."

"Yes sir."

"Will you help me arrest those fugitives?"

"It would be an honor, sir."

"I parked my car outside the Jewish district. After we get in, you will direct me to the Solomonson's home."

⌘⌘⌘⌘⌘⌘⌘⌘

Siegfried and Judah followed the grandfather and Sarah into their apartment. An old woman, who lay crying on the couch when they arrived, sprang up. "Thank God you're both safe."

"Everyone," said Siegfried forcefully, "The Nazis will soon be here. We must leave. Pack one small bag of personal items and get back here as soon as you can."

The family scattered to their rooms.

Siegfried telephoned Heinrich Mayer. "I have three patients for the infectious disease ward. They are contagious and need an ambulance." Sarah then returned with her bag and Siegfried handed her the phone. "Please give the doctor your address."

When the old woman returned, Siegfried told her about the attack on her relatives. After the grandfather joined them, Siegfried spoke to the family "Help is on the way. We'll soon take you to safety."

Siegfried saw the grandfather pick up his Torah and approached him with his arms outstretched. “Please let me carry that for you. It was enough you protected it from those savages.”

He said, “I rescued it before those godless brutes set our Synagogue on fire,” as he handed the scroll to Siegfried.

Siegfried walked back to the window and said, “The ambulance arrived. It’s best if your neighbors don’t hear us leave. Follow me out quietly.”

Everyone filed out of the house and crowded into the ambulance. Heinrich Mayer, wearing a white lab coat, closed the rear door. Siegfried sighed when they began moving, then offered a silent prayer of thanks to God for helping him save the old man, his granddaughter and the old woman from harm.

⌘⌘⌘⌘⌘⌘⌘⌘

Wassermann unlocked his car and got behind the wheel. After Schmidt got in and closed his door Wassermann barked, “Which way to the Solomonson’s house?”

Schmidt pointed saying, “Take that street into the Jewish district.” He then told him how to circumvent burning buildings and streets clogged with rioting Nazis. Half an hour later, Schmidt pointed to a departing ambulance. “The Solomonsons live there. Park in that space.”

Schmidt led Wassermann into the Solomonson's apartment. They found it empty. "Damn it, I should have known better."

"What do you mean, sir?"

"That ambulance took the subversives to safety. I should have let you check the apartment while I followed it."

⌘⌘⌘⌘⌘⌘⌘⌘

Gazing at the young woman seated opposite him in the ambulance, Judah became conscious of her silent dignity. Each breath seemed to say, *Look at me. I make a difference in an indifferent world.* She looked into his eyes, causing him to blink. Her face brightened into a warm smile as she moved to sit next to him, took his hands into hers, and whispered, "May Adonoi bless you and all your generations for risking yourself to save our lives."

The anger, fear, and pain of Judah's fight for life drained from his body. *This could not have been an accident. God must have planned to bring us together. Perhaps it's silly, but I believe she is my beshiert... my soul mate... ordained by Adonoi to be at my side forever.*

Siegfried flashed a smile at the young pair, then said, "My name is Siegfried Mannheim, and this is my friend Judah Isaacson." Speaking to the old man he said, "Please introduce your family, sir?"

"Of course, Mr. Mannheim, but first let me thank you for coming to our aid. We would have perished if you and Judah hadn't helped us." He turned to Judah. "You are the son of Joshua, member of Beth Shalom Synagogue, right?"

"Yes sir, I am."

"My name is Mendel Solomonson. I knew your blessed father well, may he rest in peace. The Jews of Austria will be proud when they hear of your bravery in the face of great danger." Still looking at Judah, he continued, "You met my precious granddaughter, Sarah. She has the heart of an angel and the soul of David. Sarah came to live with us after the Nazis murdered her parents in Germany."

Mendel then looked at an elderly woman sitting next to him. Patting her face he said, "This is Rachel, the love of my life. We're married almost sixty years. I couldn't imagine living another day without her at my side." He then faced Siegfried, and asked, "Mr. Mannheim, what will happen to us now?"

"We're taking you to our hideout, then we'll get you out of the country."

After the ambulance pulled up to the back entrance of a hospital, Siegfried led everyone into Heinrich Mayer's hideout.

Judah expected to find resistance operatives assembling weapons or counterfeiting Nazi documents. What he found was a medical treatment center, several patient rooms, and a central nurses' station. He looked at Siegfried. "Didn't you tell us this is a hideout?"

"It is, but we never know when the Gestapo may invade." Siegfried stepped behind the nurse's station and moved a large patient-scheduling blackboard out of the way. He then grasped a huge bookcase, previously hidden by the blackboard, pressed a concealed button, and pulled the bookcase open like a door. After Judah entered the hideout Siegfried asked, "Is this what you were expecting?"

"Yes, it is." Counterfeiters were preparing what looked like forged passports. He saw no one assembling weapons, but several machine guns hung on the wall. "Where are Otto and his family?"

Siegfried lifted a carpet, opened a hidden trap door in the floor, and motioned Judah to walk down the stairs and into a corridor. He followed them down, saying, "This is our most secure area. We can replace our weapons and fake documents, but if the Nazis capture our fugitives, they will torture them for information then kill them."

"Did you dig out this area?" asked Judah.

"No, that would have been impossible. Fortunately, the hospital sits over a large storage area. We found it by chance while repairing damage to the clinic floor."

Siegfried opened the last of many doors along the corridor and invited Judah to enter.

"Judah, it gives me great pleasure to introduce Otto Klein. Otto, please meet Judah, Joshua Isaacson's son."

Judah embraced Otto. "It's a great honor to meet you, sir. You risked your life, and the lives of your family, to save my father from Schwartz and Heintz's attack. I shall always be in your debt."

"Judah joined the resistance tonight, Otto," continued Siegfried, "and fought off three Nazis to save Sarah Solomonson's life. We brought Sarah and her family here for safekeeping. You will soon meet them."

9th November, 1938 – Vienna – 11:00 PM – Mayer experiences Kristallnacht

Mayer was reading a newsmagazine to relax before going to sleep when he heard people rejoicing in the street. He went to the window and saw SA troopers laughing, singing, and waving Nazi flags as they promenaded toward the Jewish District. When Mayer looked in that direction, he saw fire and smoke rising over the area. Seeing a friend walk by, he opened his window. "Hey Fritz, what's all the excitement? Are you celebrating the Beer Hall Putsch anniversary?"

"No, we'll teach those Jew swine a lesson. One of them murdered a big shot in Paris. Come join us, it should be fun."

"I'll catch up with you after putting on my clothes."

He dressed quickly, then joined the crowd. The closer he got to the District, the noisier it became. After getting there, Mayer saw a gang of six surround what appeared to be a husband, wife, and their two children. He couldn't believe his eyes when three of them seized the children and forced them to watch while two men clubbed their parents with heavy wooden sticks. *This is wrong. We shouldn't be doing that to children.*

Mayer kept walking, then slowed seeing one of his SA friends point a gun at the back of an old Jew's head. He paused when his comrade gave an old woman, possibly his wife, a knife and said, "Cut off this Yid's beard and side curls or I'll kill both of you." Mayer covered his mouth in amazement when the old man smiled and gently nodded his head, giving her permission to comply with the order. *It makes no sense. His love for her must be greater than his obedience to Judaism.*

Moving on, Mayer saw four men force three Jews wearing long black coats and velvet skullcaps to watch as their house of worship crumbled into a huge ball of fire. When one of them turned away, a Nazi pounded his body with a nightstick, saying, "Never again will you use that place to make Passover bread with the blood of sacrificed Christian children."

Mayer had seen enough. He turned to flee the madness, shielding his face from fellow Nazis still rushing toward the violence.

The sounds faded then Mayer sensed a mysterious power beckoning from behind. When he turned, he saw the strange prisoner who had unnerved him on the day of his fifteenth anniversary. The blazing buildings created a mystical aura around the old man, compelling Mayer to kneel. The captive spoke in a thunderous voice, enunciating every word with awe-inspiring clarity. "Do not kneel before me for I am mortal. Beg God's forgiveness. You have done evil and greatly offended Almighty God."

Mayer's mind drew him back to the night of The Beer Hall Putsch. He watched in horror as SA troopers followed his orders to slaughter Solomon Weisskopf. Mayer cringed seeing himself delight in his wife's heartache as she lay on her beloved's dismembered corpse. His eyes filled with tears as he looked to heaven and begged for mercy.

... his body shook.

... his soul screamed for release from wickedness.

... his mind went blank.

10th November, 1938 – Vienna – 2:30 AM – Avram and Eszter experience Kristallnacht

Avram woke to shrieks and laughter from the street. He walked to the window and held back a scream seeing Aryan youths brandish flaming torches. They yelled, "Out with you Jew swine. Leave our country."

He woke Eszter, saying, "Get dressed."

Hearing loud pounding on the front door, he clutched at his heart then went downstairs. "What do you want?"

"It's Wilhelm Braun and Rupert Freund, your Great War friends."

Avram opened the door. "Why are you here? You could be killed."

"We're taking you to safety," said Braun.

Freund added, "There's a murderous pogrom spreading throughout the Reich. No Jew is safe. Get dressed, bring Eszter, and come out to our car."

Avram ran back up to the bedroom. "Wilhelm and Rupert are here. We must leave." He dressed, then they dashed down the stairs and into the street. "We're grateful for your help," said Eszter after getting into the huge Mercedes limousine.

"Where are you taking us?" asked Avram.

"Out of harm's way," answered Freund. "We'll bring you both home as soon as this pogrom ends."

Avram's blood froze seeing a man run at one of his Jewish friends wielding a thick wooden club. *What is...?* Moments later, his friend's blood covered them both. "Eszter, whatever you do, don't look out the window."

"It's too late." Tears streamed down her cheeks.

Avram took her in his arms. Her sobbing subsided.

Freund turned to Avram. "Lower the shades over the back windows."

Avram did so.

Eszter remained motionless, her face buried in his chest.

Avram lifted his shade again and trembled. The limousine stopped beside his synagogue. Hungry flames shot through a huge Star of David adorning the top of the grand entry. Brown shirted troopers clutched the Rabbi and elders, forcing them to watch as their house of worship burned. They cheered when the front of the building exploded into a sea of flames. Avram sobbed. *Has the world gone mad?*

Pleasure seekers ran into the street to gawk at the devastation, blocking the limousine's way forward.

A blond SA trooper gazed at the limo. Avram drew back. *He's looking at me*.

The blond grinned as he walked toward the car. Avram gripped Eszter, terrified he would wrench both of them out of the car.

The trooper stopped at the front passenger window and gave a Nazi salute. "I'm sorry for delaying you, Herr Freund. We'll clear a path."

Avram sighed and kissed his wife.

Seconds later, the limousine began moving. When it stopped, Avram glanced outside hoping the violence had ebbed. It had not. His heartbeat raced seeing six SA troopers drag an old friend and his family from their home. One of the Nazis pounded his friend's head with a nightstick. Blood cascaded from his cracked skull, then floated down and coated the perpetrators and victims in a deep red hue. His comrade slumped to the ground.

Why is this happening? Avram had seen enough. He lowered his window shade.

Wilhelm Braun drove to an outskirt of Vienna untouched by violence and ushered the pair into his house. "Avram and Eszter," said Freund's wife, rushing to meet them. "I brewed tea to calm your nerves. The wireless reported horrifying news from your district. You are safe here. Stay as long as you want." They remained until radio reports confirmed the savagery ended. Then Braun drove them home.

Avram and Eszter were unharmed, and their home was unscathed, but the horrific events they witnessed on the fifteenth anniversary of Adolf Hitler's Beer Hall Putsch haunted their dreams for the rest of their lives.

⌘⌘⌘⌘⌘⌘⌘⌘

Elisabeth spent the evening listening to graphic radio reports of the pogrom with the Kreutzers.

Her in-laws cheered Nazism's long-awaited triumph over Judaism.

Elisabeth openly shared in their delight.

Rachel's mind balanced precariously on the edge of an abyss, powerless to voice her anguish over the plight of her beleaguered people.

At long last, safely tucked in Elisabeth Billingsworth's warm bed, Rachel vented her thoughts.

Could success at Evian have prevented this cold-hearted cruelty?

Would the democratic nation's condemnation of Hitler have averted this massive tribute to anti-Semitic hatred?

Will this night of anguish provoke a pitiless world into action?

If not now... when?

If not the world's democratic nations ... who?

11th November, 1938 – Vienna – 8:30 AM – Siegfried goes to England

After rescuing Mendel Solomonson, his wife, and granddaughter Siegfried overnighted in the hideout. The next morning Heinrich asked him, "Did the Nazis see you last night?"

"I'm sure they did."

"You must leave Austria as soon as possible. I'll have Elisabeth arrange it."

After getting Heinrich's message, Elisabeth told Irena she'd do some early holiday shopping in Vienna. When her plane landed, she took a taxi to Heinrich's hospital and headed to his clinic. Heinrich sat down with her and said, "The Gestapo hasn't stopped hunting for Siegfried. We daren't allow him to leave."

"I thought that might be the case." She opened a bag and took out face paint and old women's clothes. "This will disguise him."

Heinrich went into the clinic to fetch Siegfried. When he found him he said, "Elisabeth is here and wants to see you." As they were walking back, Siegfried remarked, "I remember when Elisabeth interviewed me for my MI6 position. It surprised me when she revealed she was Jewish."

Heinrich stopped dead in his tracks and looked at Siegfried. "I never knew that."

When the pair walked into the room, Heinrich said, "Elisabeth will disguise you."

Elisabeth applied cosmetics, had Siegfried slip into a dress, and then stepped back to examine him. "Let's see if this disguise works before sending you out." She then asked Heinrich to bring in Gandalf, a resistance comrade who'd known Siegfried for many years. "Gandalf, meet Helga, she's our newest underground member."

Heinrich told everyone how he'd brought Siegfried and the Solomonson family to the hideout. Siegfried remained silent for half an hour, then asked Gandalf, "You didn't recognize me, did you?"

"Not until you spoke, old friend."

Elisabeth then told Siegfried, "If you remain silent, it should be safe for Gandalf to drive you to a small airport outside Graz. I'll arrange for an MI6 plane to pick you up there and fly you to England." She then left the hideout, bought gifts for friends and family, and returned to Berlin.

The next morning, Gandalf and Siegfried set out for Graz. They'd driven about fifteen miles when traffic slowed to a crawl. After inching forward for almost an hour, Siegfried caught sight of four Gestapo agents checking every vehicle. He began sweating. Worried the perspiration would ruin his makeup, he forced himself to relax. A Gestapo agent approached the car and compared both their features against an artist's sketch he held. He then pointed at Siegfried and barked, "Get out of the car."

"My mother is sick," said Gandalf. "I'm taking her to a hospital."

When the agent moved to pull Siegfried out of the car, Gandalf exclaimed, "Please be careful, sir. My mother may have Typhus. I must take her to the hospital." The Nazi stepped back and snapped, "Wait here."

After he left, Siegfried asked, "Should we run for it?"

"No, if we do they'll kill us both. Stay calm."

Siegfried closed his eyes and concentrated on relaxing his mind and body. A few minutes later, shots rang out. Siegfried slid down in his seat, afraid the Gestapo was shooting at him.

Another agent ran up and waved Gandalf on, yelling, "Go now."

Siegfried sighed when the car moved forward. "That was a lucky break."

Siegfried smiled. “That was due to Heinrich. He sent two of his agents to track our progress and cause a distraction if the Gestapo stopped us.”

“I hope we aren’t stopped again. My makeup can’t take much more of this.”

Gandalf smiled, then laughed. “Just like a woman to worry about her makeup.” Siegfried also laughed, releasing his pent up anxiety.

Gandalf took back roads the rest of the way to Graz, then they overnighted at his house. The next morning, he drove Siegfried to a nearby airport where he boarded a small MI6 plane. Turnbey met him when he landed in London and showed him to his car. After they got in, he asked, “Will you return to Vienna as an agent?”

“Yes, I have much to do there.”

“Then I’ll take you to MI6 headquarters, where a doctor can alter your facial features. After that, we’ll take your picture and forge Nazi papers to give you a new identity.”

They agreed Siegfried’s new name would be Willy Labandter, a Christian life insurance agent. It took several weeks for his surgery scars to heal. He then returned to Vienna.

10th November, 1938 – Vienna – 9:30 AM – Wassermann reports on the Kristallnacht attack

Wassermann, still fuming the morning after Kristallnacht, strode into Schlossburg's office. "I saw four Jewish parasites launch an unprovoked attack on several brave Nazis last night. They killed three of them. We must act quickly to bring those antisocials to justice."

"Tell me what you know."

"Werner Schmidt, one of those injured, gave me the names, addresses, and descriptions of an old Jew and his granddaughter. He didn't recognize the two men who assaulted him, but knew where the old Jew and his granddaughter lived. We drove there and saw an ambulance leaving their building. We didn't realize it then, but that's how the four fugitives escaped." Wassermann handed Schlossburg several pieces of paper. "Here's what we remembered."

Schlossburg read Wassermann's report, making copious notes in the margins "I need you to fill in all the details while they're fresh in your mind."

The pair spent the next two hours reviewing everything Wassermann and Schmidt saw on Kristallnacht. Schlossburg then compiled detailed descriptions of the unidentified Jews and the ambulance. "Look this over, Wassermann, then tell me if I missed any details."

After reviewing Schlossburg's descriptions, he handed the pages back. "I have nothing to add, sir."

"Good, I'll give this information to a Gestapo chief. He'll have an agent find photos of the old man and his daughter. His artist will sketch likenesses of the unidentified Jews from your descriptions. Then, several agents will be assigned to find the fugitives."

"I could have apprehended them last night if I'd had agents working for me."

Schlossburg thought for a moment. "How many do you need?"

"I could use four, adding more as our workload increases."

"I'll talk with General Heydrich and get back to you."

Heydrich approved Wassermann's personnel request, and Wasserman hired police officers Franz Schwartz, Rolf Heintz, and Max Littner, along with civilian Werner Schmidt.

10th November, 1938 – Vienna – 9:00 AM - Mayer wakes up after Kristallnacht

Claus Mayer woke thinking his Kristallnacht recollections were a nightmare. Then the truth dawned on him. *That was no dream... I lived through it... did I really see the strange prisoner? How did I get home?*

He got out of bed and attempted to perform the daily ritual that had purged his mind of compassion since 1923. It was no use. The prisoner's lingering hold on him blocked Mayer's ability to concentrate. Dismayed, he bathed, dressed, and headed for the door.

When he stepped into the street, the stench of smoldering bodies and buildings filled his nostrils. He gagged, ran back into his apartment, wet a small towel with diluted eau de cologne, held the makeshift mask over his face, and walked out to the waiting limousine.

Mayer felt physically sick and mentally anguished when he arrived at the Rothschild Palace. Eichmann approached him. "You look like you saw a ghost, Claus. Were you caught up in the demonstrations last night?"

"Yes, were the Jews responsible for it?"

Eichmann put his fingers to his lips. "We'll talk inside," then followed Mayer into his office.

Mayer slumped into his chair. "Sit down for a moment, Adolf. I'm feeling nauseous from that smell." He took a cigarette from Göring's elegantly adorned holder, offered one to Eichmann, and lit both of them. Mayer drew the smoke deep into his lungs, hoping it would overwhelm the sickening taste. It did not.

"What caused all the destruction last night?" asked Mayer, forcing himself to continue.

"Heydrich told me Göring is with the Führer today to discuss that. I'll attend a meeting at the Reich Air Ministry tomorrow to go over their conclusions. I'll fill you in when I return."

When Eichmann got back, he called Mayer into his office. "A Jew assassinated a German diplomat in Paris on the seventh of November. On the ninth, Hitler left the Bürgerbräukeller Putsch anniversary event early. Goebbels then told attendees to retaliate for the assassination by initiating spontaneous demonstrations in the Jewish District. The protests grew so rapidly that Heydrich had to cable all State Police Chiefs, ordering them to safeguard foreigners and keep the flames from spreading to non-Jewish properties. The morning after the riots, Hitler instructed Göring to take advantage of the pogrom by speeding the departure of Jews from the Reich."

"Hitler wanted to do that since the Evian Conference. Did he tell him what to do?"

"He ordered Heydrich to arrest as many able bodied Jews as he could, then hold them at Dachau until their families arranged for them to leave the Reich. He also barred Jews from owning any businesses and levied a one billion mark fine on the Jews to pay for the damage they caused."

"It's about time," said Mayer with as much fervor as he could muster. Eichmann spent another half hour reviewing outcomes from Göring's meeting, then Mayer went back to his office, closed the door, and sat down.

I've blindly obeyed Hitler's dictates for far too long. Last night's pogrom, and the measures imposed on Jews to punish them for our own misdeeds, proves it. But what choice do I have? I built a successful career implementing Hitler's anti-Semitic programs. Resign now and I lose everything. It will be just like 1923. I cannot allow that to happen.

On 15 November, President Roosevelt responded to Kristallnacht by reading a statement to the media harshly denouncing the anti-Semitic violence in Germany. He also recalled Hugh Wilson, his ambassador to Germany.

U. S. Immigration restrictions remained unchanged.

Feeling exhausted, Mayer decided he needed a rest. He returned to Eichmann's office. "I haven't relaxed since before moving to Vienna, and I'm dog-tired. There's little of importance for me to do over the next few days, so I'll take a short vacation."

"You *do* look worn out, Claus. Forget about work for a while. I'll take care of anything requiring your attention."

Mayer called for his limousine and spent the entire drive home thinking about Elisabeth. Although he hadn't seen her since their weekend in Lausanne, he felt strangely drawn to her. As soon as Mayer entered his apartment, he dialed the Kreutzer's number.

"Elisabeth, I'm glad you're there. Is everyone all right? I've been too busy with the aftermath of Kristallnacht to ask after my friends' welfare."

"We're all fine, Claus. Living far from the Jewish District, we were in no danger. Were you hurt during the fighting?"

"No, I slept like a baby all night," lied Mayer.

"When will we see each other?"

"That's why I called. I've taken a few days off and wondered whether you'd like to spend them with me?"

"That sounds wonderful. Before I forget, Reichsminister Göring invited me to a small party at Carinhall tonight. He told me he was thrilled we were seeing each other and hoped you'd escort me."

"Yes, when should I get you?"

"Don't bother. Your apartment is on my way to Carinhall. I'll have my limousine get you."

22nd November, 1938 – Berlin – 8:00 PM - Mayer and Elisabeth visit Carinhall

Elisabeth's chauffeur knocked on Mayer's door at eight. He strode out to her limousine wearing a white shirt and dinner jacket, black bow tie, and black trousers with braid down the side seams.

After settling in the limousine, Mayer smiled at Elisabeth. "You wore that dress the evening we met." He took her hands in his. "Although I haven't seen you since Lausanne, you have constantly been on my mind. I treasure the days we spent together, and would like to see our relationship grow. I hope you feel the same way."

After all this time, I thought Claus saw me as a fleeting fancy. He wants us to fall in love and I will do all I can to make that happen. "My darling, you've made me very happy."

Mayer drew the blind, blocking the driver's view of them, took Elisabeth in his arms, and kissed her. She closed her eyes, forcing her mind to form the image of Benjie Kornblum's face. The pair nestled for a while, then Elisabeth said, "It will take us about two hours to get to Carinhall. It has quite a history. Göring built it around a log cabin he used on his hunting trips. It's about ten miles inside the national game preserve through which we're now driving. He named it in honor of Carin, his first wife."

"I knew her well," said Mayer. He told her how he'd saved Göring's life during the Beer Hall Putsch, then added, "After learning that the Government toppled the Nazi Party, Göring asked Carin to make their assets available so I could arrange for their escape from Germany. If you're ever in my office, I'll show you the magnificent cigarette box she sent me as a thank you for saving Göring's life."

"No wonder the Reichsminister speaks so warmly of you."

The car continued through a thin forest of pine and scattered birch, then stopped at a fortified gate. A concrete and steel fence stretched in both directions. Luftwaffe troops carrying machine guns guarded the entry. One of them approached the limousine, his jaw set. "Let me see your authorization to enter?" The driver rolled down his window and handed him Elisabeth's invitation. He checked it against a list, then looked at the darkened back passenger window and barked, "Show yourselves." When Mayer opened the window, the guard snapped to attention, gave a straight-arm salute, barked, "Heil Hitler," and waved them through, adding, "Enjoy the party Herr Oberst," with a smile.

After the limousine passed through two more security checkpoints, Carinhall came into view. It was a richly detailed huge structure constructed of wood and stone. Mayer said, "This is the first time I've seen this place. It certainly personifies the full measure of Göring's extravagance in fashion and personality." A long line of limousines inched forward, dropping elegantly dressed guests off at the front door.

Entering the seventy-two foot by thirty-eight foot reception area, known as the *Jaghalle,* Elisabeth recalled trembling on her first visit there in 1936. The unvarnished supremacy of its soaring raw oak log walls terrified her. A massive roaring fireplace, that could reduce an entire family to ashes in a matter of seconds, added to her dread.

⌘⌘⌘⌘⌘⌘⌘⌘

Ghosts of Teutonic Knights, that appeared to be one with the primal splendor of the *Jaghalle*, exhilarated Claus. He sensed that Carinhall embodied the grand spirit of Germany's legendary prehistoric roots.

⌘⌘⌘⌘⌘⌘⌘⌘

The divergent emotions felt by Elisabeth and Mayer on their first visits to Carinhall exemplified the dualistic nature of the Nazi state. The unfaithful languished under its unbending code of beliefs while the faithful thrived because of them.

Inside, Göring's mansion was teeming with guests. The stylish crowd was a veritable who's who of international politics.

"Ambassadors from all four corners of the globe are here, Claus, but I've seen none of our top Nazi leaders. Where's the Reichsminister?"

"He was delighted when I called to let him know I'd join you, but wasn't sure he could spend any time with us. He's meeting in his private quarters with Hitler and his general staff."

"I hope we can share a drink with him."

"Me too. Would you like to show me around his mansion?"

"Yes, I would."

The first floor seemed to have miles of corridors, each lined with original art. Mayer was astonished to see paintings by German and Italian masters alongside crudely painted works by modern German artists. In another area, he saw tapestries of naked women labeled with the names of virtues such as goodness, mercy, and purity.

While gazing into a glass case, exhibiting precious gifts presented to Göring by world leaders, a voice thundered from behind them, "Elisabeth and Claus together holding hands. I'm overjoyed you both came this evening."

They turned to see Göring grinning at them. He kissed Elisabeth's hand, then shook Mayer's. "I've always worried that your single-minded sense of duty would turn you into a lonely old man. I'm glad Elisabeth is making sure that won't happen."

"Thank you Herr Reichsminister. Elisabeth brightens my life whenever she's beside me. I'm the luckiest man in the Reich."

Elisabeth's eyes glistened at Mayer's flattering remark. She then asked, "Do you have time to share a drink with us, sir?"

"Unfortunately not. When I excused myself, the Führer insisted I return quickly. One day, when things become more settled, you must both spend an evening with my wife Emmy and me."

"I'll remind you of that, Herr Reichsminister," said Elisabeth.

Göring smiled, kissed Elisabeth's hand again, and hurried away.

"I hope you don't mind, but I'd like to go home before dinner is served. I'm exhausted, and we still need to talk about plans for our time together."

"That's fine, Claus. I wasn't hungry, and you look worn out."

⌘⌘⌘⌘⌘⌘⌘⌘

Mayer dozed off soon after they got into the limousine. His head slipped onto Elisabeth's shoulder. She smiled looking at him sleeping peacefully next to her. *He's made me feel so calm and contented today. I can't believe he is the same person who treated Papa so cold-heartedly during the Putsch. It's becoming difficult for me to hate him.*

Rachel's guilty conscience toppled her mood. A tear flowed down her cheek. *Claus became a Nazi, attacked our home, and held the purging of my people from Germany as his greatest goal. After Hitler is deposed, I will insist that MI6 lock him away in a cold dark cell for the rest of his life. He deserves no better.* A torrent of tears gushed down her cheeks. She found a handkerchief in her bag to wipe them from her face. The movement was enough to waken Mayer.

He said, "What's the matter, why are you crying?" in a raspy voice.

"It's nothing, my darling. I'm glad we're together, and you love me. I often cry when I am happy."

⌘⌘⌘⌘⌘⌘⌘⌘

Mayer kissed her tears, finishing the work her handkerchief began. "Promise me you'll tell me if I ever make you unhappy. I couldn't bear the thought of you being sad, especially if I'm the cause." Mayer held Elisabeth tightly, convinced she was not weeping tears of happiness. His heart ached. *What is the key to your unhappiness? Are you hiding something? How can I make you happy? Will you ever open your heart to me?*

After a few minutes he asked, "Have you visited Murano, my love?"

"No, where is it, in Italy?"

"Yes, it's a picturesque small island a short vaporetto ride from Venice."

"Vaporetto, what's that?"

"It's a water taxi. I first visited Murano after Hitler came to power. It is such a romantic spot, and I dreamed of sharing it with someone I adore. Will you help me realize that dream?"

"Of course, sweetheart, I would love to visit Murano with you."

The next morning, Mayer called Eichmann to let him know he would vacation in Murano with Elisabeth. Eichmann told Heydrich, who phoned Mayer to offer his private plane for the trip.

24th November, 1938 - 7:30 AM - Mayer and Elisabeth vacation in Murano

"The flight in the General's airplane was a real treat," said Elisabeth as they walked toward the waiting limousine. "But you haven't told me where we'll be staying."

"I called Vincenzo Amarati, a close friend of mine, to ask if we could stay in a small bedroom on the second floor of his glass shop. It overlooks the Grand Canal. You will love the view. It's breathtaking."

"He has a glass shop?"

"Yes, he comes from a line of glassblowers dating back several centuries. Many people visit Murano to buy its unique glass creations. I go there to enjoy its beauty."

Vincenzo embraced Mayer when he arrived. "Claus, my friend, it has been far too long. And this attractive lady must be Miss Billingsworth." Looking at her with a smile, he continued, "Murano is too romantic for a man alone. I'm glad you accompanied Claus. He appears so much happier than the last few times he visited me."

"Please call me Elisabeth, and thank you for allowing us to stay with you, Vincenzo."

"That is my pleasure. You and Claus are always welcome. Please stay as long as you want."

A few days later, Elisabeth stood on the balcony watching small boats cruise along Murano's Grand Canal while she waited for Mayer to awaken. Glimpsing through the fine lace curtains, she saw him smile up at the ceiling

She had mixed feelings. He was wonderful, taking her on romantic walks along Murano's canals. They even took a vaporetto to Venice then rode a gondola under the Bridge of Sighs. "Local legends say lovers will have eternal love if they kiss on a gondola at sunset under this bridge," said Mayer as took her into his arms and kissed her while the shadows lengthened over Venice.

Pushing the curtains aside, Elisabeth said, "My love, this is the best vacation I've had in years. And the beauty of our ride beneath the Bridge of Sighs shall be in my thoughts forever."

"Come here my love. We have unfinished business from last night."

Elisabeth laughed coquettishly as she joined him on the bed. "I can't believe you, Claus. This vacation has liberated the wild beast in you."

"Are you complaining?"

"Not at all, but General Heydrich's plane will soon take us back to our busy lives."

Mayer's smile vanished. "I don't want to leave. Nothing would make me happier than to live with you above Vincenzo's shop for the rest of my life. He wouldn't mind."

"You know that's impossible. You have important work awaiting you, and I must return to England."

"Why is that?"

"I must look in on my home, and my family is there."

Mayer got out of bed. "My darling, please join me on the balcony so we can talk."

Elisabeth smiled. "You'd better put something on or all of Murano will see your crown jewels."

"Complaining again?" chuckled Mayer as he pulled on a bathrobe and headed outside with her. "Sweetheart, I've been doing a great deal of thinking and have come to a very important decision," said Mayer after they sat.

"What's that, my love?" `

"Until we met, I had only one purpose, to serve our Führer and the Third Reich. While serving the Führer remains an important part of my life, it leaves me unfulfilled. You make me complete as a person. I adore you and want you to be my wife."

Elisabeth said nothing for over a minute. "I also love you, my dearest, but cannot make that commitment."

"Why not? What could stand in the way of our getting married?"

"I'm British, not only by birth, but by choice. I love Britain as you love the Fatherland, and my family there cherishes me. They do so *despite* my service to our Führer. Although Nazism's goals and methods are repugnant to them, they turn a blind eye so long as I stay true to my birthright."

"What does that mean?"

"I'm free to serve the Führer while in Germany, but must keep my British citizenship and never become involved with, or discuss, my Nazi activities while at home."

"But if we marry…"

"... To marry you," interrupted Elisabeth, "I must choose you over my parents. That's a step I won't take."

I don't want to lose Elisabeth, but I also won't give up my position of power in the Party to marry her. "Elisabeth, I will not allow my marriage proposal to come between us. If you agree, we can just continue loving each other."

⌘⌘⌘⌘⌘⌘⌘⌘

Elisabeth hugged Mayer on that picturesque balcony above Murano's Grand Canal. "Yes, my love, I can continue loving you." *I don't hate Claus anymore, and enjoy spending time with him, but marriage is out of the question.*

CHAPTER ELEVEN -- HITLER'S JANUARY 1939 REICHSTAG SPEECH

30th January, 1939 – Berlin – 11:00 AM

Two months after Mayer returned from Murano, Eichmann walked into his office. "Göring wants to see me in Berlin at eleven tomorrow morning and asked that you join me."

"Is there a problem?"

"Not at all. He applauded my work in Vienna and told me the Führer approved changes I would enjoy. He provided no more details over the phone."

The next morning, Göring's secretary knocked on his door. "Herr Reichsminister, Lieutenant Eichmann, and Oberst Mayer are here for your 10 o'clock meeting. Shall I have them join you?"

"By all means."

Göring gazed at them with the look of a proud parent as they walked in and took their seats. "The Führer applauds your work in Vienna as the best way to purge Germany of its Jews. He asked that I replicate that model throughout the Reich, so I signed an order establishing the Reich Central Office for Jewish Emigration in Berlin, under General Heydrich's command. Adolf, you'll administer our plans to rid the Reich of its Jews, directing Section IV B4 of that office in your new capacity as Obersturmbannführer."

"I'm honored, Herr Reichsminister, and will do all I can to earn your trust," said Eichmann.

"I now have a special treat for you both," continued Göring. "As you know, the Führer will address the Reichstag today. His speech should be of particular interest, so I've reserved front row seats in the gallery for you." Göring handed them their tickets. "You'd better hurry so you can be in place before he speaks."

After they took their Reichstag seats, Mayer turned to Eichmann. "Congratulations on your promotion. You deserve it." His smile vanished when he leaned toward him and whispered, "What did you tell Göring? I never supported your department."

"Claus, my friend, I know when a man is in love. After returning from Murano, all you talked about was Elisabeth and your hope to marry her. That won't happen with you in Vienna and her in Berlin. I knew Heydrich was considering my reassignment to Berlin..."

"... and you thought if I accompanied you I could spend more time with Elisabeth and convince her to marry me."

"Is that something you'd be willing to consider, or am I off the mark?"

"I'm deeply in your debt Adolf."

"Now that that's settled we'd better be quiet. The Führer is here."

Hitler walked in posing as an unassuming observer. He stood scanning the audience, as if he was sniffing out their hopes, dreams, and fears. Then, when the hall became silent, he spoke in slow soft tones. Mayer strained to hear his first words.

"Members of the Reichstag. Six years ago, when thousands of National Socialist fighters marched through the Brandenburg Gate to express their joy at my becoming Chancellor, it seemed only a miracle could save our great nation."

Hitler's voice became louder, and his gestures more forceful.

"Before I took office, the Jews thought they were seeing the final flickers of our Nazi dream. They knew that once our dream died, they could destroy Germany and all Europe. During those dark days, I worried for the future of my people. But today we can all appreciate the full meaning of those pious words: *What a change, by the grace of god.*"

His voice moderated. "In the course of my life I was often a prophet. During my struggle for power, the Jews received my prophecies with contempt. They laughed when I predicted I would take power and then settle the Jewish problem. For some time now, they have muted their laughter. Today, I will again be a prophet."

Hitler's voice rose to a feverish pitch.

"Europe will not have peace until I settle the Jewish question. We must break away from the notion that our dear god intended the Jews to be parasites living off the productive work of others. Jewry must adapt itself to respectable and constructive labors as do other people or it will eventually succumb to a crisis of unimaginable proportions. Nations are no longer willing to die on the battlefield so this predatory international race can profiteer from war and satisfy its Old Testament vengeance. The battle cry *workers of the world unite* will yield to a higher calling: *Workers of all classes and of all nations unite to recognize the Jews as your common enemy.*"

All in the Reichstag stood, roaring approval for their Führer's words. Hitler raised his hand to silence them. They listened in rapt attention as he raised his voice to declare: "If the international Jewish financiers plunge the European nations into yet another world war the result will not be the Bolshevization of the earth, and thus the victory of Jewry, *but the annihilation of the Jewish race in Europe.*"

The Reichstag shook as delegates jumped to their feet, raised their arms in the Nazi salute, and repeatedly screamed Sieg Heil. Thunderous applause shook every bone in Mayer's body. Hysteria infected his mind. Hitler was his personal savior, the redeemer of the

Aryan race. Mayer and the crowd were one, their hysteria galvanizing his body and mind. He was on his feet screaming "Sieg Heil." in unison with the assembly. Never had he felt so powerful. Nothing could stand in his way. Mayer was fearless. He would rule the world. The animal leapt into his throat, amplifying every sound.

In the heat of that moment, Mayer's mind swept him back to Kristallnacht, and the strange prisoner. This time, all the old man said was, "When will you, at long last, mend your evil ways?"

Mayer found himself back in the Reichstag, Claus' inner voice once again claiming victory over Hitler's demonic hatred. He saw himself as an alien being in a world gone mad. He looked at Eichmann, who was still one with the others. Claus' soul was free of its shackles. Fear replaced fearlessness. He glanced at those around him. A*nyone can see I am no longer a true believer*. He clapped and cheered, now feigning emotion... hoping others could not see the obvious. *Claus is faking it. Claus is no longer a devoted Nazi. Claus will no longer fight world Jewry as a devoted anti-Semite*. Even as Claus' thoughts swore blasphemy, Mayer's shouts pledged undying loyalty to his Nazi god.

⌘⌘⌘⌘⌘⌘⌘⌘

The radio broadcast of Hitler's Reichstag speech electrified much of Germany's citizenry.

Otto and Irena Kreutzer were on their feet, bellowing reverence for their deity's words.

Elisabeth, compelled by her MI6 responsibilities, could do no less.

Rachel trembled, her voice muted by the deafening silence of a pitiless world.

⌘⌘⌘⌘⌘⌘⌘⌘

"The Führer was in top form today," gasped Eichmann as he accompanied Mayer out of the Reichstag building. "There has never been a speaker with such passion before, and there may never be another in our lifetimes. Remember this day. You will tell your grandchildren you were there when the Führer gave his ultimatum to the Jews. It will go down in history as one of his greatest speeches."

"I couldn't believe it," replied Mayer, certain Eichmann could tell his words lacked conviction. "It felt as if we were reliving the Führer's Beer Hall days, and even better, it laid the groundwork for your work at the new RHSA office."

"*Our* work," replied Eichmann with a hearty laugh.

"Let's go out for an expensive dinner, Adolf, to celebrate. I'm buying, then I'll call Elisabeth to let her know of our plans."

The next morning, a hotel employee handed Mayer a message from Göring. He went to Eichmann's room. "Göring asked me to meet with him at ten this morning. Do you have any idea what he wants?"

"I called him last night requesting your transfer to my new RHSA office. I expected him to approve it on the phone, but he was evasive, saying he had to talk with the Führer before deciding."

"What do you think is going on?"

"If you move back to Berlin, Göring probably wants you reporting to him instead of me."

Later that morning, Mayer met with Göring and accepted his invitation to move to Berlin as his special assistant. *What an opportunity*, thought Mayer, once again shaking off the remnants of his latest rebellion against Hitler. *This move will allow me to do more for the Nazi Party... but it won't make it any easier for me to marry Elisabeth.*

CHAPTER TWELVE -- HEINRICH'S CLINIC IS THREATENED

9th February, 1939 – Vienna Austria – 9:00 AM - Wassermann raids Mayer's clinic

Two months after Kristallnacht, Schlossburg called Wassermann into his office. "The Gestapo completed their analysis. Eyewitnesses reported that the Solomonsons and their accomplices drove toward Vienna's Central hospital, but nobody saw them beyond it."

"So you're saying they're inside that hospital?"

"That's the Gestapo's best guess, and you should begin there."

Eager to apprehend the Jewish subversives, Wassermann ordered Max Littner, his senior Gestapo agent, admitted as a member of the hospital's staff. It took less than a day for him to discover the Infectious Disease Clinic was the only area closed to inspection.

After hearing the news, Wassermann directed agents Rolf Heintz and Franz Schwartz to watch the corridors around the clinic. Two weeks later, Wassermann called all four agents to his office. "Heintz, did you confirm that the Jews are hiding in that clinic?"

"No sir. Visitors aren't allowed in, and security guards seal off the hallways whenever the clinic admits new patients. They say it's the only way to make sure others aren't infected."

Wassermann turned to Schwartz. "How about you, do you think our Jews are there?"

"I don't know, sir."

Banging his fist on the table, Wassermann bellowed, "That's where they are, and we will expose those subhumans tomorrow." He turned to Schmidt. "The clinic's employees haven't yet seen us, so it's best if we go in alone." Addressing the others he added, "I want the rest of you covering the adjacent corridors to make sure nobody escapes."

The next morning, Wassermann rang the clinic bell. A woman wearing a white lab coat opened a small door at eye level and asked, "May I help you, sir?"

"We're Gestapo agents, here to investigate your facility. Open the door." Wassermann smiled inwardly, satisfied he had struck an ominous tone. He expected it to open. Instead, the view hole slammed shut.

Wassermann was about to bang on the door again when the woman reappeared. "I'm sorry, sir. The clinic had a typhus outbreak. Berlin issued strict orders banning visitors until it's safe."

Striking an angry tone, Wassermann said, "I'm with the Gestapo. Open this door at once or I must break it down."

"I have no authority to do so, sir. If you wish, I can ask Dr. Mayer, our Director, to talk with you."

Wassermann's temper exploded. "Get him here, *now*."

Heinrich's face was flushed, his eyes bloodshot, and shirt drenched with perspiration when he opened the small window. "Yes, may I help you?"

"I'm Wassermann, with the Gestapo. We must conduct a routine search of the clinic. Let us in at once, or I shall break in and arrest you all."

"I'm sorry Inspector, we admitted a patient with typhus last week. When I reported that two members of my staff became infected, Berlin ordered us to quarantine our facility. If I allow you in, the infection could spread to you, your staff, and the hospital's visitors."

Wassermann scratched at his cheek. *If he's telling the truth, and my forced entry results in the spread of typhus, it could mean my job... or worse...*

"If we're done here, Inspector, I must go back to my patients. They are gravely ill and need my full attention."

"To whom do you report?" asked Wassermann angrily. "I must speak with him."

"Fritzendorff, he's with the Reich Ministry of Health. He is out of the country on a special assignment for the Führer, and won't return for several weeks. By that time, we should have contained the outbreak and you'll be able to inspect my clinic. Please call me in three weeks. Excuse me while I tend to my sick patients." Heinrich nodded and slammed the small door shut.

Wassermann fumed, caught between his fear of confronting Heinrich's authoritative presence and his wish to prove Mayer was hiding subversives. Frustrated at his own failure to act decisively, Wassermann lashed out. "Schmidt, stay in the area. Don't let those vermin see you. Keep your eyes open, taking notes on any comings, goings, or unusual activity. I'll have you relieved in three hours; report to me at once, I'll be in my office." He turned and stormed away.

9th February, 1939 – Vienna, Austria – 11:00 AM - Heinrich Mayer moves his fugitives

Knowing the Nazis could stumble onto their hiding place, Bleimann and Heinrich drew up an emergency escape plan for their fugitives. When Bleimann heard about the Gestapo's attempted raid, he set the plan in motion by dispatching ten resistance fighters to the hospital basement. They wore full-face gas masks, rubberized protective coats, and carried commercial spraying equipment. Approaching Schwartz and Heintz, one of them said, "The Reich Ministry of Health ordered us to decontaminate in and around the Infectious Disease Clinic. You must clear this hallway until we complete our work."

"That's out of the question," replied Schwartz. "Our chief must relieve us before we can go."

"We use a very strong chemical that burns skin, eyes, nostrils, and other exposed areas of the body."

"We'll stay here and take our chances," said Heintz.

"Suit yourselves."

Schwartz and Heintz protested until the noxious fumes blinded them. They then squealed while scurrying away. Eight squad members entered the clinic, leaving two outside to stand guard. Those inside took off their protective outerwear and masks, then helped Heinrich and his fugitives into them. They all exited the hideout, strode through the deserted halls, and stepped into a large paneled truck parked outside a rarely used hospital exit. The vehicle drove off when a squad member closed the back door.

Heinrich maneuvered his way through Vienna, making sharp turns at frequent intervals to make sure nobody was following them. When he was confident they were alone, he headed south.

They reached the outskirts of Graz two hours later. Heinrich parked in a forest several miles from the university. He then took a bicycle from the truck, rode to the school, and left a note for the Medical Administrator that read, "The package arrived and needs your attention." He then bought sandwiches at a nearby restaurant and bicycled back to the paneled truck.

"Now we wait," said Heinrich as he climbed in and handed out the food. "A friend will soon get you." After the fugitives left, he drove back to Vienna and returned to the clinic early on Friday morning.

Wassermann was livid when he stormed into Schlossburg's office on Friday afternoon. "I knew I should have broken into the clinic yesterday and arrested Mayer."

"What's the matter?" asked Schlossburg calmly.

"I went back to Mayer's *so called* Infectious Disease Clinic today and he let me enter."

"That was a problem?"

"Of course not, but we searched the clinic and found nothing."

"Calm down Peter, you're making no sense. There must have been something in there."

"Yes, they had medical facilities, and were treating people with infectious diseases, but I found no trace of the Jews. Then, that pig nurse Rheinbaum wouldn't let us go until she'd given each of us shots using large painful needles."

"You couldn't just walk out?"

"No."

"Peter, you're leaving something out."

Wassermann's voice became timid when he continued. "Mayer didn't allow us in, we broke down the door. Someone must have contacted the authorities because an SS officer arrived soon after we entered. He accused us of posing an unacceptable health risk to the people of Vienna."

"And?"

"And he ordered us to receive the shots, or else."

"Or else, what?"

"They would arrest us for endangering the people of Vienna. Then, Rheinbaum made us take down our pants, in front of the SS officer, while she injected us all in the buttocks."

Schlossburg burst out laughing.

"Damn it, Ernst, it's *not* funny."

"I know, but you must admit it could amuse someone not as involved as yourself."

Wassermann glared at his boss.

"Peter, I'll help you sort this out, but I need more information."

After bristling for several more minutes, Wassermann told him he assigned two agents to guard the clinic door. Then a fumigation team sprayed outside the clinic to contain a typhus outbreak, forcing the agents to leave.

"Did your agents see the crew again?"

"No, they were blinded by the fumigation spray."

"So, they didn't see them leave the building?"

"That's right."

"Did anyone else see them leave?"

"No."

"We have a problem, Peter."

"What's that?"

"You've given me no leads to follow, which leaves us with two possibilities. Either Mayer told the truth… and wasn't hiding subversives… or he lied and covered his tracks extremely well."

"Where do we go from here, Ernst?"

"I'll investigate, but it could take a long time."

"Damn those Jew swine," mumbled Wassermann under his breath.

12th February, 1939 – Milan Italy – Johannes and Malka flee to England

Johannes and Malka had lived in Milan for six months. During the first few months, they spent every day together. When they weren't producing stylish women's coats and dresses, they toured Milan's sights. On their four-month anniversary, Johannes made a special dress for Malka. When he presented it to her, she kissed him. He became aroused, and she didn't object when he led her to his bedroom and they made love for the first time. A few days later, Malka moved in with Johannes.

Johannes' hands shook and his eyes filled with tears when he picked up the Sunday newspaper. There, in bold lettering was the headline.

HITLER PROMISES ANNIHILATION OF JEWISH RACE IN EUROPE

The paper fell to the floor when he jumped up and screamed, "I sat still and waited for those Nazi bastards to arrest me in Vienna. *I won't do that again.*"

Johannes' shrieks brought Malka running into the living room. "What's wrong, Darling?"

"Hitler wants to kill all the Jews in Europe."

"What should we do?" asked Malka, her face losing its color.

"We must leave while we still can."

"Do you think Joshua Klein can help?"

"Yes, let's see him tomorrow."

"You're in luck, Johannes," said Klein the next morning. "A new camp is being prepared in England for Jewish male refugees."

"Only male refugees? How about Malka?"

"There's a second unrelated program for Malka, but I'll explain your program first. A transit camp is being prepared near Sandwich, Kent, in England."

"Transit camp?" asked Johannes.

"Yes, although the British remain opposed to mass Jewish immigration from Germany, Kristallnacht's violence convinced them they had to do something to help the Jews. As a result, the Secretary of State authorized United Kingdom Consulates to admit Jewish men to the new Kitchener Camp where they will await resettlement to a final destination."

"Final destination?"

"Yes, applicants must have visas permitting them to enter another country after leaving the camp. That's no problem, since the Mexican consulate approved your visa after you arrived in Milan. Would you like me to arrange for your transit visa?"

"Yes and please tell us about Malka's program?"

"The British Home Office is issuing visas to Jewish women willing to take positions as domestic service workers. We have a family in London that is looking for maids and cooks to work at their mansion in London. Should I also arrange for Malka's domestic service visa?"

"Please do."

After leaving the Jewish Committee Office, the pair went to their apartment and sat down together. Johannes was the first to speak. "Joshua is preparing the paperwork for us to enter England. If we go, I must live over eighty miles away from you. We might be free of the Nazis, but it's impossible to know how long we'll be apart. Should we go?"

"If we stay here, we will be together. However, if Hitler forces Mussolini to adopt his anti-Semitic laws, we'll have to deal with the Nazi threat. Let's go to England, where the Nazis won't be able to touch us. With God's help, we will be together after you are permitted to leave Kitchener Camp."

"I agree."

It took a week for Klein to obtain the visas for Johannes and Malka. In the meantime, they visited the French Embassy to get transit visas permitting them to travel through France to Calais, their Port of embarkation. Malka and Johannes boarded their ship on 15 February and were soon watching the European continent fade into the distance.

When the pair disembarked in Dover, Johannes said. "Now we are in a country where we can live free of fear." A ships employee pointed them to a desk where the British Immigration Officer asked, "May I please see your passports?" in English.

They gave him a blank stare.

He asked, "Do you speak English?" in broken German. When they nodded their heads sideways, he led them to another station where the officer asked for their passports in German.

Johannes surrendered them both. The official opened his first and frowned. "You may not enter the United Kingdom, Herr Kaiser. You have a C 2202 transit visa."

"I know sir. I must go to the Kitchener Refugee Camp, and my companion has a domestic service position at the Billingsworth mansion in London. Can you help us both get there?"

"Yes, I'll make your arrangements."

When the immigration officer left to set up their transportation, Johannes took Malka in his arms and held her close. He felt a lump growing in his throat. "Malka, my love, separating is difficult, but we have no choice. We must look forward to the day we can be together in a country where Hitler can no longer harm us."

A private car approached Malka's new home. The driver parked, and Malka got out. An attractive young woman came out to greet her. Speaking in German, she said, "You must be the new employee from Dover, right?"

"Yes, I arrived from Italy."

"I'm from Germany and have worked here for three months. You will love it. Mr. and Mrs. Billingsworth own this house. They are good to all the refugees they hired."

Johannes' bus, filled with thirty men bound for the Kitchener Camp, meandered through quaint English towns. Landscaped gardens racing by the window lifted his spirits. White church spires glistening in the distance made him think of Austrian villages.

When they entered an urban area, the driver called out, "We're in the town of Sandwich; you're almost home," which someone translated into German. Johannes looked out at the lovely houses, cozy corners, and mosaic like walls of timber and bricks. *I could enjoy living here*.

The bus exited the town, wound its way along another picturesque country road, then passed through a gate and stopped. The driver turned around. "Everybody out, this is the Kitchener Camp."

Johannes's jaw dropped at the sight of weather worn, identical, concrete one-story buildings stretching as far as he could see. *What a letdown from beautiful Sandwich. I hope Malka is living somewhere nicer than this.*

Entering his building, Johannes saw sixteen bunks lined up against opposite walls with a narrow walkway between them. Metal lockers covered with deep scrapes separated the beds. Looking at his new home, he wished he were anywhere else with Malka. His shoulders hunched as he unpacked his belongings into his worse-for-wear cabinet.

28th April, 1939 - Vienna Austria – 2:00 PM - Avram and Eszter are forced out of their apartment

Thirteen months after the Anschluss, the Nazis announced a new law forcing Jewish renters to move into Vienna's Jewish district by the thirtieth of April. Avram and Eszter waited until the last day before complying.

"Look Eszter, Johannes wrote us a letter," said Avram as he came in the door. "We're lucky it arrived before we left."

"You must write him our new address."

"I will," replied Avram as he opened Johannes's letter and read it aloud.

Dearest Mama and Papa,

Malka and I left Milan after hearing Adolf Hitler would annihilate European Jewry if another war broke out. The local Jewish Committee arranged for our visas to England, and we arrived here a few weeks ago. Unfortunately, I must stay in a transit camp for now, but I am safe here.

After we arrived in Milan, I wrote to you about Malka. Since then, we fell in love and look forward to marrying after I'm released from the camp.

Malka is now working as a maid in the mansion of a rich English family. We haven't seen each other since we arrived in England, but stay in regular contact through the mails. I hope we will soon be together and can't wait until you meet her. You will love her as much as I do.

Papa, you and Mama should leave Vienna. I'm afraid Hitler will start a new war and then arrest you. If you go to Milan, talk to Joshua Klein at the Jewish Committee. He helped Malka and me get to England. I am sure he will also help you.

Please write soon, letting me know you are both well.

With all my love,

Johannes

Eszter, whose eyes filled with tears while Avram read the letter, cried as soon as he finished. Avram took her in his arms. "One day we'll all live in a land where it isn't a crime to be Jewish. You'll see."

"I'm so happy Johannes found a good woman," said Eszter, wiping the tears from her eyes. "I pray they'll be united soon. Should we follow Johannes' advice, and leave Vienna?"

"All in good time, Eszter. I don't think we are in imminent danger, so we'll stay here for a while longer."

CHAPTER THIRTEEN -- THE VOYAGE OF THE *ST. LOUIS*

6th May, 1939 – Berlin – 9:00 AM – Göring asks Mayer to book passage on the St. Louis to Cuba

Three months had passed since Mayer accepted Göring's invitation to join his staff in Berlin. He spent that time closing out his affairs in Vienna, making the move, and shouldering his new responsibilities. He rented an apartment close to the Kreutzers, so he could be with Elisabeth, but Göring's assignments kept him too busy to see her very often.

Arriving at work on the sixth of May, Mayer found a note asking him to meet with Göring at once.

"Thanks for seeing me on such short notice, Claus," said Göring as he got up to shake his hand.

"It's my pleasure Herr Reichsminister."

"The Führer and I were looking forward to ridding ourselves of almost 1,000 Jews later this month, but we have a problem."

"Are you referring to the *St. Louis*, sir? The last I heard, everything was proceeding smoothly."

"Most of those who booked passage got their landing permits from Director-General Manuel Benitez Gonzalez of Cuba's immigration office. The Americans discovered he was selling those certificates for $150 or more. According to their estimates he earned over $500,000."

"Isn't that normal Cuban business practice, sir?"

"That's true, but Goebbels had sent his agents to convince the Cubans that the Jews on the *St. Louis* were criminals. When someone leaked Gonzalez's activities to the press, the Cubans held street demonstrations protesting admission of Jewish refugees, forcing the government to dismiss Gonzalez. The furor didn't die down so Cuban President Brú passed Decree 937 last Friday, rescinding all Gonzalez's landing permits."

"Does that mean the *St. Louis* won't sail?"

Göring smiled. "It will leave as scheduled."

"I don't understand, sir."

"The Führer, Propaganda Minister Goebbels, and I believe the Cuban authorities won't allow the Jews to land. We expect the captain to try disembarking them in the U.S., and the Americans will probably refuse, giving our Führer another propaganda victory."

"How may I be of help, sir?"

"Book passage on the *St. Louis* and keep me informed during the voyage. You'll travel as a private citizen, not a member of my staff."

"Yes, Herr Reichsminister."

Mayer was heading to the door when he turned toward Göring. "May Elisabeth accompany me, sir? It would be a perfect cover, two lovers on a transatlantic voyage."

"This shouldn't be a dangerous trip. Yes, have Elisabeth join you."

"Thank you, sir."

Mayer dashed back to his office and called Elisabeth. His heart raced as he dialed her number. "Elisabeth, how would you like to join me on an ocean cruise to Cuba and back?"

"Claus, I haven't seen you in weeks, and now you're making jokes."

"It's true, Göring asked me to sail to Cuba on the *St. Louis,* and you may go with me."

"That's wonderful. I'd love to accompany you."

24th April 1939 – Graz - 10:00 AM – Judah and Sarah board the St. Louis

Thinking Wassermann's fugitives might try escaping Nazi justice onboard the *St. Louis*, Schlossburg asked Heydrich to have the Gestapo double check papers of everyone arriving in Hamburg before the sail date.

After Heinrich confirmed it was still possible to buy tickets to Cuba on the *St. Louis,* he sat down with Judah in his bedroom. "The St. Louis will sail to Cuba with over 900 Jewish refugees. I could book passage for you and Sarah." He told Judah about the ship and when it would leave, then sat back. "Would you like to go?"

"Yes, but I'd better check with Sarah and her grandparents first."

Judah knocked on Sarah's door, walked in, and sat down with her. "We have lived under Heinrich Mayer's protection since Kristallnacht. Heinrich can now buy us tickets to Cuba on the *St. Louis*. Will you join me?"

"Nothing would make me happier, Judah, but I won't leave my grandparents."

"I knew you wouldn't go without them, so I asked them for your hand in marriage."

"You what?" asked Sarah, half smiling and half crying. "What's come over you? I thought you loved my grandparents as much as I do. How could you do that to them?"

"Do what? Ask for your hand in marriage?"

"Of course not silly, that's wonderful. I'm overjoyed you want to marry me, but…"

"... there are no buts. Remaining here is too dangerous. We *must* leave Austria, and your grandparents agree. They'd never forgive themselves if you didn't go with me. Their greatest wish is that we find a new life in America where we'll be free from harm and fear."

Sarah was silent for several minutes, then asked, "Do you think Graz's Rabbi could marry us before we leave?"

When Judah asked Heinrich he replied, "I must make the travel arrangements first, then I'll talk to both of you about the wedding arrangements."

Heinrich purchased tickets on the *St. Louis* for Judah and Sarah. Manuel Benitez Gonzalez, Director-General of Cuba's immigration office, issued the landing permits that accompanied the tickets. Heinrich then had travel documents forged for the couples' journey from Graz to Hamburg. They'd go as newlywed Aryan couple Julius and Heidi Bloomberg. He then invited the couple to his office so they could discuss plans for the wedding.

When they met, Heinrich turned to Sarah. “I know you wanted Graz’s Rabbi to marry you, but that’s impossible. The Nazis burned Graz’s Synagogue to the ground on Kristallnacht, then drove all the Jews out. Graz no longer has a Rabbi so a layperson must marry you. Do you think your grandfather would perform the wedding ceremony, Sarah?”

“I’m sure he would, but I must ask him.”

After Sarah’s grandfather agreed, Heinrich sent Elisabeth a coded message asking whether she could be in Graz on April 9, Easter Sunday. It was also the sixth day of Passover.

Elisabeth replied yes. She then told Irena a British school friend invited her to spend Easter with her in Vienna and flew there on April 8. Willy Labandter picked her up at the airport. While driving her to Graz he said, “We had an ulterior motive for inviting you. Sarah and Judah, whom you haven’t met, will get married tomorrow, and we thought you’d like to attend their Jewish wedding. Then they’ll leave for Cuba on the *St. Louis.*”

“That’s unbelievable. I’m also sailing to Cuba on *the St Louis*.” When Willy asked why, she said it was an MI6 assignment, without divulging her relationship with Claus. “I’d better tell Sarah and Judah I'll be on board, so they don't reveal we know each other. I'll do it before the service.

Sarah's grandfather began the wedding ceremony by saying, "During the Passover Seder we recalled how the exodus freed the Jewish people from slavery in Egypt. Sarah and Judah will also leave on an exodus…taking them from the Nazi's brutal anti-Semitism to the freedom of the New World. Let us all pray for their safe journey and a happy life together."

The wedding included many of the Jewish traditions Elisabeth cherished before leaving Germany. She had tears in her eyes when Sarah asked her to take her mother's place, at her side, as they circled Judah seven times. "One explanation for this ancient custom," said Sarah's grandfather, "is that by doing so, Sarah enters the seven spheres of her beloved's soul."

The next morning, Judah and Sarah began their rail trip to the *St Louis*. The journey was uneventful until they pulled into Hamburg. Judah then whispered, "Put on your happy face, my love. The Gestapo is checking everyone's documents at this exit. Heinrich told me they are like fierce animals, able to smell out the fear in people and turn it to their own advantage. We must beat them at their own game by acting self-assured. Can you do that?"

"That's easy. I'll tame those beasts by showing them how much I love you."

Judah smiled and hugged her. He helped her off the train, then they walked arm-in-arm chatting nonstop until a Gestapo agent snapped, “Papers please.”

Sarah flashed a coquettish smile, then handed him her documents, saying, “How are you today, officer?”

“I’m having a wonderful day, madam.”

After the agent returned Sarah’s papers, Judah handed him his, saying, “Please excuse my wife. We married yesterday, and she’s still in high spirits.”

“Congratulations to you both,” replied the agent with a bright smile… that turned into a scowl when a bald Gestapo officer glowered at him. The agent examined Judah’s papers, then handed them back saying, “Move on now, sir,” in a stern voice.

The pair was almost out of the station when the bald officer stormed after them. “Not so fast, you two. Let me see your identification papers.”

Judah felt weak-kneed seeing the bald officer lift the gun from its holster. Judah trembled as he handed him the papers.

“What is the purpose of your trip to Hamburg?”

Judah smiled, as best he could, put his arm around Sarah, and replied, "My wife and I were just married and we're on our way to a honeymoon resort outside Hamburg."

The officer barked, "You're newly married Aryans? Where is your copy of our Führer's masterpiece, *Mein Kampf*?"

Judah felt nauseous.

Sarah fished through her bag. "I know it's in here. I wanted to read it on the train, but Julius and I talked all the way here."

She was still rummaging through her belongings when the officer asked, "Would you like me to help you, madam?"

"No, that won't be necessary. I'm sure I'll find it if you'll just give me a moment."

"Hand me that bag *now*," bellowed the officer.

Judah felt his stomach flutter when the agent holstered his weapon and grabbed the handbag. The officer's facial muscles tensed as he fished through Sarah's belongings.

"It must have fallen out of your bag in the train," offered Judah.

"Perhaps it did," responded Sarah. "But I don't think so."

The Gestapo officer grinned as he held up the book. “It was here all the time, madam. You may both be on your way with my best wishes for a long and happy life together. Heil Hitler.”

The pair returned his salutation and straight-arm salute, then chatted leaving the rail station. Once they were at a safe distance, Sarah took Judah in her arms. His body was shaking.

“It’s all right now. We’re safe,” said Sarah.

“I know,” replied Judah with a shudder. “But why on earth did you have *that* book in your bag?”

“I heard newlyweds on the train say the State gives it to Aryan couples when they marry. You were in the bathroom when we changed trains in Nuremburg, so I bought it at a newspaper stand.”

He hugged Sarah. “I’m glad you found out about Hitler’s book.”

“And thank heaven I could get it. It was the last one they had.”

“Why didn’t you tell me about it?”

“I thought you’d be angry I spent our money on that monster’s so called masterpiece.”

“It may have saved our lives, my love. You did the right thing.”

13th May, 1939 - 8:00 PM - Shed 76, Hamburg Harbor - The St. Louis sets sail

The passengers applauded as the *St. Louis* weighed anchor. Those still in their cabins rushed to join their shipmates on the promenade deck. They all cheered as the ship set sail. A few had tears in their eyes.

Judah and Sarah went to the front of the *St Louis* and laughed as the stiff ocean breeze drove the late spring cold deep into their bones.

"I feel alive," screamed Sarah over the howling wind. "I could take wing and soar high above us like those seagulls," pointing to three birds flying playfully over them.

"Just think," said Judah, a lump growing in his throat. "In a few weeks we can begin our life together in America." He embraced her, tears of joy streaming down his face. "Sarah, my precious, I can't wait until we have children, lots of them. They will grow up as proud Jews. On this day, I promise Elochainu we will keep a Kosher home to honor all those who suffered and died because they were among His chosen people."

The pair went to the back of the ship and watched until Germany disappeared beneath the horizon. On their way inside the ship, they passed the social hall. A large group still celebrated the liner's departure over wine and pastries. One of them held up his hand. "Everyone be quiet." It took several attempts to silence them all. "Today is holy, like the day our ancestors escaped Pharaoh's Egypt. I'm not a rabbi, but we should thank God for saving us from the Nazis."

"He's right," said a second passenger. "Who knows a blessing for this occasion?"

Judah pushed his way to the center of the group. "We should say the *She-Heheyanu*. It thanks God for keeping us alive to reach this moment."

"I've heard it many times in the synagogue," said an old man, "but never understood its meaning. Can you say it in our language, instead of Hebrew?"

"Yes," replied Judah. "But before we do so, let's all put on a head covering to show our respect for the Eternal, our God."

Everyone, regardless of age or sex, scurried about searching for something to cover his or her head. It might have appeared amusing to a casual observer, but the participants considered it a solemn act. A few took a handkerchief, knotted the four corners, and fitted it over their heads. Others found a lace doily, using a bobby pin to keep it in place. Some ran back to their cabins to retrieve their *yarmulkes*. After everybody returned, Judah delivered the *She-Heheyanu* in German, the language spoken by most *St. Louis* passengers.

> *"Blessed are you, Almighty our God, Ruler of the Universe who has kept us alive, preserved us, and enabled us to reach this season."*

⌘⌘⌘⌘⌘⌘⌘⌘

Hans Klientraub's lips quivered as he recited Judah's prayer silently in Hebrew. The Nazis arrested him on Kristallnacht, along with 26,000 other Jews, and sent him to Dachau. While there, Klientraub witnessed the murder of fellow prisoners by hanging, drowning, and flogging. The SS released Klientraub after his family raised the funds for one ticket on the *St. Louis*. He said farewell to his wife and children with a heavy heart, planning to earn enough to pay for their tickets after he arrived in Cuba.

⌘⌘⌘⌘⌘⌘⌘⌘

The hall remained silent, Judah's prayer finding its way deep into the hearts of fellow passengers. An elderly woman wept. A young man standing next to her, who had not yet made her acquaintance, hugged her. Others, many with tears in their eyes, comforted those around them. Former strangers found support and consolation in each other's arms.

⌘⌘⌘⌘⌘⌘⌘⌘

Mayer and Elisabeth walked into the social hall minutes before Judah recited the *She-Heheyanu*. He asked, "Would you like me to get cocktails from the bar next door? We can take them out on deck to toast the sunset."

"Yes darling, that's a wonderful idea."

After he left, one passenger hushed the group and suggested a prayer.

I could join them if I make sure Claus can't see me. I'll go behind that curved stairway. After taking cover, Elisabeth smiled seeing everyone search for a head covering, then trembled when Judah delivered the prayer. Rachel's Judaism, now tucked deep in Elisabeth's mind, struggled its way into her heart. Memories of Sabbath evenings with her father came flooding back. Her lips moved, but no sound surfaced as she recited the *She-Heheyanu* in Hebrew.

After Judah finished, Elisabeth walked toward the bar and saw Mayer. Taking his hand, she led him out onto the deck. The pair sipped their cocktails while the sun set in a magnificent show of oranges, pinks, and purples. Moments after finishing her drink, she asked, "Do you mind if I go back to our cabin and take a nap? I'm exhausted."

"Of course not. Can I get anything for you?"

"No, my love, I need a little rest, then I'll be fine."

When Rachel returned to the cabin, she locked the door and covered her head with a lace handkerchief. She then recited memorized Hebrew prayers facing what she believed to be in the direction of Jerusalem as Jews had done for over two thousand years.

After Elisabeth left, Mayer looked for the ship's bridge. A uniformed officer approached him. "Passengers may go no further, sir."

"I must speak with Captain Schroeder."

"I'm the Captain, how may I help, sir?"

"My name is Obersturmbannführer Mayer. I am sailing under orders from Reichsminister Göring and may need to radiogram him without alerting the others."

"Seal your message in the envelope you'll find in your desk drawer and address it to Cabin 001. Hand it to any officer. He will deliver it to me. Is there anything else, sir?"

"Yes, if you receive any news about the Cuban situation, please have someone contact me."

"Yes, of course, sir."

On the third day of the voyage, Elisabeth was standing alone at the back of the ship when Judah approached her. He thrust something in her pocket and continued walking. She returned to the cabin, locked the door, and retrieved a crumpled piece of paper from her pocket. On one side, it said *I found this on the floor while walking past the radio office this morning.* She turned it over and found it was a radiogram to Captain Schroeder from Cuba's administrative office. *This confirms that only those passengers who posted a $500 bond, and hold landing permits from Cuba's Secretaries of State and Labor, may disembark in Cuba.*

Elisabeth felt her heart drop. *This is terrible. I had no idea the bond and alternate landing permits were required. I must help Judah and Sarah.* The next time she saw Judah she brushed up against him dropping a note into his pocket and kept walking. It said, *If I'm able to land in Cuba, I may be able to pull a few diplomatic strings. Please get me your passports, making sure nobody sees you hand them to me.*

27th May, 1939 - 2:00 PM – Cuba - The St. Louis enters Havana Harbor

The transatlantic voyage took two weeks, the *St. Louis* entering Havana Harbor on the twenty seventh of May. Most travelers crowded on deck after the engines stopped. They peered over the railings, looking for the small boats that would carry them ashore.

Captain Schroeder realized it was now high time to let his passengers know the truth. He took a deep breath, turned on the ship's loudspeaker system, and said, "Ladies and Gentlemen, I am very sorry to tell you that only those who posted a $500 bond, and got their landing permits from Cuba's Secretaries of State and Labor, may land. All others must stay on board."

Schroeder made the announcement as Elisabeth and Mayer were walking hand in hand along the promenade deck. A couple ahead of them stopped dead in their tracks. One man leaned over the railing and vomited. Others wept. An old woman collapsed, her fall broken by an attentive ship's staff member. Tears blurred Elisabeth's vision. Feeling a hollowness growing in her chest, she reflexively tensed her grip on Mayer's hand. He turned to her with concern in his voice. "Are you all right, Elisabeth? You look white as a ghost."

"I'm fine, Claus. Something I ate for lunch must have disagreed with me, and my stomach cramped."

"Are you sure? We can check with the ship's Doctor."

"No, I am already feeling much better."

Later that day, a tender tied up alongside the *St. Louis*. A ship's officer cleared twenty-eight people to board the small boat. Twenty-two Jews handed him valid entry documents. The other six were a Cuban couple and four visiting Spaniards who would return to the ship before it sailed. Claus and Elisabeth boarded after he handed the officer their passports bearing an official stamp and notice of their $500 bond payment from Berlin's Cuban embassy. The officer turned everyone else away.

"I must go to the German Embassy to communicate with Berlin," said Mayer as he settled next to Elisabeth in the tender. "You can stay with me, or go shopping. We'll meet later at the embassy."

"I'd just be in the way. After dropping you off, I'll have our taxi take me into town. I heard the stores are fantastic. I'll pick you up after I'm done."

⌘⌘⌘⌘⌘⌘⌘⌘⌘

Hans Klientraub, standing beside his distraught Jewish shipmates on the deck, watched as Elisabeth's tender bobbed toward shore. *My family in Germany is looking forward to a postcard confirming I landed in Cuba. Instead, a newspaper or radio report that only a few Jews were allowed on shore will alarm them.* Moments later, another thought crossed Klientraub's mind. *Will the Nazis let me see them before dragging me back to Dachau? If I don't see them on the dock, I may jump overboard to end this nightmare.*

⌘⌘⌘⌘⌘⌘⌘⌘⌘

After Claus stepped out of the cab, and entered the German Embassy, Elisabeth ordered the driver on to the British Embassy. Before leaving Berlin, she'd sent Turnbey a note asking how she could get help in Cuba, if she needed it. He sent her a high-level security code Cuba's British Embassy staff would honor.

After entering the building, Elisabeth went to the reception desk, introduced herself as a British agent, then handed the reception clerk a card with Turnbey's code. The clerk asked her to wait and left her desk. A few minutes later, she returned trailing behind a tall blond man with sky-blue eyes and wearing a finely tailored dark blue pinstripe suit. "Miss Billingsworth, I presume?"

"Yes, I am."

"Please follow me to my office." He walked five paces ahead of Elisabeth, opened a door, let her in, and closed it behind her.

"My name is Jonathan Kipling, no relation to the author. Please take a seat. How may I be of service?"

"If the *St Louis* returns to Germany, the Gestapo will arrest two close friends of mine as Jewish fugitives. Could you get them valid Cuban landing permits?" asked Elisabeth, handing him Judah and Sarah's passports. She then sat back.

Without looking at the documents, Kipling said, "Well, Miss Billingsworth, this whole Jewish thing is a royal mess. Citizens rallied against entry of those passengers for several weeks, and Cuban officials are unwilling to give an inch. There it is, in a nutshell. Not much we can do," concluded Kipling as he stood to hand back the passports.

Elisabeth remained seated. "May I cable my MI6 boss? *He* might be able to help me."

"MI6," said Kipling, twisting his neck as if it was sore. "You're in the… eh… in our secret service?"

"Yes, I've been an agent since 1926," replied Elisabeth coldly. "I handed the reception clerk a security code identifying me as a British government agent. You are now holding it."

Kipling glanced down at the card and grimaced. "Well, well, MI6. I say, we should be able to help you, Miss Billingsworth. Would you mind if I consulted members of our senior staff?"

"Please do, Mr. Kipling, but I must soon be on my way."

"No problem, madam. I'll be back with you shortly."

Kipling returned half an hour later. "I believe we have a solution. Our senior staff seems to think if Captain Schroeder cannot disembark his passengers here, he may try landing them in Miami. Should that be possible, the American authorities agreed to let them in… so long as nobody else learns of our arrangement."

"That will do," said Elisabeth as she retrieved the passports. She left his office and hailed a cab. When the taxi stopped, Elisabeth saw a friend step out. "Lawrence Berenson… how are you… are you still President of the Cuban-American Chamber of Commerce?" He smiled and hugged her. "No, I'm here on a mission for the American Jewish Joint Distribution Committee. I'll be meeting with President Brú to negotiate landing rights for the Jewish *St. Louis* passengers. How about you?"

She frowned. "I'm a passenger on the *St. Louis*, and that's about all I can say now. Let's get a cup of coffee so we can talk privately. Unfortunately, I must pick someone up soon, so we have to hurry."

After they sat down in a café, Berenson asked, “Are you still with MI6?”

“Yes. Do you think Brú will allow the Jewish passengers to disembark?”

“It depends on whether he’ll accept $125,000. That’s how much the Joint Distribution Committee allowed me to offer. You’re not in any danger, are you?”

“Not unless my travel companion, a top Nazi, discovers my identity.”

“I’m impressed. It sounds like you’re earning your keep as a British government employee.”

“Can you let me know whether your negotiations with Brú succeeded?”

“Not if you want to keep your identity a secret. Several Nazi agents are on the ship. Any cable from me will likely fall into their hands.”

“You’re right, it’s too dangerous. I must meet my friend and return to the ship. Good luck with Brú and be sure to visit me when you’re in London.”

The next day, Judah slipped Elisabeth a note. She went to a Ladies Room and opened it. *I joined a committee representing the St. Louis' passengers. We sent a radiogram to Brú's wife asking her to help them. It concluded with the words, "The traditional humanitarianism of your country, and your woman's feelings, give us hope you will not refuse our appeal."*

Judah later told her the passengers never received a reply.

Berenson met with President Brú on the first of June. After shaking hands he said, "Mr. President, I would like to board the *St. Louis* to allay the fears of its passengers."

Brú replied, "You may *not* get on that ship. Let's talk about the passengers. I will admit them to my country for a payment of $500 each, or $453,500."

"I'm authorized to offer as much as $125,000, sir."

"That is unacceptable. This meeting is ended."

Berenson returned to his hotel room and cabled Brú's negative response to the Committee. The next day, they sent him a cable allowing him to meet Brú's payment demand. When Berenson phoned him with the offer, he replied, "It's too late," and ordered the *St. Louis* out of Cuban waters.

After the *St. Louis* set sail for Florida, Elisabeth met secretly with Judah to let him know the arrangement she'd made with Kipling.

When the ship dropped anchor off Miami, Judah and Sarah stood together gazing at the automobile headlights rushing along Florida's shore. He pointed to them saying, "We'll soon be there, beginning our new life in America." The couple remained silent the next morning as they again focused their attention on the stretch of water between the ship and the shore, searching for the boat that would carry them to freedom. In a replay of the Cuban episode, they went from hope to despair waiting for the tender that never came.

6th June, 1939 - 8:00 PM – Miami - The St. Louis sets sail for Germany

The *St. Louis* set off on its return voyage to Germany on the sixth of June. Later that day, Judah thrust a note in Elisabeth's hand as he passed her. She opened it after returning to her room. It said a ship's delegation sent a radiogram to President Roosevelt, while they were still anchored offshore, asking for sanctuary. They received no response.

After destroying the note, Elisabeth approached Judah and Sarah on the promenade deck. She whispered, "Let's rendezvous in an hour at the back of the ship," as she passed them.

When they met, Judah said, "I'm afraid the Gestapo will arrest us when we disembark in Hamburg."

Seeing the despair in his eyes, Elisabeth tried reassuring him. "I'm sure negotiations are continuing to find a friendly port where you can land. Please try to be optimistic."

Knowing she was offering Judah false hope, Elisabeth returned to her cabin and fell on the bed crying.

Moments later, Mayer opened the door.

Damn, why didn't I lock it? She gazed up at him, tears still falling from her eyes.

He asked, "What's the matter?" as he walked over to comfort her.

"Will you still love me if I tell you something unforgivable?"

There was a knock on the door. It was the cabin attendant. Mayer tipped him, closed the door, and turned to face Elisabeth holding an unopened bottle in a bucket of ice and a corkscrew. "We're returning to the Fatherland, so I ordered champagne to celebrate."

Claus put the bucket on their writing table, took out the bottle, then grimaced while trying to dislodge the cork. It then blasted out, unnerving Elisabeth. Claus laughed watching the wine spurt into the air and onto the carpet. He filled their glasses with the escaping champagne, then turned to hand Elisabeth one of them. Claus appeared puzzled for a moment, then his expression lightened. "You can tell me anything, my darling, and I will still love you." He put down the bottle and glass, took Elisabeth's hands into his, and kissed them.

"I know I shouldn't feel sad for the Jewish passengers." Elisabeth looked at the floor then added, "But I'm worried the Gestapo will treat them badly when they land in Germany."

"That's not inexcusable, my love. You have a heart that's big enough to show concern for even them."

"Have *you* ever felt that way, Claus?" asked Elisabeth, looking into his eyes.

⌘⌘⌘⌘⌘⌘⌘⌘

I did, when Bruno feared the Gestapo would send Johannes Kaiser to Dachau. Bruno was overjoyed when I had him released. Elisabeth became upset when the Captain announced most Jewish passengers couldn't disembark in Cuba. Perhaps I can lift her spirits by admitting I'd showed concern for others.

⌘⌘⌘⌘⌘⌘⌘⌘

"Yes I have. However, I'd be in a great deal of trouble if my superiors found out."

Elisabeth's despair receded. "What did you do?"

"Are you sure you want me to tell you?"

"Yes, Claus, I do," said Elisabeth, tightening her grip on his hands.

"A Jewish family, the Kaisers, owned Der KleiderKaiser, a clothing store in Vienna. The SA staged a boycott, then a mob looted their place. A dear friend, who is Aryan, asked whether I could help them. I made it possible for him to Aryanize Der KleiderKaiser by buying it. He paid them a fair price, the store reopened, and he took them on as employees. Had I not done so, they would have lost their livelihood."

"You did that, Claus?" giving him a tender kiss on the cheek.

"Yes, and later on, when I found out the Gestapo was sending the owner's son to Dachau, I made it possible for him to leave the country. It made me glad when I learned he'd safely immigrated to Italy."

That evening, trying to fall asleep next to Claus, Elisabeth thought, *perhaps Claus does have a soul*. She reached over and gently touched his shoulder. He rolled over and took her into his arms. Elisabeth melted into his embrace. For the first time, Benjie Kornblum was not in her thoughts when they made love.

On the ninth of June, Judah secretly passed a note to Elisabeth telling her the *St. Louis'* passenger committee sent radiograms requesting safe haven to British Prime Minister Neville Chamberlain, the governments of France, Belgium, and Holland, and civic and religious leaders throughout Europe. The passengers paid for the radiograms by selling their jewelry, cameras, and clothes to crewmembers.

Four days later, Captain Schroeder received a cable from Morris Troper, the European director for the American Jewish Joint Distribution Committee, saying that the governments of Belgium, Holland, France, and England offered sanctuary to all the Jewish passengers.

After Captain Schroeder announced the news, the Jewish passengers organized a party to celebrate in the social hall. They cheered, cried, and embraced each other when one of them read Troper's cable aloud. Judah held Sarah tightly as he whispered, "I pray we aren't disappointed again when one or more of those countries change their mind."

Judah and Sarah rejoiced when they joined the 214 Jewish passengers entering Belgium. After disembarking, Judah fell to his knees and kissed the ground. He then stood up and joined the other passengers reciting the *She-Heheyanu* prayer once again.

20th June, 1939 - 10:00 AM - Berlin - Mayer Reports to Göring on the voyage of the St. Louis.

Göring's secretary called Mayer the morning he returned from the *St. Louis*. "The Reichsminister would like to see you."

He started toward his office with a smile on his face and a spring in his step. *Life always seems brighter after spending time with Elisabeth.* He slowed his pace. *I walked in on her crying, but her sadness lifted when I told her I rescued Johannes Kaiser from being sent to Dachau.* Mayer paused. *I also felt better after making that admission.*

He was still cheerful when Göring's secretary showed him into his office. "Herr Reichsminister, it's wonderful to be back in the Fatherland."

"Welcome home Claus. Come in and sit down," said Göring, as he stood to shake his hand. "How is the ever delightful Fräulein Elisabeth?"

"She's well and overjoyed to be home after our long voyage."

"Before getting down to business, I must ask when you will announce a wedding date."

There's nothing I'd like more. It seems Göring feels the same way. "We've talked about it, but aren't ready to set a date, sir."

"That will disappoint the Führer. He sees you as the ideal couple… an exemplary Nazi with classic Nordic features, marrying a beautiful Aryan princess bride. After the wedding, he hopes Elisabeth will become his goodwill ambassador to Britain, helping to convince the English that an alliance with us is in their best interest. One final word on this, be sure to invite the Führer when making your wedding arrangements. He wants to honor you both with his presence."

"Of course, Herr Reichsminister. You will also be one of our honored guests, and I hope you'll consider being godfather to our firstborn."

"That goes without saying, but you realize the wedding must come first." Göring broke into a hearty laugh, his chest heaving up and down, and his face turning bright crimson.

After recovering his composure, he continued. "Claus, I thank you for the many cables you sent from the *St. Louis*. They allowed me to keep the Führer informed about the voyage's progress. He was appreciative that your updates reached him ahead of the international press reports."

"As always, Herr Reichsminister, it was my honor to serve the both of you."

"The Führer decided that Germany must occupy Poland sometime this year. He is certain England and France will ignore our invasion as they did when we seized Austria and Czechoslovakia. Since I'm not convinced they'll do so, I proposed that you first visit England to gauge their probable reaction to an attack before Hitler makes a final decision, and he agreed."

"I'll be honored to do so, sir."

"Wait until August, Claus. That's a better fit with his plans."

12th July, 1939 – Vienna – 9:00 AM – Avram and Eszter Kaiser leave Vienna

Two months after the Nazis forced them to move into Vienna's Jewish district, Avram and Eszter's life under Nazi rule became more treacherous.

"I'm sick of being cooped up in this apartment," said Avram with a sigh. "If I don't go outside, I will…"

"… it's too risky. You know how the Nazis attacked our Jewish friends when they went out on the street."

"Don't be silly Eszter," barked Avram. "I came to no harm on the western front during the war. A short walk in Vienna won't be the end of me either." Then he left, slamming the door.

Avram's mood improved as soon as the cool morning air drove the musty apartment smell from his nostrils. Feeling better, he walked out of the Jewish District. Mayer felt guilty as he a kept walking. *I shouldn't have treated Eszter so badly. She was only thinking of my safety and is probably upstairs crying.*

He pivoted, bumping into a police officer following him. The officer fell to the ground with a loud thump. Avram helped him up saying, "I am so sorry, sir. I didn't mean to hurt you. Is there anything I can do?"

The officer's face turned red. "You're Kaiser, the Jew who owned Der KleiderKaiser, right?"

He replied, "Yes, I am," sorry he hadn't followed Eszter's advice to stay at home.

A tall man with a Nazi Party pin fastened to the lapel of his jacket pushed his way through the gathering crowd. "Make that Jew scum clean the street."

"Yes, do as he says. Get on your knees and begin," said the officer.

Avram answered without thinking. "Is that how you treat a soldier who battled Germany's enemies during the Great War?"

"I don't believe you fought in the war," answered the policeman, rolling his eyes. "The commandant will decide your fate." He grabbed Avram's shirt collar and pulled him toward the police station. When they arrived, he told the Commanding Officer, "This Jew says he was a soldier in the Great War. *I don't believe him.*"

"What proof do you have?" asked the commandant.

"Please release my right hand, sir, and I'll show you."

When the commandant nodded toward Avram, the arresting officer swaggered over to unlock his handcuff. Avram then bent down to pull up his right pant leg.

The commander gasped after seeing a large irregular gash that disfigured his calf. "You got that during the war?"

"Yes, and after I killed the French bastard who wounded me, three more came at me. I killed all three before they could take aim."

"Did they send you home?" asked the commandant.

"Yes, and it took eight months to recover. When I returned to duty, they wanted to give me a desk job, but I insisted on rejoining my regiment. That was the least I could do after being out of the war for so long."

The commandant and his men walked to the other end of the station, then looked like they were arguing.

Avram felt his chest muscles tighten when they returned. The commandant said, "A Jew died shielding me from a grenade, when I fought in the Great War. I know I should follow my officers' advice and send you to a concentration camp, but I'll show my gratitude for that Jew's sacrifice by letting you go." He pointed toward the door. "If any of my officers arrest you again, I *will* send you to Dachau."

Eszter had tears in her eyes when Avram walked in the door. She rushed up to him. “What happened? Where were you? I thought the Nazis killed you.”

He told her about his arrest and release from the police station. She tilted her head to one side. “But you weren’t shot during the war… were you?”

“No, but do you remember that ugly birth mark on my right calf?”

Eszter burst out laughing. “Those idiots believed it was a gunshot wound?”

“Yes, they did. It was the only thing I could think of.” Avram paused, walked over to Eszter, and took her in his arms. “I’m so sorry for being such a pig headed idiot. Can you ever forgive me?”

That evening, Avram and Eszter agreed they could no longer stay in Austria. Avram sent Johannes a brief letter telling him they were leaving Vienna. He didn’t mention the police station incident, or their having to apply for a permit to emigrate at the Rothschild Palace.

Avram and Eszter lined up for hours before gaining entry to the Palace. An officer handed him a form at the door. "Have this signed and stamped by all the Reich agencies inside. They'll tell you what to do next." He then pointed them to the first table. The local taxing agency representative combed through his records. Finding no taxes due he stamped and signed the form, then pointed Avram to the next table.

The room was deathly quiet, officials speaking in a soft monotone. Jewish pre-émigrés emulated their tone while answering questions. Avram and Eszter were about halfway through the maze of tables when Adolf Eichmann appeared. Avram recognized him from a picture in a newspaper article announcing his visit to Vienna.

Eichmann, sternly arrayed in his black SS uniform, and carrying a short black riding crop, weaved back and forth among the tables. Avram shuddered when he stopped next to a Hasidic Jew and waved his riding crop upward. After he stood up, Eichmann used his switch to steer him between the tables. The Hassid's mouth moved slightly, as if he were praying. They exited the hall through a door in Avram's direct line of sight.

The Reich utility agency representative finished his review of Avram's electric and gas bills, stamped and signed the form, handed it to Avram and pointed him to the next table. When he and Eszter sat down at the library representative's table, Avram saw Eichmann use his riding crop to steer the old man back to his wife's side.

⌘⌘⌘⌘⌘⌘⌘⌘

On their way out of the Palace Avram met the Hasid and asked, "Did Eichmann harm you?"

"No, he spoke in Yiddish, asking where I lived, and to where I will immigrate."

"Was he unkind to you?"

"No, he was most sympathetic, smiling throughout our conversation. However, I saw an emptiness in his eyes, making me believe he lacked a soul... that he would smile even as he thrust a knife deep into my heart."

⌘⌘⌘⌘⌘⌘⌘⌘

After the final representative signed and stamped Avram's form, an SS officer took it and directed the pair to another room. There, an official handed him a sheet of paper, and said, "Describe all the items you will take when you emigrate, along with its value." When Avram handed the completed form back, the officer said, "Our packer will check every item to make sure you were honest. Do you want to change anything before I look at it?"

After Avram said, "No," the official crossed out Avram's most valuable possessions and gave the form back to him. "Everything I disallowed belongs to the Reich. You may keep the rest. Wolfgang Dorst will come to your home and pack all the allowed items for you. You may leave now."

The excluded possessions were the family's valuable religious artifacts, including silver goblets to bless wine, and gold Chanukiahs to celebrate the eight-day Chanukah festival. They were in his families' possession for over four generations.

Avram became incensed at the thought of letting the Nazis steal his Judaica. As soon as he got home, he called Wilhelm Braun. "An SS officer at the Rothschild Palace ordered me to give up my family's most cherished religious works of art before I emigrate. The packer, Wolfgang Dorst, will take them when he visits my apartment. Will my Great War service excuse me from surrendering those treasured heirlooms?"

"I'll take care of it. Pack everything you want to take in suitcases. I'll pick them up tomorrow, have them stamped with official seals, and return them to you at the airport before you leave Austria."

On the day of his departure, Braun came to the airport and handed Avram the suitcases containing his Judaica. "My dear friend, it hurts me that you must suffer so at the hands of our government. You, and many of your Jewish brethren, risked your lives to protect our Fatherland during the Great War. I wish I could do more, but as you know, even these few things of value could land me and my family in a Gestapo jail."

"Wilhelm, you needn't apologize. You have my eternal gratitude for keeping Eszter and me safe during the Kristallnacht pogrom. Please go with my best hopes and wishes for you, and your family."

Avram and Eszter passed through the airport's security office. Soon after that, they were on their way to Milan, Italy.

25th July, 1939 – Kitchener Camp, Richborough Kent – Johannes finds a way out

Johannes had been at the Kitchener Camp for almost five months. He was in low spirits the day he arrived, but his mood improved when Doctor Phillip Hirsch, a close friend from Vienna, joined him there. Several weeks later, Phillip told him, "I'm getting married soon and would like you to be there."

"I'd be delighted and wish you all the happiness in the world. Is there anything I can do to help you prepare?"

He replied, "Yes," with hope in his voice. "I need a tuxedo."

"Are you serious? This is a transit camp."

"I know, but since I'm the Camp's Physician, Jonas May, the Director, made arrangements to host my wedding at his private club. His staff and their wives will wear formal clothes, so he wanted my fiancé and me to do the same."

Johannes examined his old friend's build, then asked him to turn around. "You're a little slimmer than me, but the same height. I brought my tuxedo from Vienna and will size it down for you."

"You're a lifesaver, Johannes."

Three weeks later, Jonas May sent a limousine to take Phillip, his fiancé, and Johannes to his private club. When Johannes got in the car he exclaimed, “Irma, what a surprise. You are Phillip’s bride?”

“Yes, sit next to me so we can talk.”

“When did you two meet?” asked Phillip.

“Johannes was one of my best friends, in Vienna. I saw him last in 1935 after I left Germany,” said Irma.

“Your accounts of Nazi violence against German Jews terrified me,” said Johannes. “If only I’d acted then, my family and I would have left Austria before the Anschluss.” He then turned to Phillip. “Did you meet Irma in Germany?”

“No, Jonas introduced us at a restaurant in Sandwich, where Irma is Maîtres D.”

“How bad was it in Vienna after the Anschluss?” asked Irma with a frown.

Johannes told her about his encounters with the Nazis, his experiences in Italy, and his relationship with Malka.

“Why isn’t Malka here?” asked Irma, scowling at Phillip.

“It’s not his fault,” said Johannes. “She lives and works in London. It was impossible for her to attend the wedding.”

"All right Phillip, but you must seat Johannes next to me, at the main table."

"We placed Jonas next to you. He made it possible for us to get married at his private club. We can't move him now, can we?"

"You're right, but make sure Johannes sits next to him."

What a perfect opportunity. Perhaps Jonas can order my release from the camp.

Jonas spoke little German, and Johannes still felt uncomfortable speaking English, so he made him aware of his presence with smiles and hand gestures.

The next day, Johannes asked a Viennese friend, with the best command of English, to go with him to Jonas' office.

"Mr. May, I sat next to you at Doctor Hirsch's wedding yesterday," said Johannes through his interpreter.

"Yes, I understand you and Irma were close friends in Vienna."

"That's right, sir."

"Can I do anything for you, Johannes?"

"Yes, I have a visa to enter Mexico, but cannot leave England until I complete my fashion design training in a London academy. Can you get me released so I can do that, sir?"

Jonas thought for a few moments. "Let me give the Under Secretary of State for Home Affairs a call. He's a close friend, and may help you."

After finishing his telephone call, Jonas turned to Johannes with a wide smile. "It's arranged. Do you have your passport with you?"

"Yes, sir," said Johannes, handing it to him.

Jonas wrote the following on a blank page:

The condition attached to the grant of leave to land is hereby varied so that the holder will emigrate from the United Kingdom on completion of his training.

Signed Jonas May, for Under Secretary of State, Home Affairs.

Johannes left the camp the next day and took a bus to London's East End, home to many Yiddish speaking refugees. He rented a small apartment, then found a job as a tailor working for another Viennese refugee. Missing Malka, he wrote her a letter inviting her to spend a weekend with him. She replied she would visit him that Saturday at about 11 in the morning.

Johannes eagerly awaited her arrival. There was a knock on the door and his heart jumped when he opened it. Malka's long black hair glowed under the single light hanging in the windowless hall. Her eyes glistened in the thin ray of sunlight shining through his apartment. Her smile was radiant, warming his heart.

Johannes kissed Malka's eyes, tasting the sweetness of her tears. She entered his room, and he closed the door. They walked to the bed together and made love. Two souls became one as they rediscovered each other.

Hours later, exhausted from their lovemaking, Johannes and Malka fell asleep in each other's arms. They exchanged their first words after waking up, alternately laughing at the funny things that happened to them since their last meeting, and crying tears of joy at being reunited.

"Malka, I can't live without you any longer," said Johannes. "We must get married soon or I'll go mad."

"Not yet, my precious. I asked the Billingsworths to bring my mother to England under the domestic helper program. She now works for them as their cook. They paid for my mother's passage from Vienna, and I volunteered to stay on until we work off those costs. That's the least I could do after all the kindnesses they've shown me."

"You're right. I'd have insisted on doing the same for my own parents." Johannes paused and took Malka's hands in his. "After we marry, I'll gladly share our home with your mother. She's alone and belongs with us."

Malka took Johannes in her arms. "You're a good man. Few would accept another's family member into their home sight unseen."

13th August, 1939 - Berlin – Mayer and Elisabeth discuss going to England

Two months after they disembarked the *St. Louis*, Elisabeth told Mayer she was planning to visit London.

"I also need to spend a few days there. The Reichsminister wants me to speak with our people at the embassy, and I'd like to meet your parents."

"They'd like to meet you. How about leaving later this week?"

"I have a few more loose ends to tie up, but Thursday or Friday would be perfect for me."

Elisabeth's expression deepened into a frown, "We've known each other for over a year, yet you've never mentioned your family. Are your parents still alive? Do you have brothers or sisters?"

Mayer looked down at the floor. "The last time I saw them was in 1926, at a party my parents threw to celebrate my brother Heinrich's graduation from Medical School."

"Why has it been so long?"

Mayer's eyes filled with tears when he replied. "Heinrich learned I became a Storm Trooper, at that party. Shocked by that news he gave me an ultimatum, leave the Nazis or we would no longer be brothers. I told him I would make any sacrifice in Adolf

Hitler's name to safeguard our Fatherland's rebirth. He kissed me and whispered 'so be it' in my ear. I haven't seen him since that day."

Is it possible? Could Claus be our Heinrich's brother?

⌘⌘⌘⌘⌘⌘⌘⌘

Mayer and Elisabeth sat together for a long time, saying nothing. He wondered how different his life would have been if he had never met Ernst Röhm. She wondered how different her life would have been if Claus had Heinrich's strong moral values. Both felt compelled to continue their pretense, fearing the worst if the other learned their true identity.

14th August, 1939 – Vienna – Wassermann confronts Schlossburg for not finding Heinrich Mayer

General Heydrich was furious when Heinrich Mayer's fugitives slipped through Wassermann's fingers at Vienna's Infectious Disease Clinic. Wassermann, eager to restore Heydrich's faith in him, asked Schlossburg to seek new clues to the escapees' hiding place. His boss gave him four. Wassermann pursued each one, but none of them led to the fugitives.

After the fourth aborted try, Wassermann barged into Schlossburg's office, planted his hands on his desk, and glared down at him. "It's been months since Mayer fled, and he's still at large because of your worthless investigative work. Perhaps General Heydrich should replace you with someone more dedicated to Adolf Hitler's dream of a Jew-free Reich."

Schlossburg exploded from his seat, baring his teeth. "If you *ever* dare address me with such disrespect again, I'll have you disciplined by the best in the Gestapo."

Wassermann stepped back and took a deep breath. "I apologize, Ernst, but you haven't given me a decent clue to Mayer's whereabouts in eight months. What makes you think you'll ever find him?"

"I trust in my instincts and have solved every case assigned to me. I *will* soon locate his hiding place." Schlossburg narrowed his eyes. "You acted like a hothead when you dealt with Heinrich Mayer. Had you remained clear-headed at Vienna's Infectious Disease Clinic, you would have apprehended him… and the General wouldn't be questioning *your* performance."

Wassermann turned and skulked out of his office.

The next day, Schlossburg's temper subsided, and he presented Wassermann with a new lead to the fugitive's whereabouts.

CHAPTER FOURTEEN – WASSERMANN SEEKS HEINRICH

15th August, 1939 - A Train on its way to Graz

"You look troubled, sir, if you don't mind me saying so?" said a woman sitting opposite Wassermann in a train hurtling toward Graz.

Annoyed at having his thoughts interrupted, he looked up intending to scream at her. His anger melted seeing her long blonde hair, smooth white skin, sky-blue eyes, and wearing a form-fitting black outfit.

"I don't mind at all, madam. I've been hunting a dangerous fugitive. My last four attempts to arrest him failed because of flawed intelligence. You saw me venting frustration at the source of that information."

"Oh, my, are you a police officer?"

"To put it more precisely," he replied with as much authority as he could muster, "I'm a Gestapo agent pursuing vicious Jewish fugitives." To his delight, her expression grew from admiration to reverence.

"You're a Gestapo agent tracking the vermin that would destroy all our Führer has done to restore Germany?"

"Yes, madam, and I'm delighted by your support. Too many citizens cringe when I approach them. They should be like you, secure knowing anyone loyal to Adolf Hitler has nothing to fear. I will purify the Reich so we can take our rightful place as the world's greatest nation."

Wassermann's companion raised her arm in the Nazi salute, followed by a crisp "Heil Hitler," which he returned. She then extended her hand saying, "May I shake your hand as a true loyalist to the Nazi cause?"

His breast swelled with pride as he replied, "Madam. My name is Peter Wassermann, and I am honored to make your acquaintance."

"I'm Ingrid Stoller, and the honor is all mine. Where will you apprehend those criminals?"

"In Graz, Ingrid, if I may call you that?"

"Please do, I live in Graz and work at the Medical University. What can I do to help you?"

"I believe Doctor Heinrich Mayer, the fugitive I am seeking, is there." He fished in his jacket pocket and pulled out a picture. "Have you seen or met this man?"

"Oh my dear," replied Ingrid, the blood draining from her face. "I know him well, but his name isn't Mayer, it's Kupp. He joined the University earlier this year, and treats patients with communicable diseases. They seal his clinic off to keep them from spreading."

"That's him," said Wassermann, as he moved over to sit next to her. "That filthy scum changed his name to evade capture. He ran a similar facility in Vienna and escaped as we were closing in on him."

"What can I do to help you bring him to justice?"

"I *will* need your help, but must first tell the conductor to cable my men in Vienna. After they get to Graz, we'll work up a plan to arrest Mayer. In the meantime, perhaps you can suggest a nice restaurant where we can eat lunch."

"I know just the place. It's a short walk from the railroad station, and even closer to my apartment. How about having a glass of wine there after lunch?"

"I would enjoy that," said Wassermann, raising his hand to hail the conductor. He penned a note to his agents and handed it to him. "At our next stop, send this cable to Vienna's Gestapo headquarters. It concerns a critical national security matter." He took out his Gestapo badge to show his identity.

The conductor took the note, gave a straight-arm salute, and barked "Heil Hitler."

The train made several more stops. When they arrived in Graz, Wassermann approached the stationmaster, identified himself, and asked when his Gestapo agents would arrive. "They'll get here at six-thirty, sir." Wassermann asked Ingrid to write her address on his business card and handed it to the stationmaster. "When they pull in, direct them to this location."

Someone knocked on Ingrid's door at seven. "Are you ready for us, sir?" asked Max Littner.

Wassermann shot out of bed. "Get us a table for six in the restaurant. It's to your left after leaving this building. I'll meet you there in a few minutes."

"Yes sir," replied his four agents in unison. Heintz added, "Take your time, boss. We'll order a drink while we wait." A snicker wafted through the door.

"Oh my, your men are brazen."

"Boys will be boys, but they'll be laughing on the other side of their faces before we're finished with this assignment."

She covered her mouth and giggled. "We had fun this afternoon. Allow them to have their little joke in peace. They're very jealous of you."

"You're right, I'll let it go this time."

"We have Mayer and his nest of Jews where we want them," said Wassermann as he sat down with his agents in the restaurant. "Miss Stoller will soon be here. She is bringing a blueprint of the hospital's layout to show us the location of all the hideout's exits. After that, we'll decide how to execute our mission."

"Right on cue," said Ingrid, approaching Wassermann's table with a smile. He and his four agents stood. After Wassermann introduced her, she bent over the table, smoothed out a large drawing, pointed out Heinrich's hiding place, and described the best way to reach each of its exits.

"We're in luck," said Wassermann. "The clinic has only three avenues of escape. Heintz, you cover the outside door on the east; Littner wait at the outside door on the north; and, the rest of us will attack through the inside entry. We'll meet here for breakfast at seven." Turning to Ingrid, he continued. "Would you like to join us, then direct us to the Medical University?"

"Yes."

The next morning, Wassermann, his agents, and Ingrid set out for the hospital in a large automobile he'd borrowed from Graz's Gestapo headquarters. He asked her to let him know when they were getting close to the hospital.

Five minutes later, Ingrid said, "We'll be at the Medical University after turning right at the next street."

Wassermann parked and had everyone congregate next to the car. "Ingrid, please show Littner and Heintz the best way to their exits." After she did, he told the pair, "We'll break down Mayer's inside door at nine, then get ready to capture anyone who tries to escape. If you have no questions, walk to your posts."

They both said, "Yes sir," as they left.

"Ingrid, please come into the hospital with us, point out our best route to the clinic, then go to your office."

Pouting, she said, "But, I was hoping to join you for the arrest."

"It's dangerous, and you're too important to the Nazi cause."

Ingrid beamed. "Do you think so, Peter?"

"Of course my dear, we couldn't have organized this operation without your help."

Ingrid, Wassermann, Franz Schwartz, and Werner Schmidt entered the hospital at eight fifty five. Ingrid directed them toward the clinic, then turned and left. Less than a minute later she came running up behind them, whispering, "Peter, Peter, stop, you must stop."

He and his two agents turned to face her.

"I saw a frequent clinic visitor enter the hospital. He's following me. Let's hide in this office until he passes, then you can push your way in when they open the door for him."

Someone walked past the office as Ingrid was closing it. He didn't appear to see her.

⌘⌘⌘⌘⌘⌘⌘⌘

There was a knock at the clinic door using a prearranged pattern. Otto, who was closest to the entrance, asked, "Heinrich, should I get that for you?"

"Yes, I'm inventorying medical supplies. Check through the view hole. If it's a friend, open the door. Tell me when it's safe."

⌘⌘⌘⌘⌘⌘⌘⌘

Wassermann heard someone knock twice, three times, and then once. He then heard what sounded like a small door opening and remembered the view hole in Mayer's Vienna hideout. *I have you now, you Jew-loving bastard. You're not getting away from me this time.* "Is everyone ready? We go on my signal," whispered Wassermann. "Ingrid, go to your office."

Ingrid pouted, but said nothing.

⌘⌘⌘⌘⌘⌘⌘⌘

Otto recognized Willy, smiled, and opened the door, saying, "It's good to see you Willy." He then clasped him in a friendly hug, blocking the entry. When Otto let him go, and the door was closing, Wassermann kicked it open. He and his men raised their guns and pushed the pair into the hideout.

"Not a word or I'll shoot," growled Wassermann in a low whisper. "Put your hands on your heads and face the wall."

⌘⌘⌘⌘⌘⌘⌘⌘

Heinrich listened for the laughter and friendly banter that always accompanied Willy's visits, but there was none. He stopped inventorying, crawled closer to the main entrance, and heard shuffling feet and whispers. Acting on instinct, He crept back into the clinic, then dashed toward the east exit.

⌘⌘⌘⌘⌘⌘⌘⌘

"Tie these two up, Schwartz," whispered Wassermann, "while I check for others."

In the next room, he saw the tops of two heads behind a large couch. "Come out from behind there. I won't hurt you if you don't resist."

An elderly couple stood up, and she asked, "Is my Otto all right?"

"We won't harm him, so long as you do everything I say." Wassermann turned to Schmidt. "Tie this pair up while I look for others."

⌘⌘⌘⌘⌘⌘⌘⌘

Heinrich opened the east door and gasped. A snarling Gestapo agent was aiming a gun at him. "Don't even think about escaping. Turn around and raise your hands or I'll shoot."

⌘⌘⌘⌘⌘⌘⌘⌘

Wassermann saw nobody in the other rooms. He spotted a sign pointing to the north exit and followed it. When he opened the door, Littner turned to face him. "No one came this way. Did you capture anyone?"

"Yes, we have four in custody. Wait here a few more minutes, then join us."

Wassermann took a few steps toward the east exit when Heintz yelled, "Stop, you bastard," and a shot rang out. He ran toward the gun blast and found Heintz outside the east exit standing over a body lying face down in a pool of blood. “The bastard tried to run,” said Heintz. “All it took was one shot. I got him through the heart.”

Wassermann used his right foot to turn the body face up, then shrieked. “Damn it, that’s Mayer, the Jew-loving pig. I’d have given anything to spend a few hours getting back at him for the trouble he caused us. Can you believe it, he’s Oberst Mayer’s brother? Claus is one of our finest patriots, and his brother is the worst traitor.”

“How do you know Oberst Mayer isn’t in sympathy with him?” asked Heintz.

“The Gestapo kept an eye on them for years. They never caught them together and didn’t even find a note passed from one to the other. It’s all for the best. This pig is dead, giving us more time to find other traitors. Dispose of the corpse, Heintz. If the resistance finds his body they’ll make a martyr of him.”

“It’ll be my pleasure, sir.”

Wassermann walked back into the hideout and gathered all his agents. “Help me return these prisoners to Vienna. They may be the key to arresting more troublemakers.”

CHAPTER FIFTEEN - CLAUS AND ELISABETH GO TO ENGLAND

16th August, 1939 – London – 9:30 AM - Elisabeth meets with Turnbey

Elisabeth felt out of sorts for several weeks. She was irritable, tired, and nauseous. Certain her symptoms were remnants of a lung infection she caught after disembarking the *St Louis,* she didn't mention it to Mayer.

Heydrich's airplane whisked Mayer and Elisabeth to London Airport. They landed at eight in the morning. When their limo stopped at the German Embassy, Elisabeth said, "I'll go shopping, spend time with my parents, and pick you up here at noon. After that, we can enjoy the weekend at my parents' beach house."

"That sounds perfect," said Claus, removing the Nazi Party Swastika pin from his jacket collar. "It's best if I don't wear this until we get back to Germany."

She kissed him and he got out. After he disappeared into the building, Elisabeth ordered the driver to drop her off at a store several miles from MI6 headquarters. She told him to pick her up there at eleven thirty, then hailed a cab and walked into MI6s 54 Broadway offices at nine thirty.

"I didn't expect you so soon," said Reginald Turnbey, greeting her in the reception hall. "It's good you're early, we have a great deal to discuss. When are you planning to see Mayer?"

"He's meeting with his people at the German Embassy. I'll pick him up there at noon, then we'll spend the weekend at the beach." She took documents from her bag and handed them to Turnbey. "To save us time, I've drafted this list of items Heinrich needs for his Graz hideout."

He looked at the list, then faced her. His expression was grim. "We decoded a communiqué from Willy Labandter. The news isn't good. He's on his way to warn Heinrich that a Gestapo agent may soon arrive in Graz to arrest him and his fugitives."

When she winced Turnbey asked, "What's the matter?"

"Last week, Claus told me he has a brother named Heinrich. It may just be a coincidence, but he's a doctor who loathes the Nazis. Can we check whether Claus' brother is our Heinrich Mayer?"

Turnbey leaned back in his chair, stroking his beard. "What could you do with that information?"

Elisabeth said nothing, turning her head away.

He walked around his table, pulled up a chair, and sat down in front of her. She gave him a pained smile.

"What have you done? Did you allow your love affair to become more fact than fiction?"

She felt like the ground was sinking beneath her.

"You must know how important it is to keep your feelings hidden while in the field. If you're not careful, Mayer will discover your identity as an agent."

"You're right, Reg. I apologize. My emotions have been out of control. I don't know why." Her eyes teared.

"You *have* fallen in love with him, right?"

Elisabeth looked down, "Yes."

Turnbey strode back and sat down in his chair. "We must decide whether it's safe for you to return to Germany as an agent. I will ask you a few questions. Answer them carefully. Your life depends on it."

Elisabeth looked at him. "Please go ahead."

"Do you want to continue working for us as Elisabeth Billingsworth? If not, you can have your identity back and spend the rest of your life as a civil servant somewhere in the British Commonwealth. Your father could join you, and you'd never have to spy for us again."

"No, that's out of the question. The Nazis accept Elisabeth as a bona fide supporter of their regime. I can't give up on her now. It would be unfair to all the Jews I could still rescue from those monsters."

"Are you sure?"

"Yes, I'm sure."

"Second question: Can you become more detached about your relationship with Mayer?"

Elisabeth looked away from Turnbey for a few moments, then faced him again, her jaw set. "Absolutely not. If I'm in the same room with Claus and don't express my love for him in so many ways… a touch, a look, a special smile… he'd know something is wrong."

"If he discovers you're an MI6 agent, would Mayer tell the Gestapo?"

Elisabeth answered immediately. "No, he knows what they would do to me, and I sense he loves me too much to let that happen. Also, Claus could be questioning his loyalty to the Nazis."

"What makes you say that?"

"I became despondent when the *St. Louis* turned for Germany with all the Jews still on board. Claus caught me crying in our cabin and asked why I was so sad. I told him I feared for the safety of the Jewish passengers and asked whether he'd ever felt the same way. He confided that he'd helped a Jewish family in trouble with the Nazis on two separate occasions. Had the Nazis discovered either incident, they would have dismissed him." She paused for a moment. "They could have shot him as a traitor."

Turnbey stroked his beard for several minutes, then looked Elisabeth in the eye. "I believe you've made the case for returning to Germany as an MI6 operative. Do you agree?"

"Yes I do."

"We must still discuss how you'll manage your relationship with Mayer, but that's best left for another day."

There was a knock at the door. Turnbey's secretary walked in and said, "Minister Churchill found out Miss Billingsworth is here and would like to meet with her at around eleven. Is that possible?"

"Yes, I'll talk with Ian until then," answered Elisabeth.

16th August, 1939 – London – 9:30 AM - Mayer meets Winston Churchill

When their limousine stopped at the German Embassy, Mayer kissed Elisabeth and got out. He walked into the building, talked with the reception desk officer for a few minutes, then headed back to the front door. *I wonder what Elisabeth would think if she knew I was meeting with Winston Churchill's aide*. Seeing that her taxi had left, he went outside, found a payphone, took a slip of paper out of his jacket pocket, dropped some coins in the slot, dialed a number, and spoke in German. "My name is Claus Mayer. May I please speak with Mr. Ian McAllister?" The operator switched him to someone speaking German. He repeated his question, listened for a moment, and then replied, "Yes, I'll be glad to hold."

When Ian answered, he said, "I'm Claus Mayer. We talked in Munich last year and agreed to seek each other out if the occasion presented itself. I'm in London, have a few hours to spare, and wondered whether we could get together?"

"I'll be with my boss at ten. We could talk until then." McAllister was silent for a moment, then added, "Come to think of it, Churchill might be interested in meeting you."

"Tell me where you're located and I'll take a taxi."

"It's best if I send a car for you. You'd be in a heap of trouble talking German to a London cabbie now."

Less than half an hour later, Ian met Mayer in the entry hall at 54 Broadway. He escorted him past a sign marked Broadway Press, and they made their way to his office. "It's a pleasure to see you again," said Ian as they sat. "What's on your mind, Claus?"

"This may be a perfect time for us to trade information, as we did in Munich. I have it on good authority that Hitler will soon launch an invasion. Does that surprise you?"

"Not really," said Ian with a smile.

"What will Chamberlain do if we attack?" asked Mayer, leaning toward him.

"I don't know, but he risks losing his seat as Prime Minister if he *doesn't* take action. Mr. Churchill, a rival for his position, has often insisted that Parliament take a strong stand against Nazism. If Chamberlain refuses to act against Hitler's aggression, Churchill will surely replace him as Prime Minister. Believe me when I say Winston has the ability, will, and backbone to see England victorious against Hitler, no matter how long it takes."

"Well said, Ian," trumpeted Churchill as he breezed through Ian's door and sat down next to Mayer chomping on his trademark cigar. "I understand you wanted to meet with Ian, Herr Mayer. What's the nature of your visit?"

Ian translated Churchill's question into German, then summarized their discussion in English, for him.

"So, Herr Hitler thinks he can gobble up more European real estate without upsetting the British, huh?" asked Churchill, in a mocking tone. "Had I been the PM at Munich, I'd have told your Führer where to shove his fucking pact."

"It's a distinct pleasure to meet you, Mr. Churchill. About Munich, your Prime Minister handed my Führer valuable real estate without so much as a whimper. Hitler now believes Chamberlain is reluctant to act against Germany, regardless of what he does. Failure of the Evian Conference *convinced* him that the democratic world loathes the Jews as we do, but lacks the backbone to do anything about it."

Churchill took the cigar out of his mouth and responded in a soft monotone. "Do you really believe that bucket of horseshit you slopped all over my brand new shoes?" His eyes closed to a squint as he glared at Claus.

Churchill's intensity surprised Mayer. Copying his intonation, he replied, "I do. The facts speak for themselves."

Churchill glowered at Mayer for a few more moments, then laughed so forcefully he had trouble catching his breath. "Ian, get me a damn drink, will you?"

McAllister pulled a bottle of whisky from his credenza, filled half his glass, added water, and handed it to him. Churchill drank the entire glassful as if it were his last, put it down, and turned to face Mayer. "Where did you find this fellow, Ian? I like him. He may be a Naaaazi, but I *still* like him." Göring later told Mayer that Churchill drew the word Nazi into an insulting taunt, knowing how it infuriated Hitler.

"That's high praise coming from you, sir," said Ian, slanting his head.

"All right, Mayer," continued Churchill, "let's get down to brass tacks. Are you bastards ready to exterminate every Jew that doesn't get out of your way?"

"What makes you say that, Mr. Churchill?"

"I have my sources. Now answer the damn question."

"Before responding, sir, tell me *why* you care."

"Because I have immense respect for the Jews; it borders on love for the buggers. They enriched every civilization that allowed them in, and their reward was never-ending persecution. You must know they survived every people that tried to annihilate them. What makes you think your civili…" Churchill paused for a second, "… your regime will be any different?"

Mayer squared his back and replied, "Because it's a question of us, or them. They are at the root of all our problems. When they're gone, we'll be free to build our Thousand Year Reich."

"BULLSHIT," bellowed Churchill, his eyes burning with rage. "You can't believe that crap. It worked on the illiterate Russian peasants, and appears to work on your people, but it's a damn load of horseshit. There aren't enough Jews in the world to cause problems anywhere... especially in your Naaaazi police state.

"Hitler won't stop after conquering Poland," continued Churchill. "He'll order his Wehrmacht into Russia, and all its bordering states. If he's successful, he'll add millions to his Jewish population. What will he do then? Exterminate them all. It's too ridiculous to contemplate. Even your lame brained Führer isn't that wacky. Get me another drink, Ian."

After downing his second drink, Churchill stood up, strode over to Mayer, and extended his hand. "It's been a distinct pleasure meeting you, Mayer, and I hope we meet again. Give my best wishes to Miss Billingsworth. I can understand what she sees in you."

Astonished, Mayer stood to shake Churchill's hand and mumbled, "How…"

"… how do I know her? Elisabeth's parents and I run in the same social circles, so it's been my pleasure to know her since she was a child bouncing on my knee." Churchill then marched out of the room.

"Quite a whirlwind, that man, huh?" said Ian.

"I'm more than impressed, though he could launder his language." Both men laughed.

A few minutes later, they heard sounds of a disturbance outside and Churchill burst back into the room. "Damn it, Claus that's *not* all. I can see you're a decent fellow. I saw it in your eyes right off, and won't take my leave of you until we come to an understanding."

Mayer hid his surprise at Churchill's sudden return.

"You Naaaazis hate *all* Jews regardless of where they are, but if they're dead, or live elsewhere, you dislike them a little less. Does that sum up the Naaaazi view, Claus?"

"Yes, Mr. Churchill, it states our position."

"Then Hitler must slaughter every Jew he inherits. What choice does he have? Will he grant them German citizenship? Of course not, He built the Concentration Camps all over his Reich to punish any Jew unable or unwilling to leave. With that in mind, will you blindly follow your Führer's orders, no matter how heinous they become?

"Now on to our understanding. If your Führer launches a new war, England will kick your Naaaazi butts into the last century... and that's true even if the rest of the free world doesn't join us. It may take years, but when we're done, our troops will crap all over your Naaaazi flags right in the middle of fucking Berlin. After that, you'll pay for every Jewish life you took on your unholy quest. Let me repeat that, just in case I wasn't clear. We will hunt down and hang every fucking Naaaazi who took part in the 'annihilation of the Jewish race in Europe'. None of them will survive to tell their grandchildren how much fun it was murdering Jews. Is that clear?"

"Yes sir, abundantly clear," replied Mayer without wincing... openly. On the inside, he trembled, knowing he'd have to share Hitler's responsibility for the slaughter of countless helpless Jews.

"One final thought, Claus," said Churchill, looking deeply into his eyes. "You're not like those other inbreds in Berlin. You undoubtedly followed orders that would make the skin of any normal person crawl, and ignored your conscience until now, but once those acts become horrific enough your inner voice will awaken. It may have already done so. I know, because I can see it in your eyes. I'm also convinced Elisabeth couldn't love someone who thinks like those evil sons of bitches in Himmler's SS.

"Heed my words, don't get sucked any deeper into that viper's nest created by your Führer. Instead, use your position of power to fight his regime. Few others would dare, but I know you have the bollocks to do it. When you're ready do so, contact Ian. I'll be Prime Minister soon, and could use a level-headed fellow like you on my side."

⌘⌘⌘⌘⌘⌘⌘⌘

Churchill stood, walked over to Claus, bent down, and shook his hand. At that moment both men sensed the highest level of respect possible between two people.

Churchill prayed Claus would heed his warning.

Claus prayed for the strength to do it.

Churchill gave Claus a pat on the cheek, stood up, and walked out of the room.

16th August, 1939 – London –11:00 AM - Elisabeth meets with Winston Churchill

“Miss Billingsworth is here to see you,” said McAllister’s secretary.

McAllister walked to his door and shook Elisabeth’s hand. “Come in and take a seat. Minister Churchill was in meetings all day. I expect him at any moment.”

“It’s wonderful to be back in England, but this may be my last time.”

“You’re right. I met with Claus earlier today. He confirmed Germany would soon launch an invasion.”

“Claus...” muttered Elisabeth. “... Claus Mayer?” she repeated loudly, her eyes wide open.

“Yes, we met in Munich last year...”

Churchill strode in, interrupting McAllister. He walked over to Elisabeth, who was now standing, shook her hand, and sat down next to her.

“I had the pleasure of meeting your friend Claus Mayer earlier today.”

“You too?” said Elisabeth with a gasp, as she took a seat.

“Yes, and I’m more than impressed with him.”

"I don't understand."

"As I was saying before the minister joined us," interjected McAllister, "Claus and I met in Munich. We exchanged information and agreed to meet again when the opportunity presented itself. Well, he called me this morning, and I arranged for a car to pick him up at the German Embassy."

"That scoundrel, he never told me."

"It's best if you don't let him know we met," said Churchill. "He isn't aware you're with MI6, right?"

"That's right, sir. What did you discuss?"

"We had two conversations. First, we discussed Herr Hitler's planned invasion of Poland. Then I left the room, turned our tête-à-tête over in my mind, and returned."

"Why, sir?"

"I'm a good judge of character. Claus Mayer strikes me as a decent fellow, not a run of the mill Naaaazi. As we talked, I realized his conscience is beginning to bother him."

"How did you conclude that, sir?" asked Elisabeth, leaning toward Churchill.

"I saw it in his eyes when I told him his Führer must murder Jews by the millions after conquering Poland and Russia. That was when I sensed he may be on the verge of rebelling against Hitler."

"Are you certain?"

"I can't say I'm certain, but many years of experience tell me it's a real possibility. I also told him his sense of right and wrong would soon bother him and suggested he contact Ian when that day comes."

"You did? What was his reaction?"

"He didn't dismiss it, but I got the impression he'd agree to my offer if an unpredictable event turned him against the Naaaazis."

Churchill's answer intrigued Rachel. "How do you think I should treat him when we meet later today?"

"First, I need to know the nature of your relationship?"

"It's complicated, sir."

"Just put it into words, Elisabeth. I'll tell you if I have trouble understanding any part of it."

"He invaded our home during the Beer Hall Putsch and physically abused my father. Although I detested him, it was my responsibility, as an MI6 agent, to set aside my feelings to make him fall in love with me. I forced myself to sleep with him during a weekend we spent together in Lausanne after the Evian Conference."

"Did you still hate him, at that point?"

Rachel was silent for several moments, collecting her thoughts. "I wouldn't call it hate, but it wasn't love either." Elisabeth then lapsed into silence.

"Go on," said Churchill.

"Claus walked in after the *St. Louis* had turned east, returning over 900 Jews to Germany. I was crying in our cabin and he asked why I was in tears. I replied it saddened me that the authorities would mistreat the Jews when they disembarked."

"What was his reaction?"

"I expected him to reprimand me, but he didn't. He said my response was understandable... which took me by surprise. When I pressed him, Claus confessed he'd helped a Jewish family in trouble with the Nazis on two occasions."

"How did you feel about that?"

"The MI6 agent in me became convinced Claus was transforming himself into a better person, someone I could love. But the young woman he'd wronged during the Beer Hall Putsch still wouldn't accept him."

"How about when I said Claus' conscience may emerge?"

"It *confirms* he's becoming a better person, but Claus must prove he's turned his back on the Nazis before I can open my heart to him."

"When you're together later today show him you love him. That will make it easier for him to turn against his Führer."

CHAPTER SIXTEEN -- CLAUS AND ELISABETH

20th August, 1939 – London – 8:30 AM - Mayer and Elisabeth return from the beach

After meeting with Churchill, Elisabeth took a cab to rendezvous with her limousine and ordered the driver to pick Mayer up at the German Embassy. The limo returned them to Elizabeth's mansion, where they got into her car. Mayer then drove them to the Billingsworth's beach house in Southwold.

Elisabeth forgot about MI6 for three glorious days, during which she felt like she was living in a fantasy world. Silver sand, blue water, candlelight dinners, moonlit walks, and interludes of lovemaking that elevated her to levels of sensuality she never knew existed.

After their weekend, Mayer drove them back to Elisabeth's mansion. A beautiful young maid met Elisabeth at the door. Speaking in German, she said, "Welcome home Fräulein Elisabeth. My name is Malka. My mother and I work for your parents. They sent us to take care of you while you are here. Your father asked that you call him as soon as you get home."

"Thank you, Malka. Herr Mayer will also stay while I'm here. He's bringing in our baggage. Please show him to his bedroom while I call my dad. He's in the blue bedroom, at the top of the stairs, and I'm in the next room on the right."

Elisabeth went into the library, opened a hidden panel, stepped into a soundproof room MI6 built for her, closed the panel, and called Turnbey on a secure phone.

"Do you have any updates?"

"Yes, I learned our Heinrich *is* Claus's brother."

"How about Willy Labandter, did he arrive in time to warn him about the Gestapo agent?"

"He got there too late. The Gestapo broke into the hideout."

"So Heinrich, Willy, Otto and his parents are now Gestapo prisoners?"

"The Gestapo killed Heinrich. The others are prisoners."

"Are you sure? How do you know he died?" asked Elisabeth in a shaky voice.

"Someone who escaped capture told us. She couldn't see what happened, but heard everything. When Heinrich attempted to escape, a Gestapo agent ordered him to stop, then shot him in the heart."

"Who killed him?"

"All we know is at least three Gestapo agents raided the hideout."

"Who told you Heinrich died?"

"Hertha Rheinbaum, Heinrich's head nurse. She hid when the Gestapo attacked. Hertha was never an agent, but adored Heinrich and wanted to work with us after he died." Turnbey remained silent for a few moments, then said, "You know who Willy Labandter is, right?"

"I coordinated Siegfried Mannheim's escape to England after Kristallnacht. He underwent facial surgery, and we changed his name to Willy Labandter. He knows more about our Austrian underground network than anyone else in MI6."

"If the Nazis break him, they could destroy that entire operation."

"What's the likelihood of that happening?"

"It's just a matter of time. The Nazis are experts at using torture to make their captives talk."

"How about Otto and his parents, are they all right?"

"Yes they are, at least for now."

"We *must* get them out of there, and I could help," said Elisabeth.

"I'm listening."

"When I was with Churchill last week, he told me he met with Claus. It was his impression that an unforeseen event could turn him against Hitler. If that's true, Heinrich's murder, at the hands of the Gestapo, may help me convince him to work with us… but I'd have to divulge my identity as an MI6 agent."

While she waited for him to respond, Elisabeth imagined Turnbey sitting back in his chair and stroking his beard. After several minutes he said, "MI6 director, Admiral Sir Hugh Sinclair told me Churchill wants Mayer to become our covert agent. I didn't think that was possible. However, your suggestion, to have Mayer work with us, changed my mind. It's a viable option, so go ahead."

"I can't tell him the bad news, then immediately ask him to become our agent. His brother's murder would weigh too heavily on his mind, making it difficult for him to take that second step. I'll tell him, let it sink in, then ask for his help with the rescue."

"I agree."

20th August, 1939 – London – 10:00 AM – Mayer learns of his brother's fate

Elisabeth began shivering as soon as she hung up the phone. She'd loved Heinrich as a brother since they first met two years earlier. His loss deeply saddened her. That, plus her fear Mayer would reject her, when she admitted her MI6 responsibilities, terrified Elisabeth. She forced herself to calm down before looking for him. She found him eating breakfast on the patio. "I'm glad you ate while I was on the phone."

He jumped up. "You look and sound like you saw a ghost." Mayer took her in his arms. She melted into his embrace, then stiffened up and gently pushed him away. "Claus, we must talk."

Mayer knit his brow as he held her at arms' length. He was about to speak when she put two fingers over his mouth and whispered, "Please, darling, don't say another word. Just sit and hold my hands."

When Elisabeth sat down, Mayer pulled his chair in front of hers. He then sat, cupped her small hands in his, lifted her fingers to his mouth, and kissed them.

"Claus, we've reached a moment few others must face. What I'm about to say may end our relationship."

Confusion showed in Mayer's eyes as she painstakingly recounted Rachel Goldstein's story, beginning with the Munich

Putsch, and ending when they met at Irena's welcome home party. He remained silent until Elisabeth finished. His eyes, which remained riveted on hers while she spoke, didn't move. "Why did you wait until now to tell me?"

"That's the hardest question of all, my dearest. Please be strong."

Elisabeth squeezed his hands. "I was on the phone with a dear friend. He told me your beloved brother, Heinrich… he was mur… the Gestapo… they… they… murdered him."

Mayer stared blankly at her, saying nothing. His voice was raspy when he finally said, "No… it can't be… that's impossible."

Still squeezing his hands, she whispered, "It's true, his head nurse heard the gunshot blast that killed him. She contacted MI6 as soon as it was safe and they told me."

Mayer frowned, then asked, "Why was he killed?"

"He'd been hiding Jewish fugitives for over a year."

Claus' face paled. "Of course he was. He always helped others, even if it meant risking his own life." He was silent for two minutes, then added, "When Heinrich was a child he was almost killed by an oncoming train while pushing a brute, who had often beaten him, to safety. Heinrich was always a much better person than me." His eyes filled with anguish as he added, "I need time to think."

"Let me know what I can do to help you."

⌘⌘⌘⌘⌘⌘⌘⌘

Mayer turned, walked slowly back into the house, and sat on the edge of the couch. He trembled as his mind reacted to news of his brothers' death. *Why did those bastards kill Heinrich? He was the best man I know.* The truth hit Claus like a thunderbolt. *I was responsible. Heinrich risked his life to rescue Jewish fugitives from Nazi hate... hate born of Hitler's obsessive dream to create a Jew-free Germany... a nightmare I eagerly supported. The strange prisoner was right. Why didn't I turn from evil long ago? Perhaps Heinrich would still be alive.* Claus felt his strength ebb. Tears fell freely from his eyes.

⌘⌘⌘⌘⌘⌘⌘⌘

Elisabeth followed Claus into the house. He was climbing the stairs one at a time, his shoulders hunched. The door opened, then closed. She sat down, uncertain what to do next. *I welcomed and feared this moment ever since I allowed myself to fall in love with him. He knows I am Rachel. Now I will find whether he loves me.* She looked up to heaven and whispered, "Please God, help me keep Claus' love." *How can I think only of myself? I must ease his despair.*

Elisabeth walked up the stairs and knocked gently on his door. The room remained deathly silent. She knocked a little louder, but heard no sound. Fear overcame caution. She turned the knob, opened the door, and walked in slowly. He sat in the dark. After turning on a small lamp, she saw his pale face and sunken eyes.

He stared at Elisabeth, saying nothing for over a minute.

She felt as if a strange force was ripping the heart from her body.

His expression lightened as he scrutinized every inch of her face. "Rachel Goldstein. I didn't know it sixteen years ago, but your goodness and indomitable spirit captured my heart on that dreadful night when I attacked you and your father. Then, last year, when Elisabeth Billingsworth entered my life, I instantly fell in love with her. That was no accident. We were always meant to be together."

Elisabeth's spirits soared hearing Claus's expressions of love. She sat down next to him and took his hand in hers. "I'm glad for every decision we made, whether consciously or unconsciously, that got us to this moment. Just think. The odds against us finding each other, and falling in love, were astronomical. You are a leader in Germany's Nazi Party, and I am a Jewess sworn to overthrow you and your regime. The fact that we sit here hand in hand, cherishing each other, defies all logic. Yet here we are." Elisabeth took Claus in her arms and hugged him.

"Thank God you are in my life," whispered Claus. "Loving you made me a better person."

Malka ran into the room. "Excuse me Fräulein Elisabeth; it's your father on the telephone. He needs to speak with you urgently."

"Please tell him I'll call back in a little while."

"Yes miss."

Elisabeth called Turnbey half an hour later. "Did you break the news to him?"

"Yes, but I still don't know whether he's willing to work with us."

"What did he say?"

"Thank God you are in my life. Loving you made me a better person."

"While that confirms nothing, it's better than a rejection."

"Did you learn more about the captives, Reg?"

"Yes, we must decide how to retrieve, or at least neutralize them."

"How can you consider killing them?" asked Elisabeth, dread in her tone.

"It's a last resort. If we rescue them that won't be necessary. However, if all other efforts fail, we must face the real possibility that Nazi torture will force Willy to divulge the identities of all our

Austrian operatives. You, of all people, must understand why we can't allow that to happen."

"Yes, I do," replied Elisabeth reluctantly. "Willy would prefer a quick death to revealing the names of his fellow agents under torture." She remained silent for a moment, then asked, "Did we hear anything about their condition and whereabouts?"

"Hertha Rheinbaum heard one of their captors say they would return them to the Rothschild Palace. Erik Blick is there. It's a good bet he'll be in charge of their interrogation."

"Erik Blick?" repeated Elisabeth.

"He's known as *The Grand Inquisitor*, a master in the art of torturing suspects. Few of his victims keep their secrets for long."

"That's terrible. We *must* get Willy out before he's interrogated." Elisabeth thought for a few moments. "Canaris is the only Nazi I know with the authority to release him. Do you know of anyone else?"

"No I don't. Is he willing to work with us?"

"He fed secret information to Churchill after Chamberlain signed the Munich Pact, but I don't know whether he'd be willing to help us rescue Willy." *Perhaps Churchill can hazard a guess*. She told Turnbey what she was thinking, then asked him to transfer her to Churchill's line.

Churchill answered. "Hello, Elisabeth. How was your weekend at the beach?"

"It was wonderful, sir." She then filled him in on Labandter's situation. "Canaris is our best bet to free him, but I'm unsure whether he would help us, or order my arrest. Based on your dealings with him, what do you recommend?"

The line was silent for over a minute before Churchill answered. "He detests Hitler, but remains a German patriot. If you ask for his help, do it *before* returning to Germany." Churchill was silent for another minute, then asked, "Will Mayer help you?"

⌘⌘⌘⌘⌘⌘⌘⌘

Elisabeth was on the phone with Turnbey when Malka walked up to Claus. He was relaxing in the living room. "Did you and Fräulein Elisabeth eat lunch today, Herr Mayer?"

"No we didn't."

"My mother is an excellent cook. She made a delicious Hungarian Goulash yesterday and could serve it when Fräulein Elisabeth finishes her call."

"That's a wonderful idea. She enjoys Hungarian cooking, and so do I."

Malka went into the kitchen and spoke in Hungarian to her mother. When she came back he asked, "You're Austrian, right?"

"Yes sir, I am."

"Have you been in England long?"

"I've been here since March, but had to leave my mother in Vienna. I told Elisabeth's parents how much I missed her, so they paid to bring her here a few weeks ago. Both of us now work for the Billingsworths, at their London mansion, to pay off her fare. They sent us here to take care of Fräulein Elisabeth while she's in England."

"Have you always worked as a maid?" ZZZ

"No, I was a seamstress in Austria."

"Why didn't both of you stay in Vienna?"

"Because we are Jewish. After we pay off my mother's fare, the Billingsworths will make it possible for us to remain in Britain. They do all they can to help Jewish victims of Nazi hate." Malka paused for a moment. "Being a good friend of Elisabeth's, you must know it was the Nazis who forced us to take refuge in England." She smiled, then looked at her watch. "If you'll excuse me, I must go upstairs to finish my chores."

⌘⌘⌘⌘⌘⌘⌘⌘

Claus went outside to the Japanese garden and sat on a bench. He thought about their Murano vacation when Elisabeth told him her parents hated the Nazi regime. *If they knew how willingly I supported the Führer's anti-Semitic campaign, they would oppose our marriage... and Elisabeth would honor their wish.*

Claus's emerging sense of right and wrong tugged at his heart. His decision, in 1926, to choose Nazism over the love of his family caused his brother's death. Now he faced another choice. Remain a loyal Nazi, and risk losing Elisabeth, or turn his back on a successful career for a chance to win her parents support.

20th August, 1939 – London – 7:00 PM - Elisabeth discusses the fugitives with Claus

When she got off the phone, Elisabeth joined Claus in the garden. "Hello darling, I'm thrilled you look so much better."

Claus smiled, rose from the bench, and hugged her. "I'm never better than when I see you."

Elisabeth sat down next to him and took a deep breath. "My MI6 boss told me the Gestapo agents who killed your brother also arrested four Jewish fugitives. They plan to interrogate them at the Rothschild Palace."

"Where was Heinrich hiding them?"

"Last year, I helped him set up a haven for Jews fleeing the Nazis in the Central Vienna Hospital. The Gestapo discovered that hideout, but Heinrich moved them to the refuge in Graz before they could raid it. Three of them were still there, with your brother, when he died."

"How about the fourth captive, was he also in hiding?"

"No, he went there to warn Heinrich that Wassermann, a Gestapo agent, would storm the shelter."

"Peter Wassermann?"

"Yes, do you know him?"

"I know of him. He's a loathsome character. Heydrich holds him in high regard because he is a fierce anti-Semite. How about the other three?"

"Otto Klein became a fugitive after rescuing an old man from two Nazis who attacked him. One of them, Rolf Heintz, drew a gun and Otto accidentally shot him with it when they fought. Heintz survived and pressed charges against Otto, implicating his parents so the Gestapo would also arrest them."

"The other Nazi was Franz Schwartz, right?"

"Yes, how did you know?"

"They're like hyenas, teaming up to commit monstrous crimes. Your friends picked the wrong Nazis as enemies."

"I suppose you are the *right* Nazi?"

"Of course," said Claus, pulling Elisabeth close to kiss her.

"Does MI6 want to rescue them?"

"Yes, and we need your help. Is that a problem?"

"How would I be involved?"

"Your participation makes it easier for us to plan and execute an escape since you know the physical layout of the Rothschild Palace and are familiar with the people who run it."

"One last question: will I take part in future MI6 operations?"

"Only if that is your wish. I can get my boss's assurance he won't use your involvement to blackmail you into further assignments. I trust him. He's a man of his word."

"That's unnecessary. If you confide in me to rescue the fugitives, I'll count on you to keep me out of trouble."

"So you'll help me rescue them?"

"If your parents knew how willingly I took part in Nazi persecution of the Jewish people, they would oppose our marriage, and you would honor their wish." He paused. "To prove my love for you, and win your hand in marriage, I will use my standing in the Nazi Party to help you thwart the Nazis and Hitler."

Elisabeth leaned closer and kissed Claus. "Is there anything you'd like to ask me?"

"I don't understand?"

"For a smart man, you can sometimes be dimwitted."

"Huh?"

"Must I say it for you?"

"Perhaps you should."

Elisabeth took his hand in hers and asked, "Will you marry me?"

"You *are* a forward little German-British hussy, aren't you?" said Claus before taking Elisabeth into his arms and kissing her.

Breathless, after a long kiss, she whispered, "I love you with all my heart, Oberst Mayer."

"Now let's get back to your problem," said Claus. "How do we rescue the prisoners?"

"We must enlist Wilhelm Canaris' help. He's the only person I know who can sign their release papers."

"You've worked with him since 1935. Why don't you call and ask for his help?"

"I don't know whether he'd risk his career to free Gestapo fugitives."

Claus remained silent for several minutes. "You're right. He may order the Gestapo to arrest *you*. We must confirm he won't do so before returning you to Germany."

"How can we do that?"

He was silent for several minutes, then said, "Call Canaris and tell him your childhood sweetheart… let's call him Cyril Gold… contacted an MI6 agent hoping he could help free his in-laws from the Gestapo." Claus paused. "It's been a long time since Gold heard from him, so he asked you to find out what happened. Tell Canaris that Gold isn't Jewish, but he married Otto's Jewish sister. After a week, I'll call a trusted Gestapo friend to find out whether Canaris ordered your arrest. That will decide whether you return to Germany. What do you think?"

Elisabeth called Canaris that afternoon. He remained silent while she told him about Cyril Gold, then said, "Let me check with Oster. He or I will call you."

Canaris called back an hour later. His tone was sober. She heard urgency in his voice.

"I'm leaving in a few minutes, so I'll be brief. First, the Gestapo will soon move the prisoners to the Rothschild Palace. The interrogation begins in three days. That's when Erik Blick returns to Vienna." Canaris was silent for almost a minute. He then spoke in a soft monotone. "If we are to succeed, we must trust each other. One of Oster's friends in the resistance told him you are his MI6 contact."

Elisabeth's heartbeat and respiration increased rapidly.

"Don't worry, we are allies against Hitler, but where does Claus' allegiance lie… with the Führer or with you?"

Elisabeth thought over the pros and cons of answering truthfully, then replied, “Claus is with me.”

“Good,” said Canaris, his tone registering surprise. “So here is how I propose we proceed.”

CHAPTER SEVENTEEN -- PREPARATIONS FOR WAR

22nd August, 1939 – The Eagles Nest – 11:00 AM – Canaris attends Hitler's meeting

Martin Bormann, Hitler's closest friend, built the Eagle's Nest at Berchtesgaden for his fiftieth birthday. That chateau-style structure, on a ridge in the mountains above the Village of Obersalzberg, served as a retreat to entertain friends and visiting dignitaries. On the twenty second of August, he met there with his military chiefs.

"My comrades," began Hitler, standing behind a huge map table. "Our day of destiny is at hand. In four days, the Reich will attack Poland, launching a historic campaign to make us master of all Europe."

"My Führer," interrupted Göring. "You must know such an invasion will lead to certain war with England and France."

"I agree," added Canaris from the rear of the room. "Are we prepared to wage a two front war with the Polish army in the east and the united English and French armies in the west?"

Hitler stepped back from the table and glared at his senior officers. "When will you fools realize I am not in the habit of losing wars?" His voice grew in intensity. "I won Austria, the Sudetenland,

and Czechoslovakia without firing a single bullet. The French and the British, who first objected to my territorial claims, soon realized I was in the right and conceded. This invasion will be no different." Hitler pounded the map table with his fist and repeated, "*This invasion will be no different.*"

Hitler's voice grew softer as he continued. "Mayer is in London gauging Britain's probable reaction to our invasion. He will report his findings before we launch our attack. Are you now ready for my report, or should we indulge in more useless banter?"

Nobody uttered a word.

"Everything I tell you this morning is confidential. The SS will kill six Buchenwald prisoners, dress them in Polish army uniforms, and transport them to a radio station in Gleiwitz, a German town on the Polish border. An SS officer will broadcast in Polish, saying he seized the radio station and is attacking Germany. The SS will leave the dead prisoners behind and return to their base. Then, we invade Poland. If Chamberlain and Daladier want to remain at peace, the Gleiwitz broadcast should give them the justification they need. Should they fight, our new *lightening war* strategy will have us in control of Poland before they can launch a counter-attack."

Hitler glared at a few of his military chiefs, then continued. "Our troops must not merely defeat the Polish. *They must annihilate them*. My SS deaths-head formations have orders to slaughter Polish men, women, and children, showing them no mercy. Only thus shall we gain the territory we need to house the German people." Hitler paused again, then said, "The SS will shoot *anyone* who interferes with my orders. Is that understood?"

A few officers replied, "Jahvohl mein Führer."

"Canaris," said Hitler. "You will go with Heydrich during the first few days of his Polish campaign, then report to me on how quickly his Einsatzgruppen cleared the conquered territories of their Jews and troublesome Catholics."

"Jahvohl, mein Führer," said Canaris.

Following the Berchtesgaden meeting, Canaris drove to nearby Munich and took a room at the Hotel of the Four Seasons. Before unpacking, he sat down to prepare a comprehensive summary of Hitler's invasion plans.

After double-checking his notes, he leaned back in his chair and closed his eyes. The last few days were exhausting. He welcomed a few minutes of quiet relaxation and fell asleep. A loud rap on the door woke him. He pulled out his service revolver and asked, "Who is it?"

"It's Hans."

Canaris holstered his weapon, opened the door, and greeted Oster. After he walked in, Canaris checked outside to see whether anyone saw him, then closed and locked the door.

"How was your meeting with Hitler?"

"It is as we thought. He'll attack Poland in four days. A sham radio broadcast, designed to make it look like the Polish started the war, will give Chamberlain an excuse to disregard Hitler's latest territorial grab."

"Did he announce plans to have the SS annihilate Polish Jews and Catholics?"

"Yes, he did. His general staff raised no objections, despite knowing Hitler will expose the Polish people to a living hell on earth."

"How can we stop this madness?" asked Oster.

Canaris gathered up his Berchtesgaden notes and handed them to him. "This summarizes Hitler's invasion strategy. Go to the Dutch Embassy, in Germany, and hand it to your old friend, the Military Attaché. Tell him I want copies distributed to the French and British military intelligence representatives in Berlin. They'll know what to do when they receive them."

"Do you think they will act with sufficient resolve to make Hitler cancel the invasion?"

“That is my hope. Only time will tell.”

Oster was heading toward the door when Canaris called him back. He pulled papers from his briefcase and handed them to him. “I also need you to deliver these documents to Claus Mayer at Vienna’s Rothschild Palace as soon as possible. They authorize release of four Jewish fugitives into his custody.”

⌘⌘⌘⌘⌘⌘⌘⌘

French Premier Daladier ordered troops along the Maginot Line to assume a war footing. The British mobilized their army and cancelled all leaves. The Admiralty put the British navy on full alert and brought all coastal defenses to battle readiness.

Both Daladier and Chamberlain publicly reiterated their promise to declare war if Germany attacked Poland. Hitler postponed his planned twenty-sixth of August invasion to review battle readiness plans and await Claus Mayer’s report on Britain’s probable reaction to his attack.

23rd August, 1939 –1:00 PM - Berlin – Claus reports to Göring on his meetings in London

The day after Claus offered to liberate Wasserman's prisoners, he flew back to Berlin in Heydrich's airplane. A limousine, waiting at the airport, took him to meet with Göring. Heydrich was with him when Claus joined them in Göring's office.

"Sit down, Claus," said Göring, "We are reviewing plans for the Polish invasion and should finish in a few minutes. Reinhard will be interested in hearing about your visit to London."

Claus shook hands with both men and sat down next to Heydrich. His blood ran cold as they continued. *What happens if they find out I freed four Nazi fugitives*? He calmed down thinking, *Elisabeth's agreement to marry me makes saving the prisoners well worth the risk.*

"Are you prepared to give us a report on your meetings in England?" asked Göring.

"Yes sir, I met Winston Churchill…"

"… you what?" interrupted Heydrich.

"I became acquainted with Ian McAllister, an aide to Churchill, before the Munich Sudetenland conference. I met with him last week to gauge Britain's reaction to our Polish invasion. Churchill walked in soon after we began."

"What was your first impression of him?" asked Heydrich.

"Our Führer is the only person who has a more powerful presence."

"What did the drunkard have to say?" asked Heydrich, with a smirk.

"He's aware we're planning to invade Poland, but doesn't seem to know when it'll occur. He's also convinced the Führer is serious about annihilating the Jewish race."

Heydrich leaned toward Claus. "Did he offer to help us?"

"No, Churchill swore Britain would defeat Germany, and then hang anyone who participated in the slaughter of our Jews."

"Don't worry," said Heydrich with a sneer, "The British are spineless. They don't stand a chance against our brave Aryan fighters. Churchill will change his tune after we conquer England and drag him to Berchtesgaden in chains. He'll stand there, hat in hand, begging for Hitler's mercy."

Claus smiled inwardly. *That's as likely as Adolf Hitler becoming a Jew.*

"Do you think the British will retaliate after we invade Poland?" asked Göring.

"Chamberlain will declare war. The French may not join him, but I'm certain the British will fight."

⌘⌘⌘⌘⌘⌘⌘⌘⌘

Following their meeting, Göring shared Claus' findings with Hitler. Undeterred, he set the first of September as the date for his Polish invasion. The Luftwaffe struck at dawn. A few hours later, the Wehrmacht attacked in force. France and Britain declared war on Germany two days later.

CHAPTER EIGHTEEN -- THE PLIGHT OF THE FUGITIVES

24th August, 1939 – Vienna – 9:45 AM – The interrogation begins

Wassermann was still in Graz when he discovered Blick couldn't interrogate the fugitives for several days. After dispatching the four of them to a nearby Gestapo facility, he left for a short vacation with Ingrid Stoller. He returned on the twenty fourth of August and ordered the Gestapo to deliver his captives to Vienna.

After hearing the detainees were at the Rothschild Palace, Rolf Heintz strode into Erik Blick's office. "Which Jew will you interrogate first?"

"I was planning on Labandter. Does it matter?"

"It matters to me. Klein left me for dead in the street. I want to make sure he pays for it."

"Give me time to think about it. I'll let you know."

"Come on Erik, you can work on Labandter later. What's the difference if you interrogate him last?"

"He strikes me as the most well-informed captive I've ever assessed for an interrogation. The others don't measure up the way he does."

"That's silly Erik, how could you tell?"

He didn't answer.

Heintz was walking out of Blick's office when he turned to face him. "You could torture Klein's parents in front of him. Then he'll be more likely to cooperate."

Blick salivated. "What an intriguing idea. If that's what you want, I'll interview him first."

⌘⌘⌘⌘⌘⌘⌘⌘

Otto Klein sat shackled to an armless metal chair in Claus Mayer's interrogation room when Rolf Heintz appeared. He walked behind him, then leaned down until his mouth was inches from Otto's right ear. "So you thought you could escape me?"

Otto didn't understand.

Heintz straightened up and walked around Otto to face him. "You don't remember me, do you?" He scowled, then raised his voice. "*You don't remember me, do you*?"

He replied in a measured and confident manner. "To tell the truth, I don't know you. You must have mistaken me for someone else,"

Heintz pulled a shiny black revolver from its holster and aimed it at his face. "Do you remember this, *Jew*?"

Otto's heart skipped a beat. He'd shot Heintz with that gun while saving Joshua Isaacson from certain death. "Yes, after shooting you I prayed for God to spare your life. He answered my prayer… you ungrateful lout."

Franz Schwartz burst into the room. Both of them attacked Otto like dogs fighting over a bone. Erik Blick stormed in less than five seconds later. "I told you bastards not to touch my prisoner. Get away from him or I'll have you both arrested."

The beatings bloodied Otto's face and nose, but his spirit remained unbroken. "You're at your best attacking helpless old men, or manacled young ones. You must be even more impressive assaulting little girls." Otto gave a hearty laugh, visibly infuriating both Schwartz and Heintz. They moved to resume his beating when Blick grabbed them by the collar and pulled them back. "Strike him again and I won't let you watch my interrogation. *Do you understand*?"

"Yes sir," said both of them clicking their heels in unison.

"Now be good little Nazis. Do what the nice man says," said Otto in a mocking tone.

Blick placed himself in front of Otto. "You watch your mouth or…"

"… or what, you'll torture me? Do your worst. I have a weak heart," lied Otto. "The better you do, the sooner I escape you pathetic apes, and your demented Third Reich. One day, you'll beg for mercy and shit in your pants on the gallows, waiting for the executioner to drop the trap door. *That* will be your crowning achievement as Nazis. Now get out of my sight, you pitiful cowards."

Sitting alone after they left, Otto Klein was pleased he had shown them neither respect nor fear. Eventually, he'd have to face torture and death, but that didn't matter. Having resigned himself to an honorable passing, he allowed himself to relax.

Otto felt calm when Schwartz and Heintz returned. Dread replaced tranquility when Schwartz dragged his parents into the interrogation room weighed down by metallic wrist and ankle restraints. The pair snickered as they pointed at Otto's anguished expression. Blick followed them in carrying a short black riding crop and closed the door. "What do you have to say, Klein? Who's begging for mercy and shitting in his pants now?"

Otto averted his eyes, silently praying for his parents' release.

"My beloved child, your mother and I are already dead. Say nothing to risk the lives of anyone able to…"

Gustav's words ended when Blick plunged the solid end of his riding crop into his mouth. Gustav fell to the floor with a thump, blood gushing from his lips. He coughed out three teeth.

Margarette spat on Blick as he walked past her. He turned toward her, wiping off the sputum. Raising his riding crop, he brought it down forcefully, stopping an instant before it ripped a gash in her left cheek. "I rarely disfigure my prisoner's faces." Turning to Otto he added, "but may make an exception later for your son's amusement." Facing Schwartz and Heintz he asked, "How would you gentlemen like to secure Otto's parents to their chairs?"

"We'd enjoy that," said Heintz.

Otto shuddered seeing the pair take pleasure in painfully binding his parents to their steel chairs. "Leave them alone. They know nothing. They have done nothing. Do what you want with me. Leave them alone."

Blick eased himself into a comfortable armchair to watch Gustav and Margarette struggle against their restraints. He straightened his clothing, then responded to Otto's plea. "Tell me what I need to know and your parents will receive medical care. I may even spare their lives. It's up to you."

"I know nothing. Hurting them won't help you. Just let them go."

Blick got up and left the room. Schwartz and Heintz followed him out.

Several minutes later, Blick returned alone. He strode over to Gustav Klein, removed his foot restraints, secured his wrist restraints to a rope and pulley assembly fastened to the ceiling, and hoisted him high enough to keep his feet from touching the ground. He then repositioned Otto and Margarette's chairs so they could view Gustav's torment.

Blick started for the door, turning before reaching it. "Please excuse me while I go for breakfast? My interrogation begins when I return. Otto, please consider whether you want this to be a long painful death for your parents, or a short interlude while they wait for me to release them."

He opened the door, walked out, and closed it quietly.

⌘⌘⌘⌘⌘⌘⌘⌘⌘

Blick walked into the adjacent viewing room. Schwartz and Heintz were watching Otto and his parents through the one-way mirror. "Go have breakfast. Come back in half an hour. That's when

I'll start the interrogation." After they left, Blick sat down and gazed at his victims. The dread, showing on their faces, electrified him. They were experiencing the most horrifying moments of their lives. The Grand Inquisitor trembled with sadistic exhilaration when Claus burst into the room.

"Did you get them to talk, Erik?"

Blick jumped to his feet. "Claus, what are you doing here? I thought you worked in Berlin."

"Canaris, the head of Abwehr Military Intelligence, called me into brief service here. He heard we captured four Jewish subversives in Graz and didn't want them killed before giving up all their secrets."

"Come now, Claus, you're familiar with my work. I've never lost a prisoner before he or she told me all they knew."

"I know that Erik," said Claus in an apologetic manner, "and tried convincing Canaris you had this situation under control. But he insisted on interrogating the prisoners at his Abwehr headquarters, without further delay."

"Is General Heydrich aware of Canaris' order?"

"Reinhard recommended Canaris to his Abwehr post, and they often talk. I can't say whether he's aware of his directive, but based on their close relationship I'm sure he wouldn't object."

"Well, that's that," said Blick, his countenance deflating like a punctured balloon. "Do you have the documents for their release?"

"Yes," said Claus pulling a wad of papers from his pocket. "Do you want to see them?"

"If you say they're authentic, that's all I need. I'll cut the old man down, but you'd better double check their restraints before they leave your interrogation room."

"Would you mind doing that for me? I'll be back soon."

⌘⌘⌘⌘⌘⌘⌘⌘

Claus strode to his old office. He'd traced those steps countless times before, but never with the thoughts now surging through his mind. *I always admired Blick for his ability to wrench the truth from suspected criminals. Now I must stand between him and Elisabeth's fugitives. No one can withstand his questioning for long... but that strange old Jew did. He overwhelmed Blick's powerful interrogation techniques. Whatever happened to him?*

Claus hadn't thought about him since Hitler's Reichstag speech. Now he couldn't get him out of his mind. He was about to open his office door when he stepped back. *That's it, Kleindienst, my former aide-de-camp, may know.*

Kleindienst sprang out of his chair when Claus walked through the door. “Herr Oberst, I’m glad to see you again. What can I do for you?”

“Many months ago, we interrogated an obstinate old Jew who caused us a great deal of trouble. Do you remember him?”

“Yes I do, sir. Blick couldn’t make the old man talk after the General promoted Colonel Kepner to replace you. Neither could Colonel Kepner, so he decided to have him shot. Then, Admiral Canaris ordered him moved to Abwehr Military Intelligence. Although the old man’s transfer surprised Kepner, he was glad to get rid of him. Can I do anything for you, sir?”

“No, I’m late for a meeting.”

How odd, pondered Claus as he closed Kleindienst’s door. *I thought I was mistaken about seeing him on Kristallnacht, believing he was still in custody... or dead. Perhaps it was him.*

Claus returned to his office and put down the sheaf of papers he’d claimed to be release documents. They were nothing of the sort. Before leaving England, Elisabeth told him Canaris would have Hans Oster deliver them to the Rothschild Palace, but they hadn’t yet arrived. Claus collapsed into his chair, exhausted.

The previous day, Heydrich’s plane had flown him to Berlin for his meeting with Göring. During the flight, Mayer asked the pilot whether he could fly him to Vienna that evening. The pilot said yes, so Claus returned to the airport at seven. Heydrich's plane wasn't there, and the airport's scheduler told him it wouldn't return until late the next day. Needing to get to the Rothschild Palace as soon as possible, and finding no other alternative, Claus borrowed the only available vehicle from Gestapo Headquarters. He then drove himself the 430 miles to Vienna in Opel's smallest and most uncomfortable car, the Kadett and arrived just in time to interrupt Blick's interrogation.

The phone rang, waking Claus. He lifted the receiver.

"Claus, is that you?"

"Yes, Elisabeth," he said drowsily.

"I wanted to make sure you arrived in Vienna. How are my four friends coping?"

"Oh my God." Claus jumped up. "They're still with Blick. I have to go, my love. I'll call you as soon as I can." Claus slammed down the phone and ran out of his office. He bounded up the stairs two at a time, tore down the hall toward his interrogation room, and threw open the door. Blick was interrogating a prisoner who was begging for mercy. He had bloody marks up and down his uncovered chest. *Is he one of the fugitives? Why didn't I look at them earlier?*

Blick was about to strike the prisoner when he saw Claus.

"Whom are you interrogating, Erik?"

"He's a trusted Viennese citizen who turned against the regime," answered Blick before smashing his rubber truncheon into the prisoner's left rib. "This traitor is coming along just fine. He'll soon be ready to tell us everything we need to know." Blick then swung the club to the right side of the prisoner's body with extreme force. "Can you believe it, he's not even Jewish. I'll never understand these people."

Claus breathed a sigh of relief.

Blick wiped the perspiration from his brow, turned to Claus, and asked, "What can I do for you, Herr Oberst?"

"The four fugitives, where are they?"

"Gestapo Chief Wassermann came by after you left and asked why I wasn't interrogating them. I told him you had orders to transfer them to Abwehr Military Intelligence. That surprised Wassermann, and he asked me to turn them over to his agents so they could get things sorted out. I saw no reason not to comply. Heintz and Schwartz came by a few minutes later and took them into custody. Do you want me to call Wassermann for you?"

"That won't be necessary. Do you know where they took them?"

"No, I don't."

"That's all right. I'll handle it from here."

Claus combed the building looking for the four prisoners, but couldn't find them. He ambled back to his office, slumped into his chair, and called Elisabeth.

"Hello dearest," said Claus with a sigh. "The fugitives vanished. I checked the building from top to bottom and…"

"… Hans Oster contacted me after our last phone call. I've been trying to reach you since then."

"What did he say?"

"He met with Canaris yesterday and brought the documents you need to release my friends. Oster couldn't find you, so he locked them in your bottom right-side desk drawer. He taped the key to the underside of the coffee table opposite your desk. Tell me when you find them."

Claus found the key, unlocked the drawer, and pulled out the papers. "Yes, I have them. What about the fugitives?"

"Earlier today, Oster told Wassermann that the people he'd captured were Abwehr spies working for Canaris. He ordered him to move them to a private room at the airport and wait until someone showed up with the official release papers. When you get there, Wassermann will release them to you."

"How will I know him?"

"I've never seen him, but Oster told me he's about your height with black hair and wears a Gestapo Chief's uniform."

"What do I do then?"

"Wait until you're relieved. As soon as I hang up, I'll call a number Oster gave me and have someone from Vienna's resistance meet you at the airport. He'll arrange for the prisoners' safe passage to London."

"I have a question before you go. They are still in Wassermann's custody, right?"

"Yes."

"So why is Wassermann willing to let me have them?"

Elisabeth laughed. "Oster handed him a forged communique from Heydrich ordering the Gestapo to give Canaris' Abwehr agents all necessary help. Oster then reprimanded Wassermann for disregarding Heydrich's directives, but said he wouldn't tell him if he followed his instructions. He complied at once."

Claus laughed, releasing his pent up tension. "Thank heaven Wassermann works for the Gestapo. He's a blithering idiot."

24th August, 1939 – Vienna – 2:45 PM – Claus meets Wassermann

"Are you inspector Wassermann?" asked Claus as he approached a Gestapo officer at the airport.

"Yes, I am."

"I'm Oberst Mayer, here to relieve you of the Abwehr agents."

"They're in there," replied Wassermann, pointing to a door at the opposite end of the hall. "Is there anything else I can do?"

"No, when I next talk with General Heydrich I'll bring your excellent performance to his attention."

Wassermann beamed. "That's very considerate, Herr Oberst. I appreciate it."

"Remember, you mustn't tell anybody about them. It's in the Reich's best interest, and your own."

"Say no more, sir."

Claus opened the door with a smile. *It's fortunate He's such a bootlicking idiot*. His grin vanished when he saw Rolf Heintz holding a gun on four people tied up in a far corner of the room.

Heintz sneered at him. "Welcome to our little party, Herr Oberst. You didn't expect to find your friends as prisoners, did you? Perhaps we're not as stupid as you thought."

Wassermann pushed Claus through the door, slammed it shut, and walked over to stand next to Schwartz.

Claus glared at Wassermann. "If you don't release these Abwehr agents, I'll have you doing latrine duty at Dachau for ten years."

"Who do you think you're fooling?" said Wassermann in a mocking voice. "We both know these Jews aren't with Abwehr." He punctuated his statement by waving a pistol, and saying, "Go stand next to the prisoners. Heintz, please tie Mayer up with our other guests."

"Don't listen to him," growled Claus. "He's a rogue Nazi working for the British. If you arrest him, I'll guarantee you a promotion and a handsome reward. All you need do is untie everyone."

Heintz winked at Wassermann. "You were right, sir; he tried to paint you as a traitor. Should I discipline him for trying to deceive us?"

"No, we'll have Erik Blick handle that. He's an expert, and will inflict maximum pain."

"You're making a big mistake, Peter." Said Claus, "I can still help you, but time is running out."

Wassermann didn't respond. Turning to Heintz he said, "Make sure they're all securely bound, then get something to eat. I'm meeting Ingrid for a late lunch."

Heintz checked everyone's ropes. He then left, turning out the lights.

"Are you all right?" asked Claus.

"My father suffered the most," answered someone. Claus assumed it was Otto. "Blick knocked out three of his teeth, then suspended him from a rope and pulley contraption. Papa was heroic, but he's now in a great deal of pain." The room was silent for a few moments, then Otto continued, "I'm glad we're out of the torture chamber, but they're taking us back there. Blick thinks I know something that could help the Nazis, but I don't. He's tormenting my parents to make me talk." His voice trembled when he added, "I want him to stop hurting them."

"Let's all stay calm," said Claus. "We can begin by introducing ourselves."

"My Name is Willy Labandter. The others in here are Otto Klein and his parents, Margerette and Gustav. Who are you?"

"I'm Claus Mayer."

"Aren't you good friends with Elisabeth Billingsworth?" asked Willy.

He didn't answer.

A few minutes later, the door opened, Rolf Heintz turned on the light, and stormed in saying, "Get up, you worthless pieces of shit. You're being moved to a more secure location, and I don't have time to play games."

Heintz strode over to Claus and kicked him in the side. "You're the worst of all. The Führer granted you powerful and prestigious positions, and how did you repay him? By supporting the filthy Jew destroyers of all we hold dear. You'll pay for your treachery."

Heintz cut the ropes from Claus' hands and feet saying, "Get up and loosen the others' restraints so they can walk. I'll be watching, so don't try to escape."

Claus stood up, saying, "Do as he says. If we don't, he'll make things even worse for us." Heintz followed behind him as he relaxed everyone's ropes.

"What should we do now?" asked Otto, nervousness ringing in his voice.

"Help your father out of the room and ask no questions. Heintz is in no mood for us. If we aren't careful, he'll shoot us all, and Wassermann will give him a medal for it."

Heintz waved his gun toward the exit. The prisoners complied, shuffling through the door one by one. Claus kept a cool head, seeking an avenue of escape as the muted procession wound its way through the empty airport lounge. Heintz herded them outside, then ordered them to stop behind a vehicle that looked like an ambulance.

"Mayer, remove your Jew friends' restraints so they can climb in."

Heintz held his gun on them until they got in, then closed the door. Seconds later, it moved.

The vehicle screeched to a stop about fifteen minutes later. Heintz opened the back door, ordered the fugitives out and into a large residence. He steered them down several hallways, then told them to stop. "Open that door, Mayer, and all of you follow him downstairs."

The five of them walked down into a big well-lit cellar. Heintz remained upstairs. "You'll be here until we move you back to the Rothschild Palace. I'll let you keep the ropes off for now. Don't make any trouble or I'll replace them. I will be outside and better not hear a sound from anyone." He then slammed the door shut.

“Damn it. There are no windows down here.” Claus pointed up the staircase they’d descended. “That’s the only way out.” He then heard the key locking their only path to freedom.

Claus asked the others to gather around him, then spoke in a whisper. “Let’s scout out the basement to make sure nobody can hear us.”

Willy approached Claus whispering, “I found this radio in that corner. If we turn it on we can speak normally.”

“Good idea,” whispered Claus, He then said, “Let’s get together by the radio to hear the news,” in a loud voice. He tuned to a station broadcasting one of Hitler’s speeches, increased the volume, and lowered his voice. “I’m sorry I couldn’t answer your question before, Willy. Someone could have overheard us. Elisabeth Billingsworth received your message and asked me to rescue you. Something went wrong with her plan, but I’m sure she’s arranging for our release.”

“Elisabeth told you about Otto and his parents?” asked Willy.

“Yes, she did.”

“What should we do now?”

“Any attempt to escape could get us killed,” said Claus. “We may have an opportunity when they move us back to Vienna.”

"You're right," replied Willy. He then turned to the others. "Would anyone like to rest? I saw mattresses behind the staircase."

"I think my parents should." Otto helped them get comfortable, then rejoined Willy and Claus. Willy found chairs, arranged them in a circle, and they sat down together. "What now?" asked Otto.

"There's little we can do until Heintz gets back, so let's talk to pass the time," said Willy. Turning to Claus, he asked, "Wassermann and Heintz seem to know you. Are you a Nazi?"

It took several minutes before he answered. "Yes, I've been one for over sixteen years. Blick reported to me until last year."

"Based on my experience, Blick must never have failed you," said Gustav Klein scornfully, as he hobbled over to join the group. Willy got him a chair, and he sat down with them.

Claus shook his head. "On one occasion, Blick couldn't even get the name of a strange prisoner. Later, when I interrogated him, he radiated a strange power that somehow took control of my mind. He's haunted me ever since that day."

Willy Labandter smiled. "I know him. He's in his sixties or seventies with thick white hair and never says very much."

"That's right, and he's about five feet six inches tall with a heart-shaped red mark on his right hand," added Claus.

"You've met Moshe Weisskopf," said Willy. "He hid in a closet with Sarah, his sister-in-law, while the Nazis kicked his brother to death during the Beer Hall Putsch."

"Tell me more about Moshe," said Claus.

"He was a coward for most of his life, but that all changed after his brother died."

"Did he become a hateful person, intent on avenging his brother's slaughter?"

"No, quite the contrary," answered Willy. "Moshe told me he swore to fight injustice using whatever power the Eternal granted him."

"I saw him a second time after running from the noise and devastation of Kristallnacht," said Claus. "The sounds faded, and I sensed something mysterious beckoning from behind. When I turned, the blazing buildings created a mystical aura that surrounded him. I felt compelled to kneel, and he told me to beg God's forgiveness for all my evil deeds. Then everything went blank. The next morning I woke up in my bed." Claus' mouth went dry when he asked, "What was Moshe's brother's name?"

"It was Solomon."

"Solomon Weisskopf?" said Claus, his voice cold with dread. "He refused when I told him to leave Germany. I booted him down the stairs and ordered my SA comrades to kill him." Overcome by guilt, Claus turned away from the others. Several minutes later he whispered, "Is it true Moshe escaped the Rothschild Palace."

"Yes," replied Willy. "He told me someone rescued him, but wouldn't give me his name. I suppose he was afraid the Nazis would capture me and I'd disclose it under torture."

"Do you know what happened to him after the Putsch?" asked Claus.

"Moshe told me he went to Poland and studied the Kabbalah under a Rabbi there."

"The Kabbalah?" asked Claus.

"Yes, he said the Rabbi taught him Mystical Judaism. I know very little about it."

"I wonder if that's where he learned to withstand Blick's brutal tortures and radiate that strange power. Moshe opened my heart and mind to the suffering I caused others."

"It looks like he changed you for the better," said Otto.

"That's my hope. I'd like to meet Moshe again and beg his forgiveness for killing his brother."

"From what I know of him," said Willy, "he will forgive you if you pledge to continue battling Nazism."

The cellar door opened and everyone looked up the staircase. There were light footsteps on the stairs. "Claus, are you down there?"

"Is that you, Elisabeth?"

"Yes, my darling," she said as she rushed over to kiss him.

Terrified, he pushed her away. "Why are you here? It isn't safe."

"Calm down, my love," she said, in a soft voice, then pointed to the stairs. A squad of men, armed with machine guns, was rushing down to the cellar. "They are members of Austria's resistance. MI6 asked them to safeguard us. We have nothing to fear."

Claus stepped back, anger cursing through his body. "We need to talk where nobody can overhear us."

Elisabeth turned to a guard. "Is there a secure location where we can speak privately?"

"Yes, we've checked the mansion, and you can use a room upstairs. Please follow me."

He led them into a small room fitted with a desk and two chairs. The guard then said, "I'll wait outside to make sure you're safe. Please knock when you are ready to leave."

Claus became enraged after the door closed. "You told me Wassermann would honor Canaris' release papers at Vienna's airport. Instead, he took me prisoner, and wanted to send us all to Blick's torture chamber. You can't imagine the diabolical tortures we would have endured. How could you allow that to happen?"

"I know how infuriated you must be, but I couldn't help it."

"Will you please explain that," said Claus coldly.

"When we were still in England together and Wilhelm Canaris returned my call, he told me Schlossburg, Wassermann's boss, discovered someone close to Hitler was sending classified German communiques to the British. Schlossburg hadn't yet identified Canaris as the guilty party, but Canaris knew it was just a matter of time before he did. He used a secure two-way radio connection with Churchill, which I'd established after signing of the Munich Pact, to develop a plan to capture or kill Schlossburg."

"How was our rescue planned?"

"When I *first* called Canaris, Churchill had already won government approval for the Schlossburg mission. After Canaris got off the phone with me he immediately radioed Churchill to delay that mission."

"Why did he do that?"

"Canaris knew Wassermann was frantically seeking a way to regain General Heydrich's confidence, lost when he allowed his Jewish prisoners to escape from the Central Vienna Hospital. When I told Canaris you would rescue Wasserman's captives, he had Oster tell Wassermann he should expose you as a traitor. Oster then took it one step further, telling Wassermann that if he *did* arrest you Heydrich would most certainly promote him to replace you. Wassermann jumped at the opportunity, saying he'd capture you while liberating the fugitives at the Rothschild Palace. Oster warned him you'd never attempt a rescue there, suggesting you *would* liberate them from a less secure location, such as Graz's airport. Wassermann agreed, moving his prisoners there as bait for your capture."

"That went smoothly, but how did you turn the tables on him?"

"Oster, who had enlisted Heintz as a spy, told him to move you and the other captives from Graz's Airport to this residence. After Heintz told Oster you were all here, Oster had me board an MI6 plane and fly to a small airport less than a mile from here. The Austrian resistance fighters, chosen for the Schlossburg mission, met me there. We all converged on Graz's airport and captured Wassermann, his agents, and Schlossburg."

"How did Oster convince Schlossburg to be there?" asked Claus.

"Oster told Wassermann to invite him, explaining that Heydrich insisted on hearing Schlossburg's firsthand account of how Wassermann captured you. Wassermann became ecstatic, telling Oster his dream of regaining Heydrich's confidence was now within reach, and he thanked him."

"I met with Heydrich yesterday. He would have arrested me if he'd known of your plan."

Elisabeth smiled. "Heydrich *didn't* know. He was too busy preparing for the invasion of Poland. We also made sure Schlossburg couldn't get to the airport before Heintz moved you. Had Schlossburg been there, he would have foiled our plan by insisting Wassermann keep an eye on you until the Gestapo returned you and the others to Vienna."

"Otto told me he was the first fugitive interrogated by Blick. That makes little sense because Blick always conducts a preliminary prisoner assessment. After talking to Willy, he would have concluded Willy knew the most about Vienna's resistance network."

"You're right," said Elisabeth, "but Oster told me Heintz convinced Blick to interrogate Otto first."

"What will you do with the captured Nazis?" asked Claus.

"They're being loaded onto our plane. After they deplane in London, MI6 will fly them to a secret prison in northern England."

Claus was silent as he thought over Elisabeth's explanation. "You couldn't tell me about Canaris' plan because he had to be certain I'd act genuinely surprised when Wassermann arrested me."

"Yes, Canaris insisted I keep you in the dark."

"I'd have done the same in his place. Sorry for not trusting you."

"I knew you'd be angry and expected you to lash out."

"What do we do now?"

"We'll use the ambulance to retrieve your car, then drive back to Berlin." She took his hands in hers and added, "Claus, my darling, I've kept the best for last. Your brother is alive."

"Are you sure? Was he badly injured?" asked Claus, his heartbeat and respiration accelerating.

"The Nazis didn't harm him. I don't have time to give you all the details now, but our MI6 plane will fly Heinrich to safety in England today."

"Can I see him before he leaves?"

"Yes, we'll stop at the small airport before getting your car."

Claus' stomach tightened. "What's the matter, Claus?" asked Elisabeth.

"Heinrich will turn his back on me."

"He's eager to see you."

"How could you know that? He could *never* forgive my evil Nazi past."

"I told him you changed for the better and risked your life to rescue the fugitives."

"But..."

"... not now, I'll answer all your questions on our drive to Berlin. We must get to the airport before the plane leaves."

25th August, 1939 – A small airport outside Vienna – 1:45 PM – Claus and Heinrich Mayer reconcile

Heinrich caught sight of Claus' ambulance as it entered the airport and sprinted toward it. Although a car almost hit him, he increased his stride.

Seeing his brother racing toward him, Claus abruptly stopped the ambulance, lost his balance while jumping out, and fell to the tarmac. When both disheveled men met, they hugged, stood back to gaze at one another, then spoke at once, drowning each other out. They embraced again, then Heinrich said, "You go first," with a smile.

"Heinrich, my brother," began Claus in almost a whisper, "I can never atone for my misdeeds as a Nazi, but my love for Elisabeth, Moshe Weisskopf's heaven-sent guidance, and your reported death by the Gestapo, changed everything. The passion I once held for Adolf Hitler is now far outweighed by hatred for him and his evil schemes."

Heinrich took his brother's hands and squeezed them tightly. "You performed monstrous acts as a Nazi, and it *will* take a lifetime to atone for them. Nonetheless, I know you are no longer evil. Elisabeth told me that the hate she felt for the malicious Nazi who raided her home many years ago is replaced by deep love for the man who now fights the scourge of Nazism at her side."

Kissing Claus on both cheeks, Heinrich added, "Yes, I forgive you, my brother." Turning to Elisabeth, he said, "And to you, the sister I always wanted, I give my undying gratitude for having the faith to fall in love with Claus."

"Where are Otto, his parents, and Willy Labandter?"

"They are already on board, and will be flown to safety in England," said Elisabeth.

"I'm sorry, sir," interrupted the pilot. "We must leave. The Gestapo could arrive at any moment."

"Of course," replied Heinrich. Facing Claus and Elisabeth, he said, "You will both be in my prayers. Take good care of each other. Hopefully we'll reunite in peace before long."

"One last question, what happened to our parents?" asked Claus.

"They're alive and well. They live in a London suburb. I'll see them when the plane lands."

"Thank God," said Claus tearfully, as his brother climbed the stairs into the airplane. He then turned to Elisabeth. "Is your father all right? I'm ashamed for having treated him so badly."

"Yes. MI6 didn't reveal my clandestine activities for fear he might accidentally tell someone. They moved him to Palestine along with several other Jews before I returned to Germany as Elisabeth. He fell in love with one of the others, and they now live happily in Haifa. I pray for an early end to the Nazis so we can be reunited."

Seeing Elisabeth in tears, Claus took her in his arms and kissed her.

Elisabeth and Claus remained on the tarmac, watching until the plane disappeared. They then walked to the ambulance and drove to get Claus' car.

"Did Heintz save Heinrich's life during the raid on his Graz hideout?" asked Claus after they began driving toward Berlin.

"Yes, Heintz blocked his way when Heinrich tried to escape, surprising both men. Your brother recovered first and asked Heintz to let him go. Remembering how Heinrich saved his life by stepping into the path of an oncoming train, when they were children, Heintz agreed to help him. Heinrich, true to form, asked Heintz to save all the fugitives, but he refused, insisting it risked all their lives.

"Heinrich realized Heintz was right and went back inside. He returned with two syringes containing clear liquids, and a quart bottle filled with a red fluid. Heinrich told Heintz to first inject him with the first syringe, to make his heart rate become undetectable. Then he told him to pour the red liquid onto his chest, turn him over, and shoot his gun into the air. After the Gestapo finished investigating the shooting, Heintz was to inject him with the second syringe, returning Heinrich's heart rate to normal."

"How did Oster convince Heintz to help him?"

"After joining Wassermann's Gestapo squad, Heintz searched for ways to profit from it. Hans Oster, always on the lookout for Nazis willing to do anything for money, put Heintz on his Abwehr payroll. When Heintz told Oster about Moshe Weisskopf's capture, Oster gave him documents, signed by Canaris, authorizing Weisskopf's release. Heintz escorted Moshe out of the Rothschild Palace, drove him to the small airport we just visited, and loaded him onto an MI6 plane. He then destroyed the release documents so nobody could tie him to the escape. Oster gave Heintz sizeable bonuses for releasing Weisskopf, for saving your brother's life, and after agreeing to take part in this rescue operation. We could never have succeeded without him."

"Why didn't you know that Heinrich survived Wassermann's raid?"

"Heintz told Oster he'd saved Heinrich, but that information wasn't relayed to MI6."

The pair was driving for about half an hour when Elisabeth said, "I felt out of sorts, after you left for Berlin, and visited the doctor."

"Did he find anything?"

"Yes, I'm carrying our child."

Claus pulled the car over, took her in his arms, and kissed her gently. "That's wonderful. When did it happen?"

"I'd like to think it was on the *St. Louis*, after you confided that you'd helped Johannes Kaiser and his family. We made love that evening."

"I'm so happy about the baby, but it changes everything. We must leave Hitler's Reich before he can harm our child. Do you think MI6 would help us?"

"Yes. Last week Reginald, my MI6 boss, became concerned that I couldn't keep my emotions in check. Afraid you would expose me as a spy, Reginald asked if I'd like to leave MI6. If so, I could settle anywhere in the British Commonwealth and work as a civil servant. Now, with our baby in the picture, I'm sure he would move us to a place where the three of us would be safe."

The pair sat silently in the car for several more minutes, then Claus asked, "Now that I'm eager to use my standing in the Party to help you defeat the Nazis, would you be content working as a bureaucrat somewhere in the British Commonwealth?"

Without thinking, Elisabeth replied, "No I wouldn't."

"So, the question boils down to whether we should bring our child into a Nazi dominated world."

"I believe we could do much to defeat Hitler, ensuring that future generations will live in a Nazi free world. That's something worth fighting for, even if it puts our unborn child at risk."

"I agree. When we return to Berlin, and announce our engagement, we'll have a special guest at our wedding."

"Let me guess, Adolf Hitler?"

"How did you know?"

"Irena said as much when I called to tell her you'd *popped the question*."

"Then, it's settled. We can't let our beloved Führer down, can we?"

DEDICATION

I owe a debt of gratitude to everyone who made publication of this book possible.

First, I thank my wife Susan for fifty wonderful years of marriage and her help in completing this novel.

Second, I thank my first critique group. Stephanie Claypool, our leader, and Carol Aronson were there from the beginning. They, and the many others who joined us, helped me finish my first draft.

Last, but not least, is the writing community in The Villages, Florida. Thanks to Steve Burt, I learned about CreateSpace, Amazon's print-on-demand technology that published this book. Thanks to the many fine writers in Phil Walker's critique group for helping me turn my first draft into this finished manuscript.

Robert Josef Konig
Bobs.historical.fiction@gmail.com

48696703R00280

Made in the USA
Middletown, DE
25 September 2017